Princess Fragrance

Created by: Thomas Astruc
Comics adaptation by: Nicole D'Andria
Written by: Matthieu Choquet & Léonie de Rudder
Art arranged by: Cheryl Black
Lettered by: Justin Birch

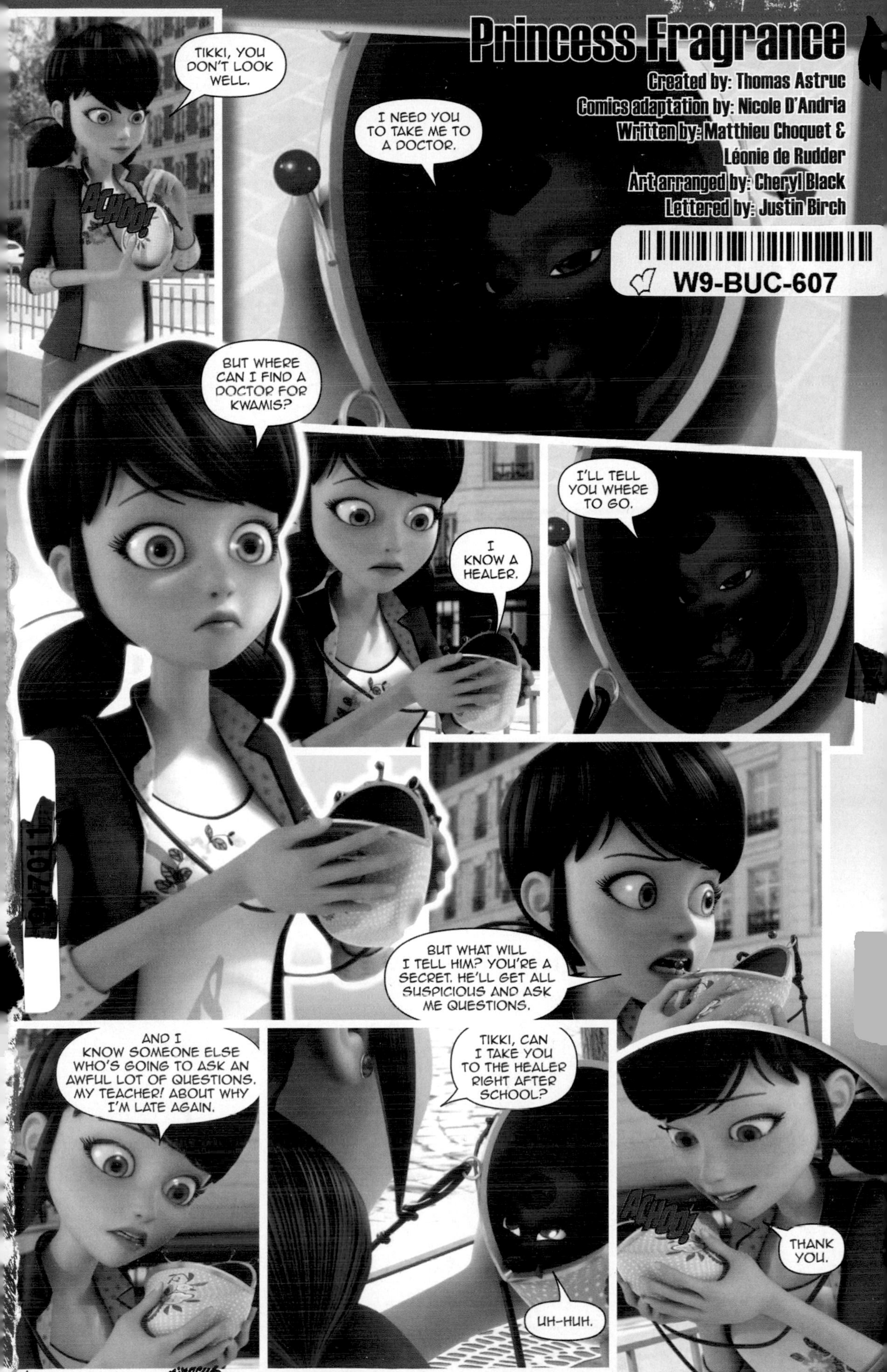
TIKKI, YOU DON'T LOOK WELL.
ACHOO!
I NEED YOU TO TAKE ME TO A DOCTOR.
BUT WHERE CAN I FIND A DOCTOR FOR KWAMIS?
I KNOW A HEALER.
I'LL TELL YOU WHERE TO GO.
BUT WHAT WILL I TELL HIM? YOU'RE A SECRET. HE'LL GET ALL SUSPICIOUS AND ASK ME QUESTIONS.
AND I KNOW SOMEONE ELSE WHO'S GOING TO ASK AN AWFUL LOT OF QUESTIONS. MY TEACHER! ABOUT WHY I'M LATE AGAIN.
TIKKI, CAN I TAKE YOU TO THE HEALER RIGHT AFTER SCHOOL?
UH-HUH.
ACHOO!
THANK YOU.

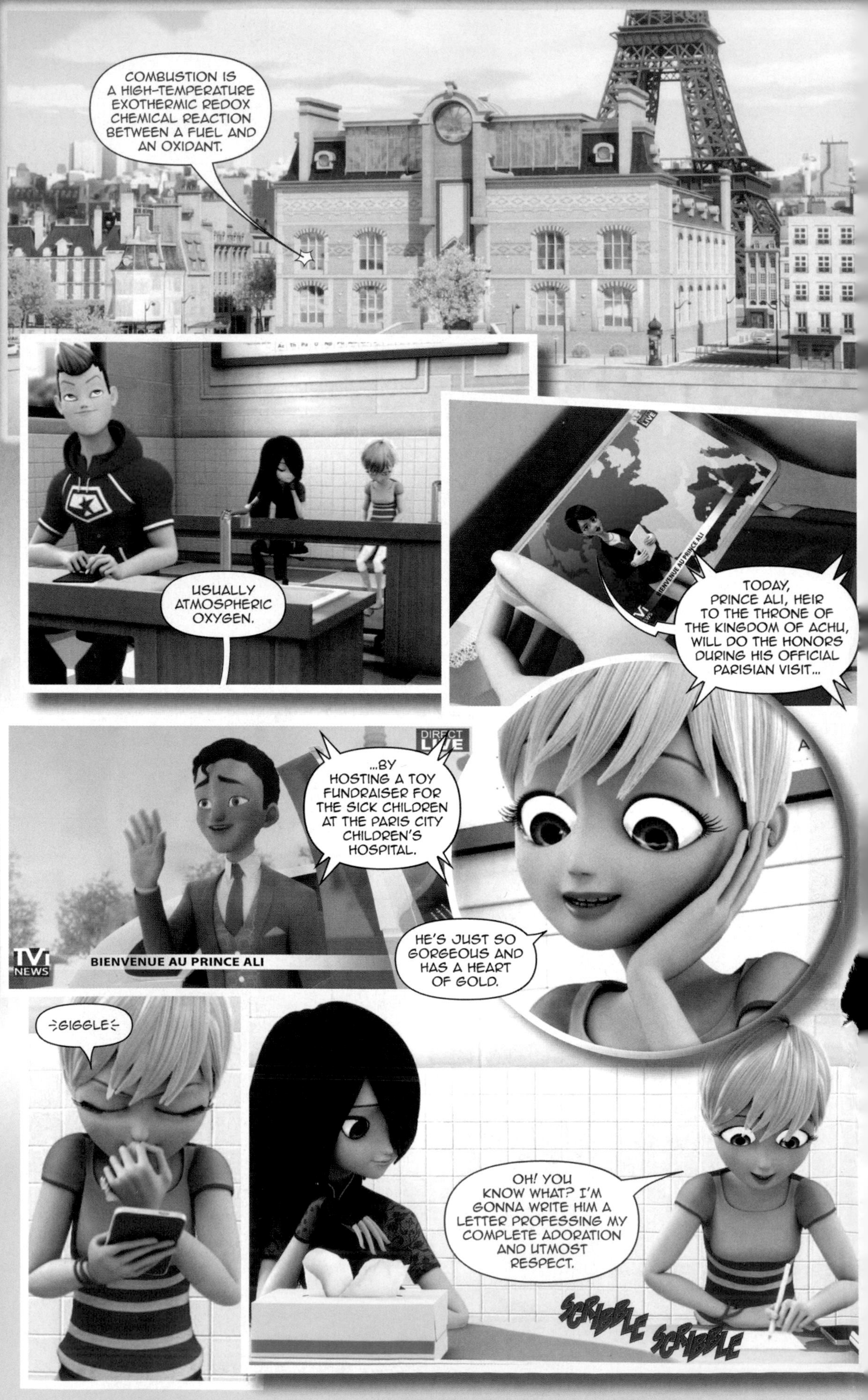
COMBUSTION IS A HIGH-TEMPERATURE EXOTHERMIC REDOX CHEMICAL REACTION BETWEEN A FUEL AND AN OXIDANT.
USUALLY ATMOSPHERIC OXYGEN.
TODAY, PRINCE ALI, HEIR TO THE THRONE OF THE KINGDOM OF ACHU, WILL DO THE HONORS DURING HIS OFFICIAL PARISIAN VISIT...
BIENVENUE AU PRINCE ALI
DIRECT LIVE
...BY HOSTING A TOY FUNDRAISER FOR THE SICK CHILDREN AT THE PARIS CITY CHILDREN'S HOSPITAL.
TVi NEWS
BIENVENUE AU PRINCE ALI
HE'S JUST SO GORGEOUS AND HAS A HEART OF GOLD.
GIGGLE
OH! YOU KNOW WHAT? I'M GONNA WRITE HIM A LETTER PROFESSING MY COMPLETE ADORATION AND UTMOST RESPECT.
SCRIBBLE SCRIBBLE

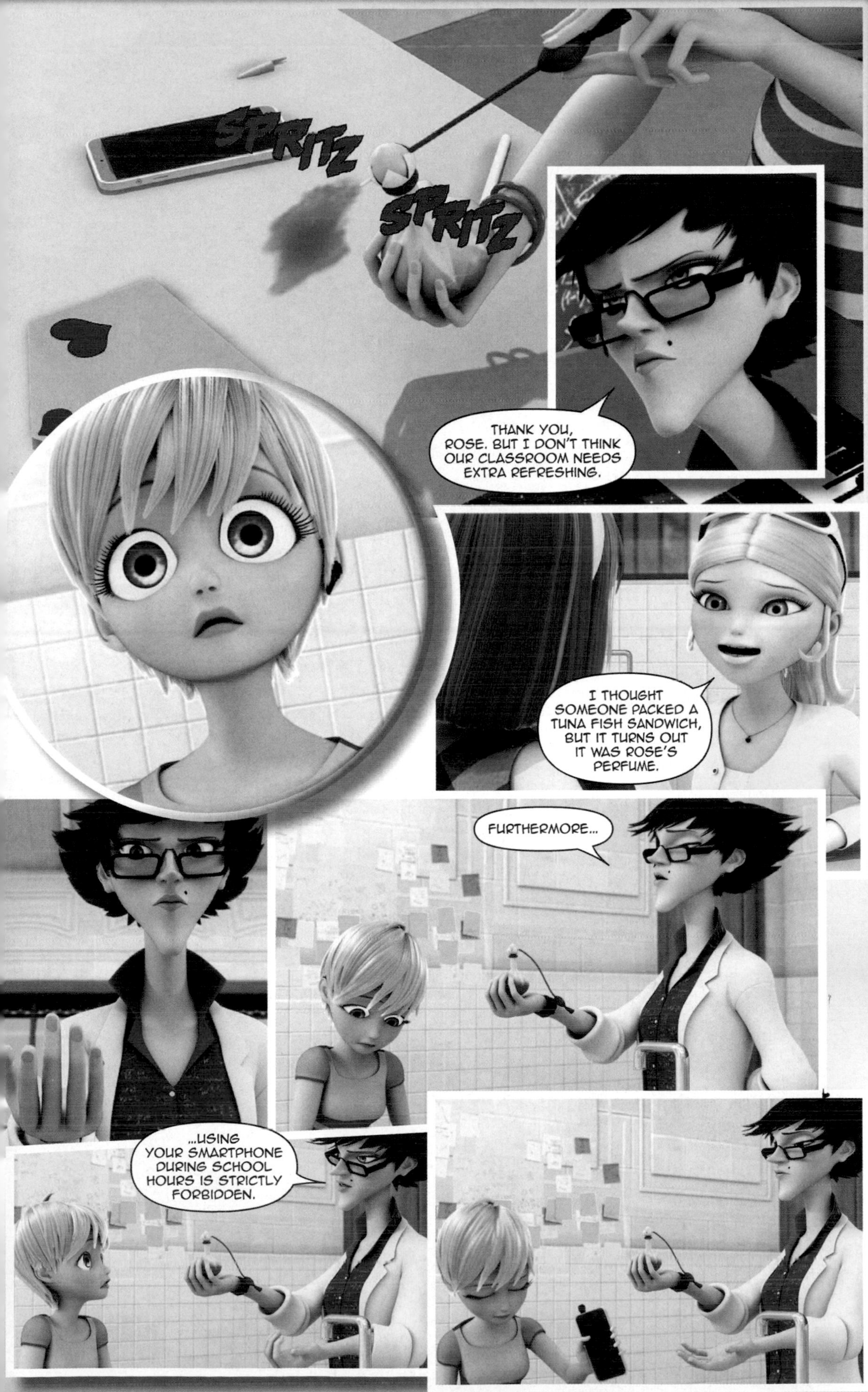
SPRITZ
SPRITZ
THANK YOU, ROSE. BUT I DON'T THINK OUR CLASSROOM NEEDS EXTRA REFRESHING.
I THOUGHT SOMEONE PACKED A TUNA FISH SANDWICH, BUT IT TURNS OUT IT WAS ROSE'S PERFUME.
FURTHERMORE...
...USING YOUR SMARTPHONE DURING SCHOOL HOURS IS STRICTLY FORBIDDEN.

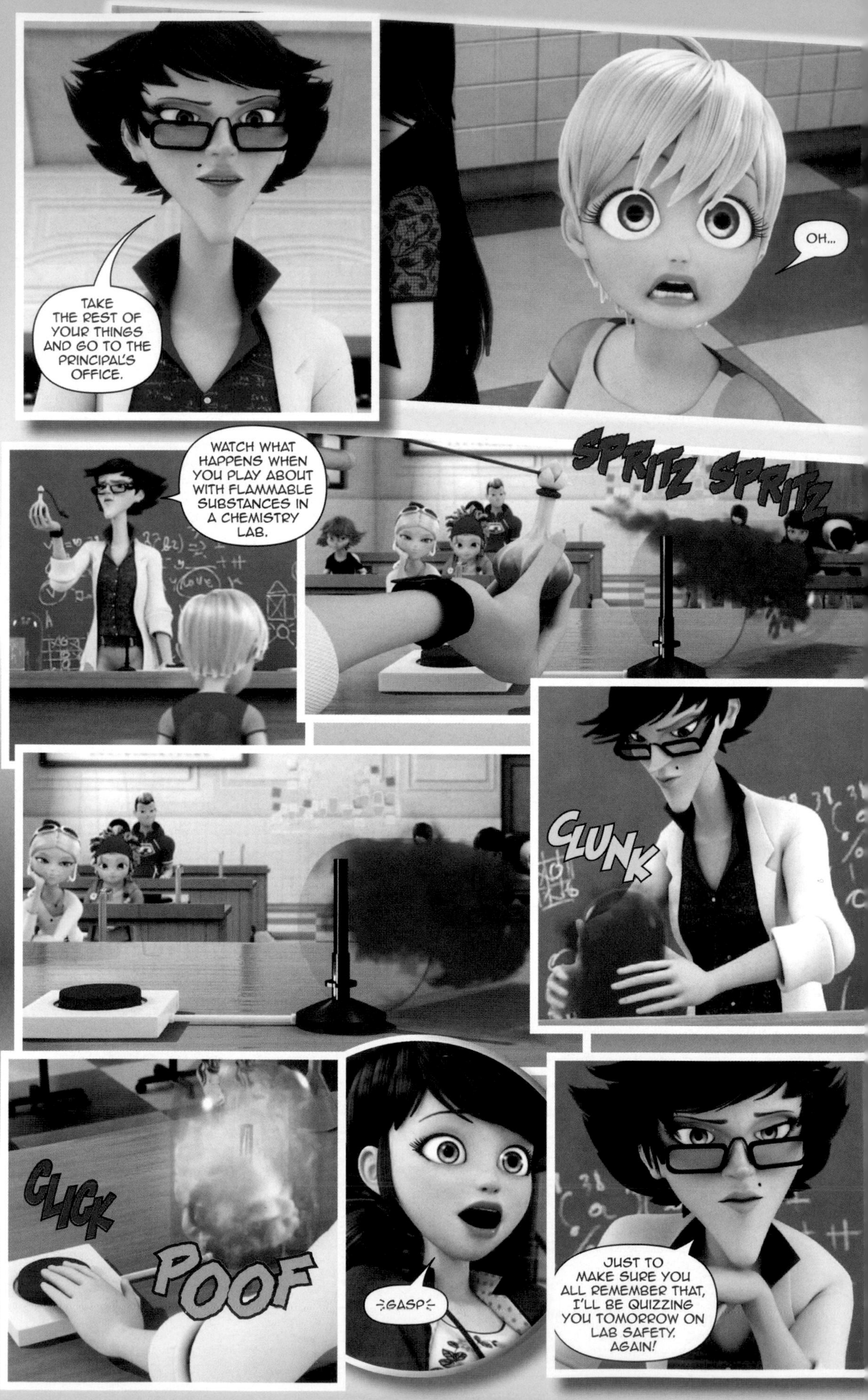
TAKE THE REST OF YOUR THINGS AND GO TO THE PRINCIPAL'S OFFICE.
OH...
WATCH WHAT HAPPENS WHEN YOU PLAY ABOUT WITH FLAMMABLE SUBSTANCES IN A CHEMISTRY LAB.
SPRITZ SPRITZ
CLUNK
CLICK
POOF
GASP
JUST TO MAKE SURE YOU ALL REMEMBER THAT, I'LL BE QUIZZING YOU TOMORROW ON LAB SAFETY. AGAIN!

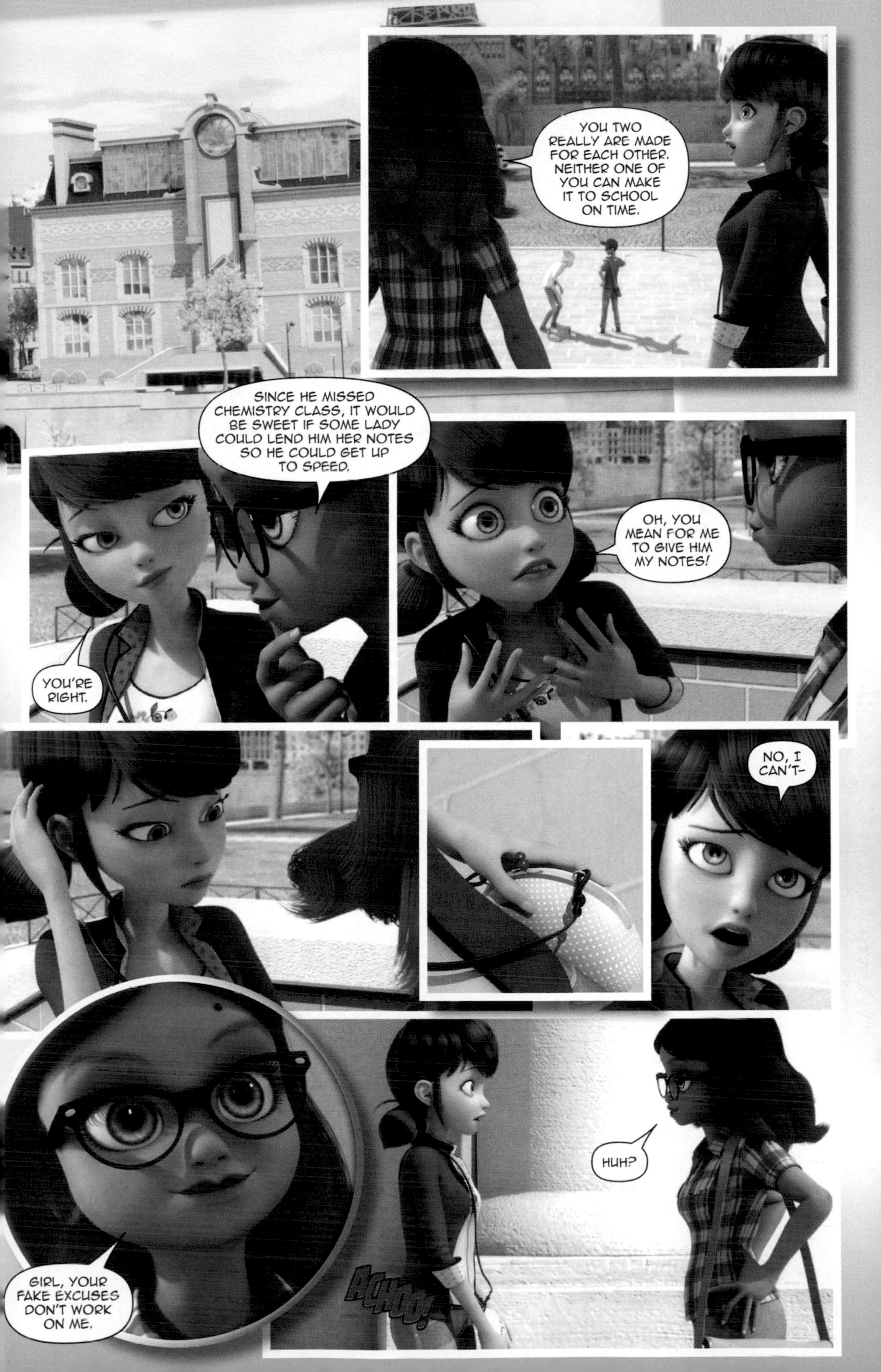
YOU TWO REALLY ARE MADE FOR EACH OTHER. NEITHER ONE OF YOU CAN MAKE IT TO SCHOOL ON TIME.
SINCE HE MISSED CHEMISTRY CLASS, IT WOULD BE SWEET IF SOME LADY COULD LEND HIM HER NOTES SO HE COULD GET UP TO SPEED.
YOU'RE RIGHT.
OH, YOU MEAN FOR ME TO GIVE HIM MY NOTES!
NO, I CAN'T-
GIRL, YOUR FAKE EXCUSES DON'T WORK ON ME.
ACHOO!
HUH?

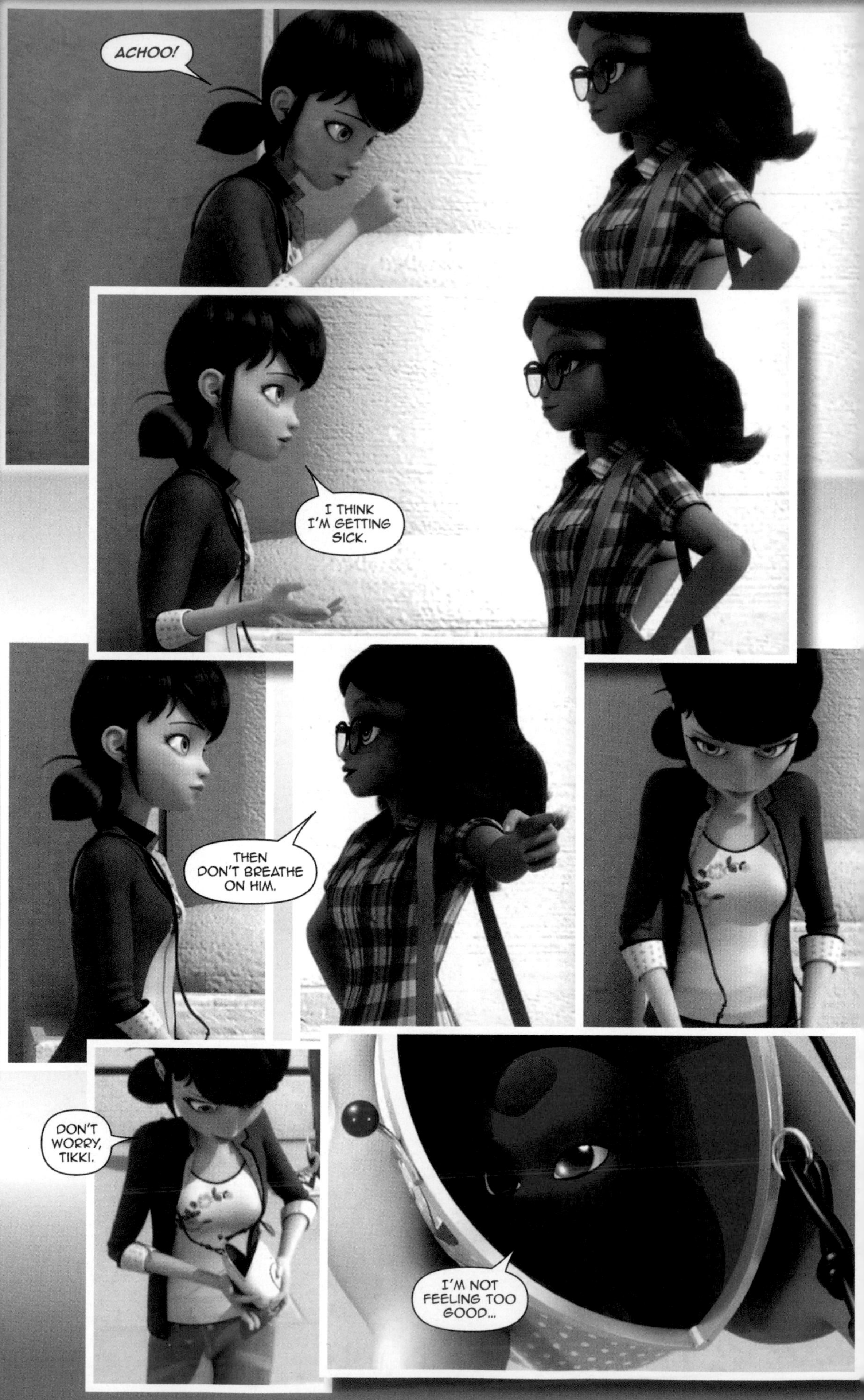
ACHOO!
I THINK I'M GETTING SICK.
THEN DON'T BREATHE ON HIM.
DON'T WORRY, TIKKI.
I'M NOT FEELING TOO GOOD...

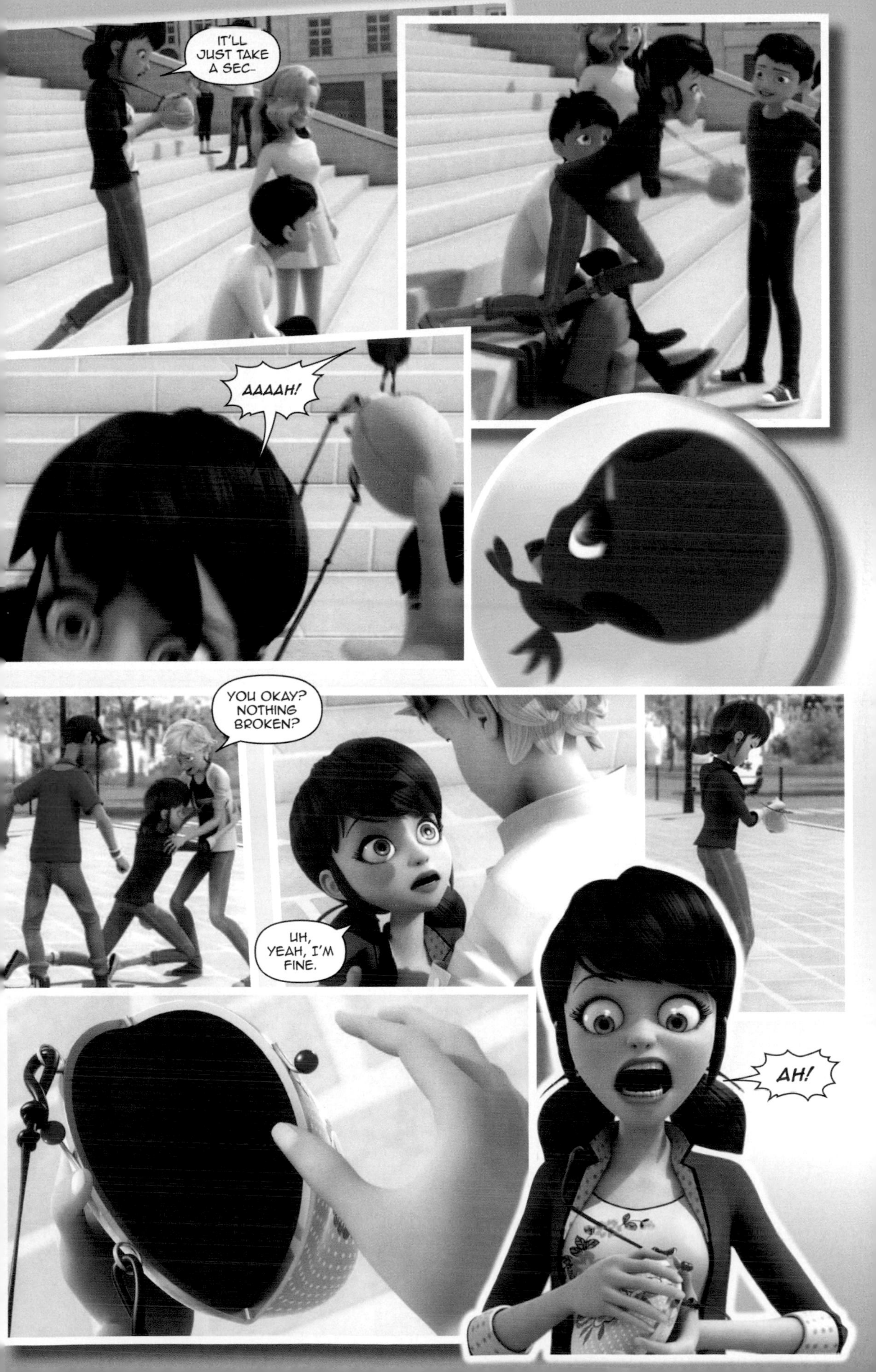
IT'LL JUST TAKE A SEC–
AAAAH!
YOU OKAY? NOTHING BROKEN?
UH, YEAH, I'M FINE.
AH!

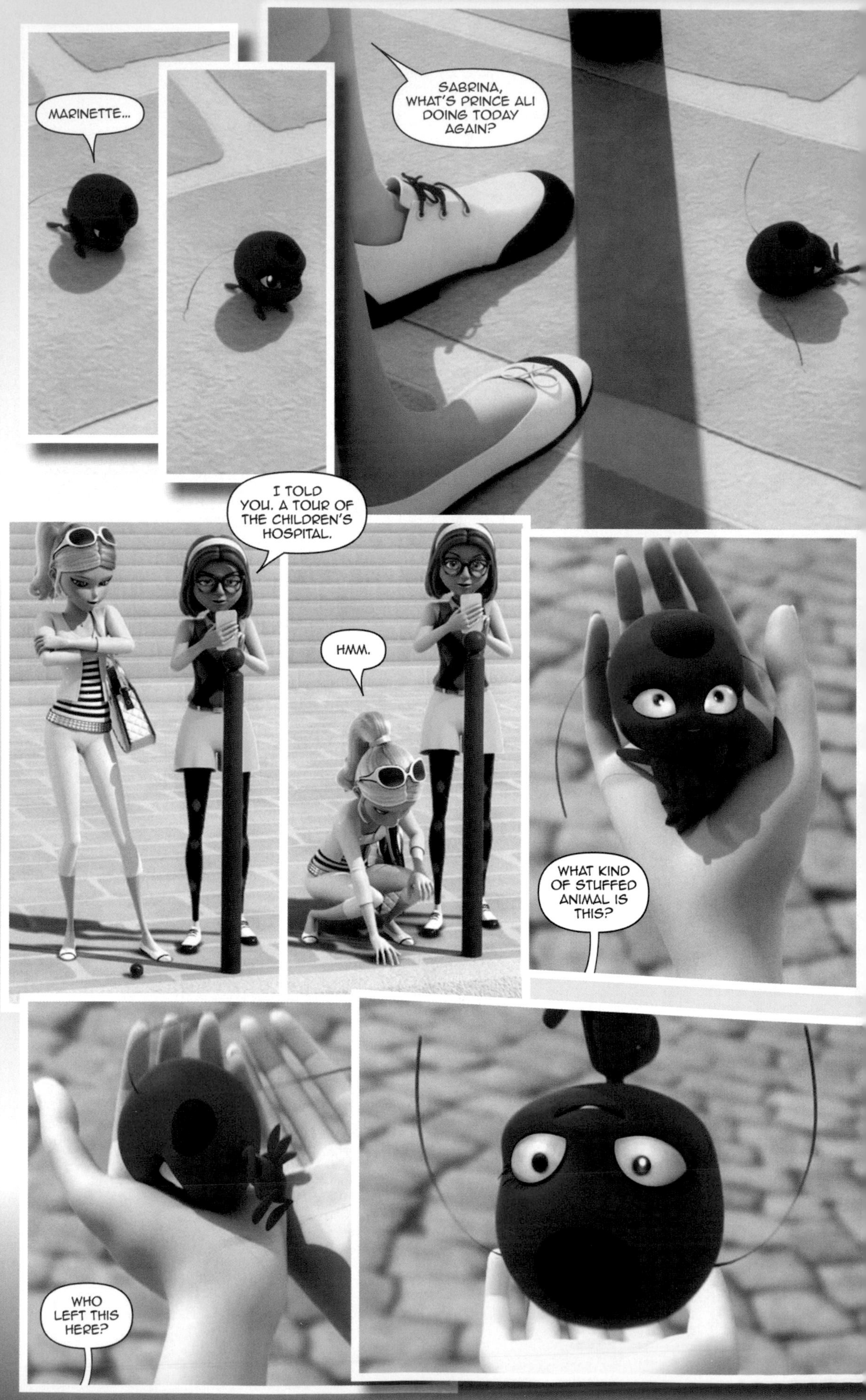
MARINETTE...
SABRINA, WHAT'S PRINCE ALI DOING TODAY AGAIN?
I TOLD YOU. A TOUR OF THE CHILDREN'S HOSPITAL.
HMM.
WHAT KIND OF STUFFED ANIMAL IS THIS?
WHO LEFT THIS HERE?

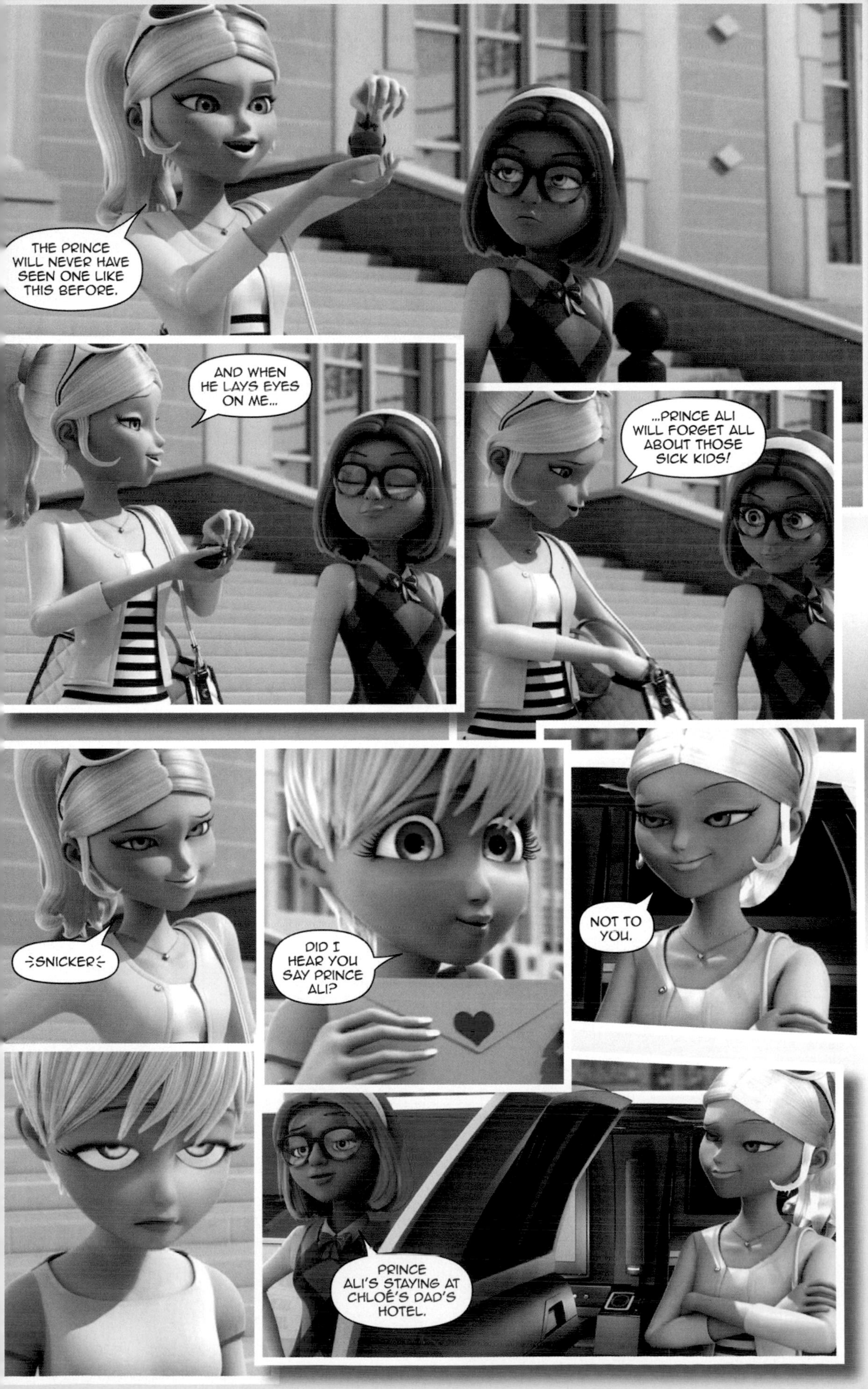
THE PRINCE WILL NEVER HAVE SEEN ONE LIKE THIS BEFORE.
AND WHEN HE LAYS EYES ON ME...
...PRINCE ALI WILL FORGET ALL ABOUT THOSE SICK KIDS!
SNICKER
DID I HEAR YOU SAY PRINCE ALI?
NOT TO YOU.
PRINCE ALI'S STAYING AT CHLOÉ'S DAD'S HOTEL.

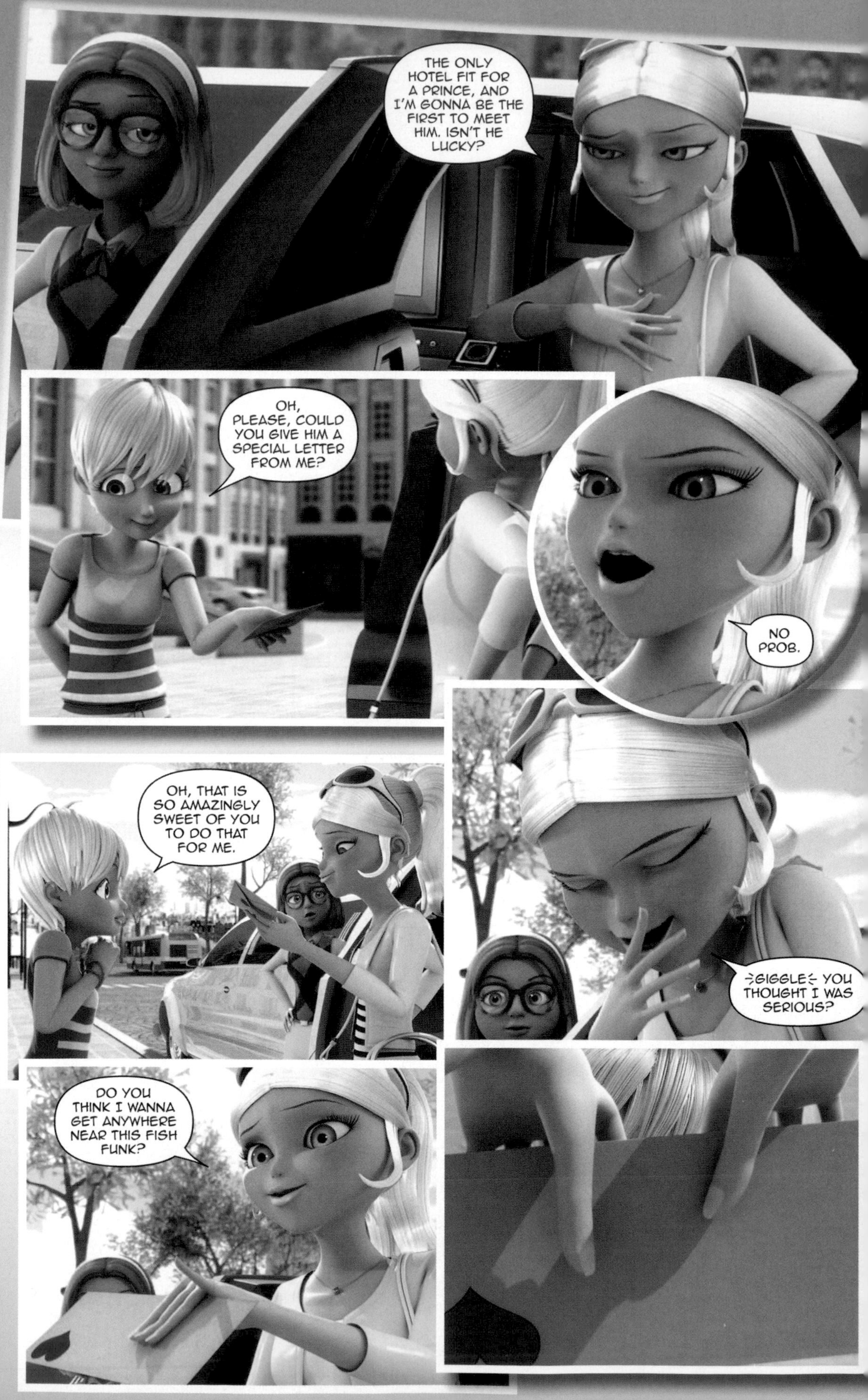
THE ONLY HOTEL FIT FOR A PRINCE, AND I'M GONNA BE THE FIRST TO MEET HIM. ISN'T HE LUCKY?
OH, PLEASE, COULD YOU GIVE HIM A SPECIAL LETTER FROM ME?
NO PROB.
OH, THAT IS SO AMAZINGLY SWEET OF YOU TO DO THAT FOR ME.
GIGGLE YOU THOUGHT I WAS SERIOUS?
DO YOU THINK I WANNA GET ANYWHERE NEAR THIS FISH FUNK?

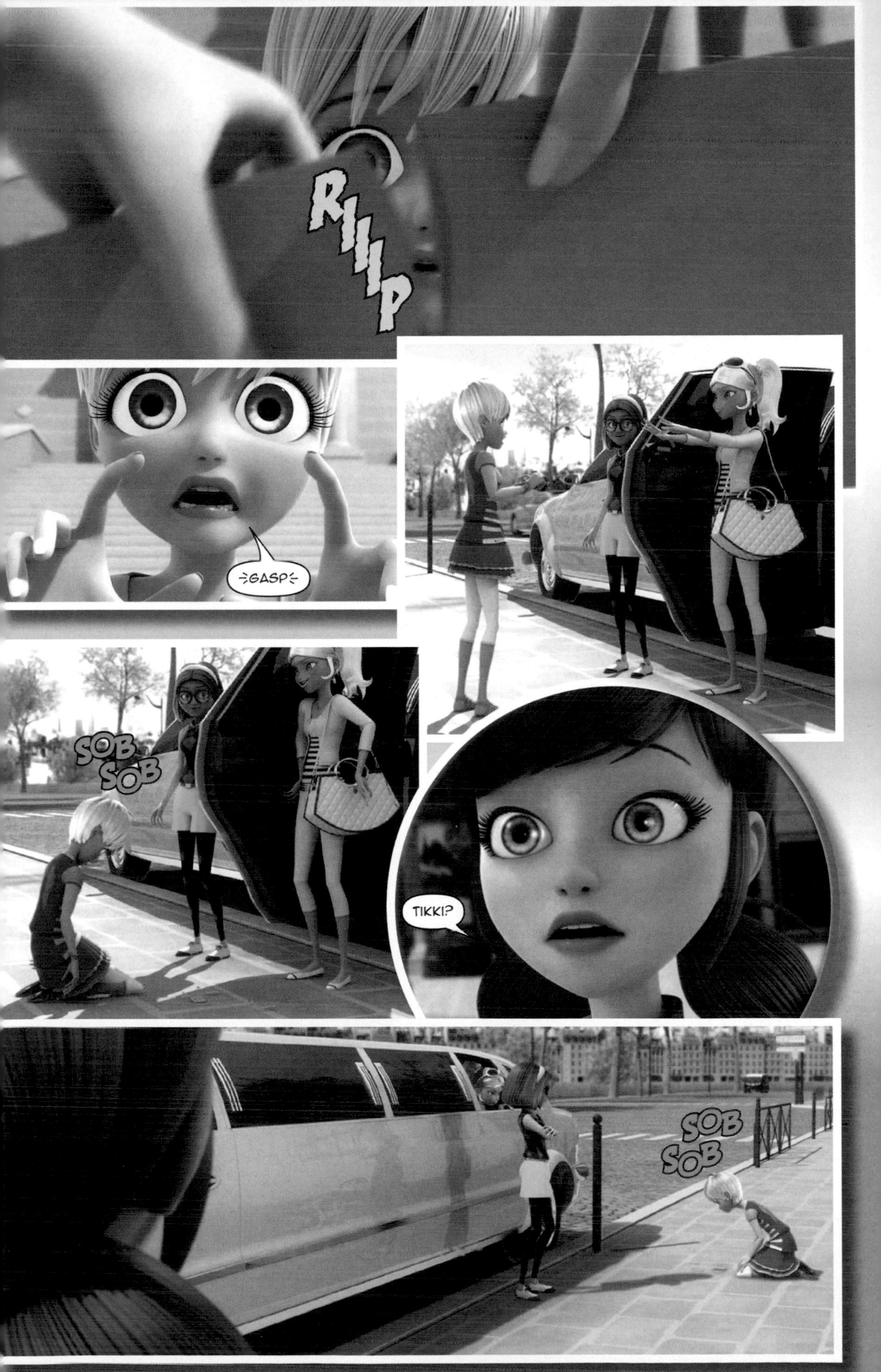
RIIIP
GASP
SOB SOB
TIKKI!?
SOB SOB

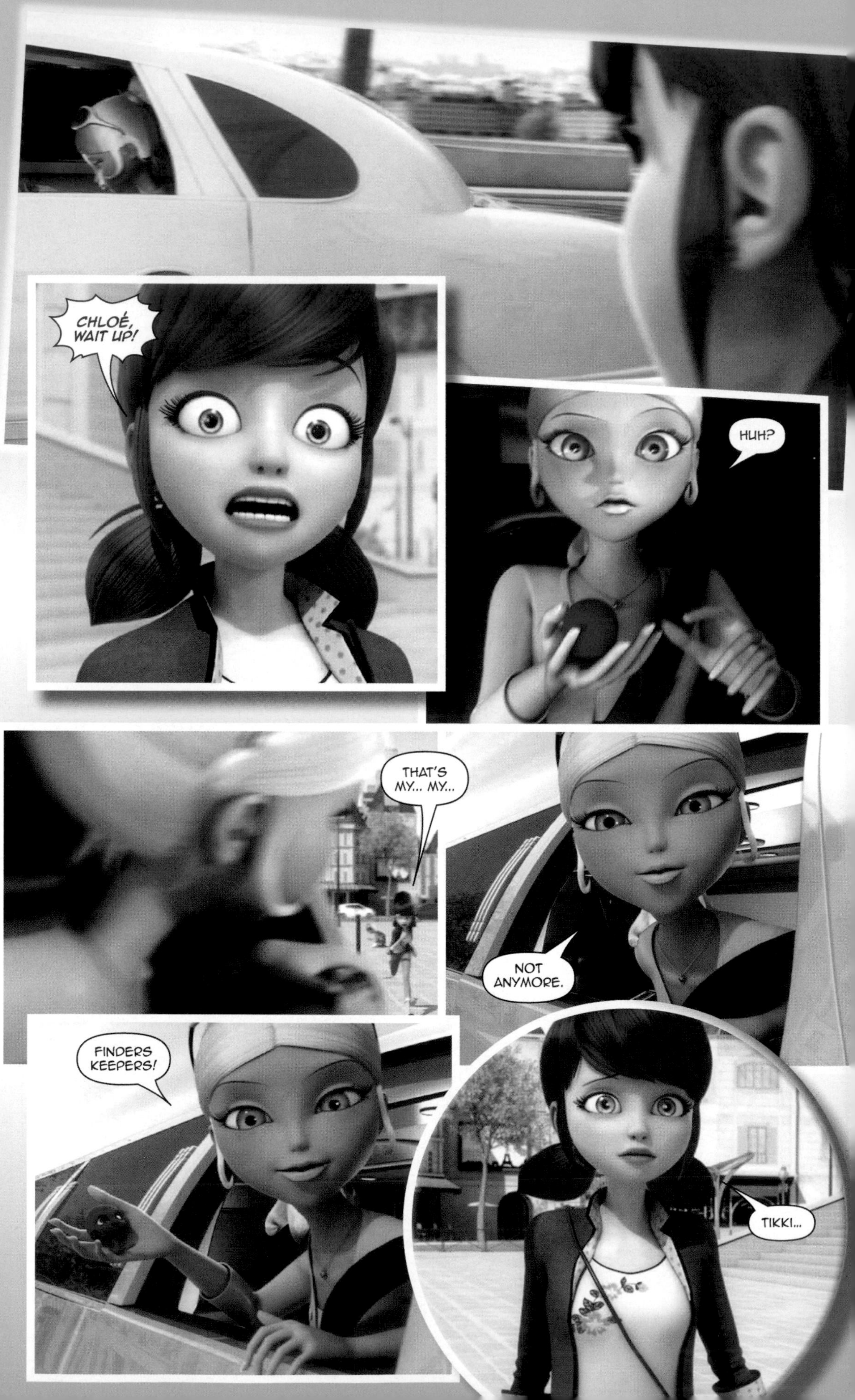
CHLOÉ, WAIT UP!
HUH?
THAT'S MY... MY...
NOT ANYMORE.
FINDERS KEEPERS!
TIKKI...

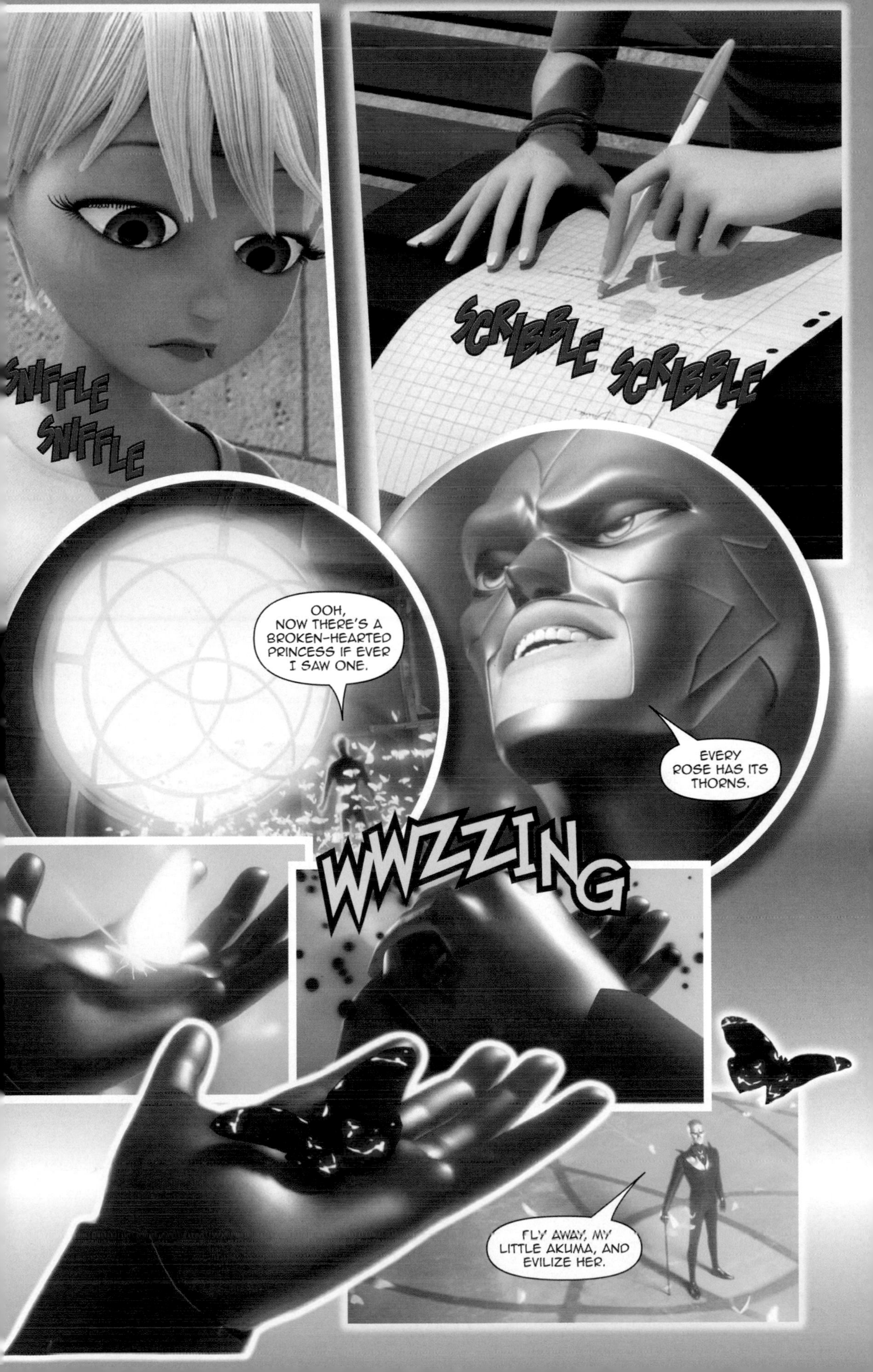
SNIFFLE
SNIFFLE
SCRIBBLE SCRIBBLE
OOH, NOW THERE'S A BROKEN-HEARTED PRINCESS IF EVER I SAW ONE.
EVERY ROSE HAS ITS THORNS.
WWZZING
FLY AWAY, MY LITTLE AKUMA, AND EVILIZE HER.

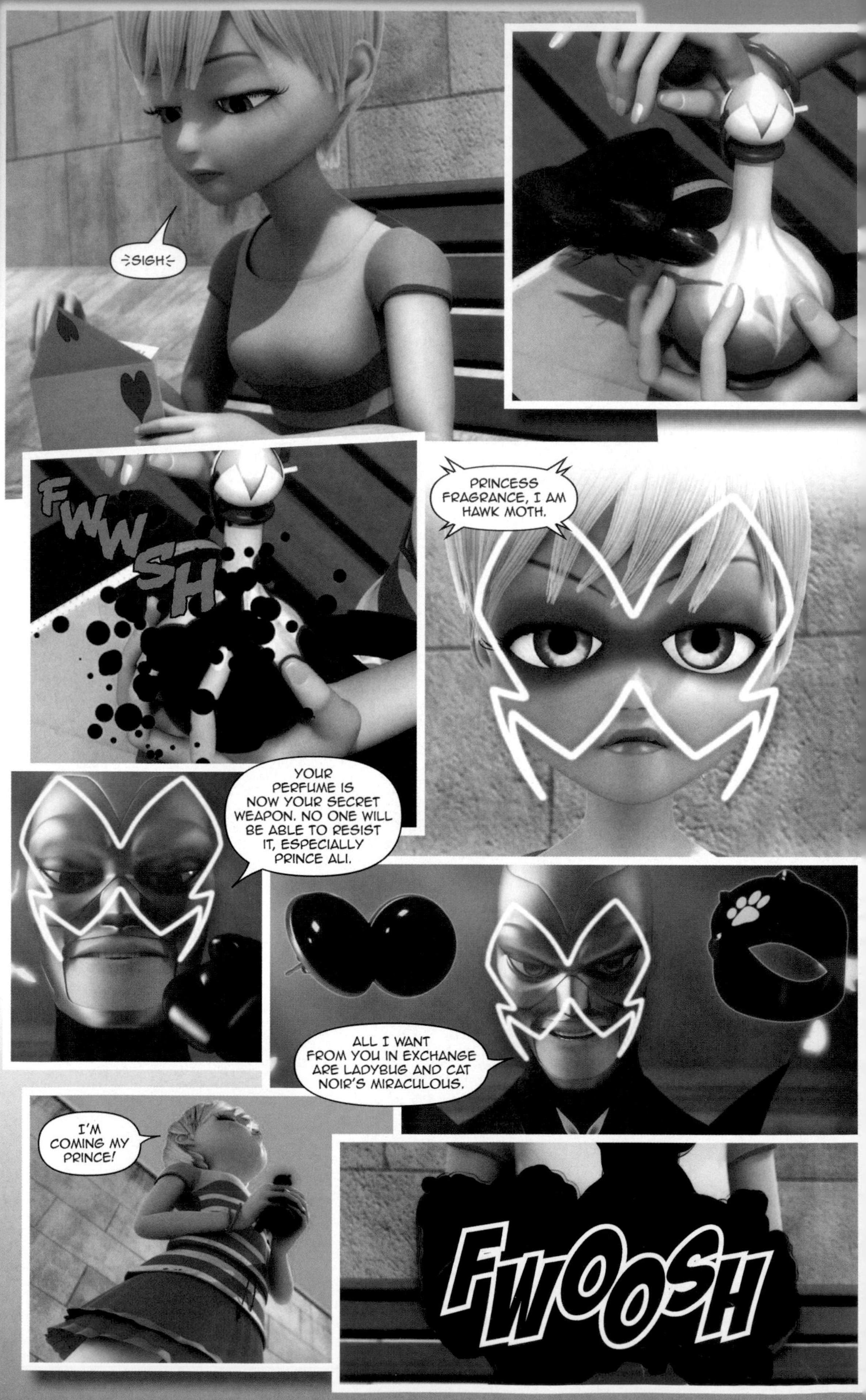
SIGH
FWWSH
PRINCESS FRAGRANCE, I AM HAWK MOTH.
YOUR PERFUME IS NOW YOUR SECRET WEAPON. NO ONE WILL BE ABLE TO RESIST IT, ESPECIALLY PRINCE ALI.
ALL I WANT FROM YOU IN EXCHANGE ARE LADYBUG AND CAT NOIR'S MIRACULOUS.
I'M COMING MY PRINCE!
FWOOSH

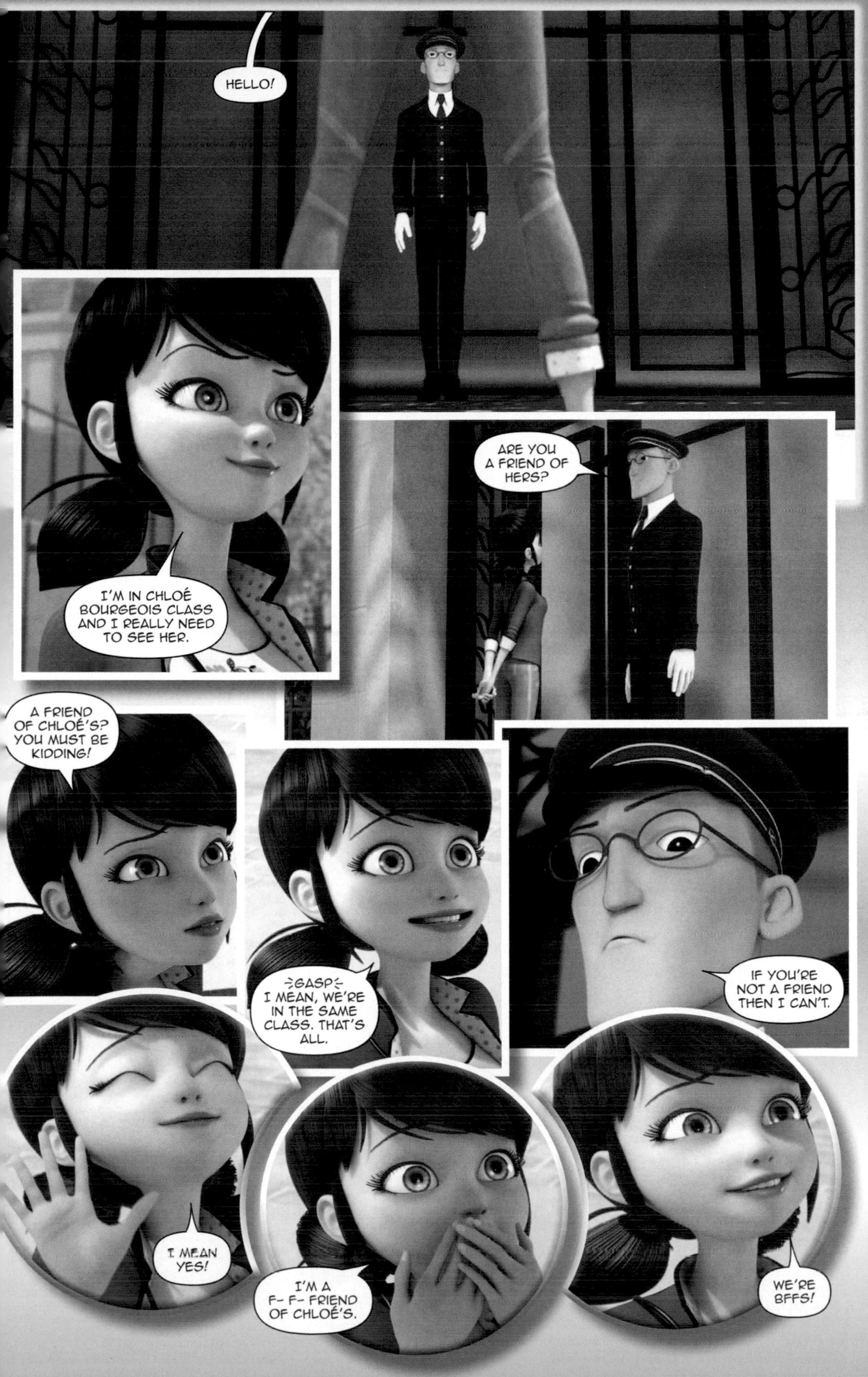
HELLO!
I'M IN CHLOÉ BOURGEOIS CLASS AND I REALLY NEED TO SEE HER.
ARE YOU A FRIEND OF HERS?
A FRIEND OF CHLOÉ'S? YOU MUST BE KIDDING!
≈GASP≈ I MEAN, WE'RE IN THE SAME CLASS. THAT'S ALL.
IF YOU'RE NOT A FRIEND THEN I CAN'T.
I MEAN YES!
I'M A F- F- FRIEND OF CHLOÉ'S.
WE'RE BFFS!

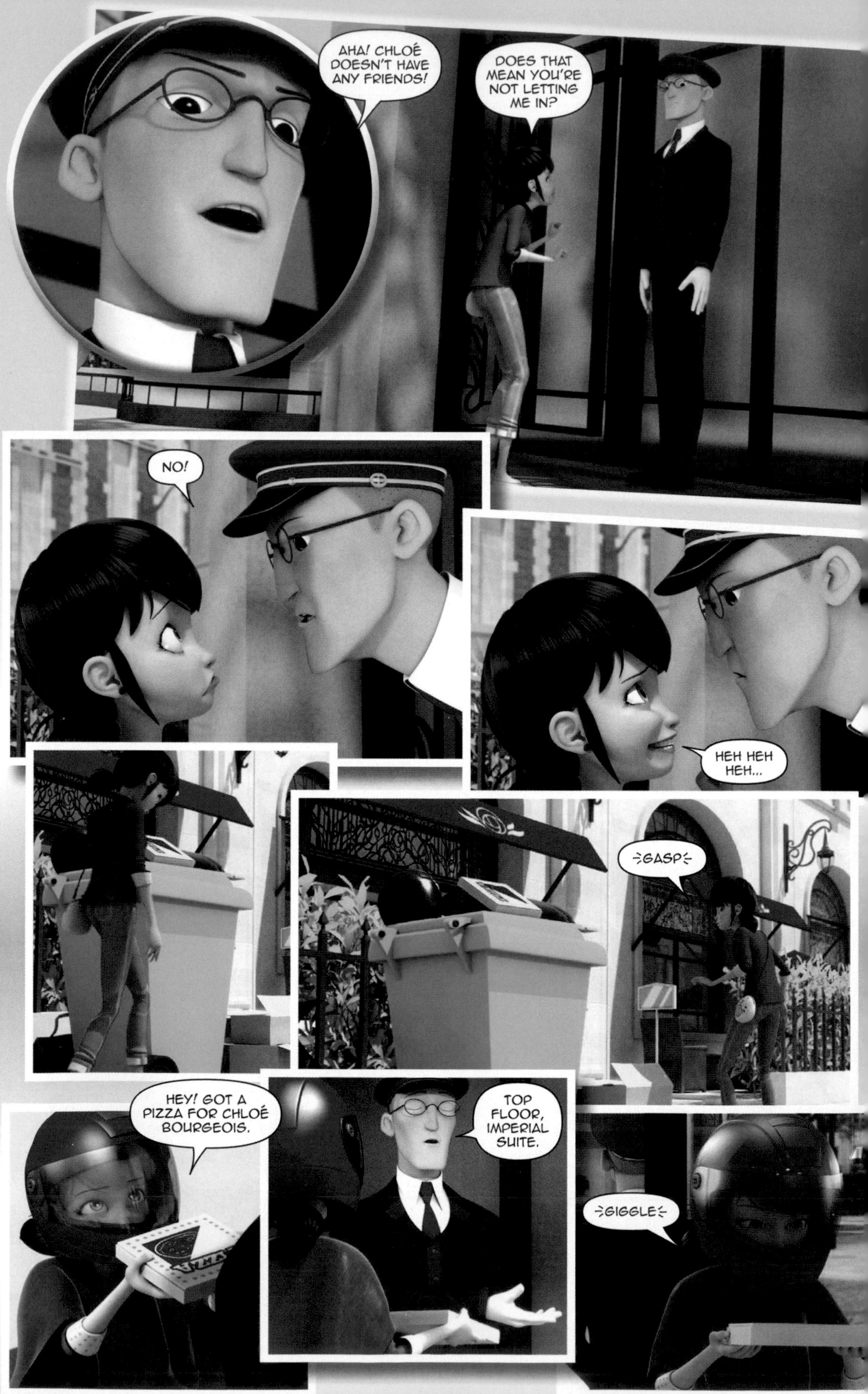
AHA! CHLOÉ DOESN'T HAVE ANY FRIENDS!
DOES THAT MEAN YOU'RE NOT LETTING ME IN?
NO!
HEH HEH HEH...
GASP
HEY! GOT A PIZZA FOR CHLOÉ BOURGEOIS.
TOP FLOOR, IMPERIAL SUITE.
GIGGLE

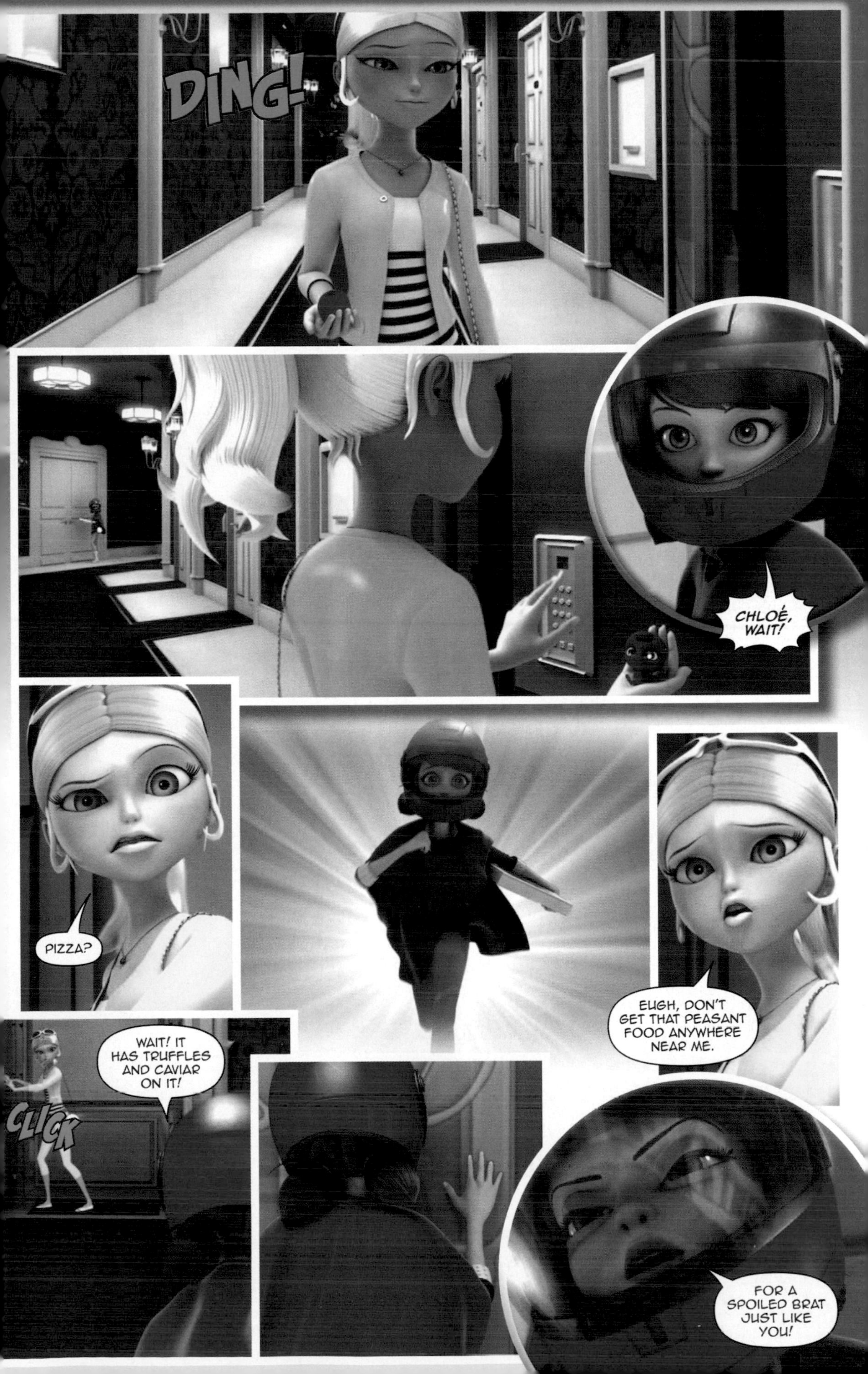
DING!
CHLOÉ, WAIT!
PIZZA?
EUGH, DON'T GET THAT PEASANT FOOD ANYWHERE NEAR ME.
WAIT! IT HAS TRUFFLES AND CAVIAR ON IT!
CLICK
FOR A SPOILED BRAT JUST LIKE YOU!

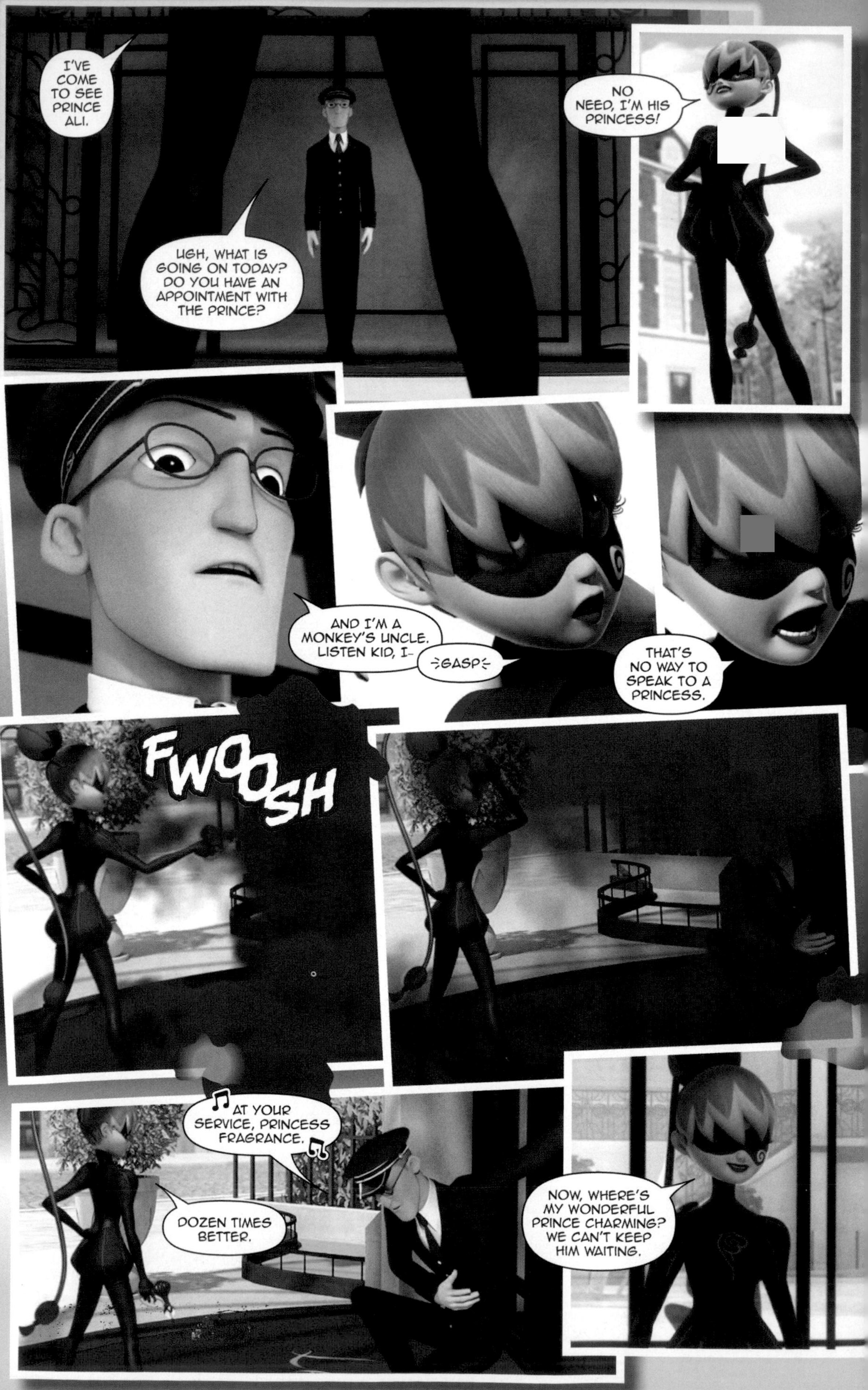

I'VE COME TO SEE PRINCE ALI.
UGH, WHAT IS GOING ON TODAY? DO YOU HAVE AN APPOINTMENT WITH THE PRINCE?
NO NEED, I'M HIS PRINCESS!
AND I'M A MONKEY'S UNCLE. LISTEN KID, I-
GASP
THAT'S NO WAY TO SPEAK TO A PRINCESS.
FWOOSH
AT YOUR SERVICE, PRINCESS FRAGRANCE.
DOZEN TIMES BETTER.
NOW, WHERE'S MY WONDERFUL PRINCE CHARMING? WE CAN'T KEEP HIM WAITING.

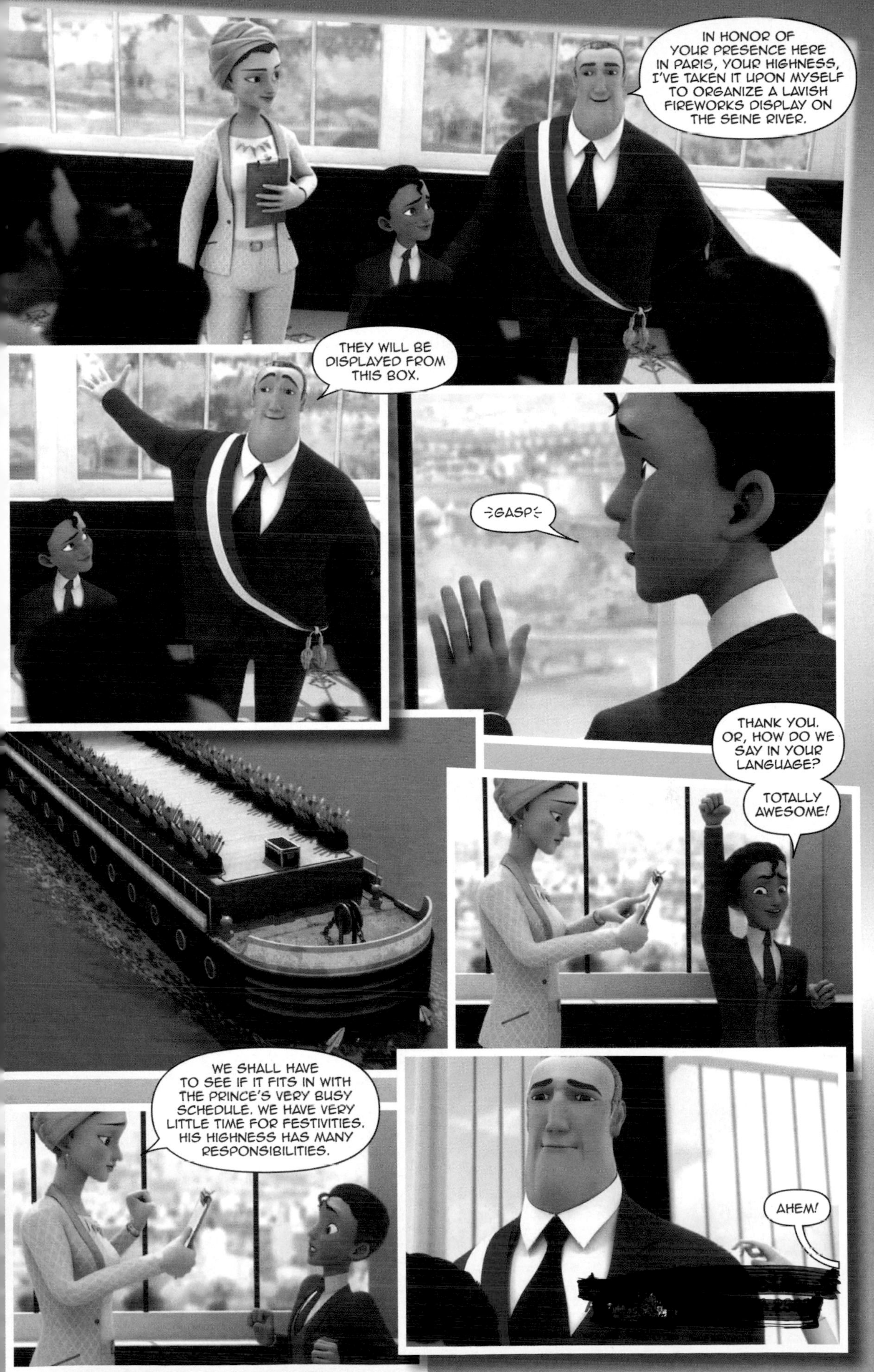
IN HONOR OF YOUR PRESENCE HERE IN PARIS, YOUR HIGHNESS, I'VE TAKEN IT UPON MYSELF TO ORGANIZE A LAVISH FIREWORKS DISPLAY ON THE SEINE RIVER.
THEY WILL BE DISPLAYED FROM THIS BOX.
GASP
THANK YOU. OR, HOW DO WE SAY IN YOUR LANGUAGE?
TOTALLY AWESOME!
WE SHALL HAVE TO SEE IF IT FITS IN WITH THE PRINCE'S VERY BUSY SCHEDULE. WE HAVE VERY LITTLE TIME FOR FESTIVITIES. HIS HIGHNESS HAS MANY RESPONSIBILITIES.
AHEM!

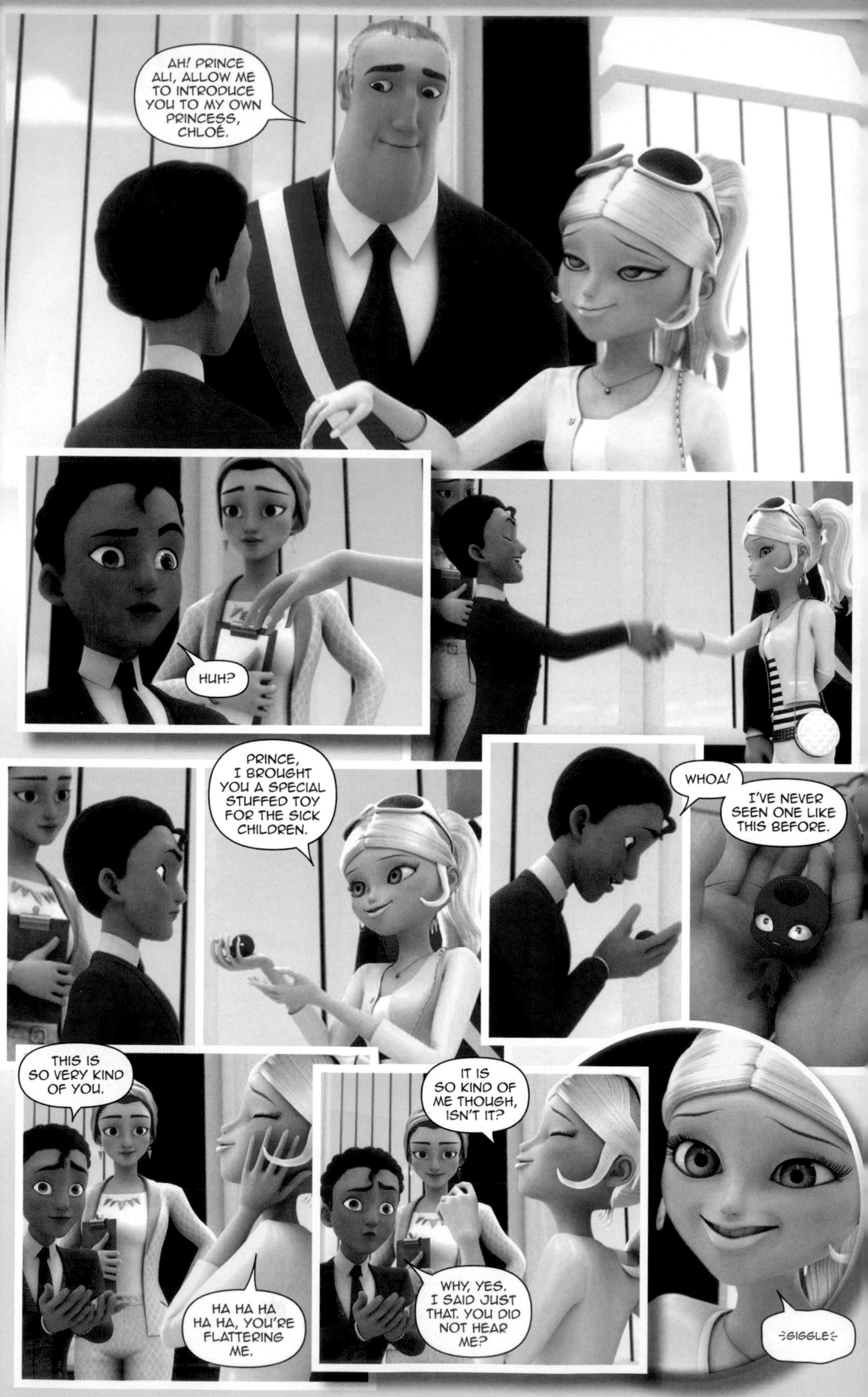
AH! PRINCE ALI, ALLOW ME TO INTRODUCE YOU TO MY OWN PRINCESS, CHLOÉ.
HUH?
PRINCE, I BROUGHT YOU A SPECIAL STUFFED TOY FOR THE SICK CHILDREN.
WHOA!
I'VE NEVER SEEN ONE LIKE THIS BEFORE.
THIS IS SO VERY KIND OF YOU.
HA HA HA HA HA, YOU'RE FLATTERING ME.
IT IS SO KIND OF ME THOUGH, ISN'T IT?
WHY, YES. I SAID JUST THAT. YOU DID NOT HEAR ME?
GIGGLE

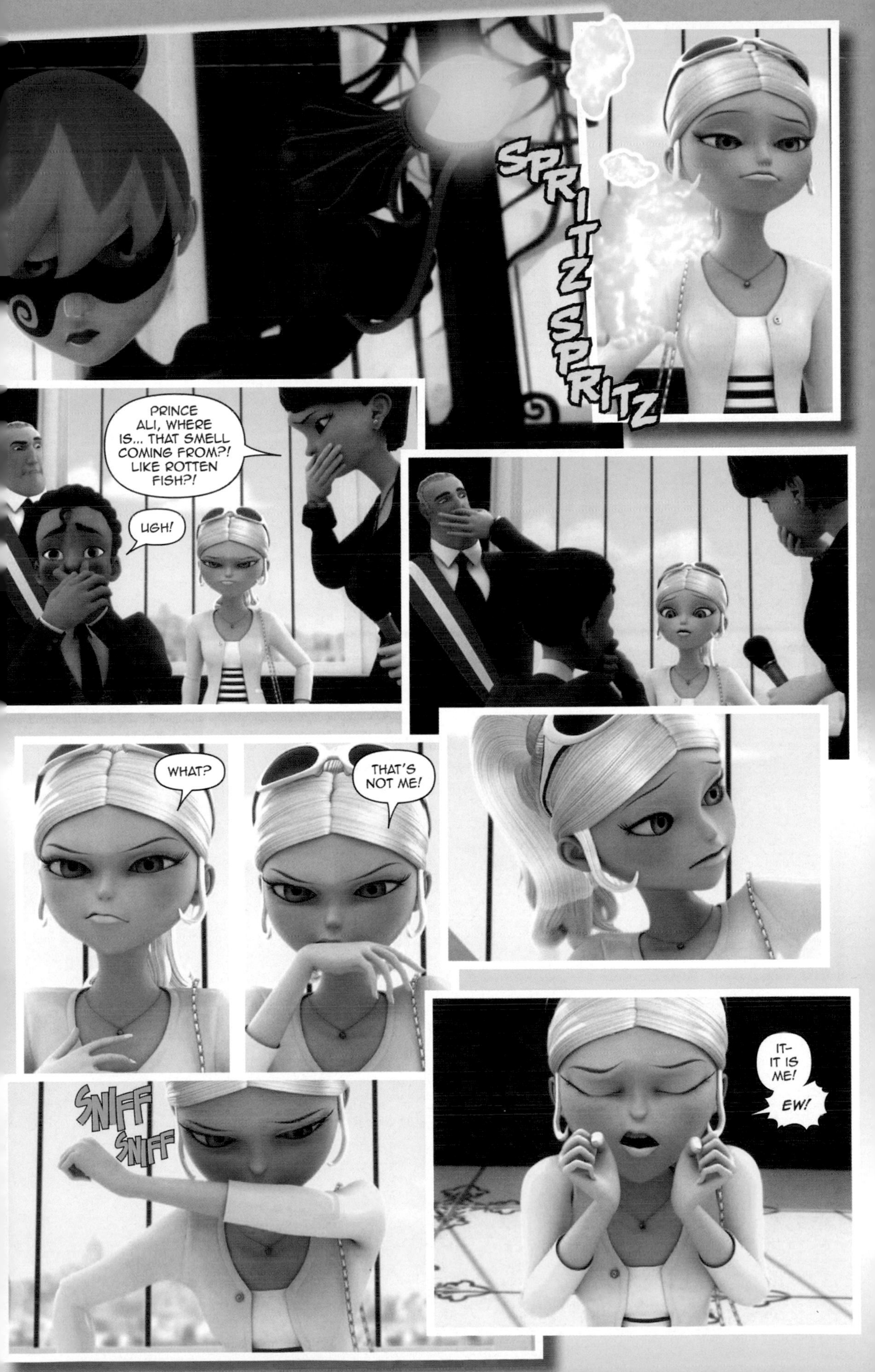
SPRITZ SPRITZ
PRINCE ALI, WHERE IS... THAT SMELL COMING FROM?! LIKE ROTTEN FISH?!
UGH!
WHAT?
THAT'S NOT ME!
SNIFF SNIFF
IT- IT IS ME!
EW!

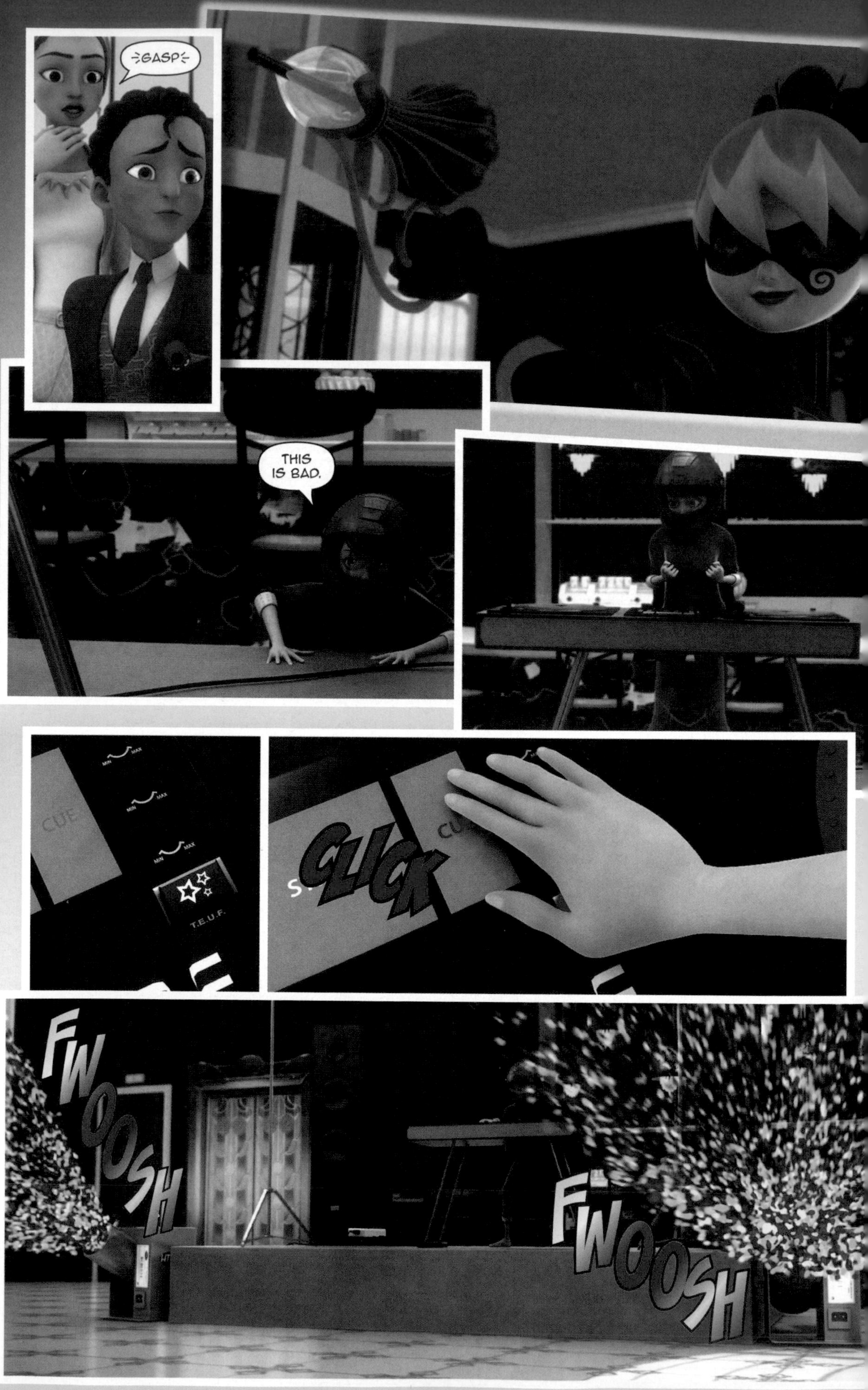
GASP
THIS IS BAD.
CLICK
FWOOSH
FWOOSH

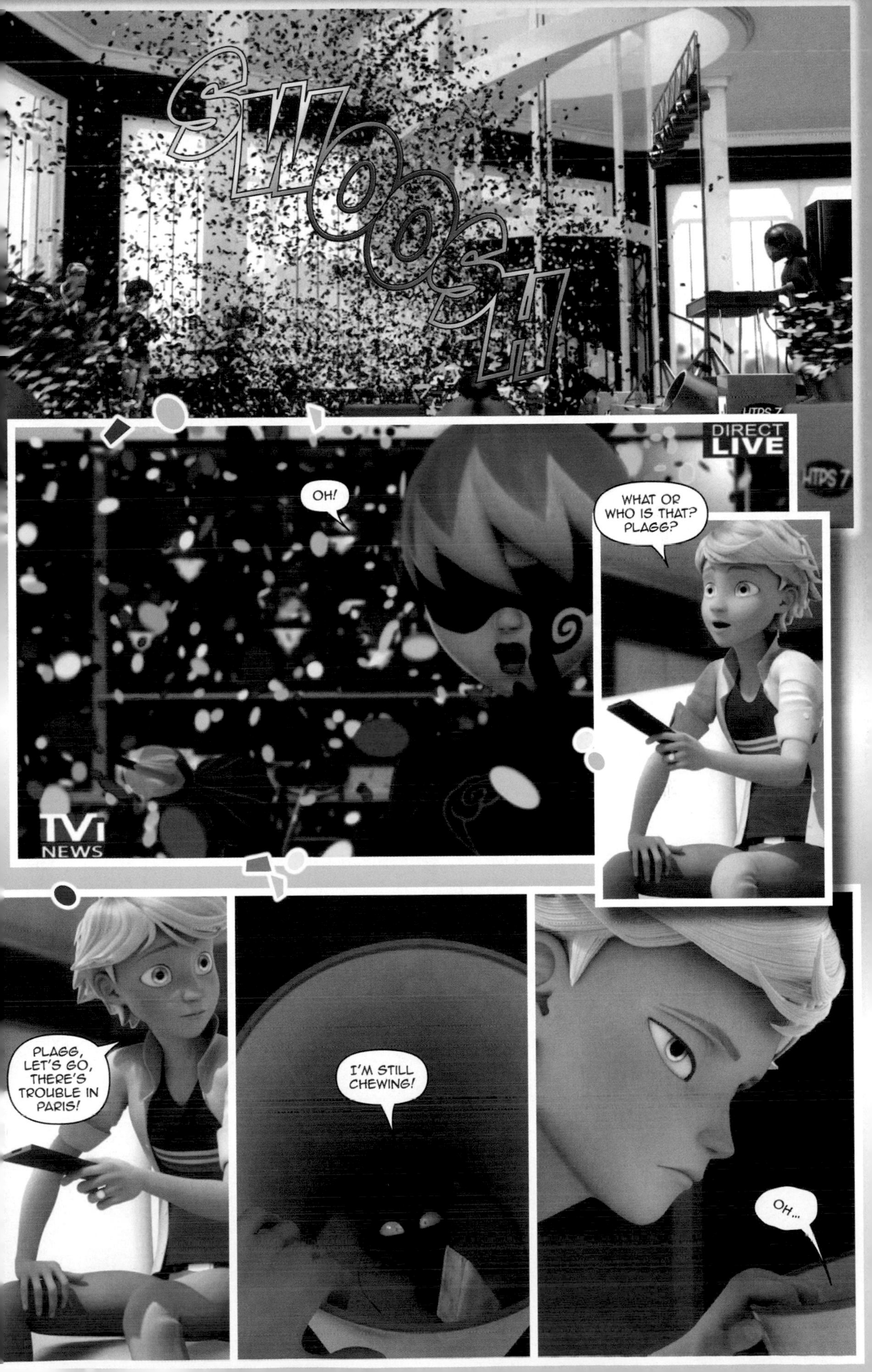
SWOOSH!
DIRECT
LIVE
HTPS 7
OH!
WHAT OR WHO IS THAT? PLAGG?
TVi NEWS
PLAGG, LET'S GO, THERE'S TROUBLE IN PARIS!
I'M STILL CHEWING!
OH...

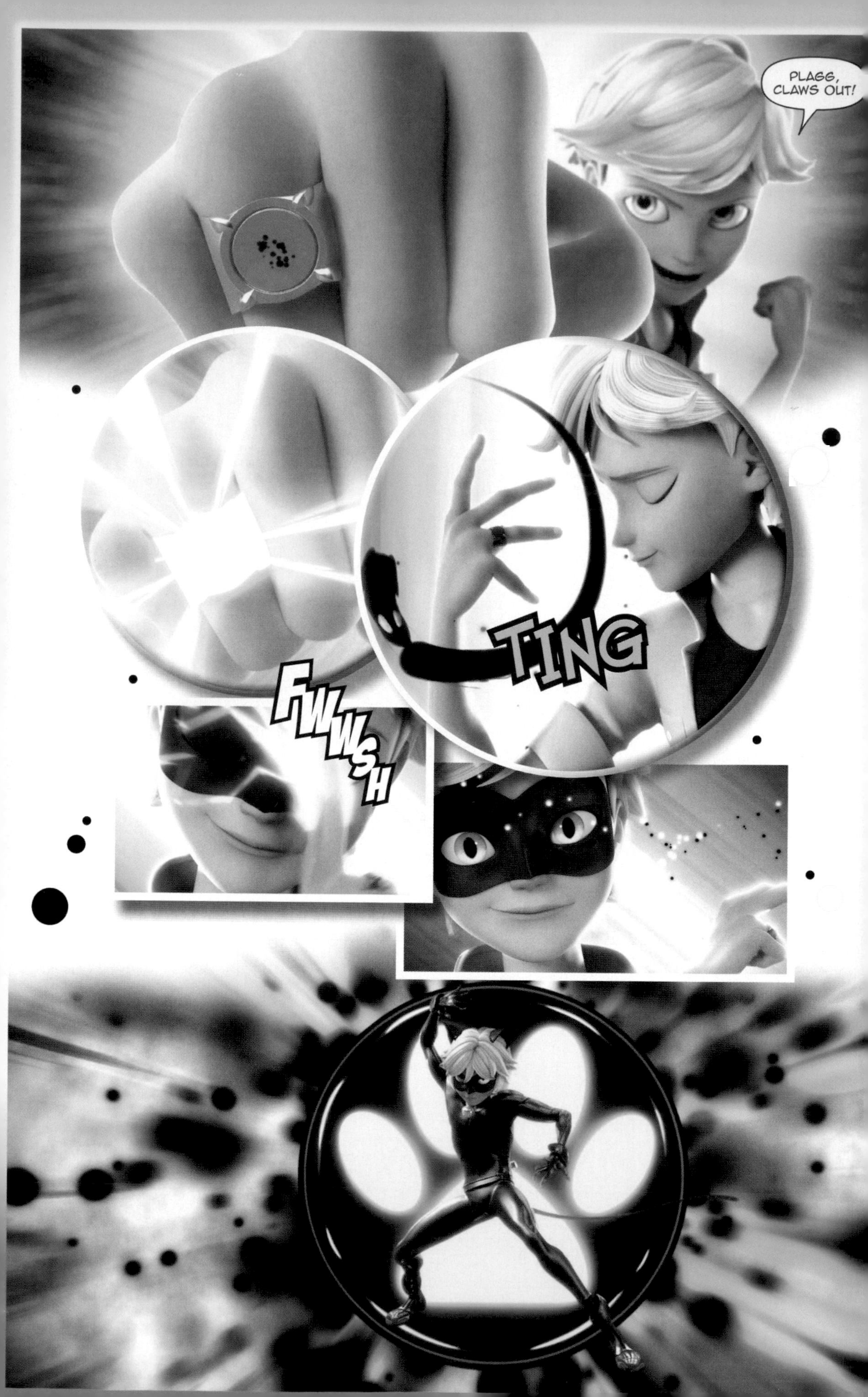
PLAGG, CLAWS OUT!
TING
FWWSH

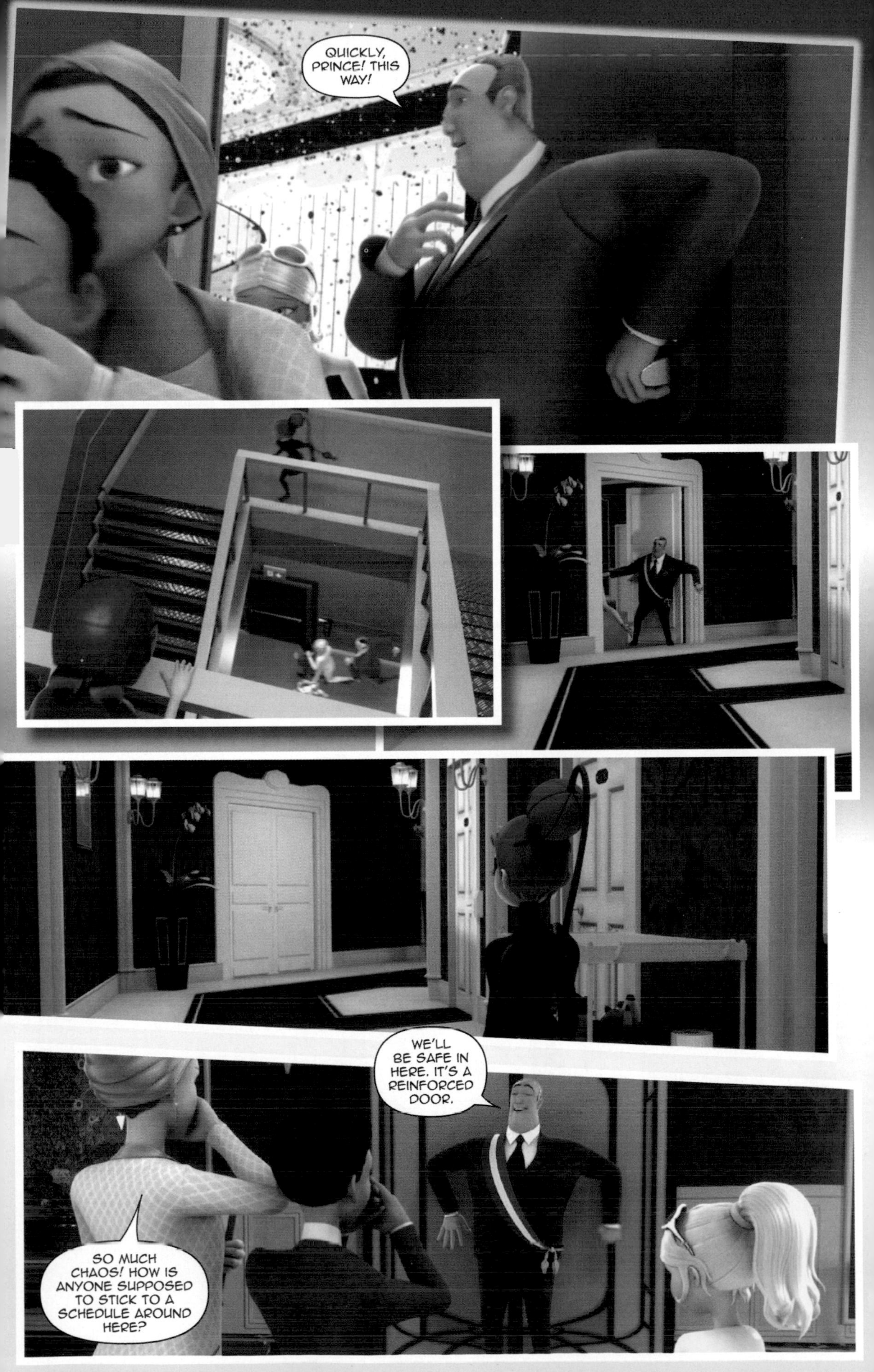
QUICKLY, PRINCE! THIS WAY!
WE'LL BE SAFE IN HERE. IT'S A REINFORCED DOOR.
SO MUCH CHAOS! HOW IS ANYONE SUPPOSED TO STICK TO A SCHEDULE AROUND HERE?

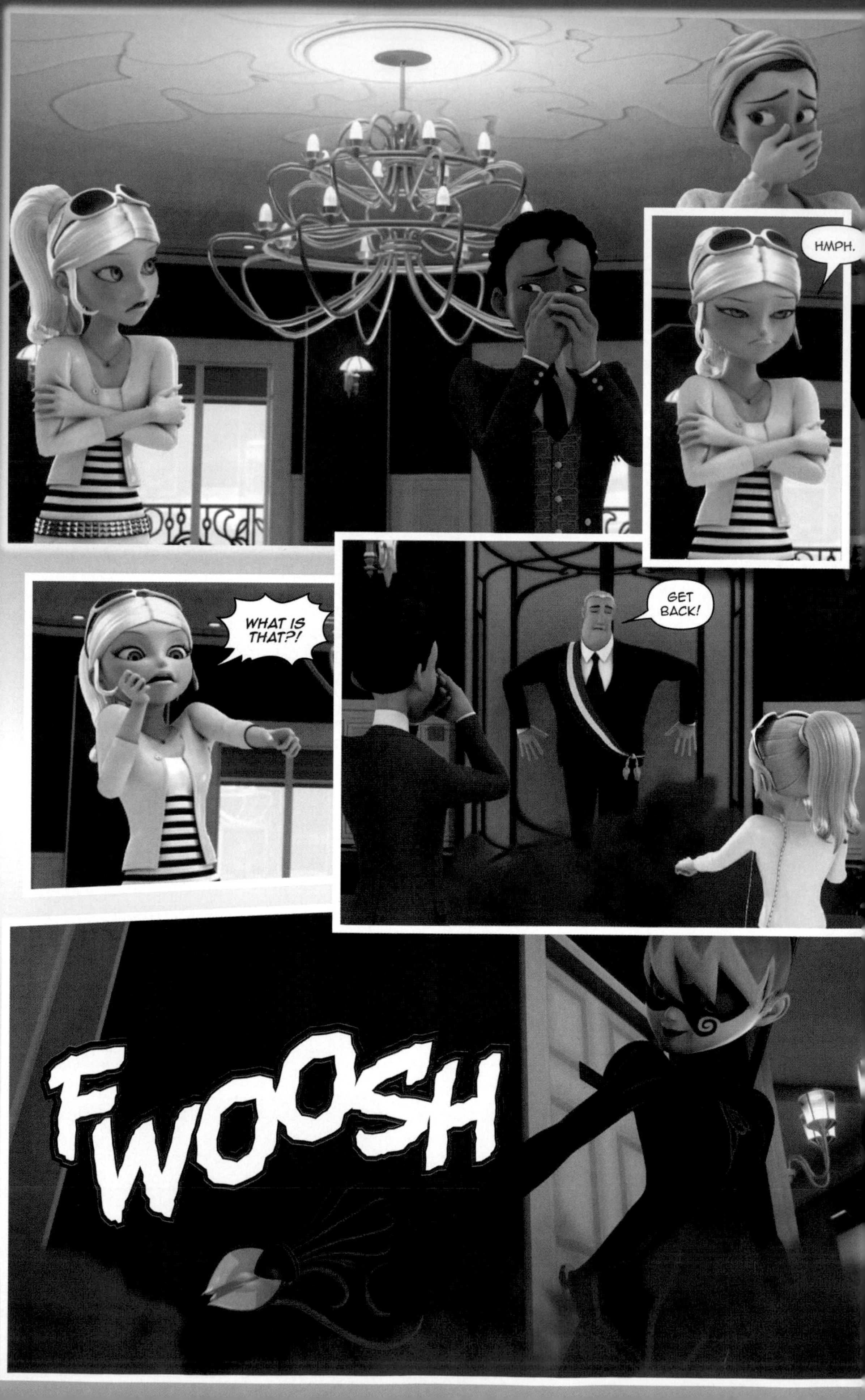
HMPH.
WHAT IS THAT?!
GET BACK!
FWOOSH

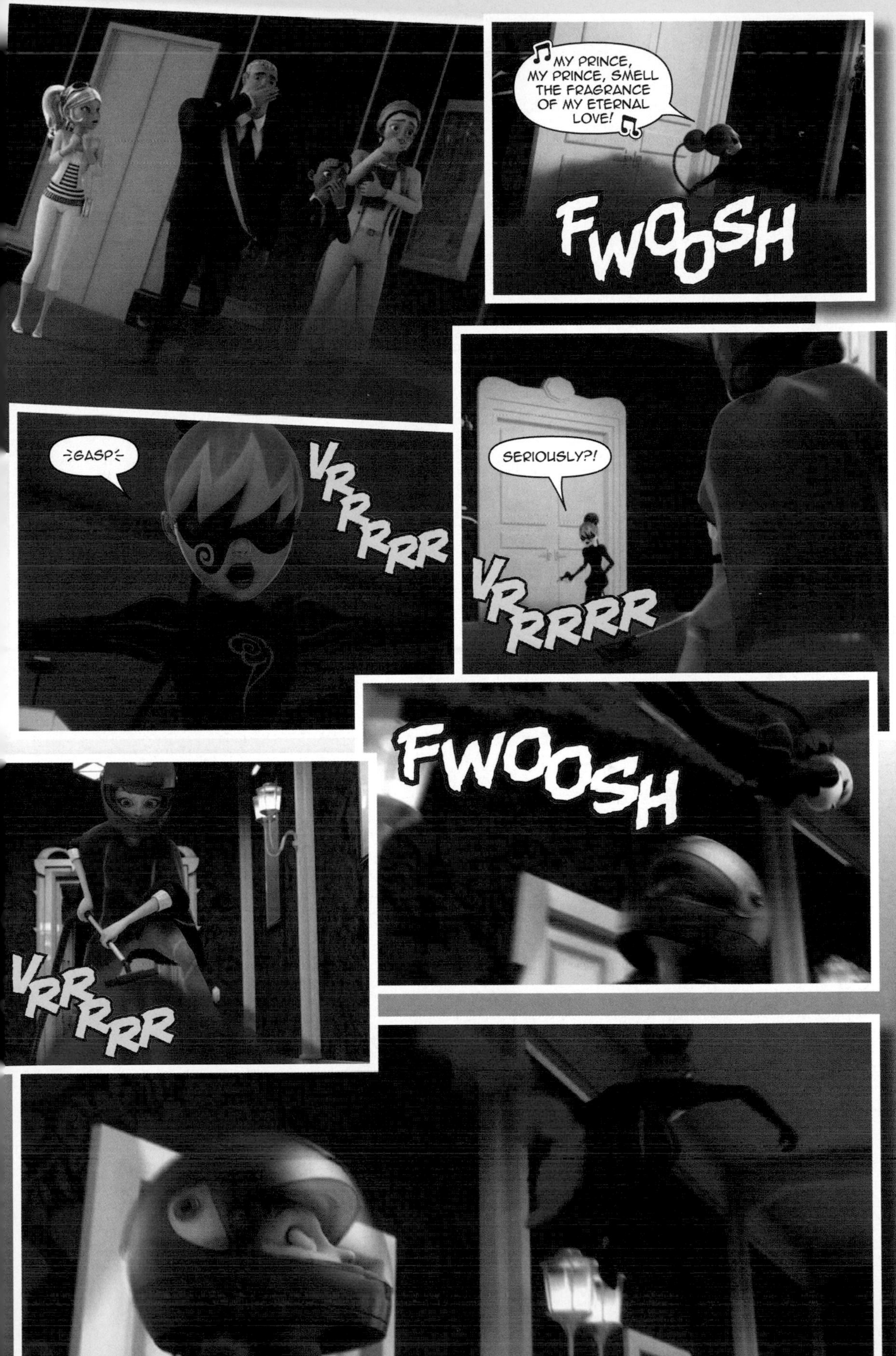
MY PRINCE, MY PRINCE, SMELL THE FRAGRANCE OF MY ETERNAL LOVE!
FWOOSH
GASP
VRRRRR
SERIOUSLY?!
VRRRRRR
VRRRRRR
FWOOSH

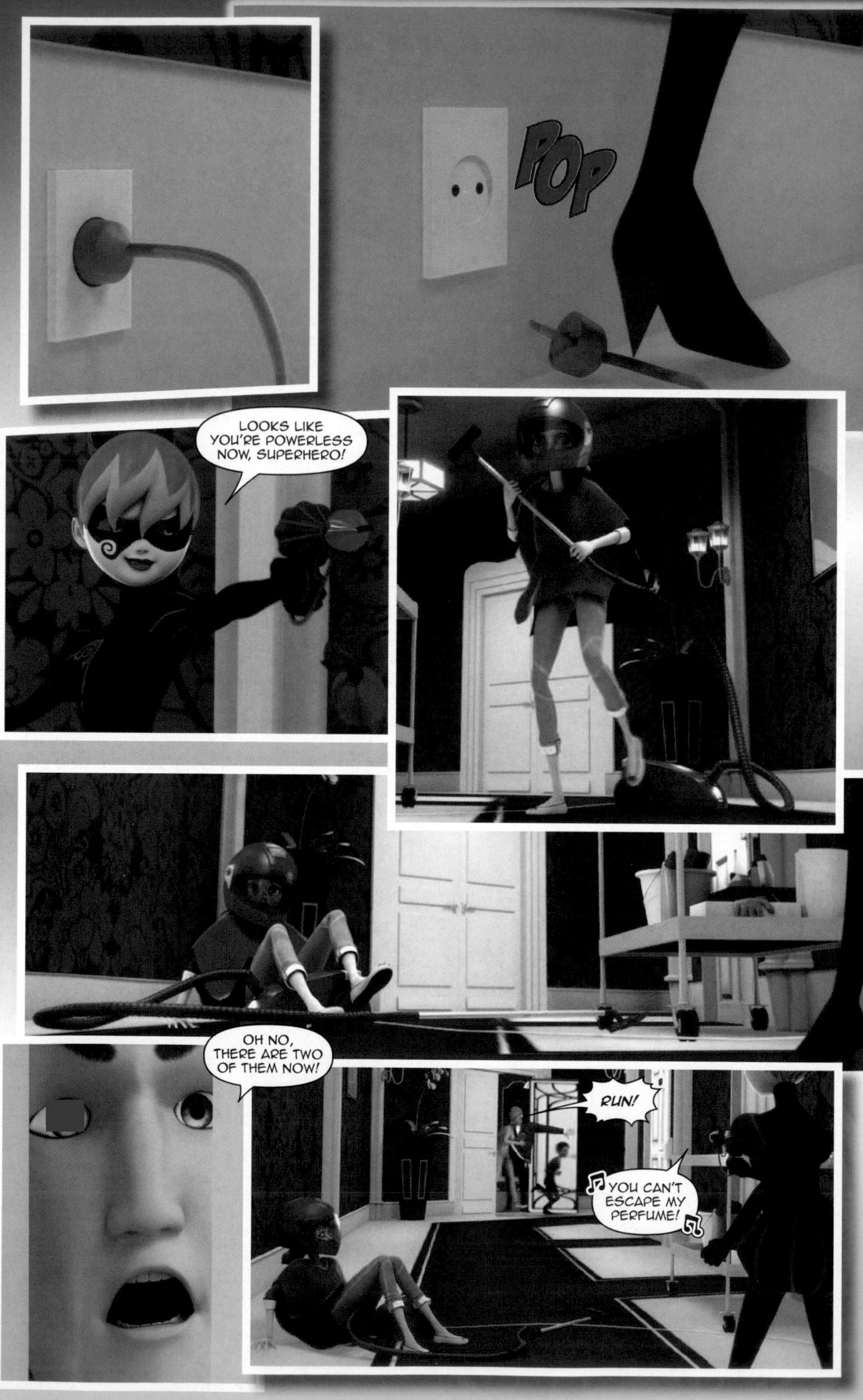
POP
LOOKS LIKE YOU'RE POWERLESS NOW, SUPERHERO!
OH NO, THERE ARE TWO OF THEM NOW!
RUN!
YOU CAN'T ESCAPE MY PERFUME!

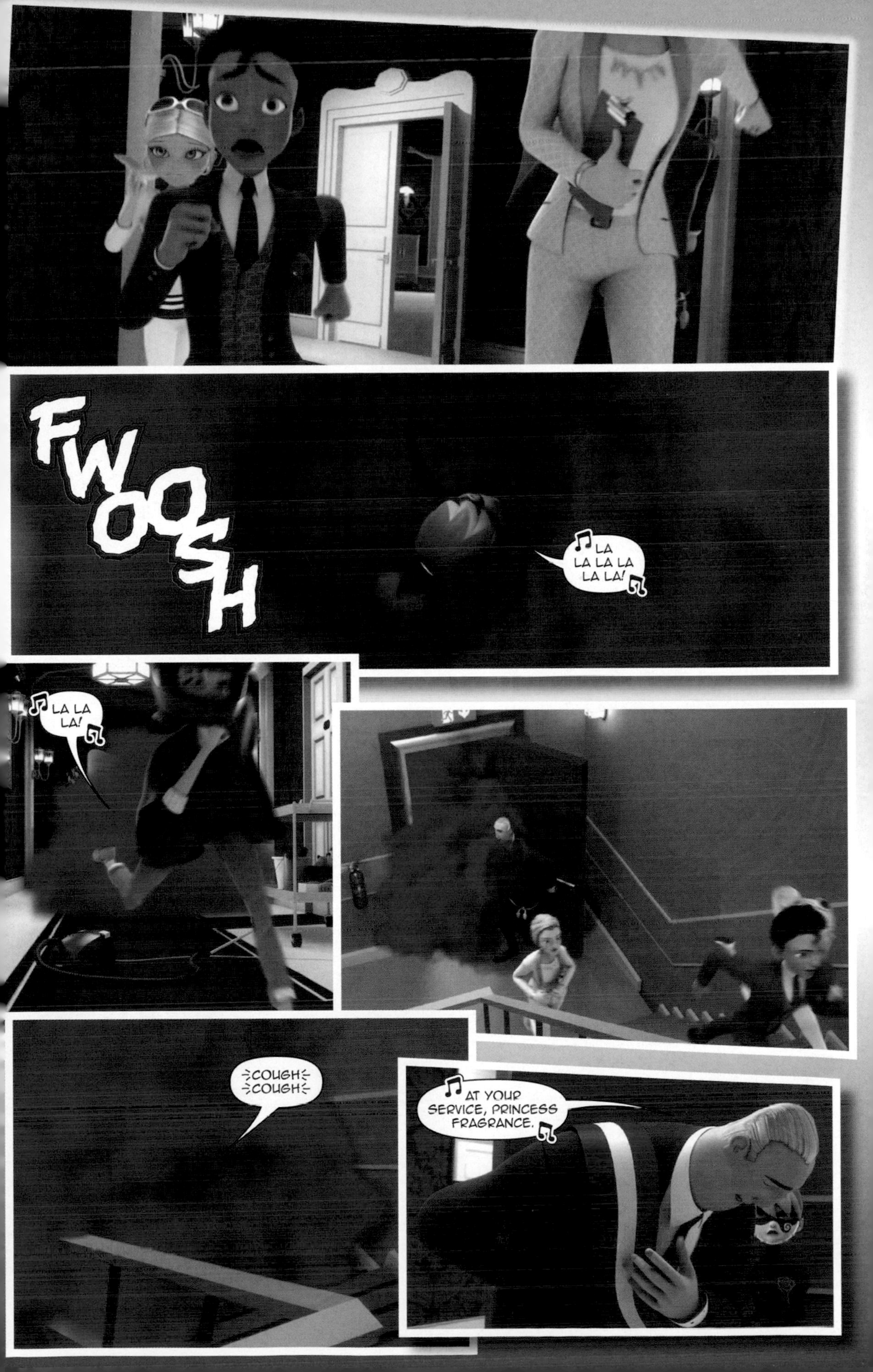
FWOOSH
LA LA LA LA LA LA!
LA LA LA!
COUGH COUGH
AT YOUR SERVICE, PRINCESS FRAGRANCE.

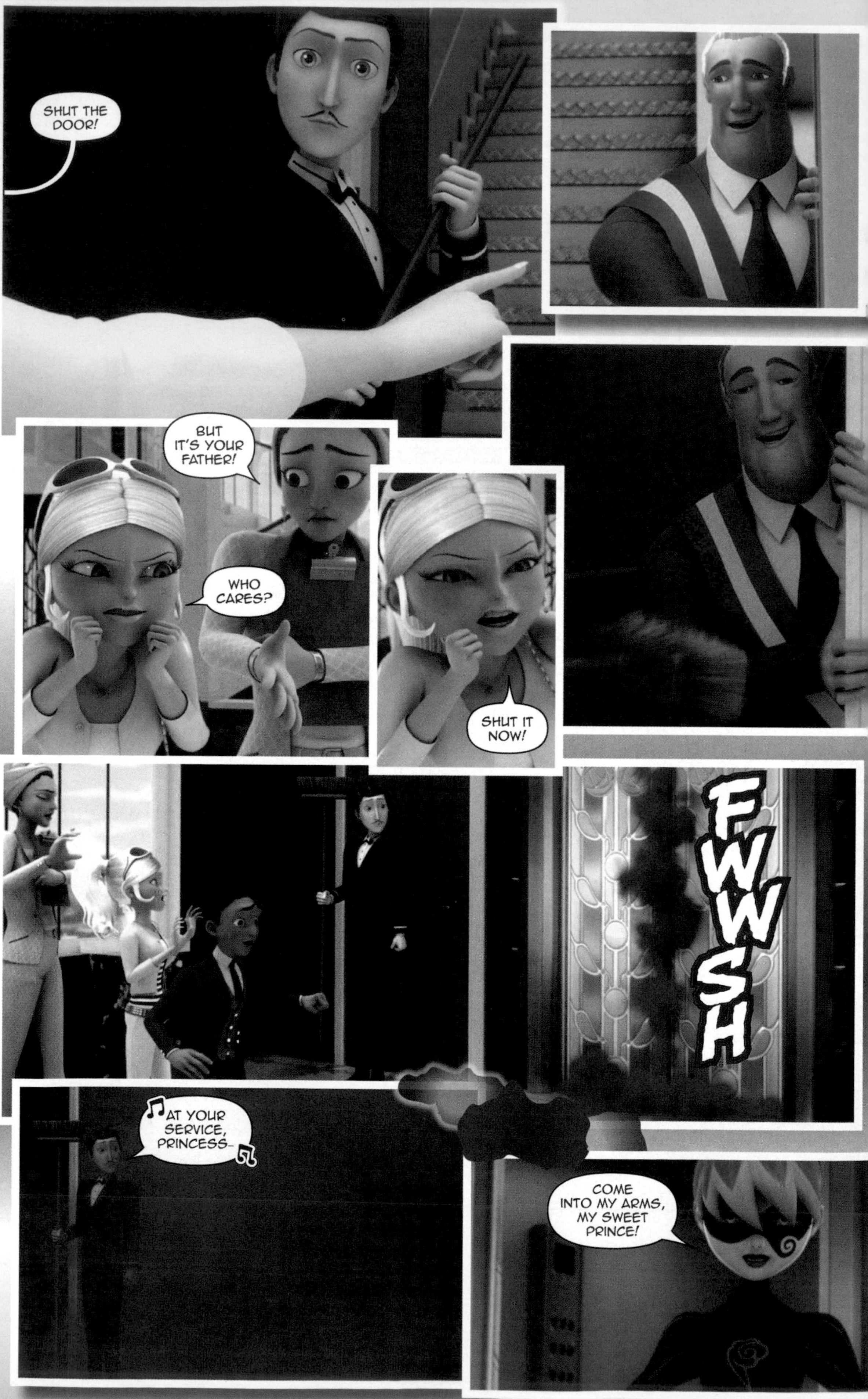
SHUT THE DOOR!
BUT IT'S YOUR FATHER!
WHO CARES?
SHUT IT NOW!
FWWSH
AT YOUR SERVICE, PRINCESS~
COME INTO MY ARMS, MY SWEET PRINCE!

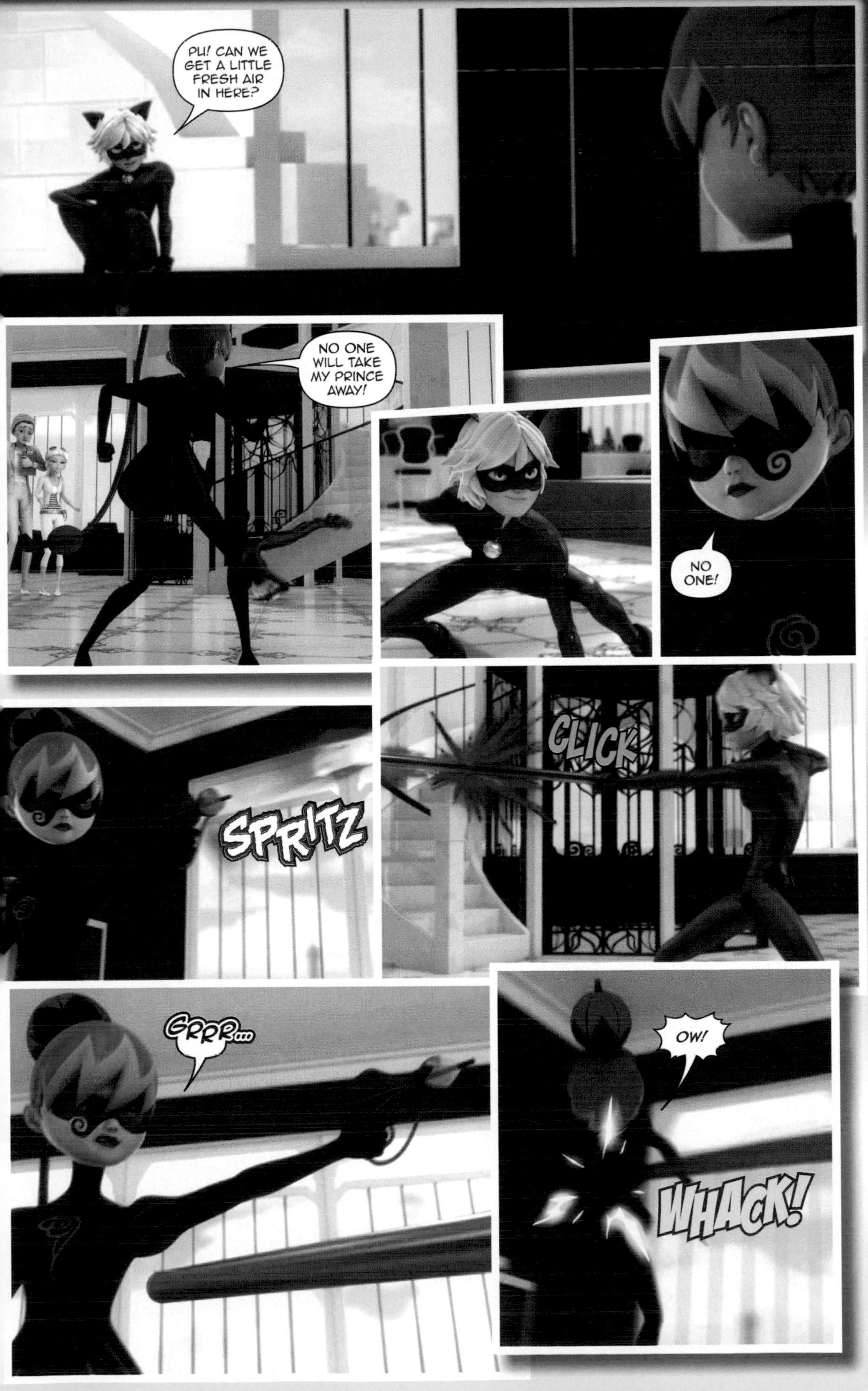
PU! CAN WE GET A LITTLE FRESH AIR IN HERE?
NO ONE WILL TAKE MY PRINCE AWAY!
NO ONE!
SPRITZ
CLICK
GRRR...
OW!
WHACK!

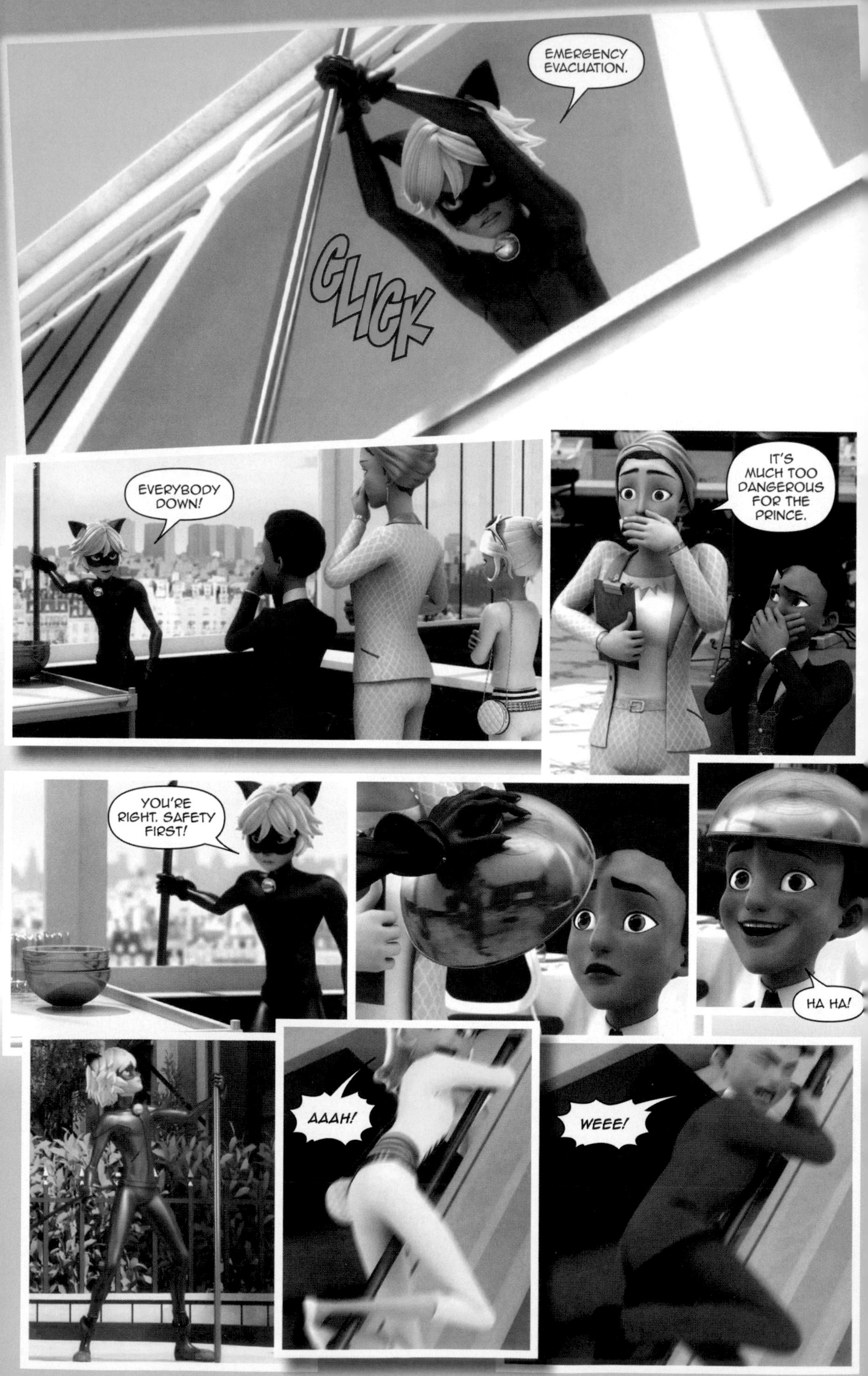
EMERGENCY EVACUATION.
CLICK
EVERYBODY DOWN!
IT'S MUCH TOO DANGEROUS FOR THE PRINCE.
YOU'RE RIGHT. SAFETY FIRST!
HA HA!
AAAH!
WEEE!

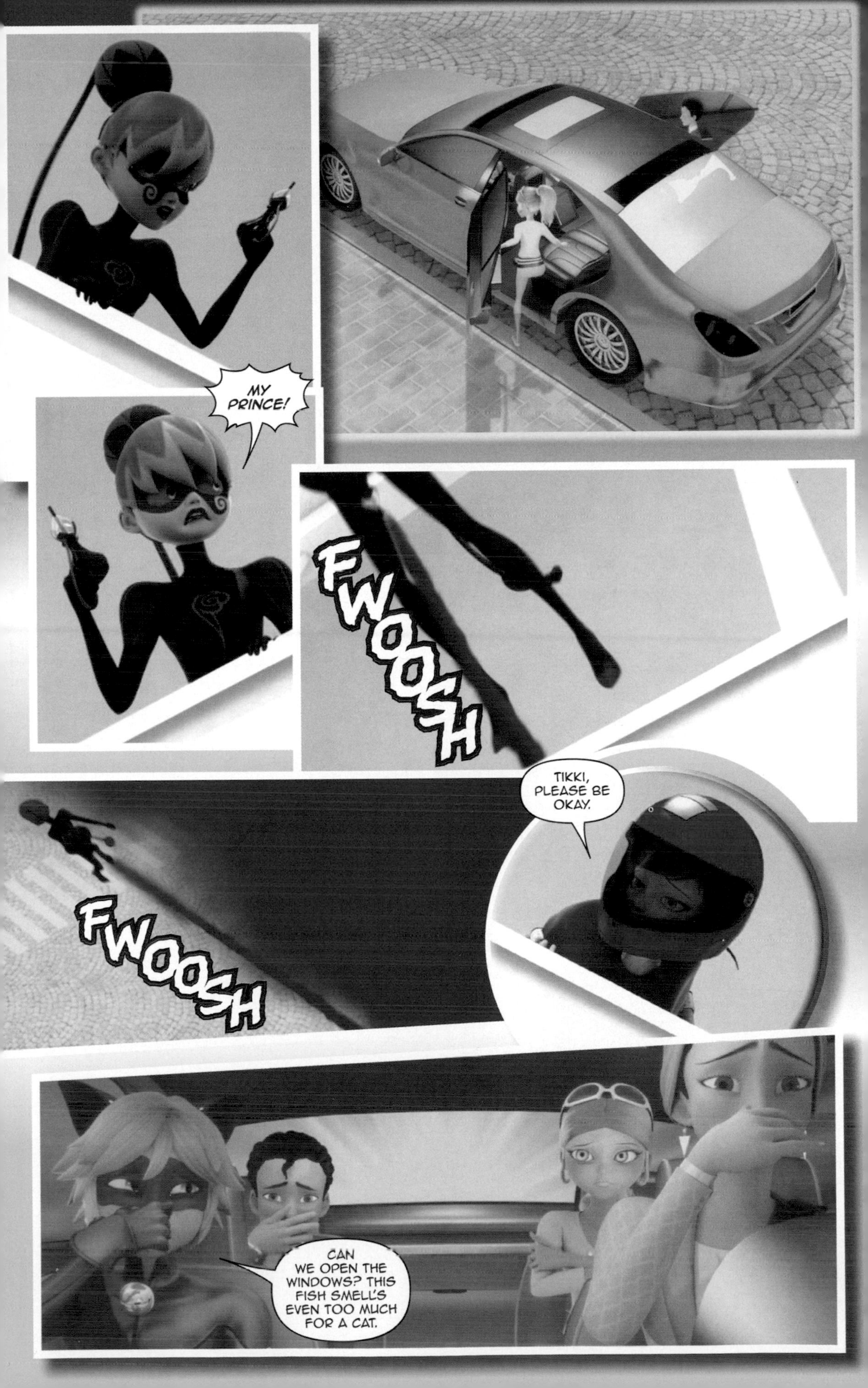
MY PRINCE!
FWOOSH
FWOOSH
TIKKI, PLEASE BE OKAY.
CAN WE OPEN THE WINDOWS? THIS FISH SMELL'S EVEN TOO MUCH FOR A CAT.

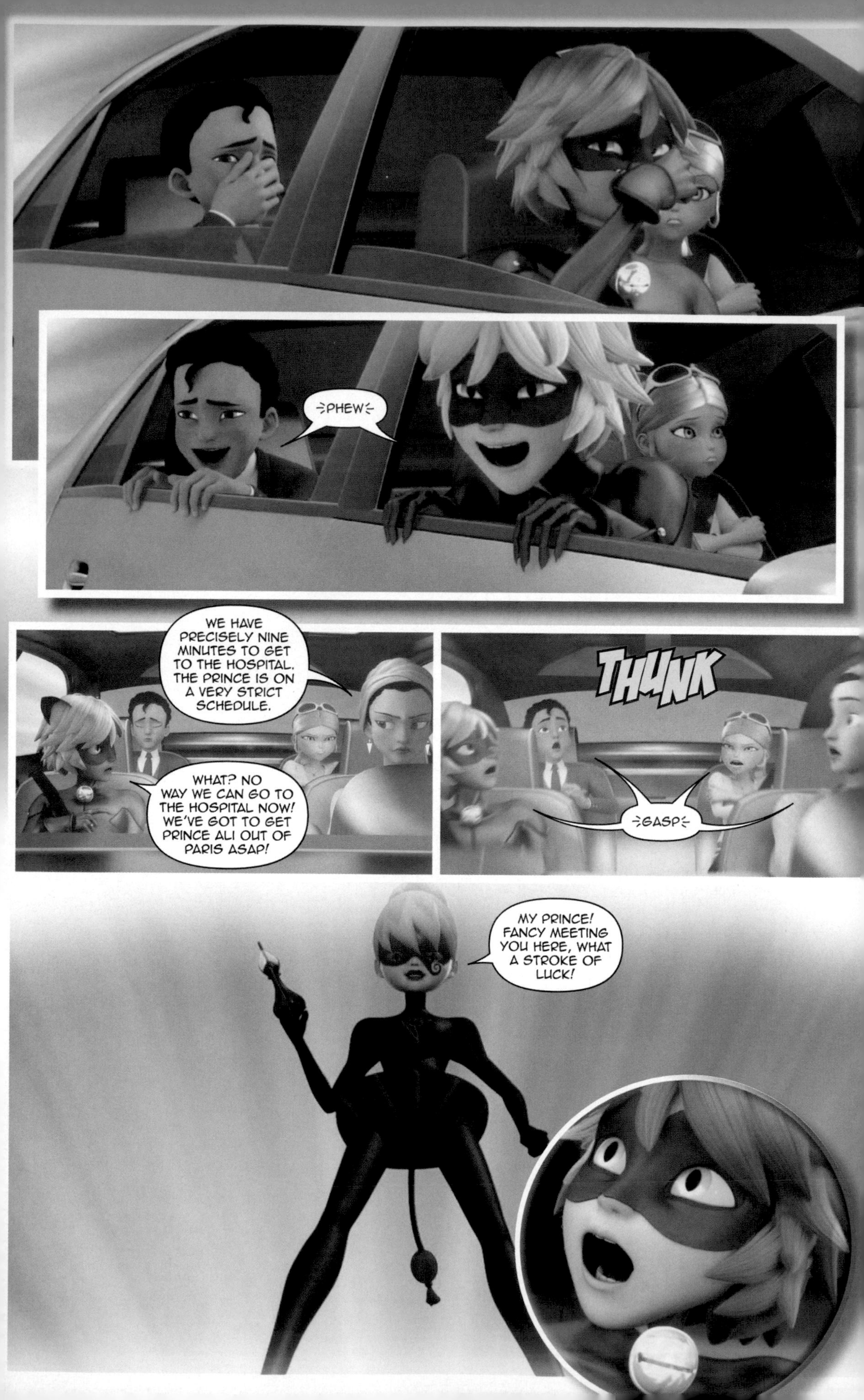
PHEW
WE HAVE PRECISELY NINE MINUTES TO GET TO THE HOSPITAL. THE PRINCE IS ON A VERY STRICT SCHEDULE.
WHAT? NO WAY WE CAN GO TO THE HOSPITAL NOW! WE'VE GOT TO GET PRINCE ALI OUT OF PARIS ASAP!
THUNK
GASP
MY PRINCE! FANCY MEETING YOU HERE, WHAT A STROKE OF LUCK!

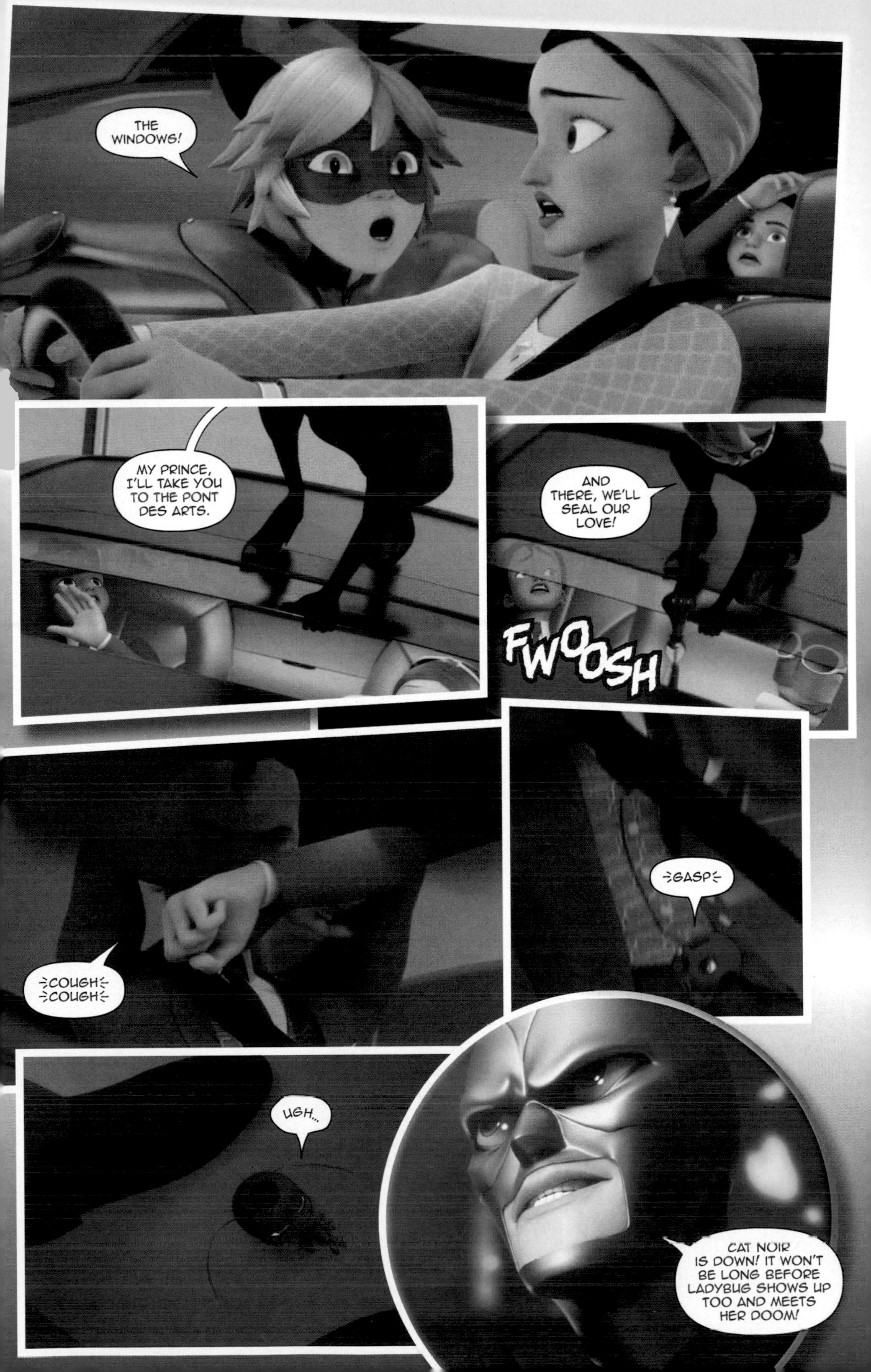
THE WINDOWS!
MY PRINCE, I'LL TAKE YOU TO THE PONT DES ARTS.
AND THERE, WE'LL SEAL OUR LOVE!
FWOOSH
COUGH COUGH
GASP
UGH...
CAT NOIR IS DOWN! IT WON'T BE LONG BEFORE LADYBUG SHOWS UP TOO AND MEETS HER DOOM!

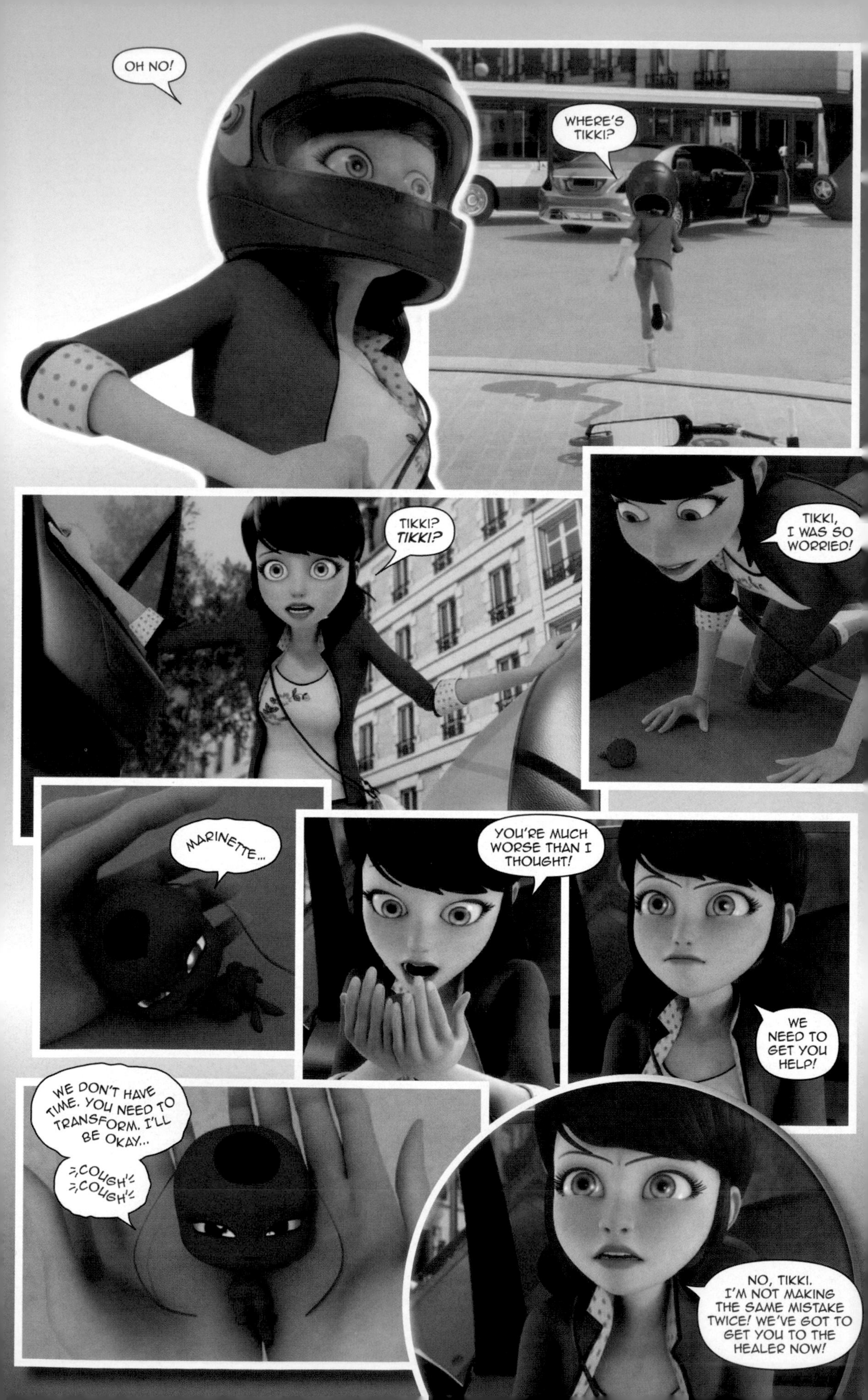
OH NO!
WHERE'S TIKKI?
TIKKI? TIKKI?
TIKKI, I WAS SO WORRIED!
MARINETTE...
YOU'RE MUCH WORSE THAN I THOUGHT!
WE NEED TO GET YOU HELP!
WE DON'T HAVE TIME. YOU NEED TO TRANSFORM. I'LL BE OKAY...
COUGH *COUGH*
NO, TIKKI. I'M NOT MAKING THE SAME MISTAKE TWICE! WE'VE GOT TO GET YOU TO THE HEALER NOW!

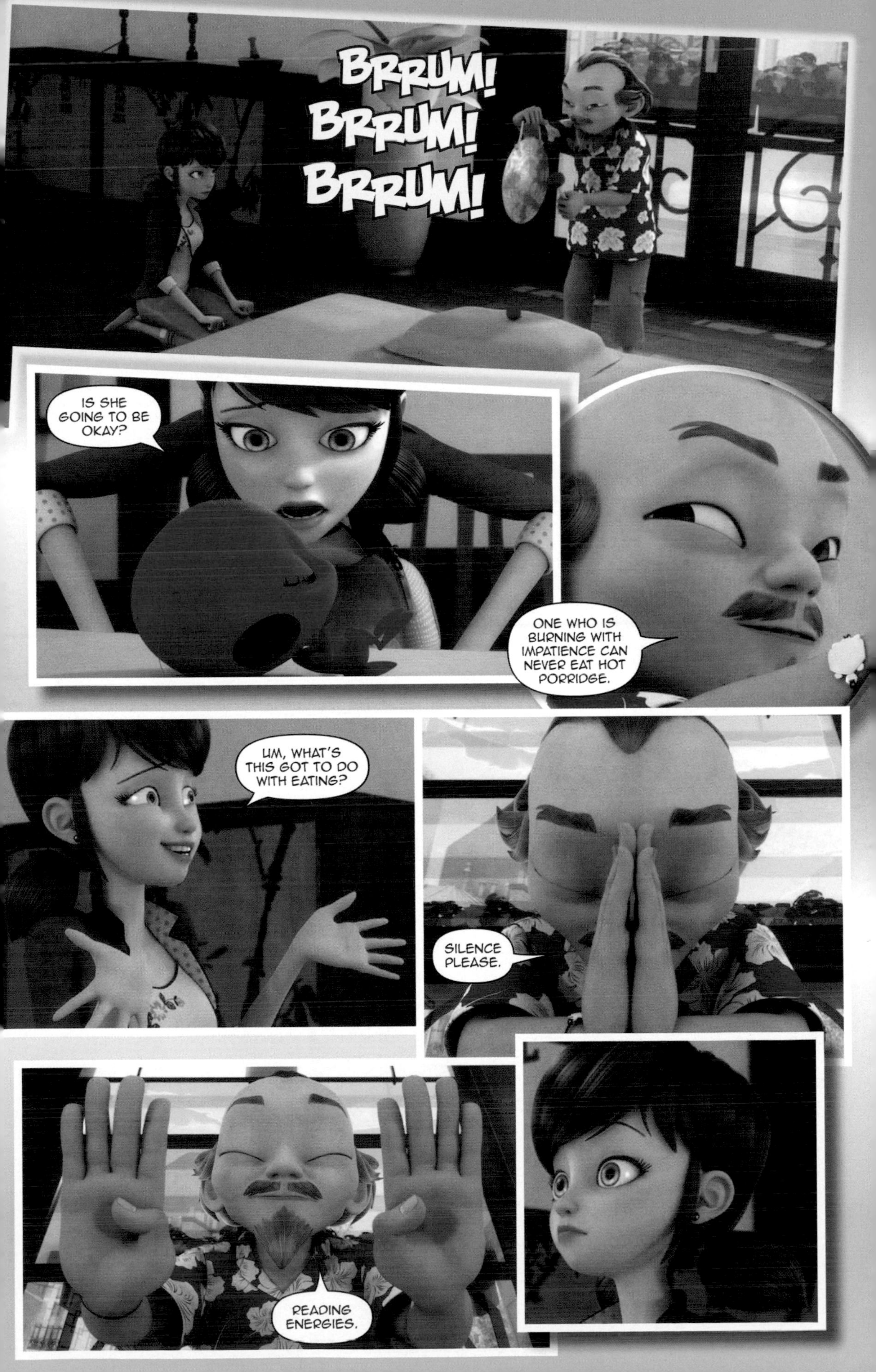
BRRUM! BRRUM! BRRUM!
IS SHE GOING TO BE OKAY?
ONE WHO IS BURNING WITH IMPATIENCE CAN NEVER EAT HOT PORRIDGE.
UM, WHAT'S THIS GOT TO DO WITH EATING?
SILENCE PLEASE.
READING ENERGIES.

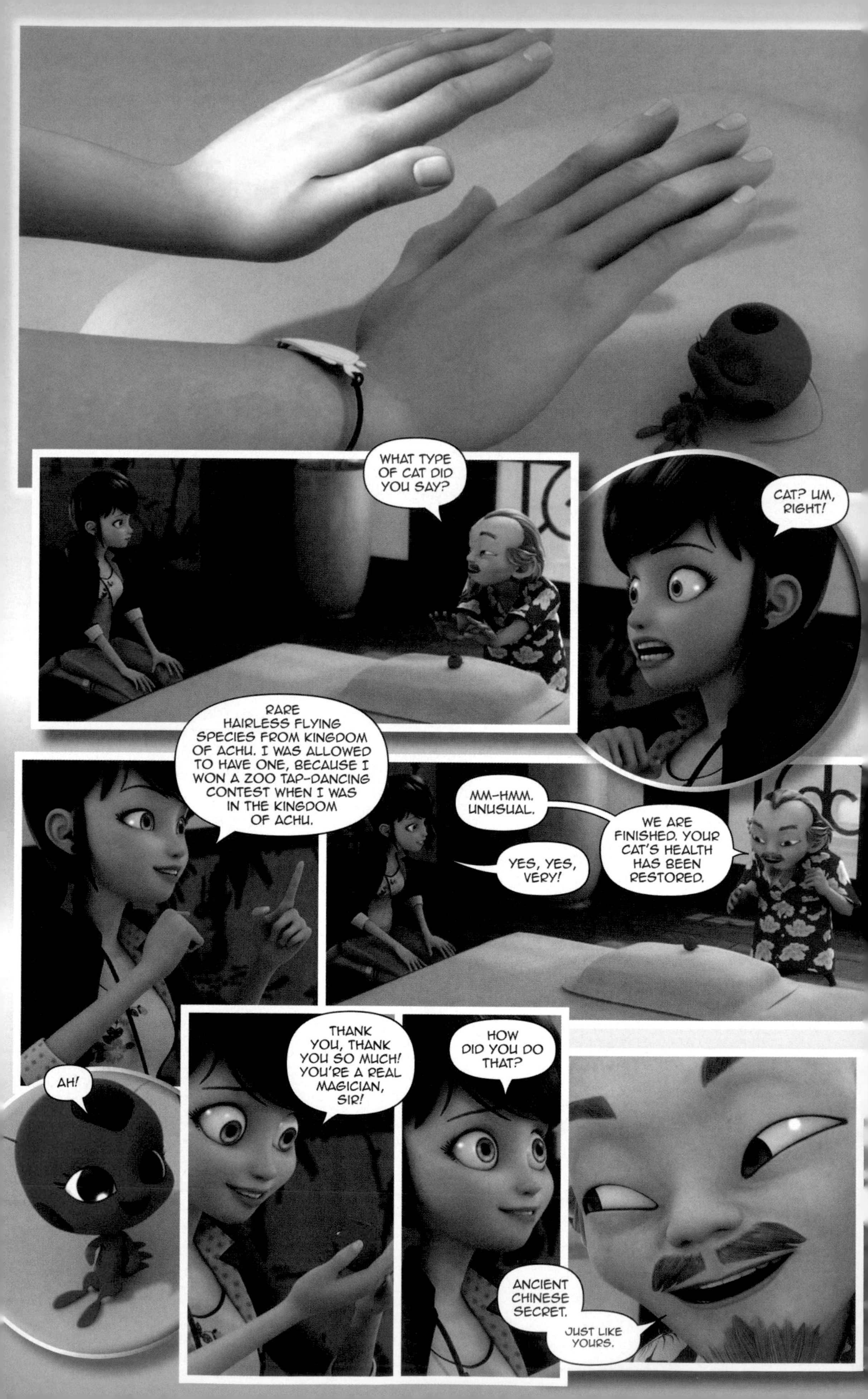
WHAT TYPE OF CAT DID YOU SAY?
CAT? UM, RIGHT!
RARE HAIRLESS FLYING SPECIES FROM KINGDOM OF ACHU. I WAS ALLOWED TO HAVE ONE, BECAUSE I WON A ZOO TAP-DANCING CONTEST WHEN I WAS IN THE KINGDOM OF ACHU.
MM-HMM. UNUSUAL.
YES, YES, VERY!
WE ARE FINISHED. YOUR CAT'S HEALTH HAS BEEN RESTORED.
AH!
THANK YOU, THANK YOU SO MUCH! YOU'RE A REAL MAGICIAN, SIR!
HOW DID YOU DO THAT?
ANCIENT CHINESE SECRET.
JUST LIKE YOURS.

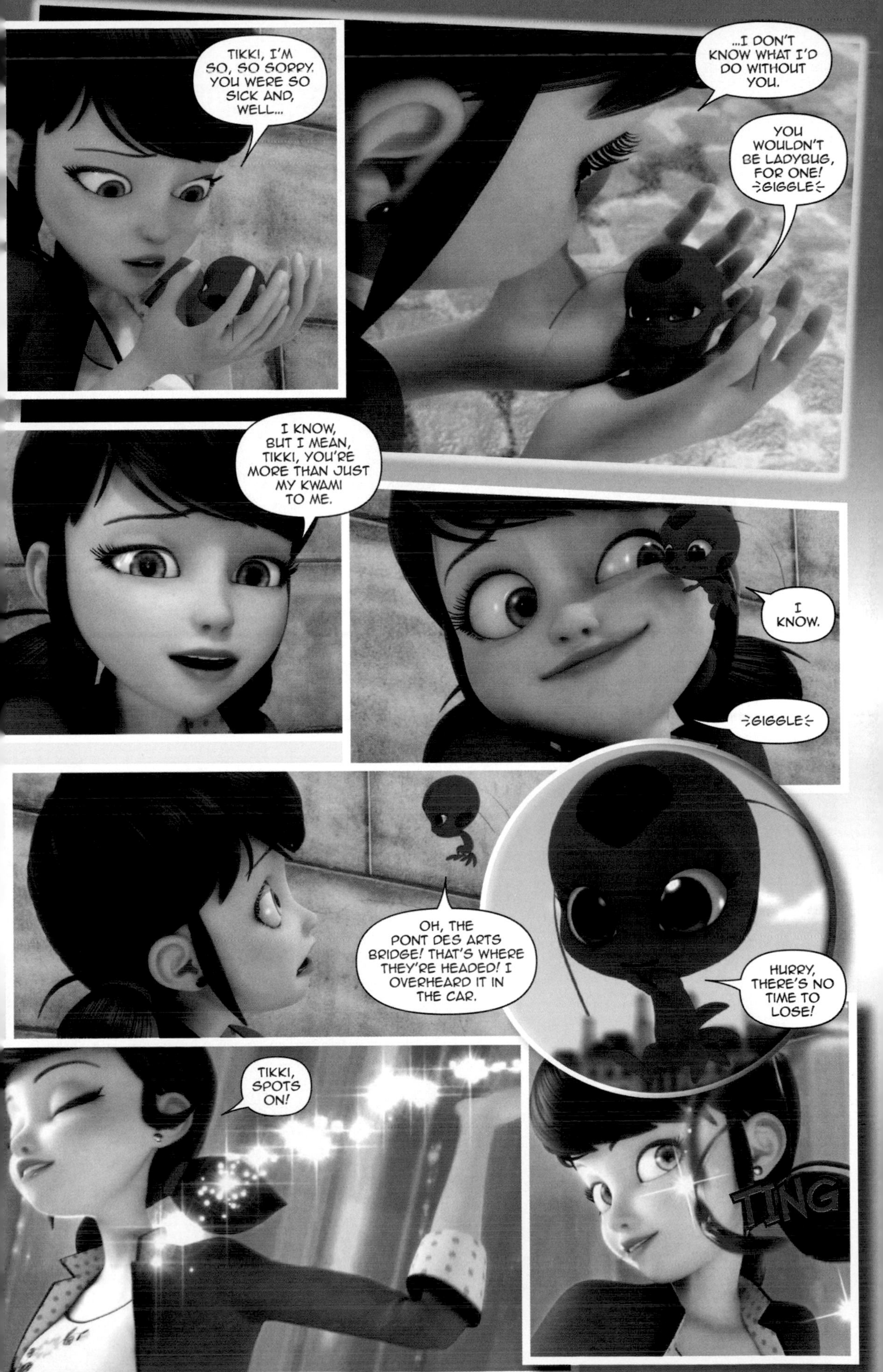
TIKKI, I'M SO, SO SORRY. YOU WERE SO SICK AND, WELL...
...I DON'T KNOW WHAT I'D DO WITHOUT YOU.
YOU WOULDN'T BE LADYBUG, FOR ONE! ⋟GIGGLE⋞
I KNOW, BUT I MEAN, TIKKI, YOU'RE MORE THAN JUST MY KWAMI TO ME.
I KNOW.
⋟GIGGLE⋞
OH, THE PONT DES ARTS BRIDGE! THAT'S WHERE THEY'RE HEADED! I OVERHEARD IT IN THE CAR.
HURRY, THERE'S NO TIME TO LOSE!
TIKKI, SPOTS ON!
TING

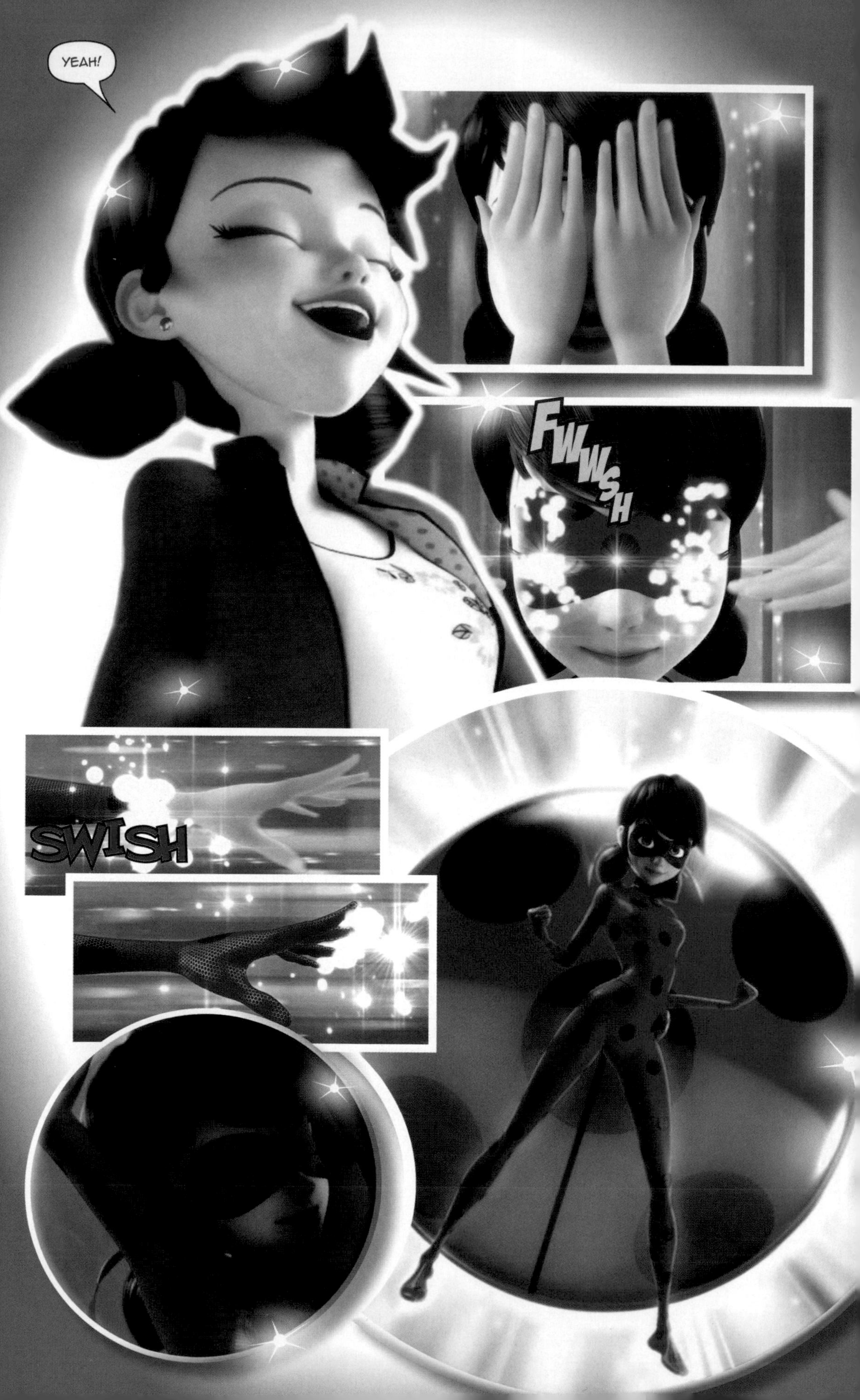
YEAH!
FWWSH
SWISH

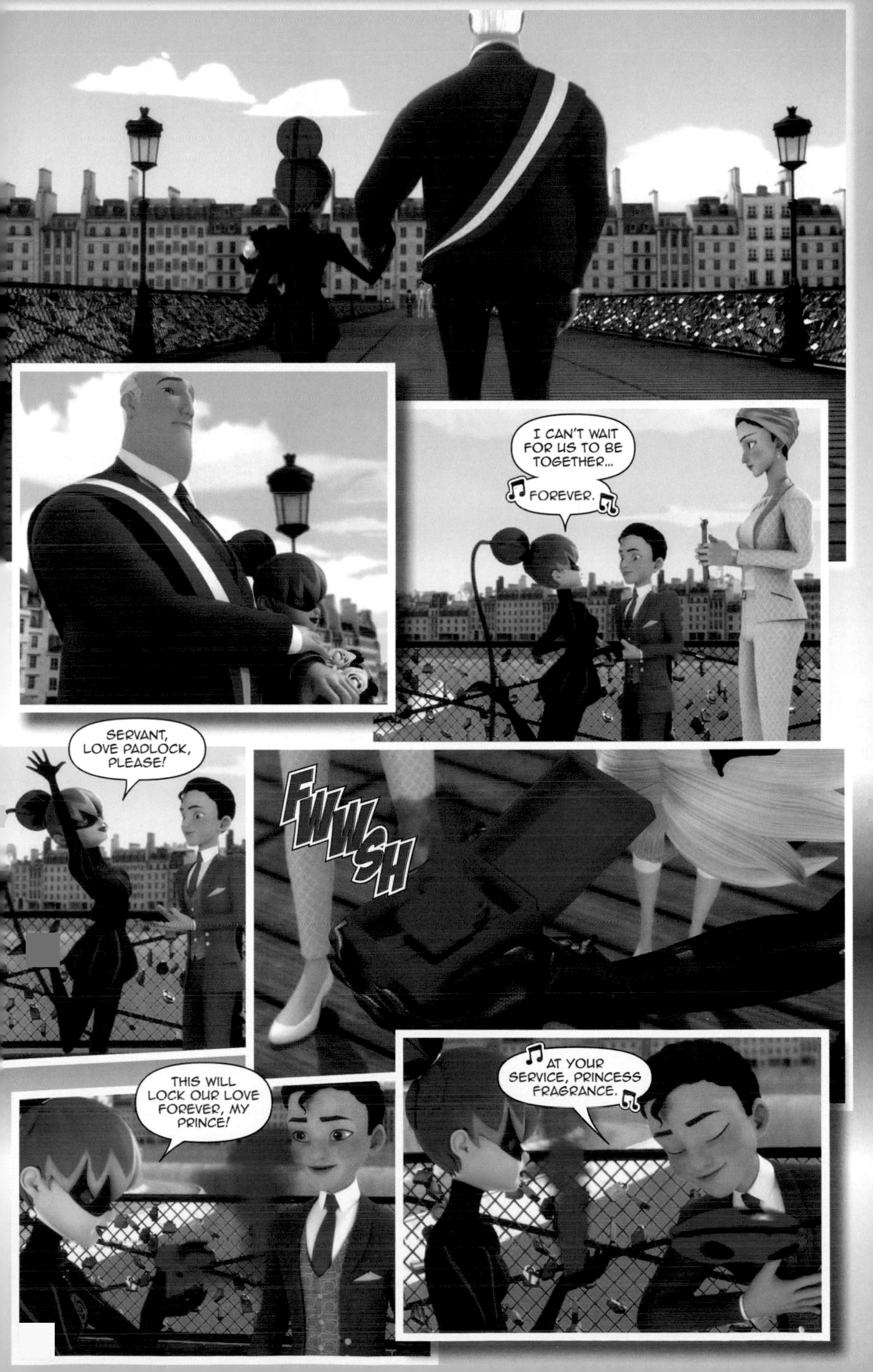

I CAN'T WAIT FOR US TO BE TOGETHER... FOREVER.
SERVANT, LOVE PADLOCK, PLEASE!
FWWSH
THIS WILL LOCK OUR LOVE FOREVER, MY PRINCE!
AT YOUR SERVICE, PRINCESS FRAGRANCE.

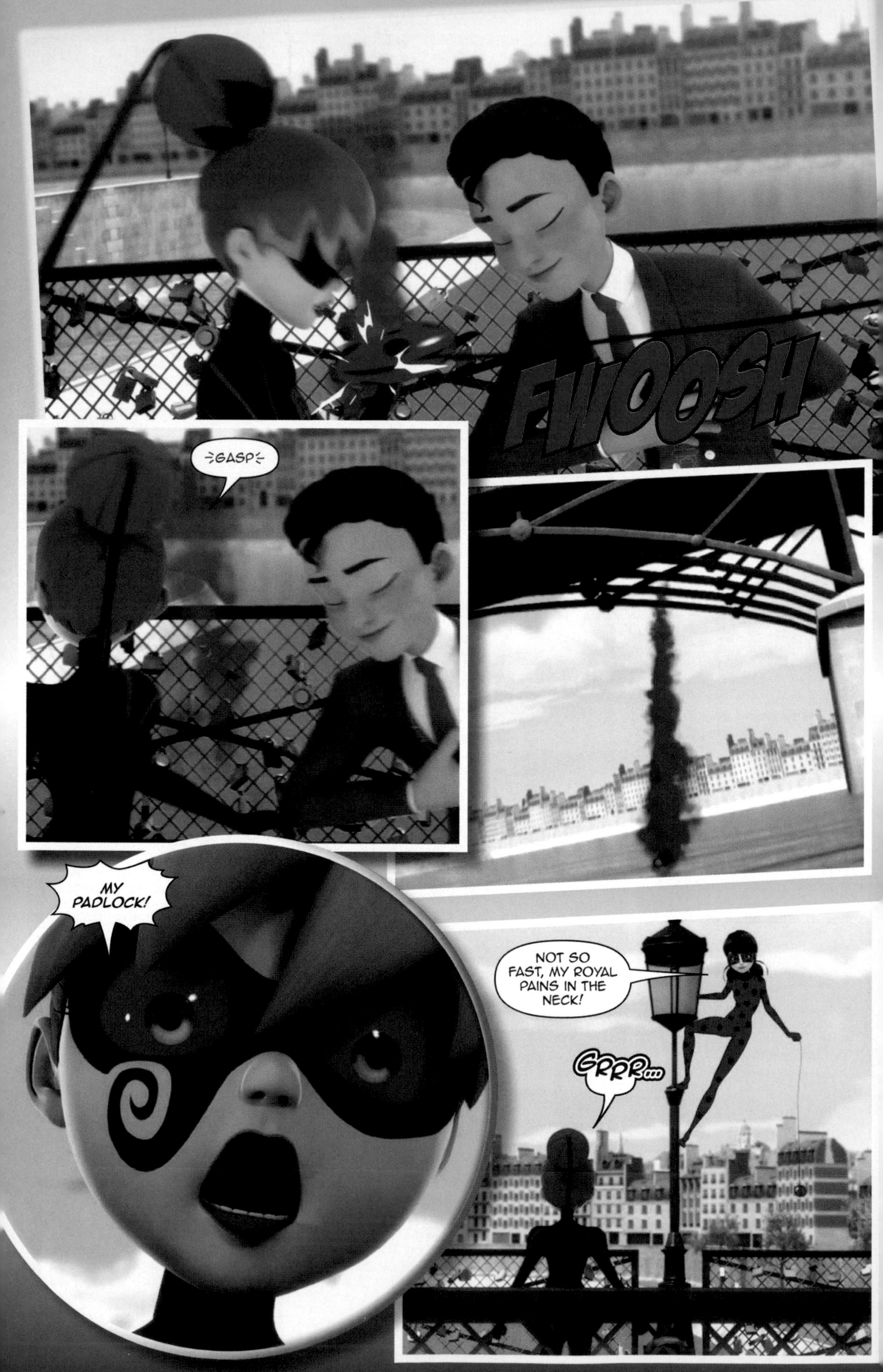
FWOOSH
GASP
MY PADLOCK!
NOT SO FAST, MY ROYAL PAINS IN THE NECK!
GRRR...

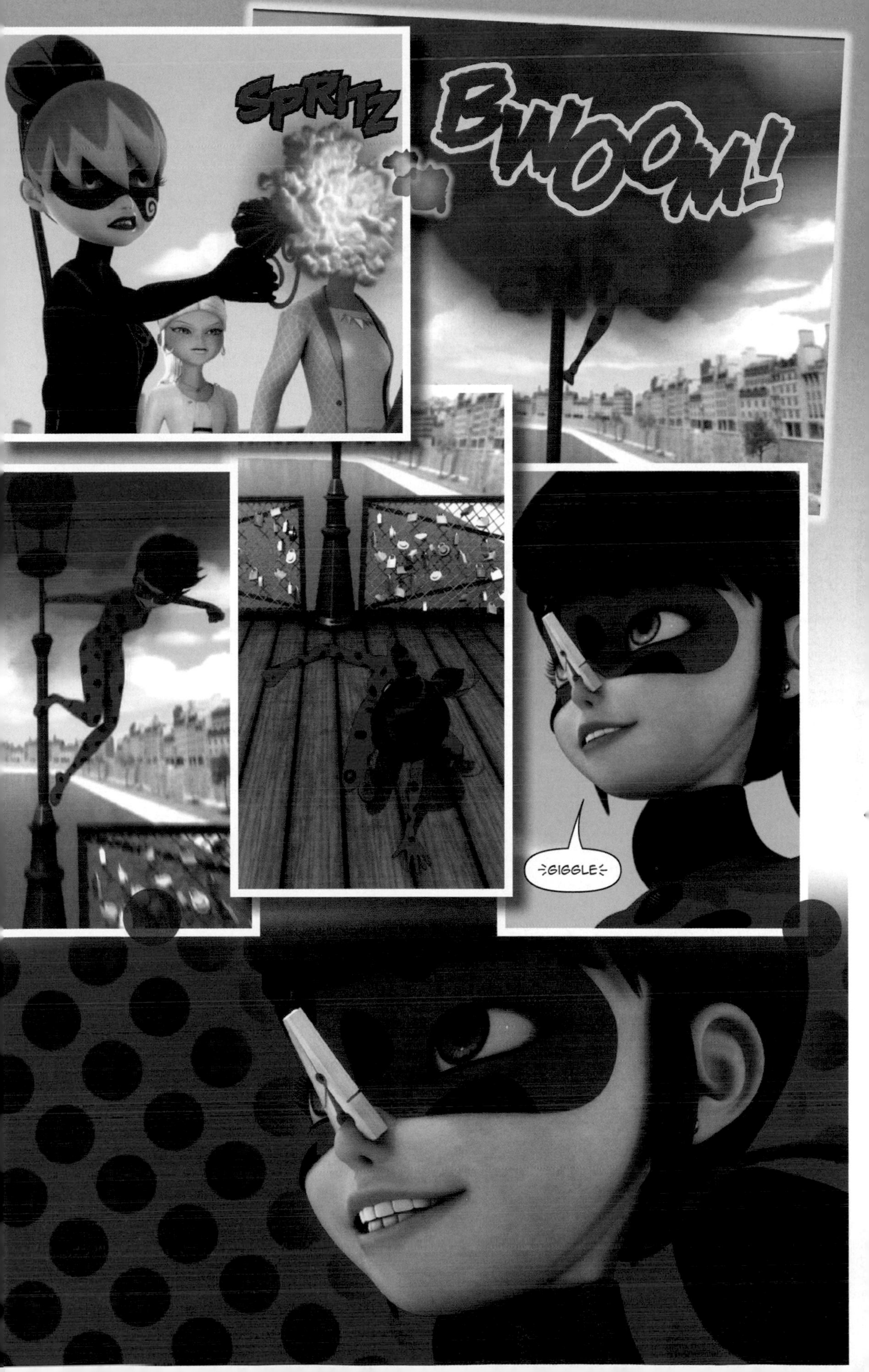
SPRITZ
BWOOM!
GIGGLE

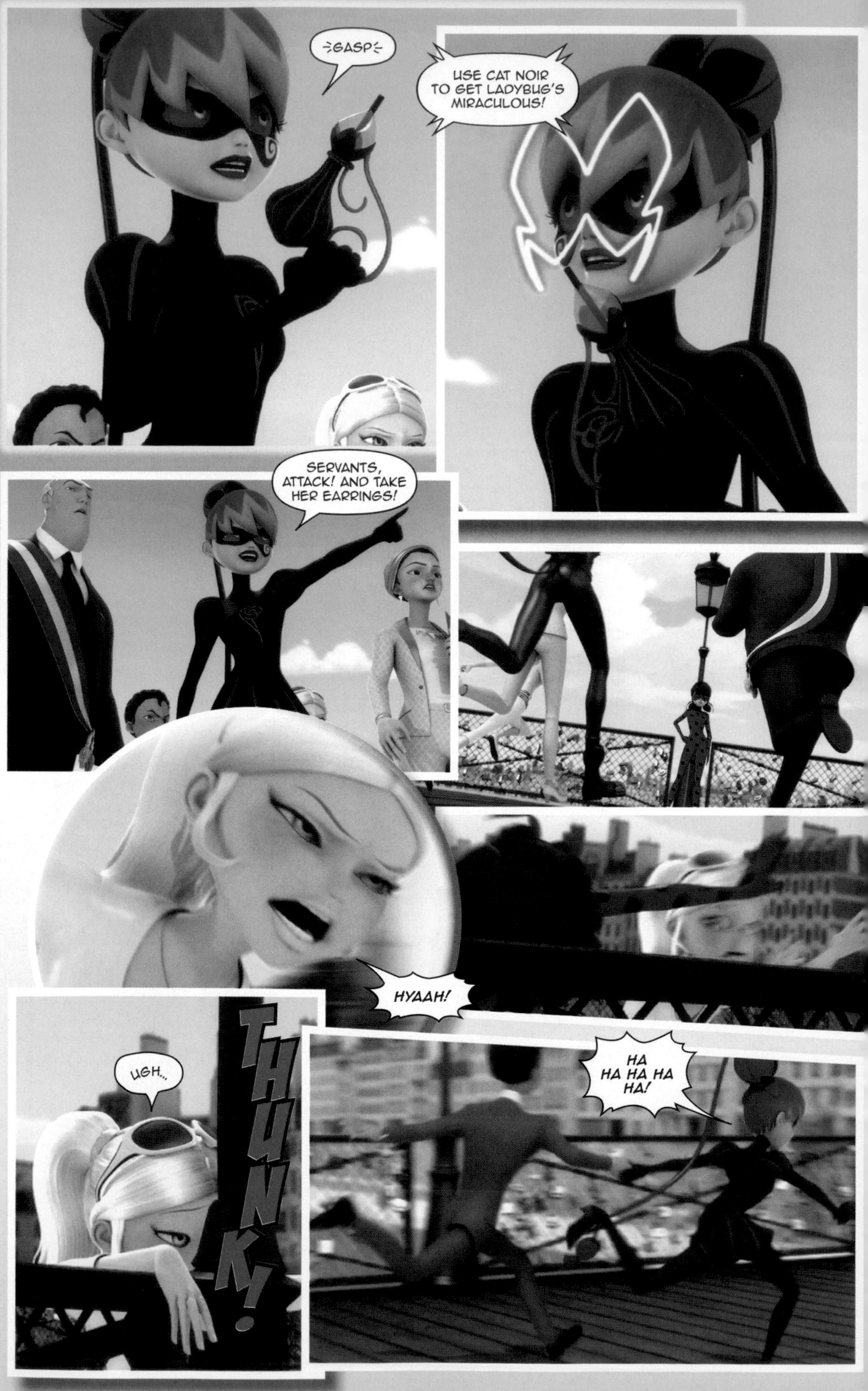
GASP
USE CAT NOIR TO GET LADYBUG'S MIRACULOUS!
SERVANTS, ATTACK! AND TAKE HER EARRINGS!
HYAAH!
UGH...
THUNK!
HA HA HA HA HA!

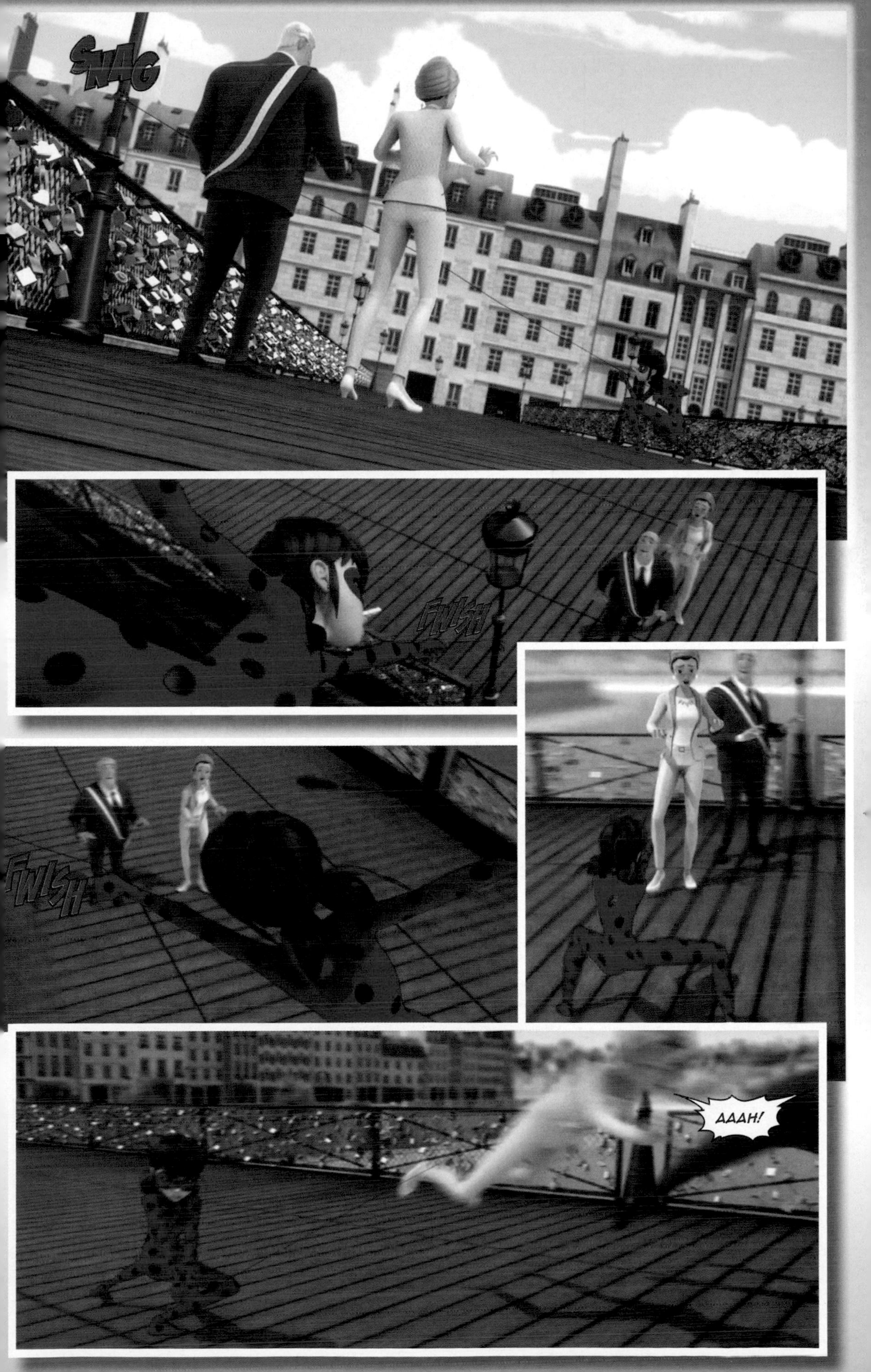
SNAG
FWISH
FWISH
AAAH!

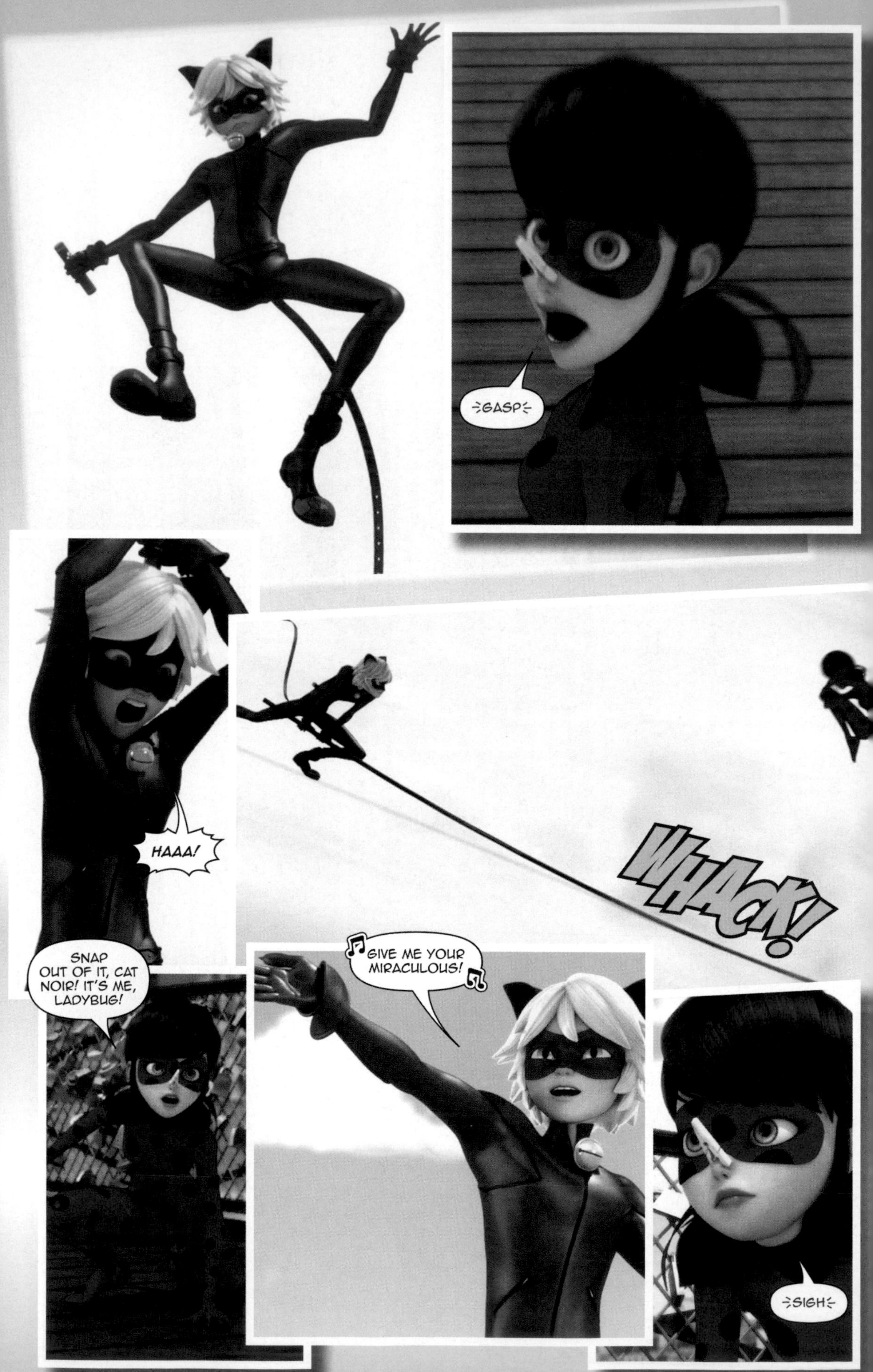
GASP
HAAA!
WHACK!
SNAP OUT OF IT, CAT NOIR! IT'S ME, LADYBUG!
GIVE ME YOUR MIRACULOUS!
SIGH

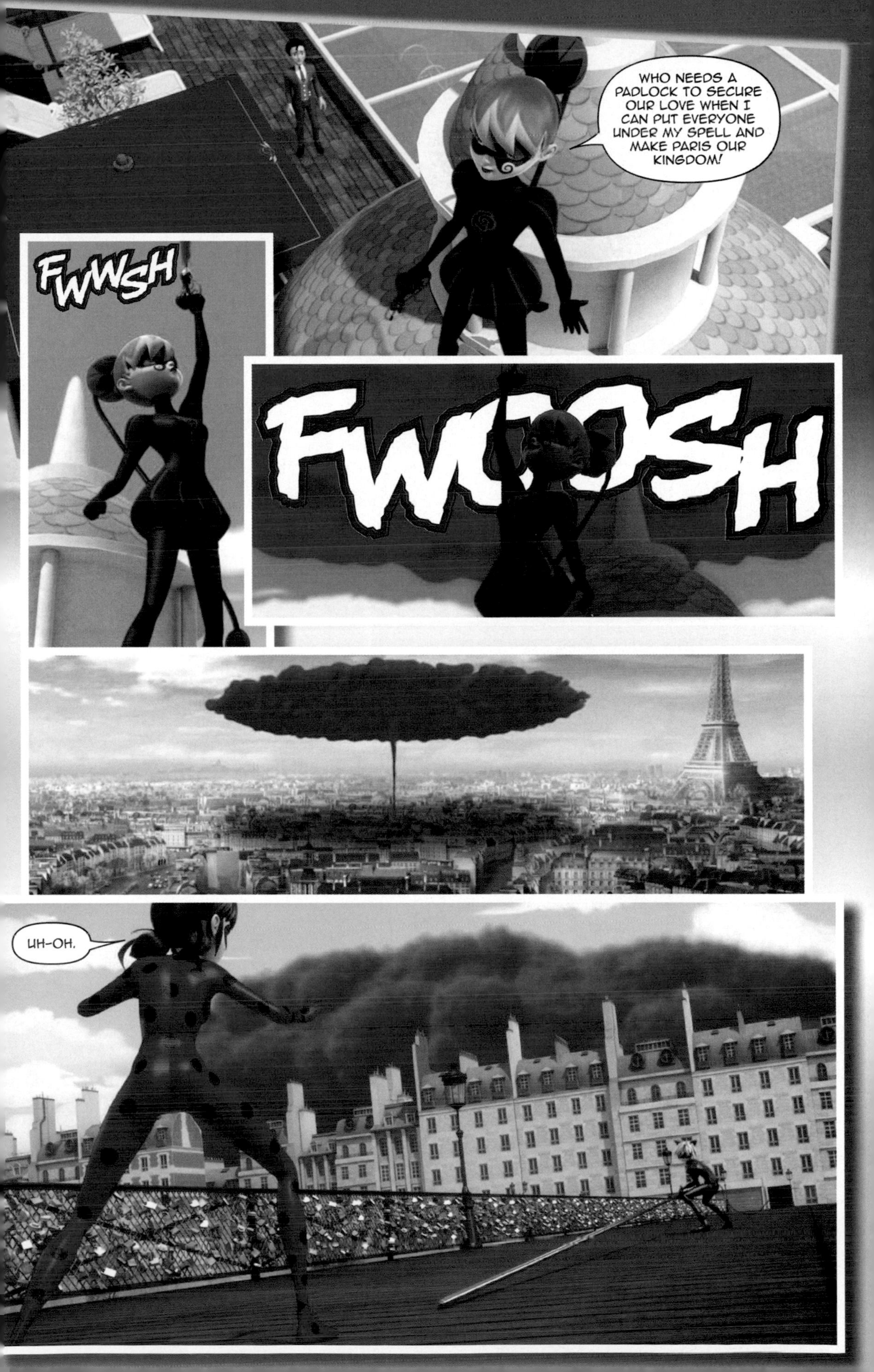
WHO NEEDS A PADLOCK TO SECURE OUR LOVE WHEN I CAN PUT EVERYONE UNDER MY SPELL AND MAKE PARIS OUR KINGDOM!
FWWSH
FWOOSH
UH-OH.

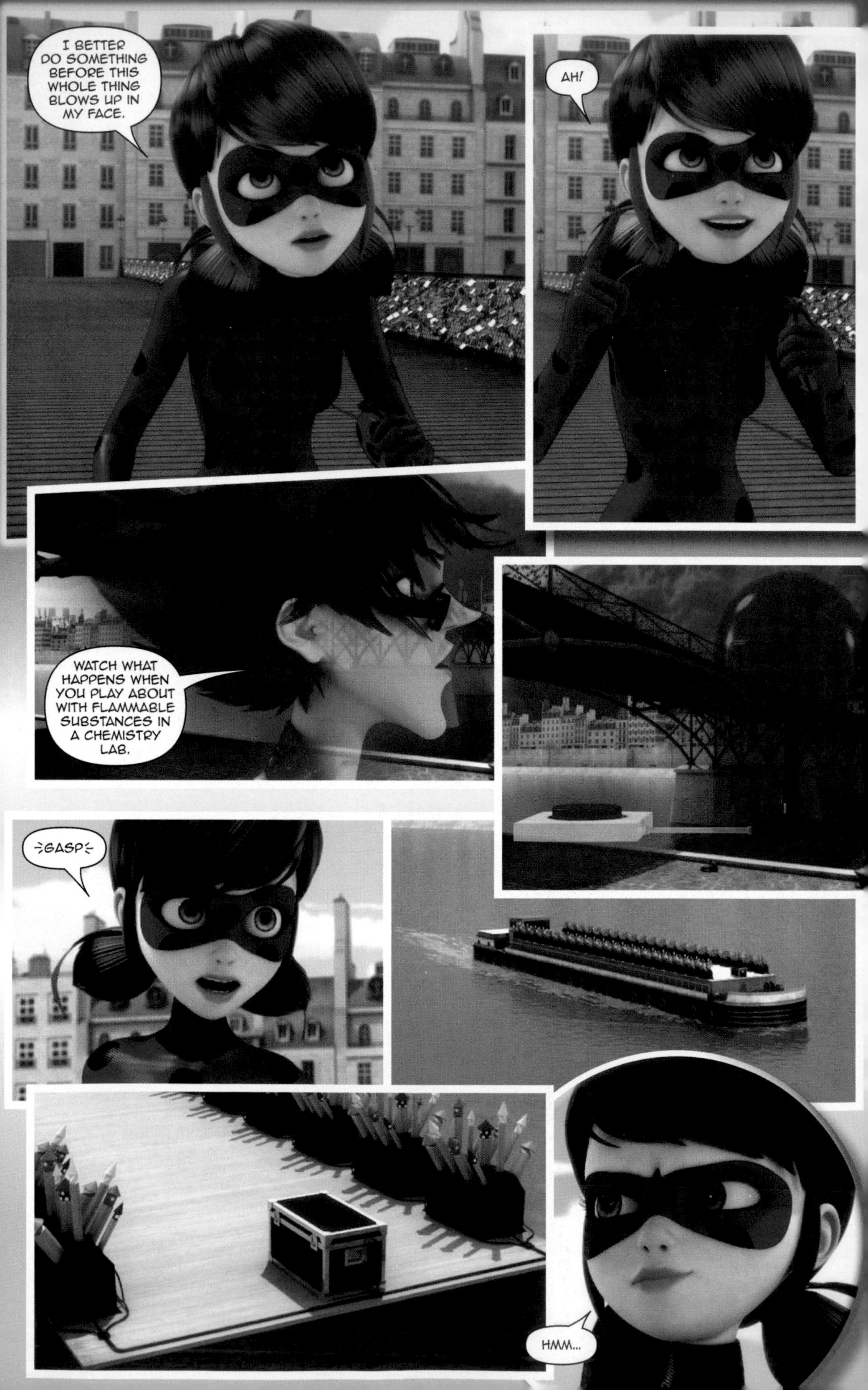
I BETTER DO SOMETHING BEFORE THIS WHOLE THING BLOWS UP IN MY FACE.
AH!
WATCH WHAT HAPPENS WHEN YOU PLAY ABOUT WITH FLAMMABLE SUBSTANCES IN A CHEMISTRY LAB.
GASP
HMM...

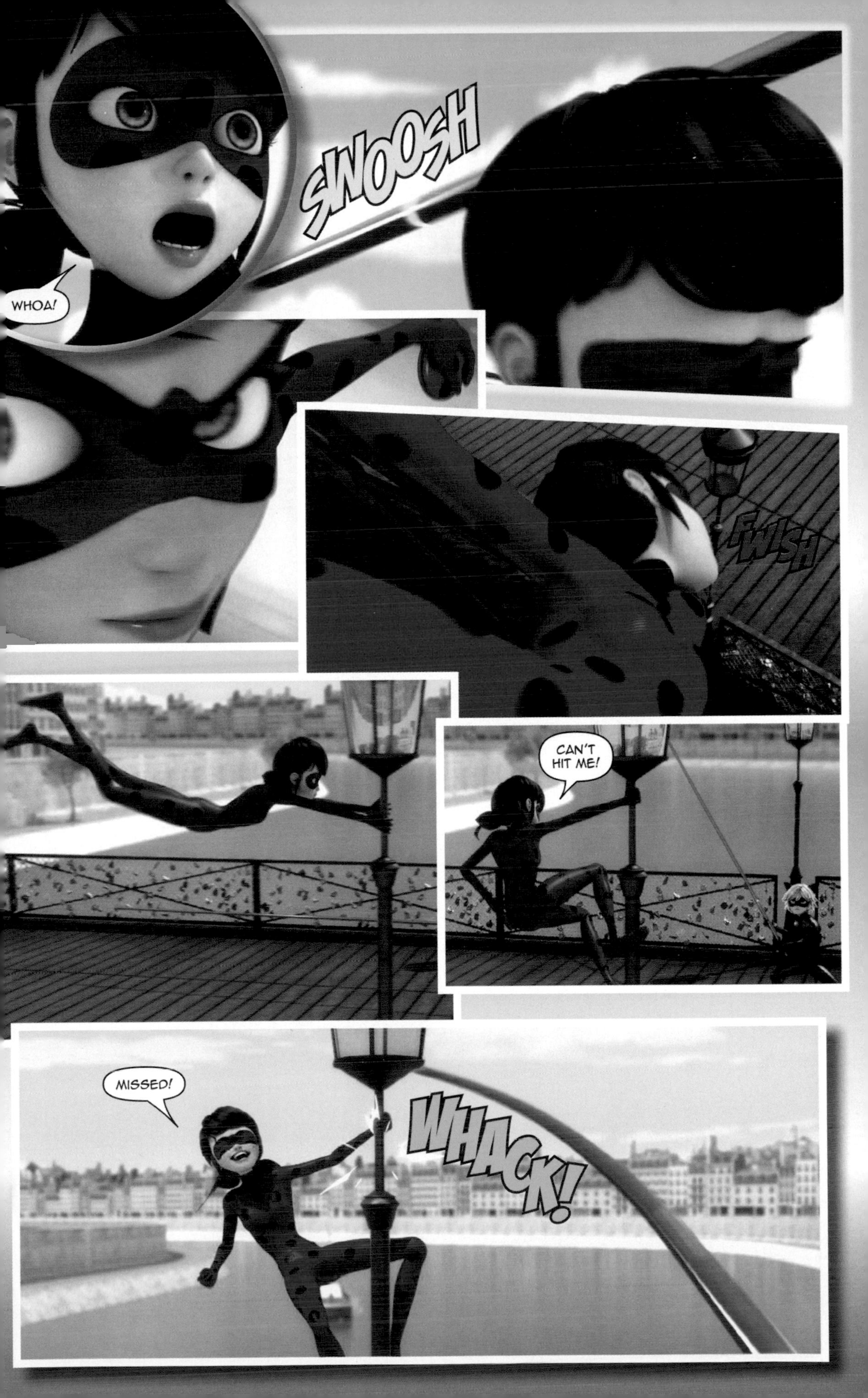
WHOA!
SWOOSH
FWISH
CAN'T HIT ME!
MISSED!
WHACK!

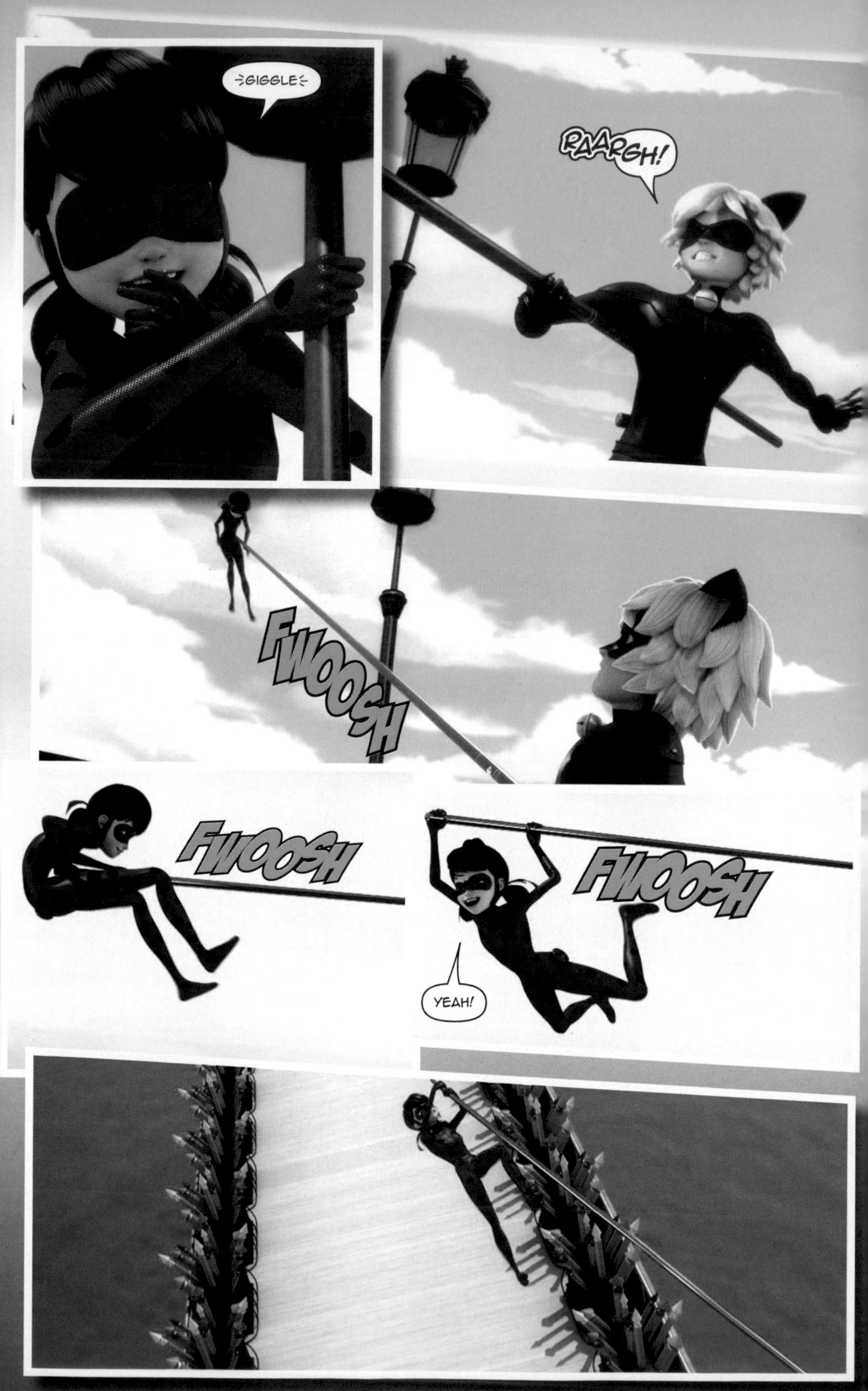

GIGGLE
RAARGH!
FWOOSH
FWOOSH
FWOOSH
YEAH!

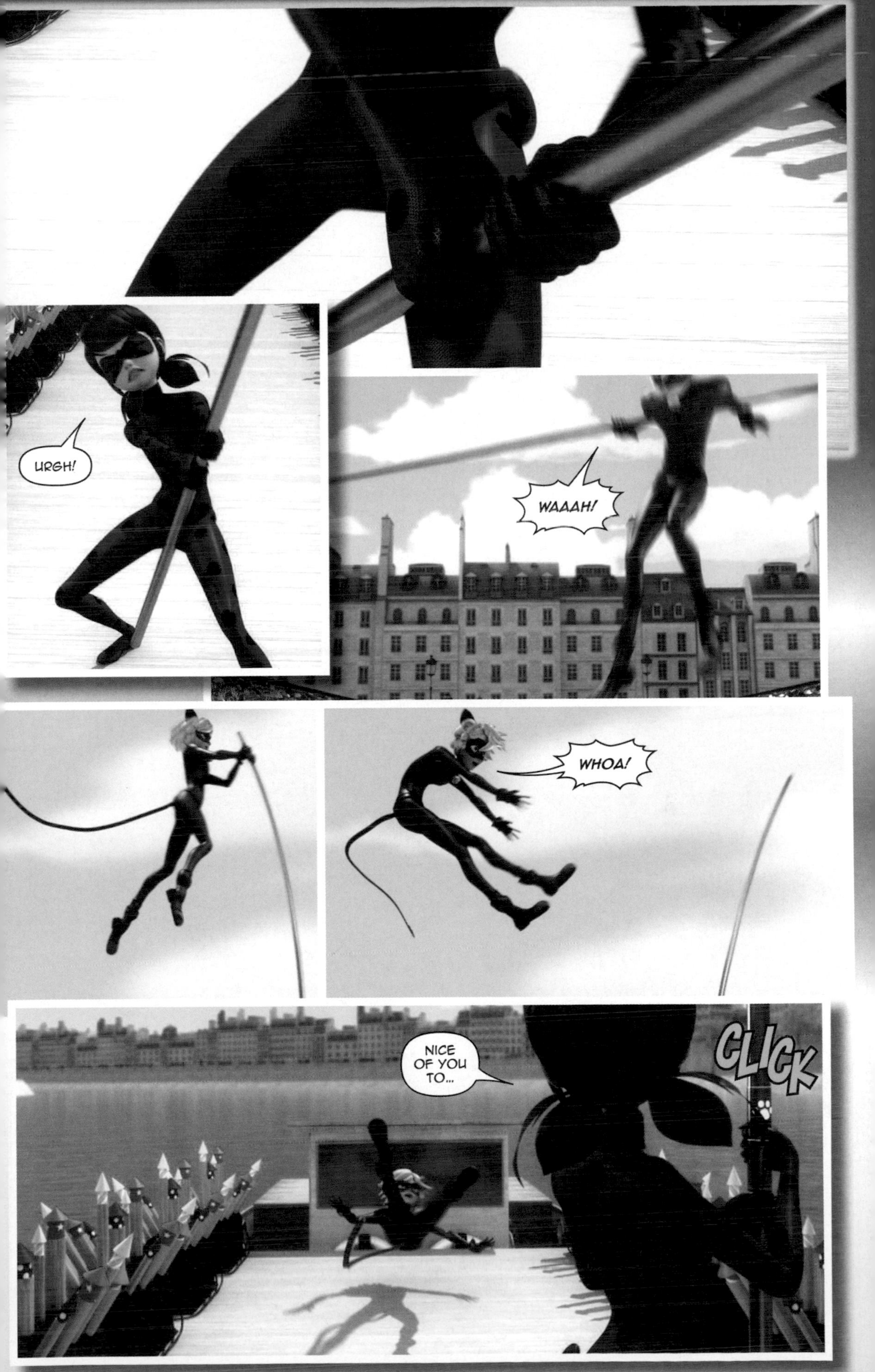
URGH!
WAAAH!
WHOA!
NICE OF YOU TO...
CLICK

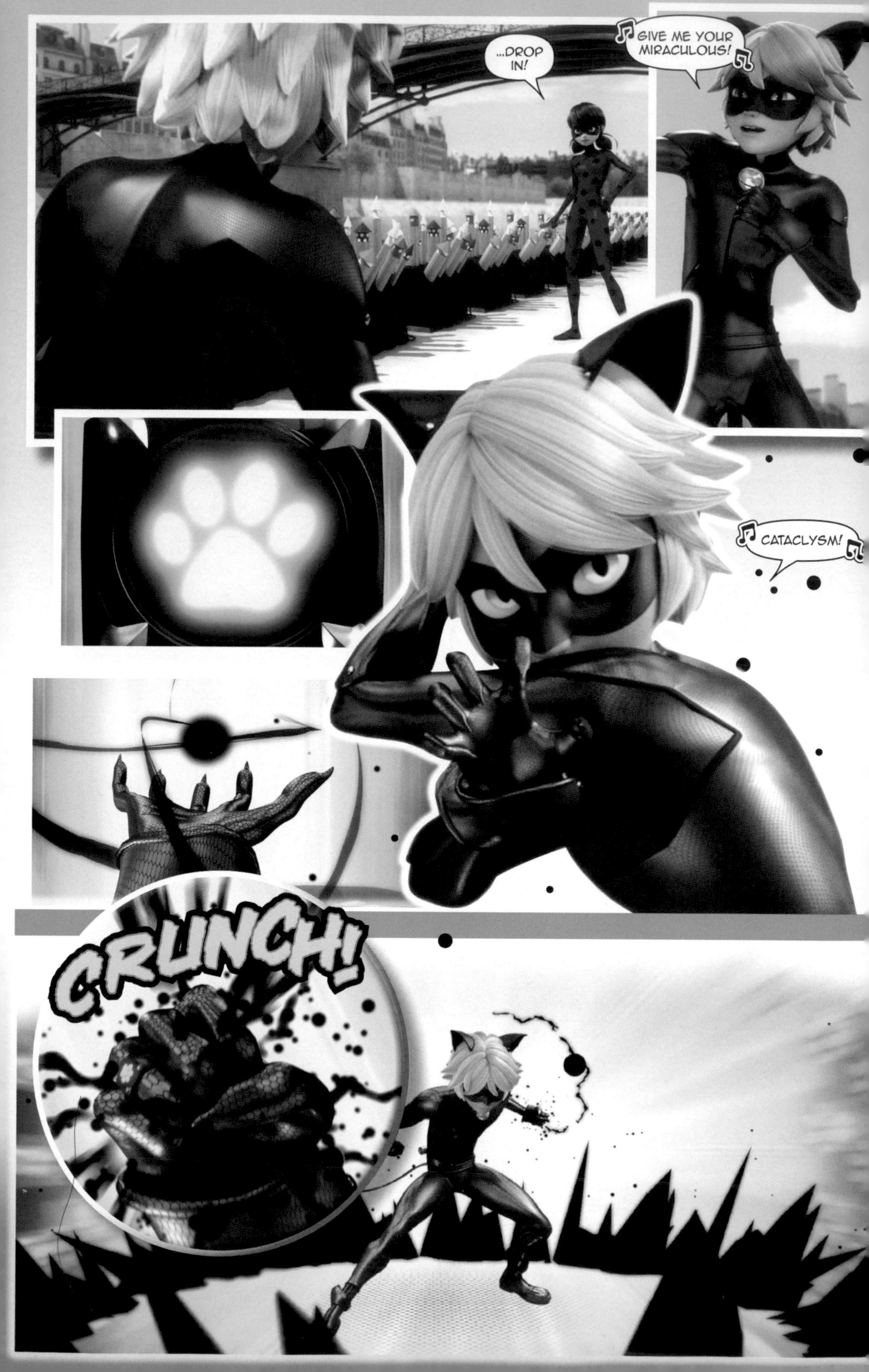
...DROP IN!
GIVE ME YOUR MIRACULOUS!
CATACLYSM!
CRUNCH!

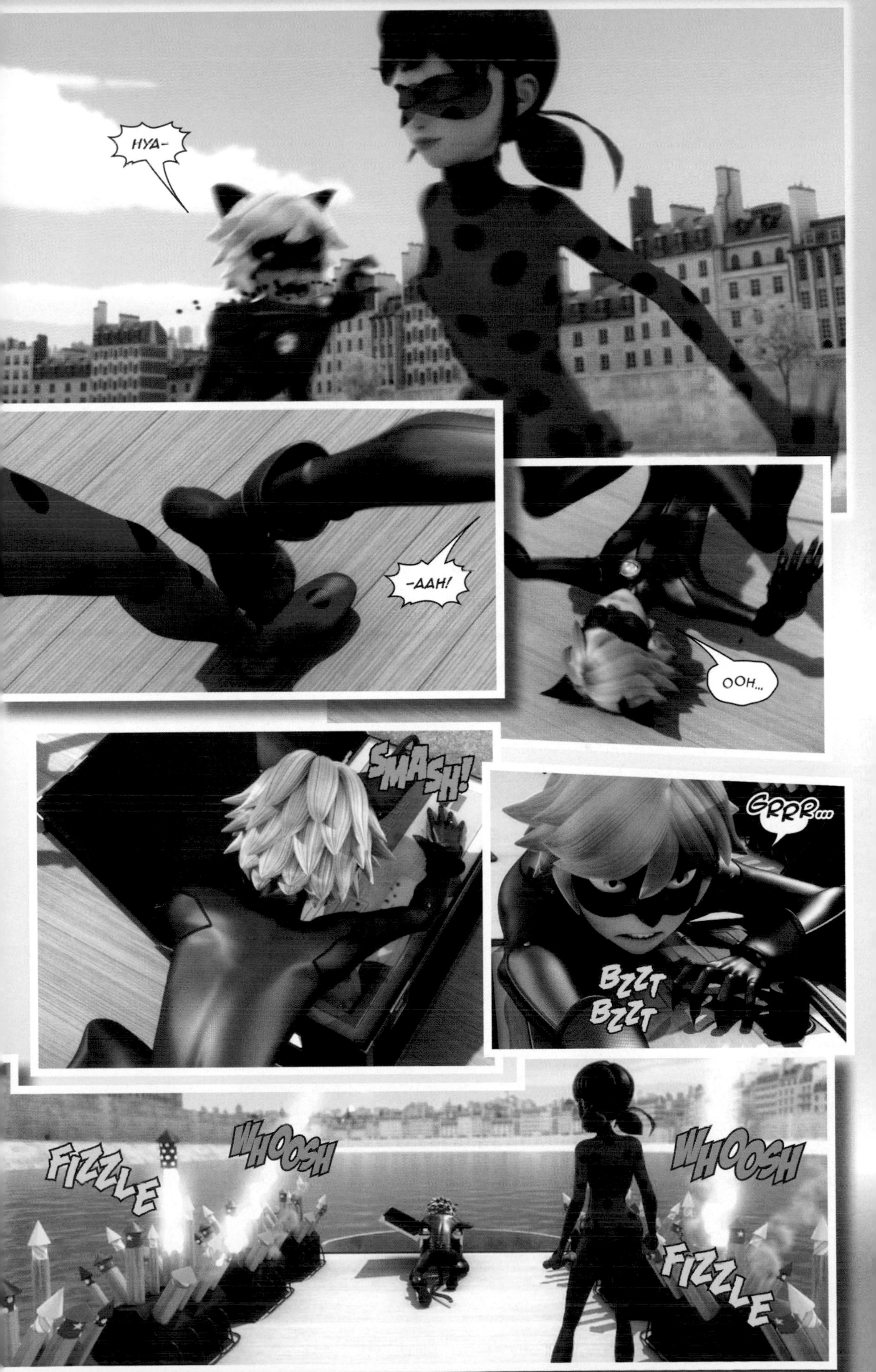
HYA-
-AAH!
OOH...
SMASH!
GRRR...
BZZT BZZT
FIZZLE
WHOOSH
WHOOSH
FIZZLE

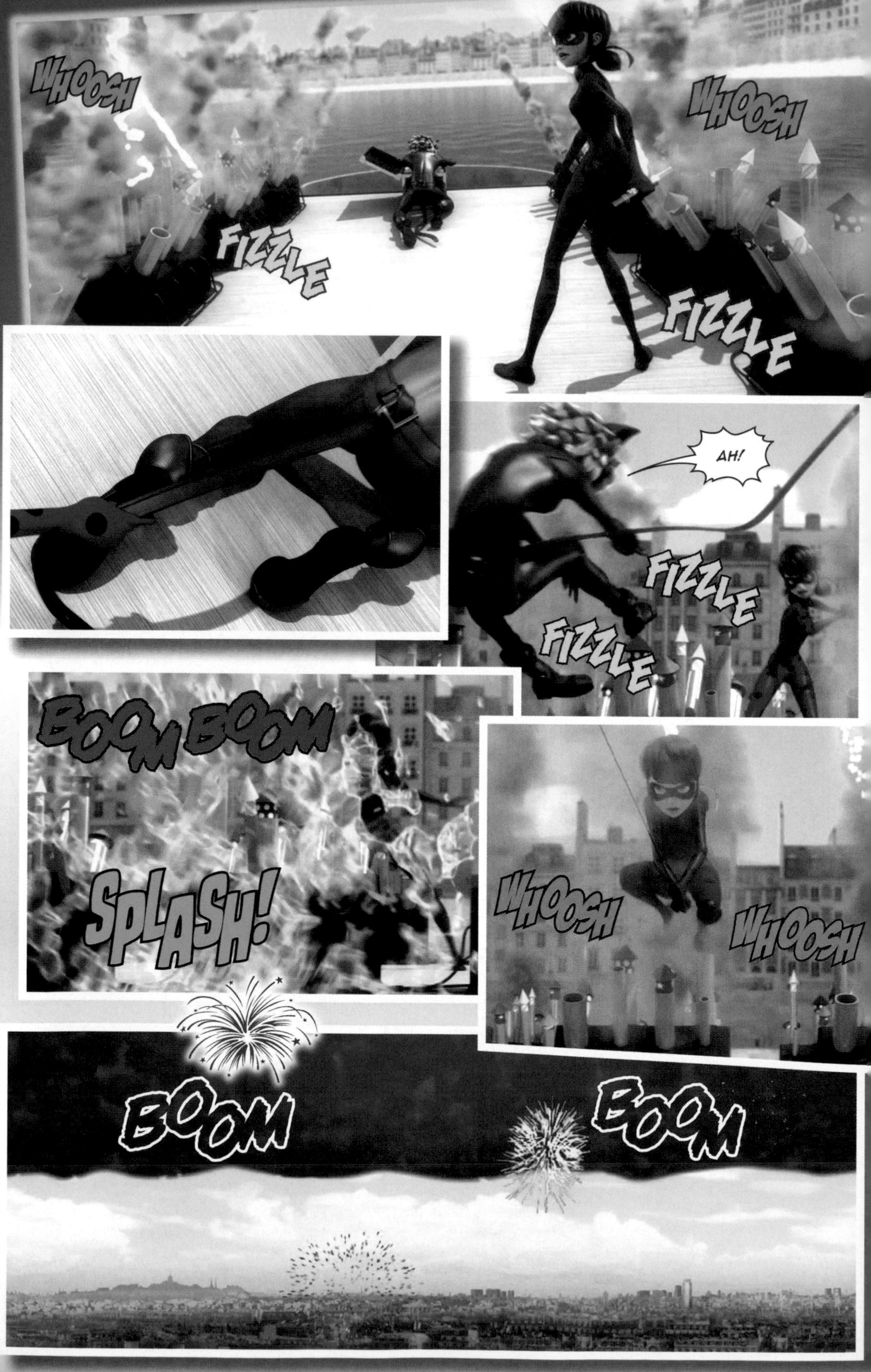

WHOOSH
FIZZLE
WHOOSH
FIZZLE
AH!
FIZZLE
FIZZLE
BOOM BOOM
SPLASH!
WHOOSH
WHOOSH
BOOM
BOOM

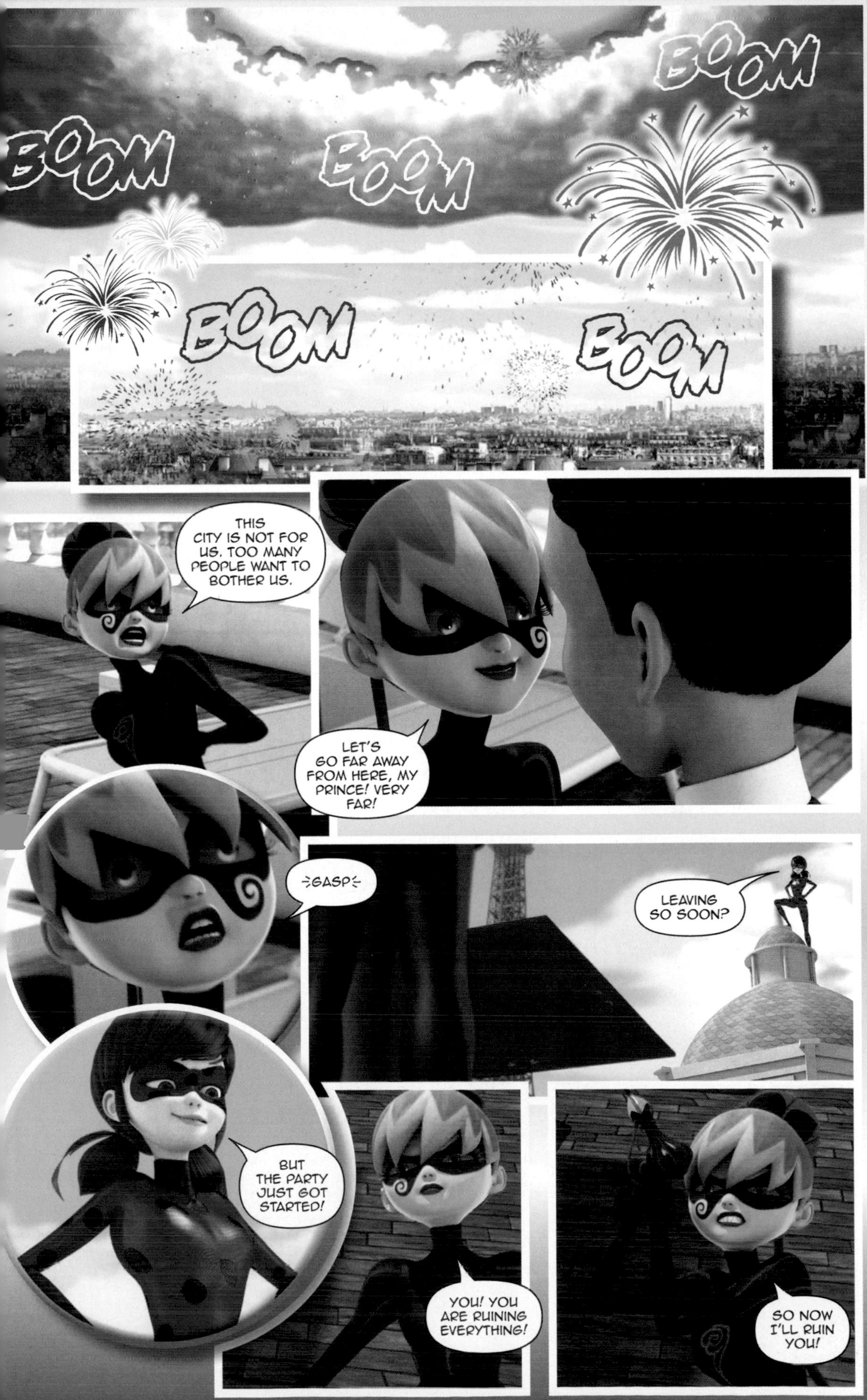
BOOM
BOOM
BOOM
BOOM
BOOM
THIS CITY IS NOT FOR US. TOO MANY PEOPLE WANT TO BOTHER US.
LET'S GO FAR AWAY FROM HERE, MY PRINCE! VERY FAR!
GASP
LEAVING SO SOON?
BUT THE PARTY JUST GOT STARTED!
YOU! YOU ARE RUINING EVERYTHING!
SO NOW I'LL RUIN YOU!

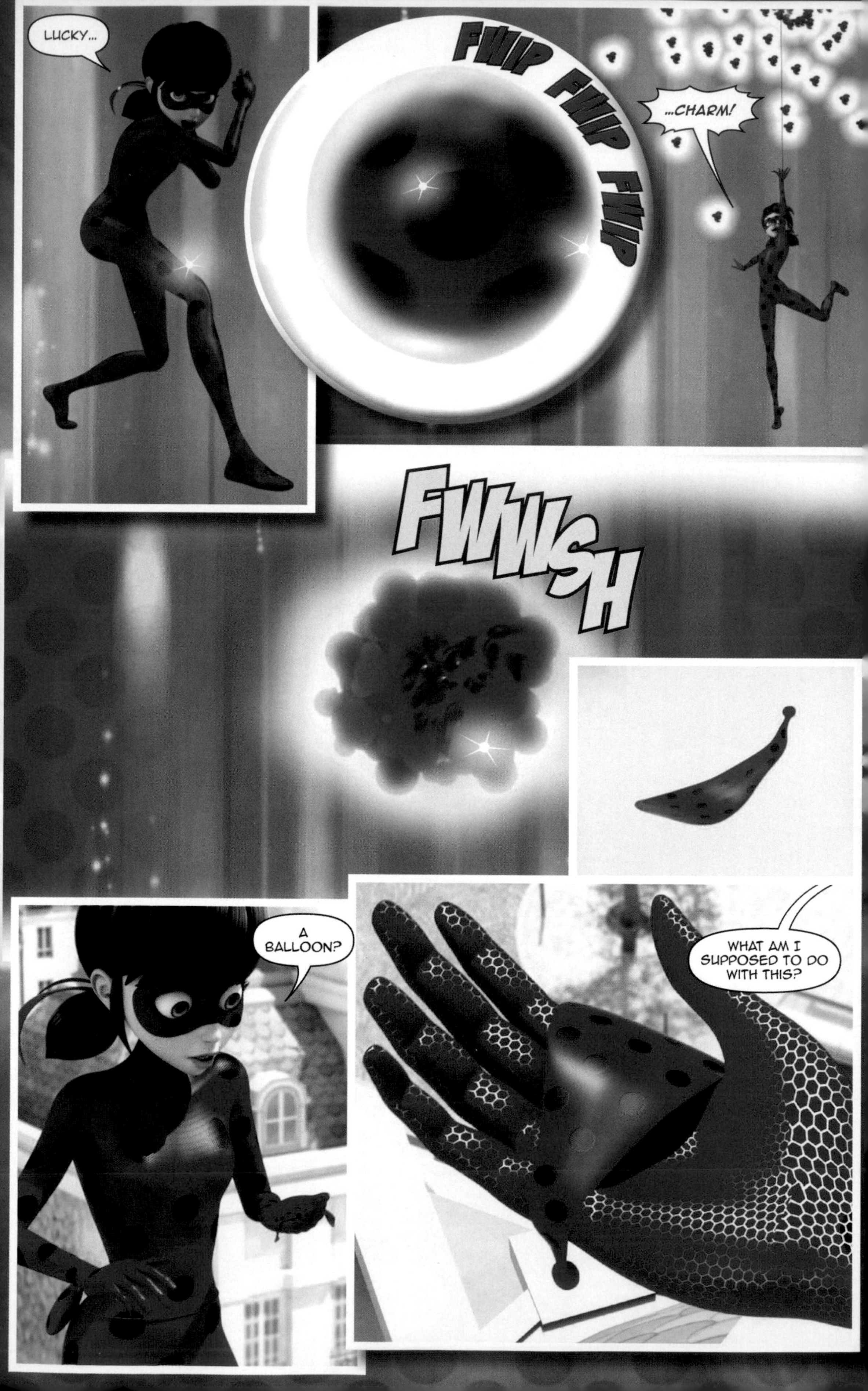
LUCKY...
FWIP FWIP FWIP FWIP
...CHARM!
FWWISH
A BALLOON?
WHAT AM I SUPPOSED TO DO WITH THIS?

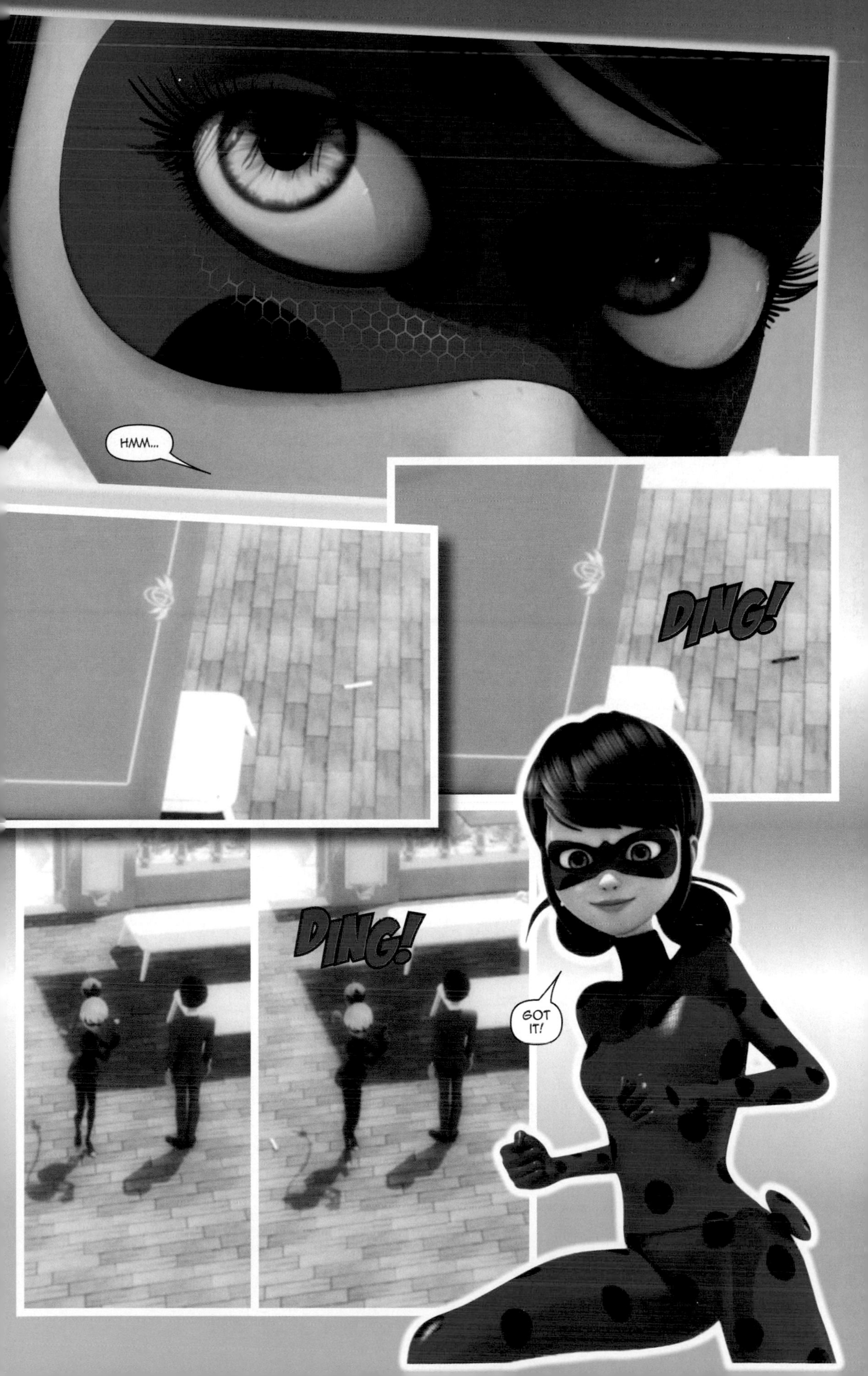
HMM...
DING!
DING!
GOT IT!

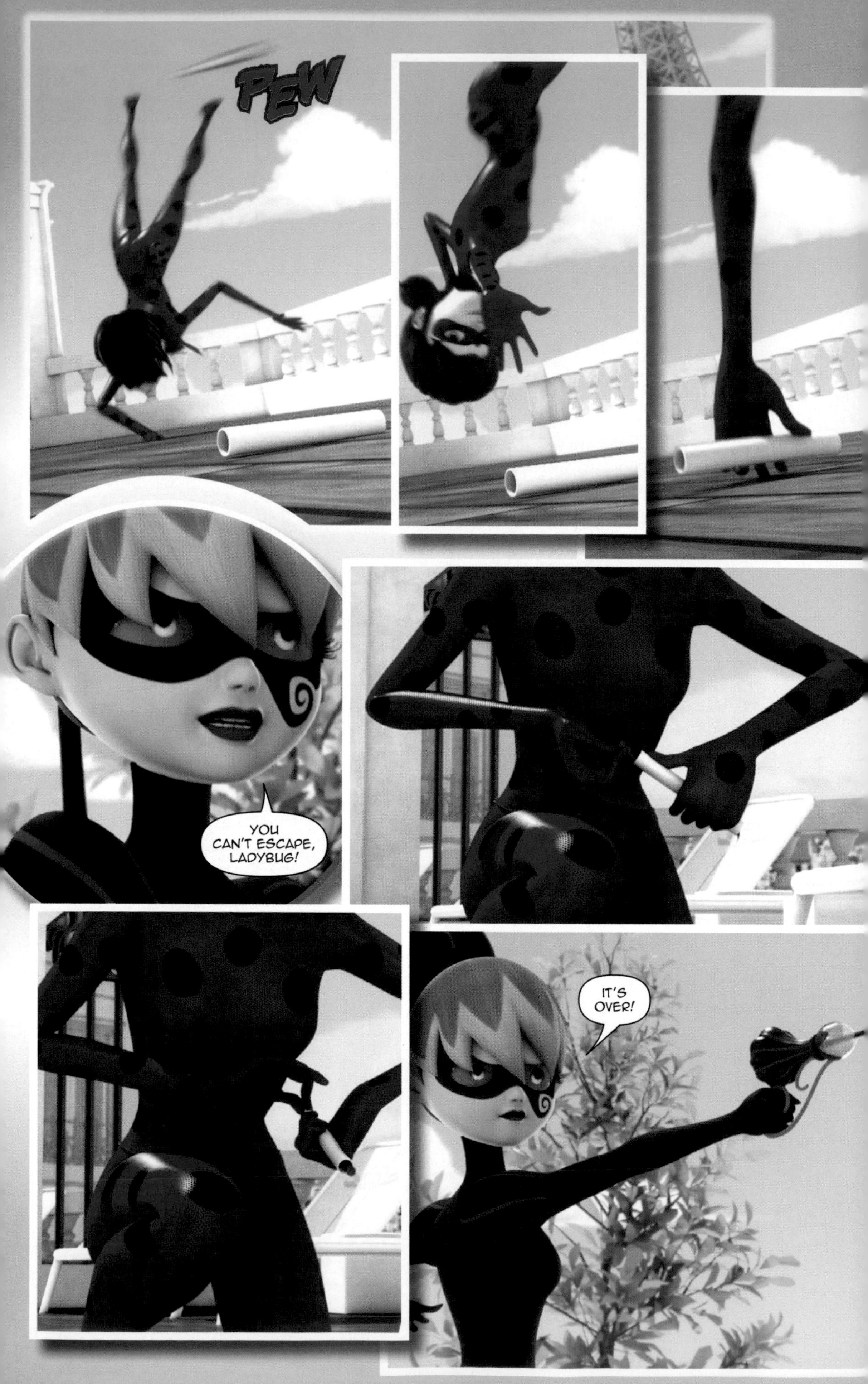
PEW
YOU CAN'T ESCAPE, LADYBUG!
IT'S OVER!

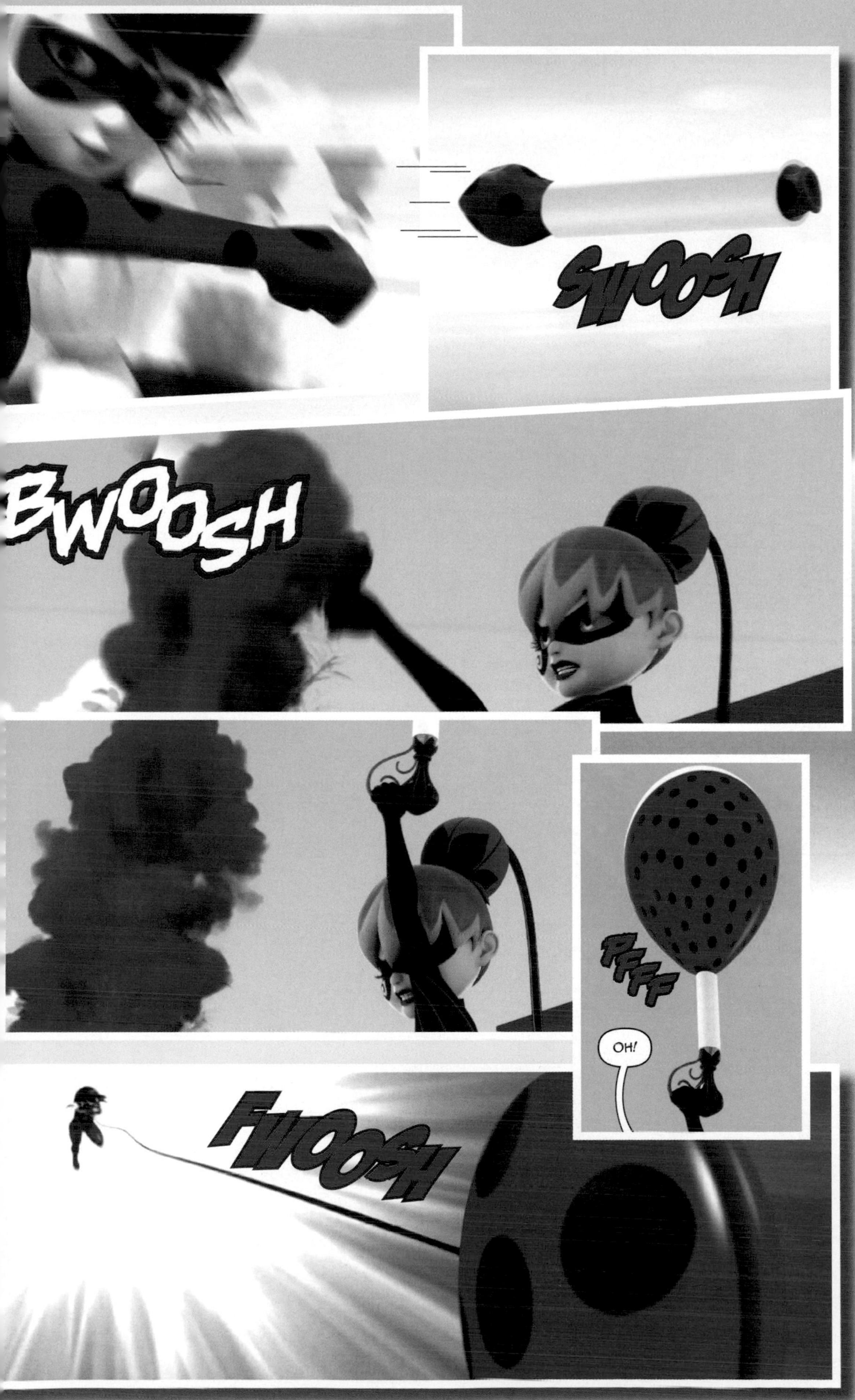
SWOOSH
BWOOSH
PFFF
OH!
FWOOSH

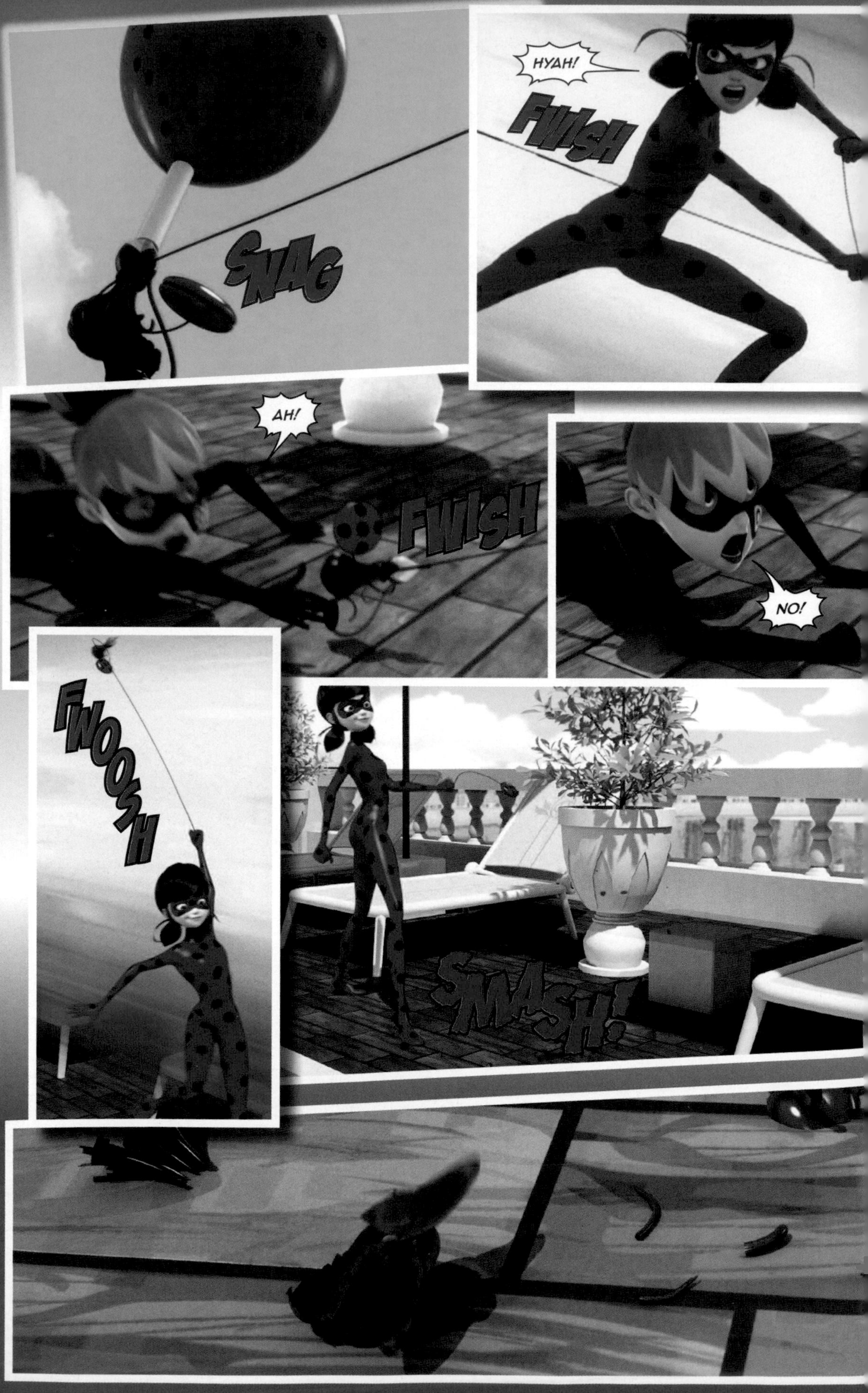
SNAG
HYAH!
FWISH
AH!
FWISH
NO!
FWOOSH
SMASH!

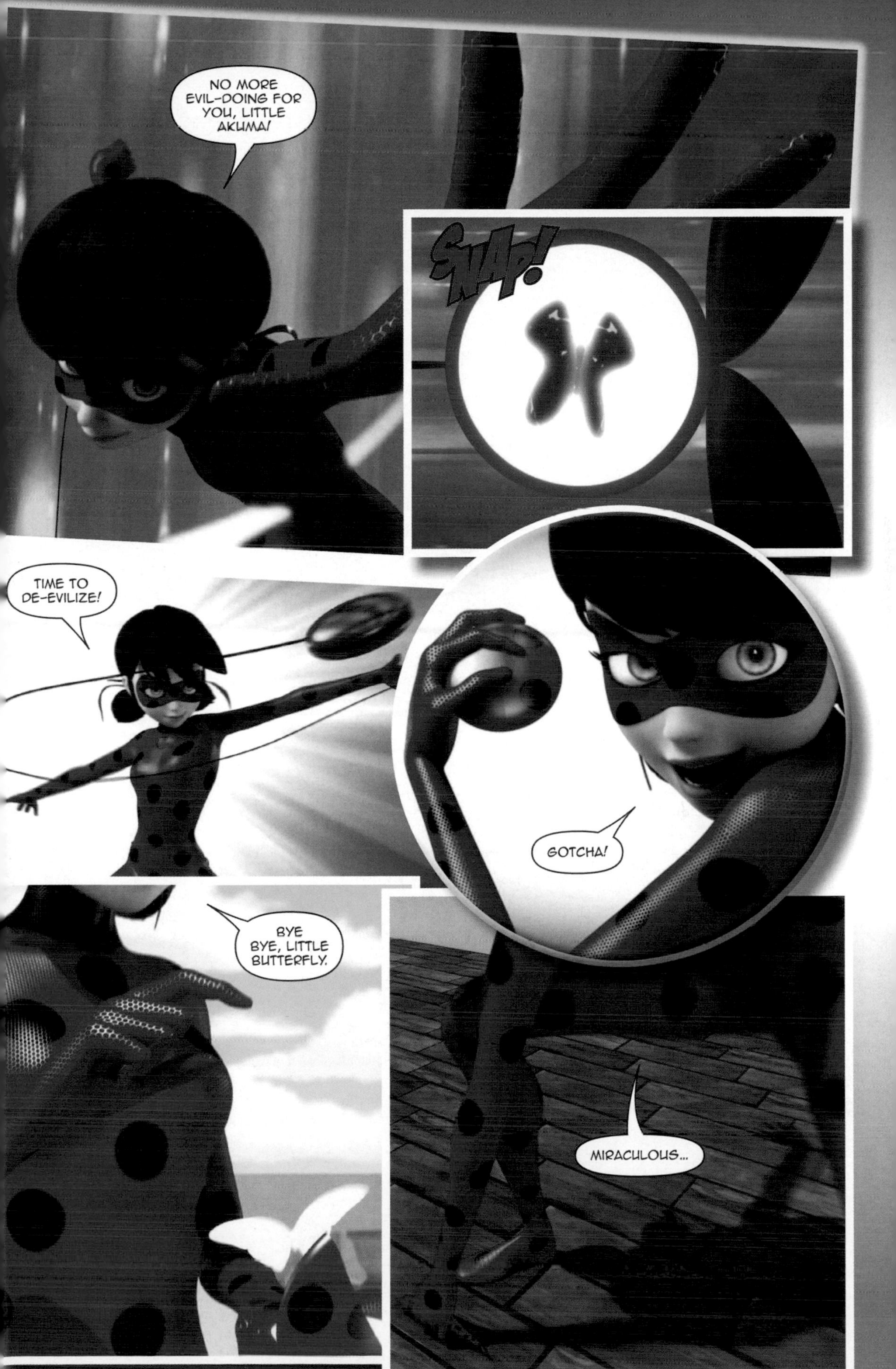
NO MORE EVIL-DOING FOR YOU, LITTLE AKUMA!
SNAP!
TIME TO DE-EVILIZE!
GOTCHA!
BYE BYE, LITTLE BUTTERFLY.
MIRACULOUS...

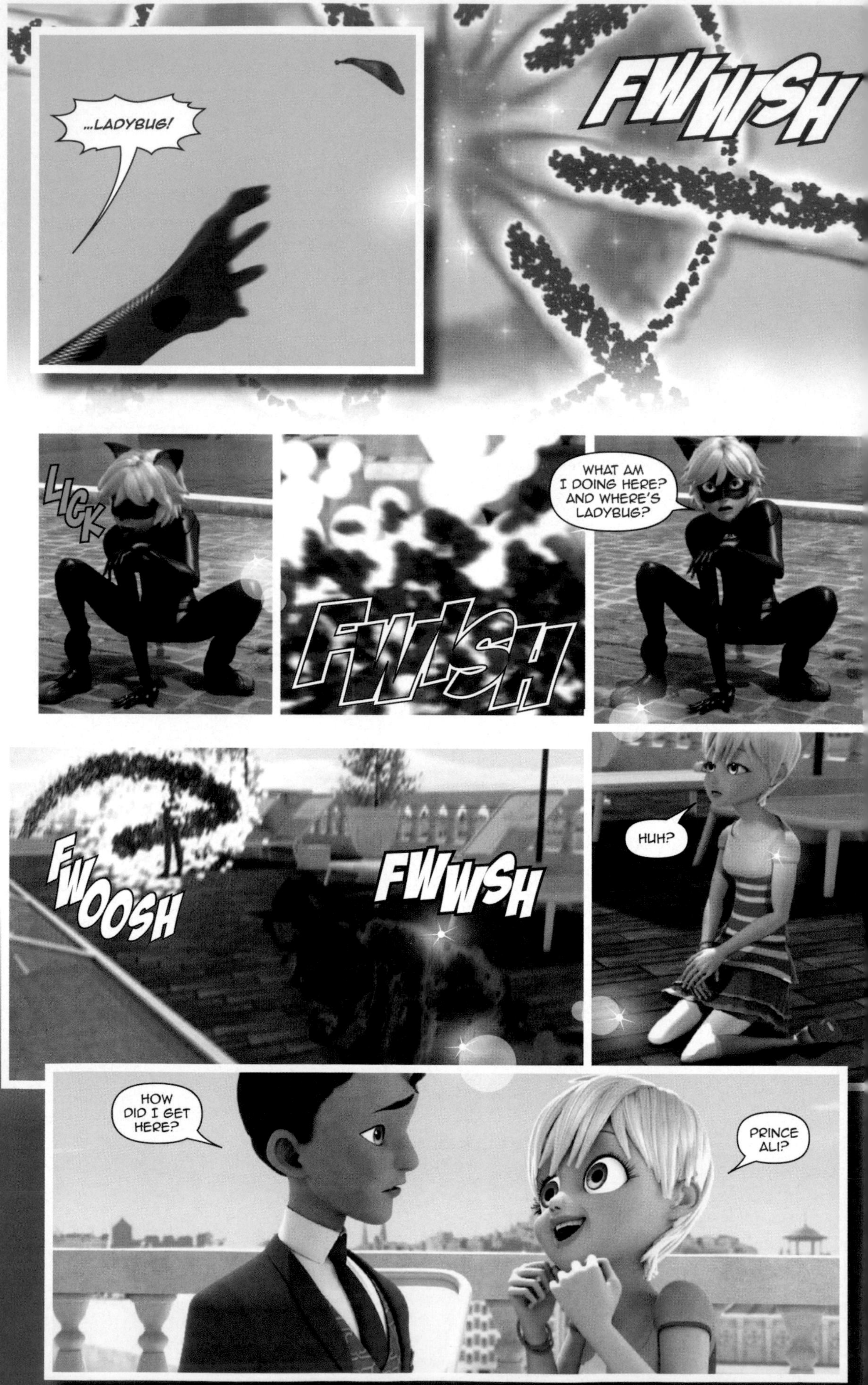
...LADYBUG!
FWWSH
LICK
FWISH
WHAT AM I DOING HERE? AND WHERE'S LADYBUG?
FWOOSH
FWWSH
HUH?
HOW DID I GET HERE?
PRINCE ALI?

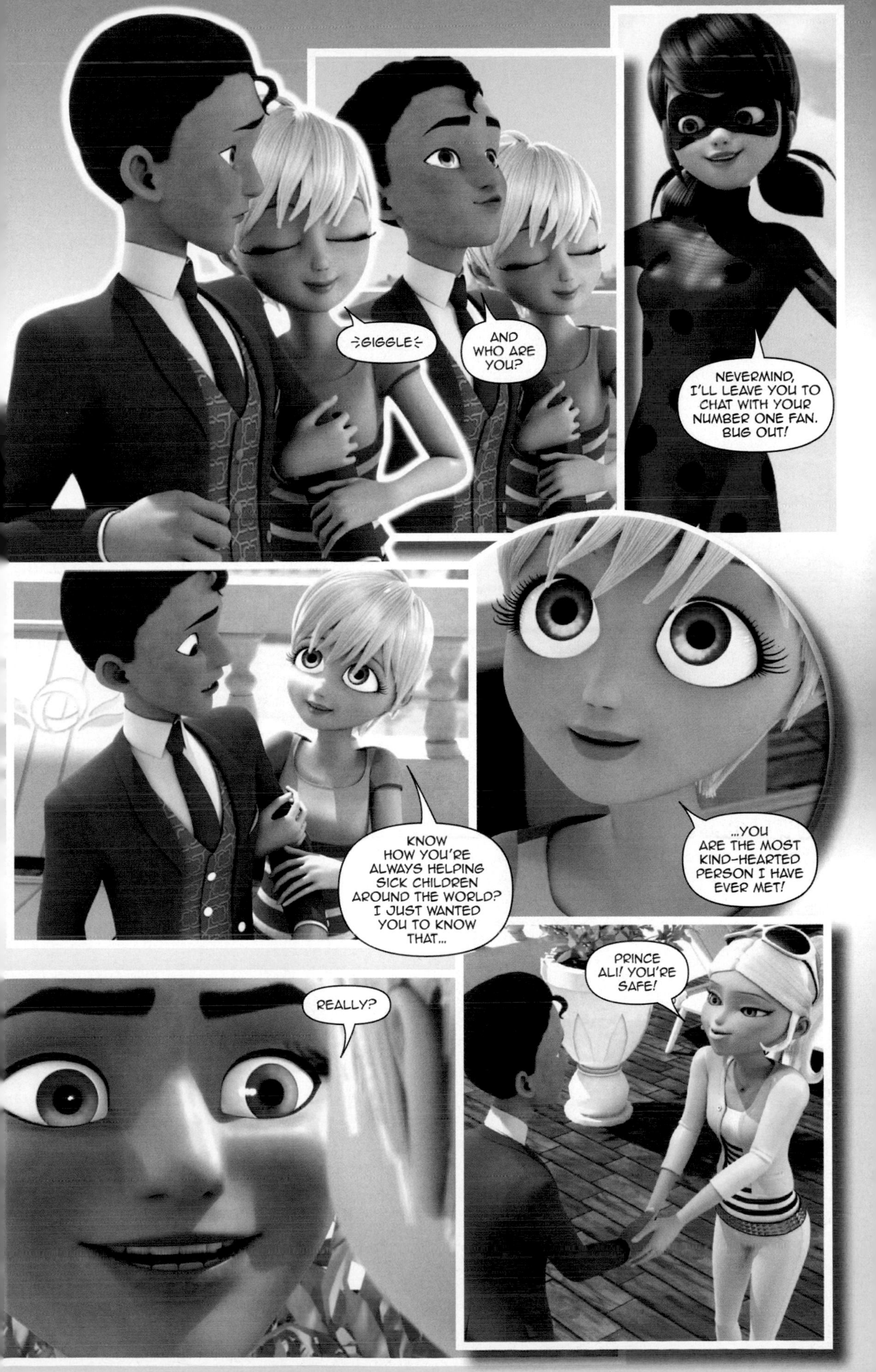

~GIGGLE~
AND WHO ARE YOU?
NEVERMIND, I'LL LEAVE YOU TO CHAT WITH YOUR NUMBER ONE FAN. BUG OUT!
KNOW HOW YOU'RE ALWAYS HELPING SICK CHILDREN AROUND THE WORLD? I JUST WANTED YOU TO KNOW THAT...
...YOU ARE THE MOST KIND-HEARTED PERSON I HAVE EVER MET!
REALLY?
PRINCE ALI! YOU'RE SAFE!

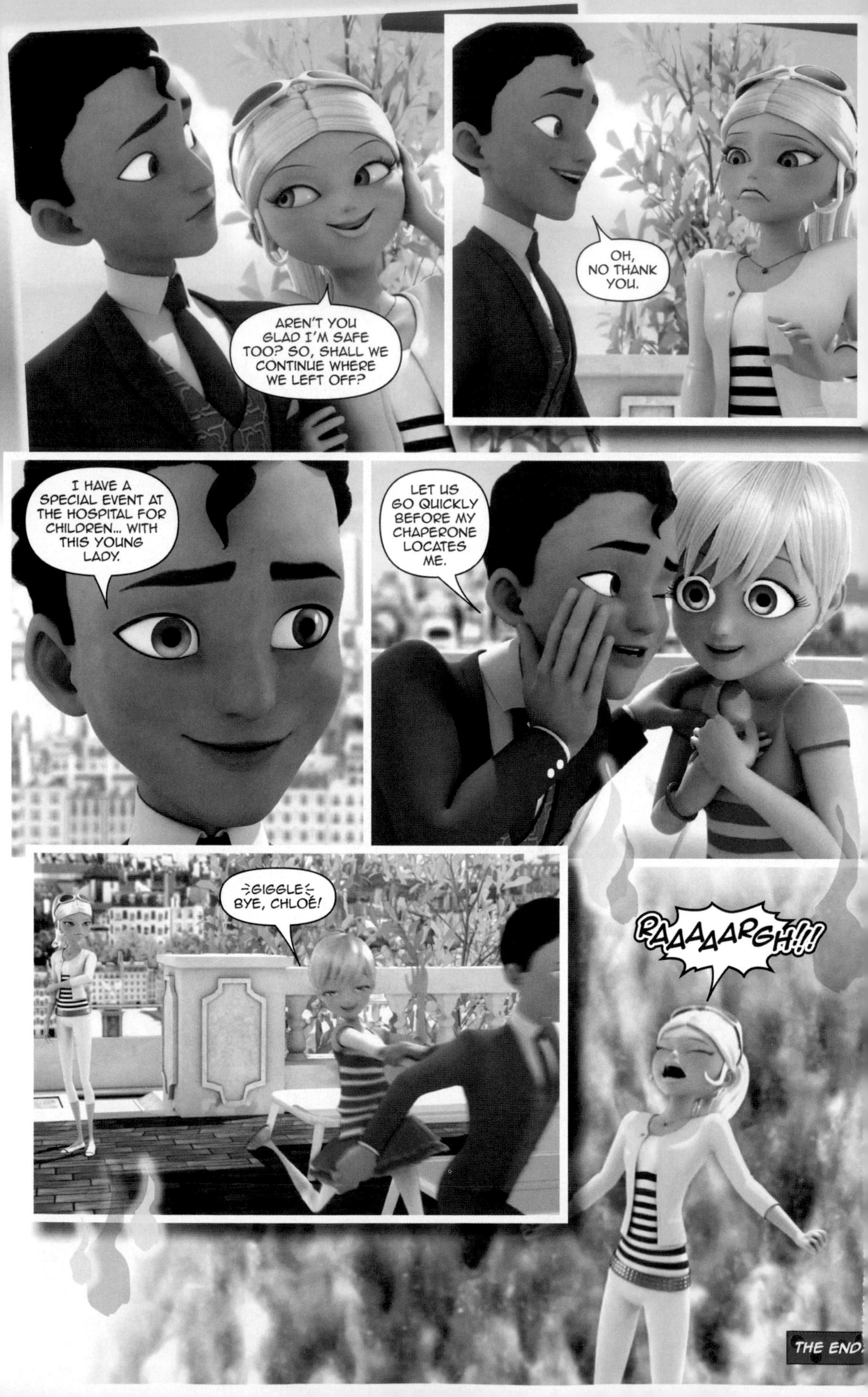
AREN'T YOU GLAD I'M SAFE TOO? SO, SHALL WE CONTINUE WHERE WE LEFT OFF?
OH, NO THANK YOU.
I HAVE A SPECIAL EVENT AT THE HOSPITAL FOR CHILDREN... WITH THIS YOUNG LADY.
LET US GO QUICKLY BEFORE MY CHAPERONE LOCATES ME.
GIGGLE
BYE, CHLOÉ!
RAAAAARGH!!!
THE END.

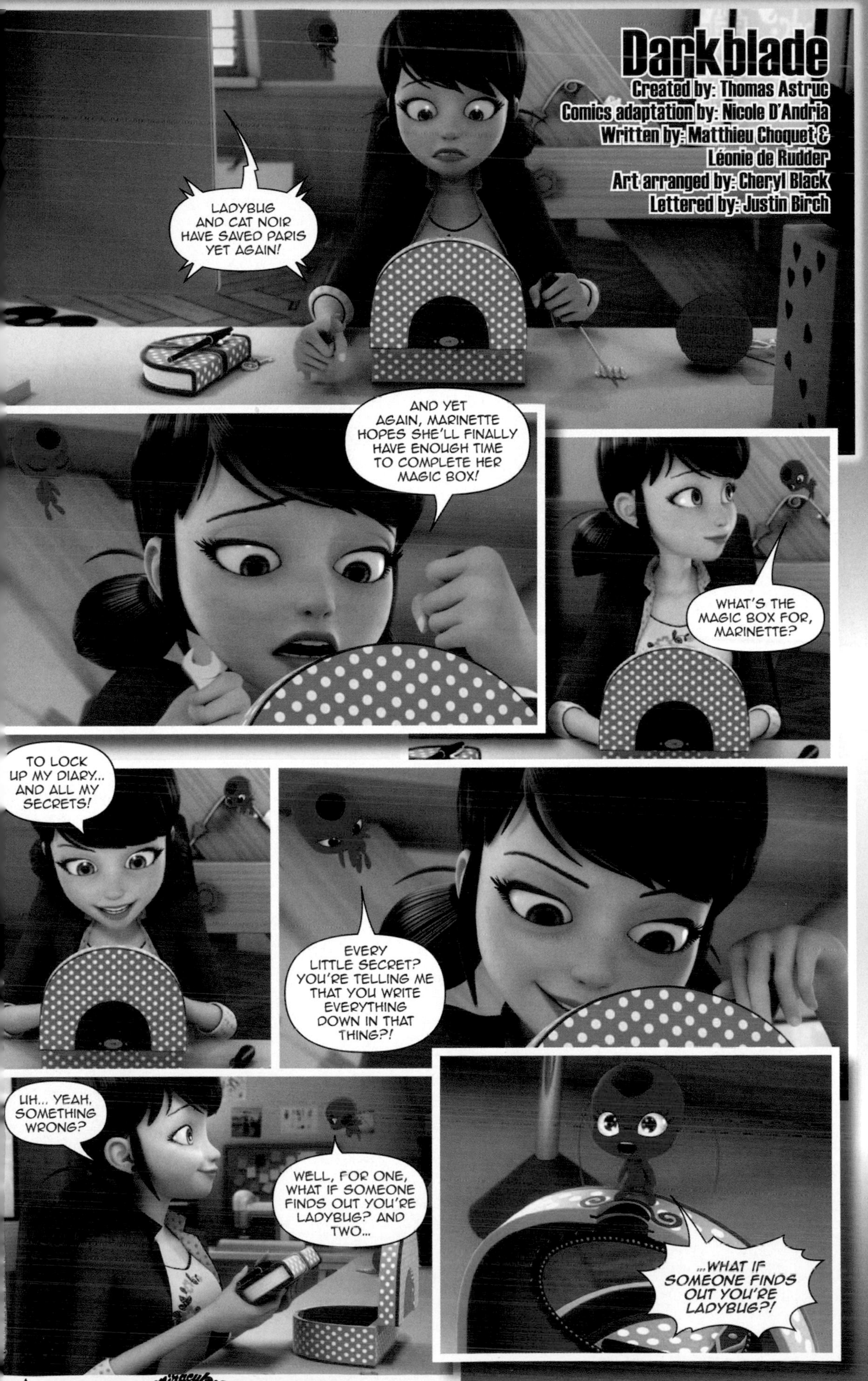
Darkblade
Created by: Thomas Astruc
Comics adaptation by: Nicole D'Andria
Written by: Matthieu Choquet & Léonie de Rudder
Art arranged by: Cheryl Black
Lettered by: Justin Birch
LADYBUG AND CAT NOIR HAVE SAVED PARIS YET AGAIN!
AND YET AGAIN, MARINETTE HOPES SHE'LL FINALLY HAVE ENOUGH TIME TO COMPLETE HER MAGIC BOX!
WHAT'S THE MAGIC BOX FOR, MARINETTE?
TO LOCK UP MY DIARY... AND ALL MY SECRETS!
EVERY LITTLE SECRET? YOU'RE TELLING ME THAT YOU WRITE EVERYTHING DOWN IN THAT THING?!
UH... YEAH, SOMETHING WRONG?
WELL, FOR ONE, WHAT IF SOMEONE FINDS OUT YOU'RE LADYBUG? AND TWO...
...WHAT IF SOMEONE FINDS OUT YOU'RE LADYBUG?!

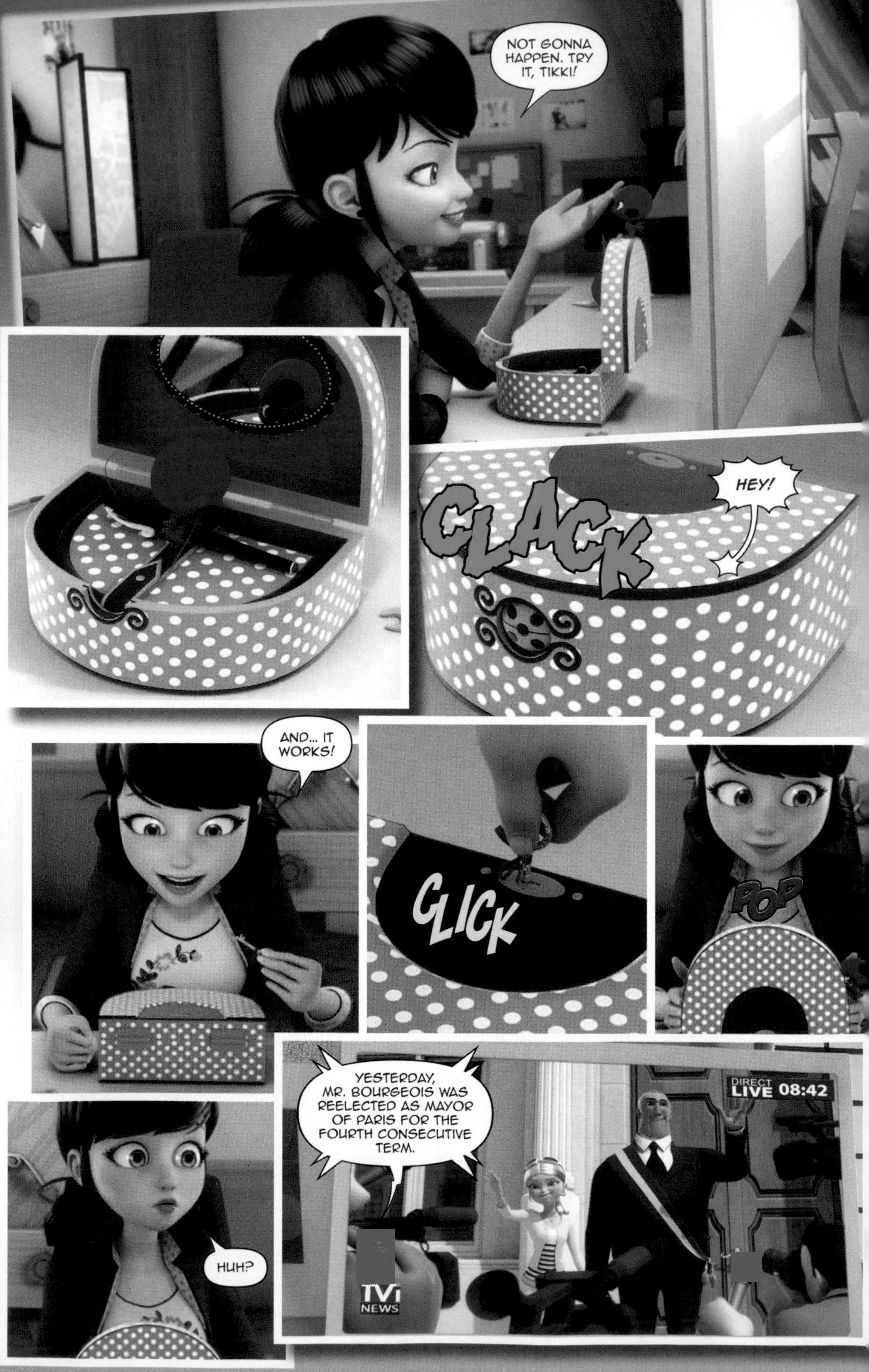
NOT GONNA HAPPEN. TRY IT, TIKKI!
CLACK
HEY!
AND... IT WORKS!
CLICK
POP
HUH?
YESTERDAY, MR. BOURGEOIS WAS REELECTED AS MAYOR OF PARIS FOR THE FOURTH CONSECUTIVE TERM.
DIRECT
LIVE 08:42
NEWS

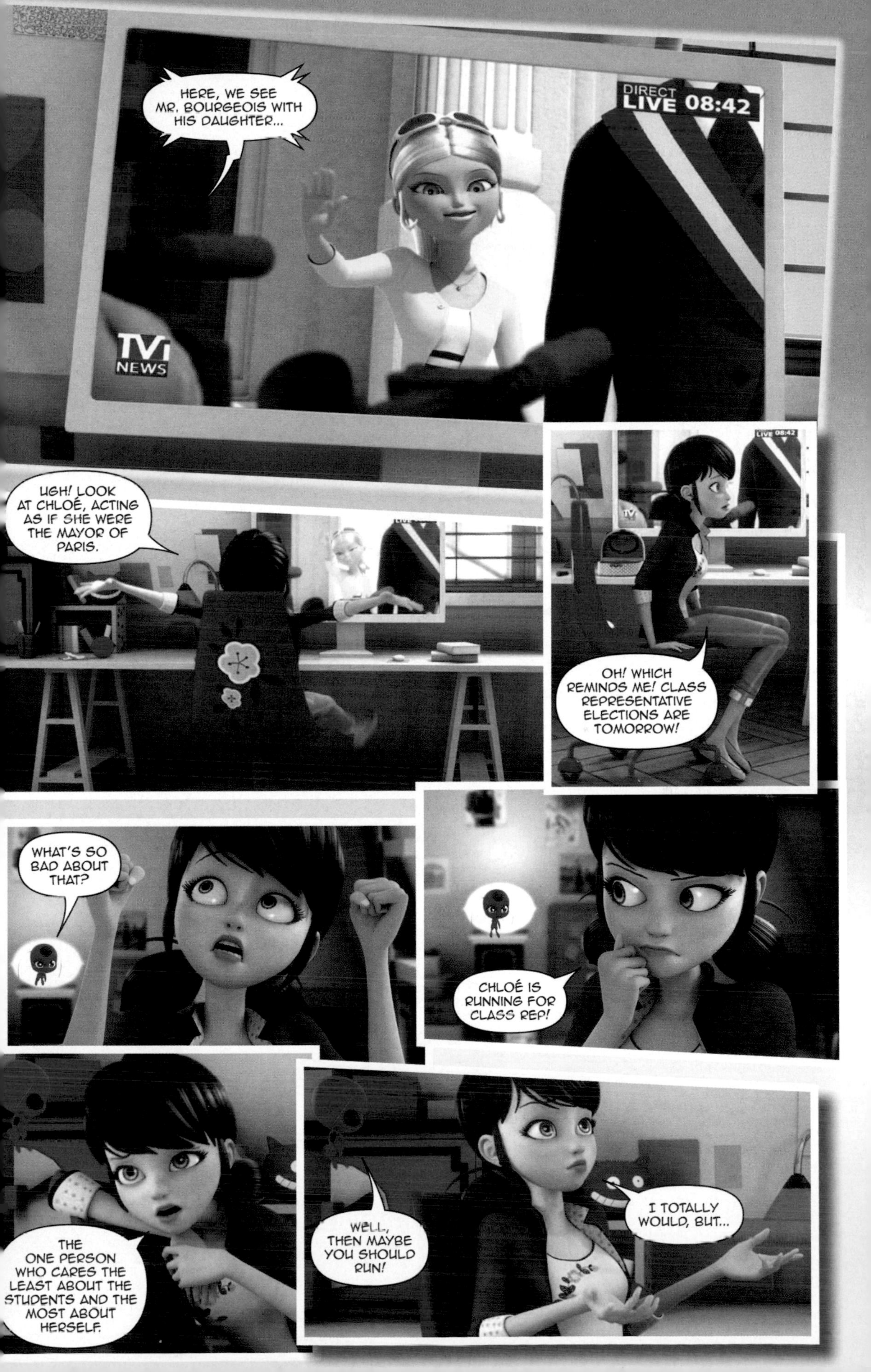
HERE, WE SEE MR. BOURGEOIS WITH HIS DAUGHTER...
DIRECT LIVE 08:42
TV NEWS
UGH! LOOK AT CHLOÉ, ACTING AS IF SHE WERE THE MAYOR OF PARIS.
OH! WHICH REMINDS ME! CLASS REPRESENTATIVE ELECTIONS ARE TOMORROW!
WHAT'S SO BAD ABOUT THAT?
CHLOÉ IS RUNNING FOR CLASS REP!
THE ONE PERSON WHO CARES THE LEAST ABOUT THE STUDENTS AND THE MOST ABOUT HERSELF.
WELL, THEN MAYBE YOU SHOULD RUN!
I TOTALLY WOULD, BUT...

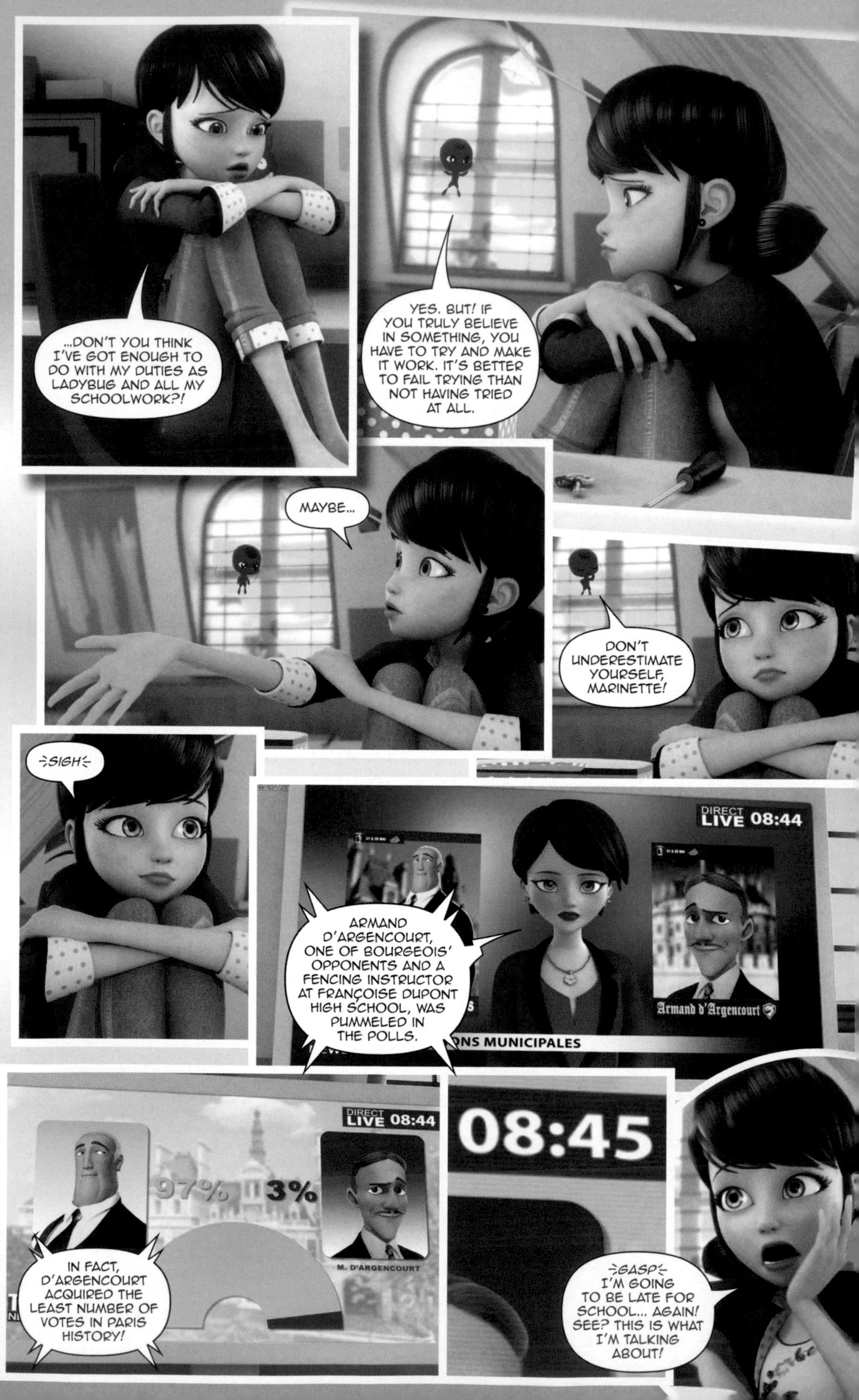
...DON'T YOU THINK I'VE GOT ENOUGH TO DO WITH MY DUTIES AS LADYBUG AND ALL MY SCHOOLWORK?!
YES. BUT! IF YOU TRULY BELIEVE IN SOMETHING, YOU HAVE TO TRY AND MAKE IT WORK. IT'S BETTER TO FAIL TRYING THAN NOT HAVING TRIED AT ALL.
MAYBE...
DON'T UNDERESTIMATE YOURSELF, MARINETTE!
SIGH
DIRECT LIVE 08:44
Armand d'Argencourt
ARMAND D'ARGENCOURT, ONE OF BOURGEOIS' OPPONENTS AND A FENCING INSTRUCTOR AT FRANÇOISE DUPONT HIGH SCHOOL, WAS PUMMELED IN THE POLLS.
DIRECT LIVE 08:44
97% 3%
M. D'ARGENCOURT
IN FACT, D'ARGENCOURT ACQUIRED THE LEAST NUMBER OF VOTES IN PARIS HISTORY!
08:45
GASP I'M GOING TO BE LATE FOR SCHOOL... AGAIN! SEE? THIS IS WHAT I'M TALKING ABOUT!

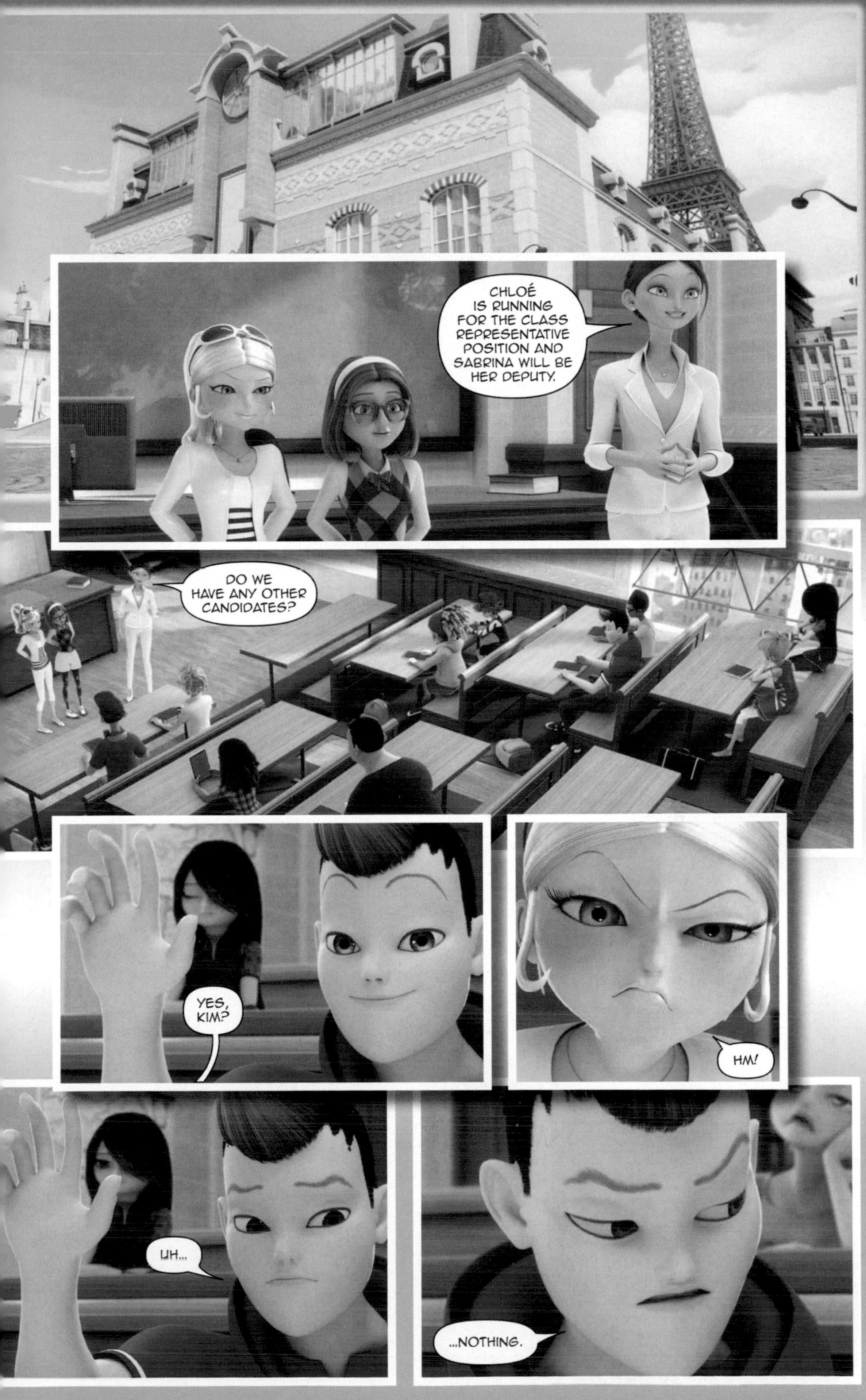
CHLOÉ IS RUNNING FOR THE CLASS REPRESENTATIVE POSITION AND SABRINA WILL BE HER DEPUTY.
DO WE HAVE ANY OTHER CANDIDATES?
YES, KIM?
HM!
UH...
...NOTHING.

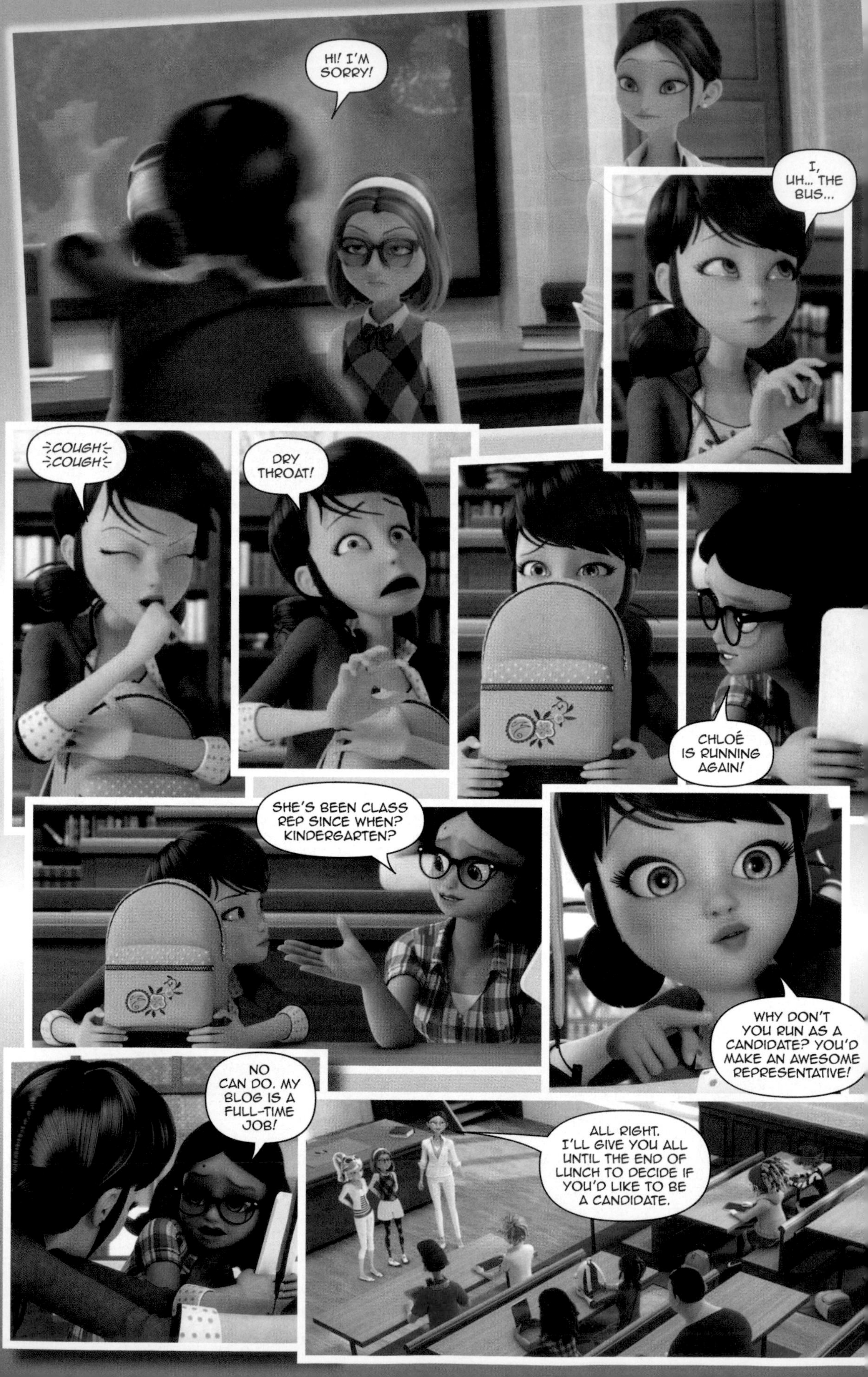
HI! I'M SORRY!
I, UH... THE BUS...
COUGH COUGH
DRY THROAT!
CHLOÉ IS RUNNING AGAIN!
SHE'S BEEN CLASS REP SINCE WHEN? KINDERGARTEN?
WHY DON'T YOU RUN AS A CANDIDATE? YOU'D MAKE AN AWESOME REPRESENTATIVE!
NO CAN DO. MY BLOG IS A FULL-TIME JOB!
ALL RIGHT. I'LL GIVE YOU ALL UNTIL THE END OF LUNCH TO DECIDE IF YOU'D LIKE TO BE A CANDIDATE.

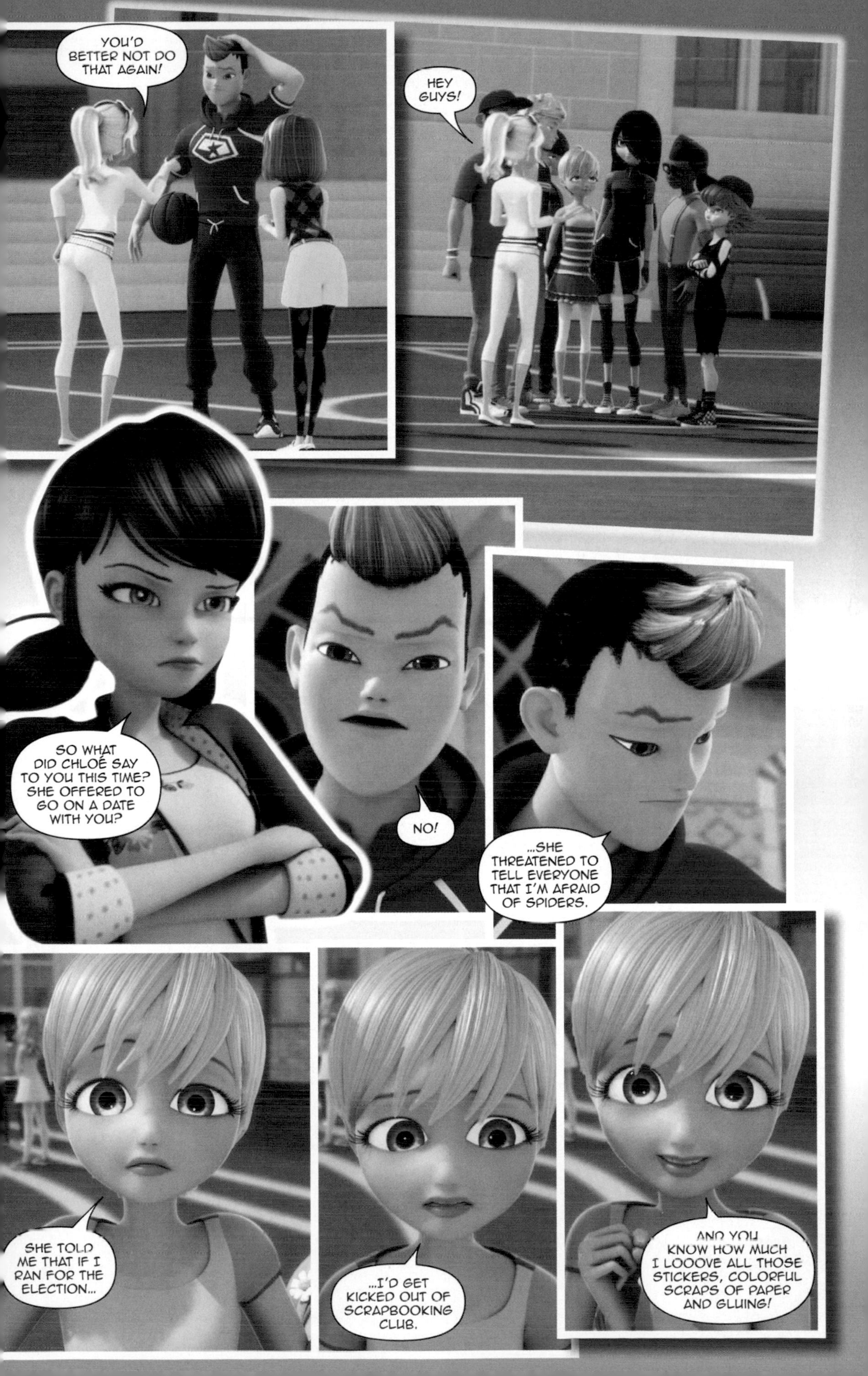
YOU'D BETTER NOT DO THAT AGAIN!
HEY GUYS!
SO WHAT DID CHLOÉ SAY TO YOU THIS TIME? SHE OFFERED TO GO ON A DATE WITH YOU?
NO!
...SHE THREATENED TO TELL EVERYONE THAT I'M AFRAID OF SPIDERS.
SHE TOLD ME THAT IF I RAN FOR THE ELECTION...
...I'D GET KICKED OUT OF SCRAPBOOKING CLUB.
AND YOU KNOW HOW MUCH I LOOOVE ALL THOSE STICKERS, COLORFUL SCRAPS OF PAPER AND GLUING!

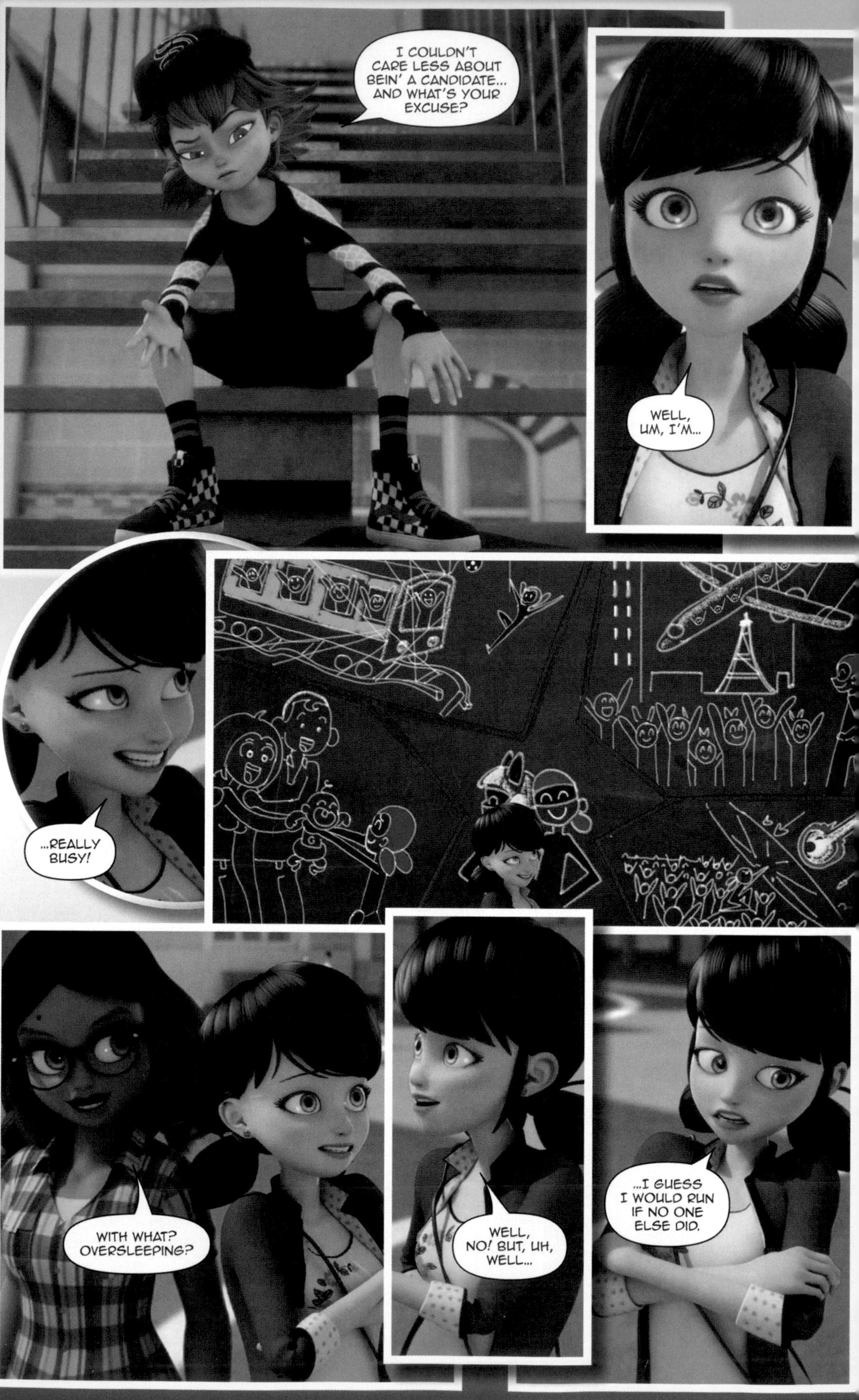
I COULDN'T CARE LESS ABOUT BEIN' A CANDIDATE... AND WHAT'S YOUR EXCUSE?
WELL, UM, I'M...
...REALLY BUSY!
WITH WHAT? OVERSLEEPING?
WELL, NO! BUT, UH, WELL...
...I GUESS I WOULD RUN IF NO ONE ELSE DID.

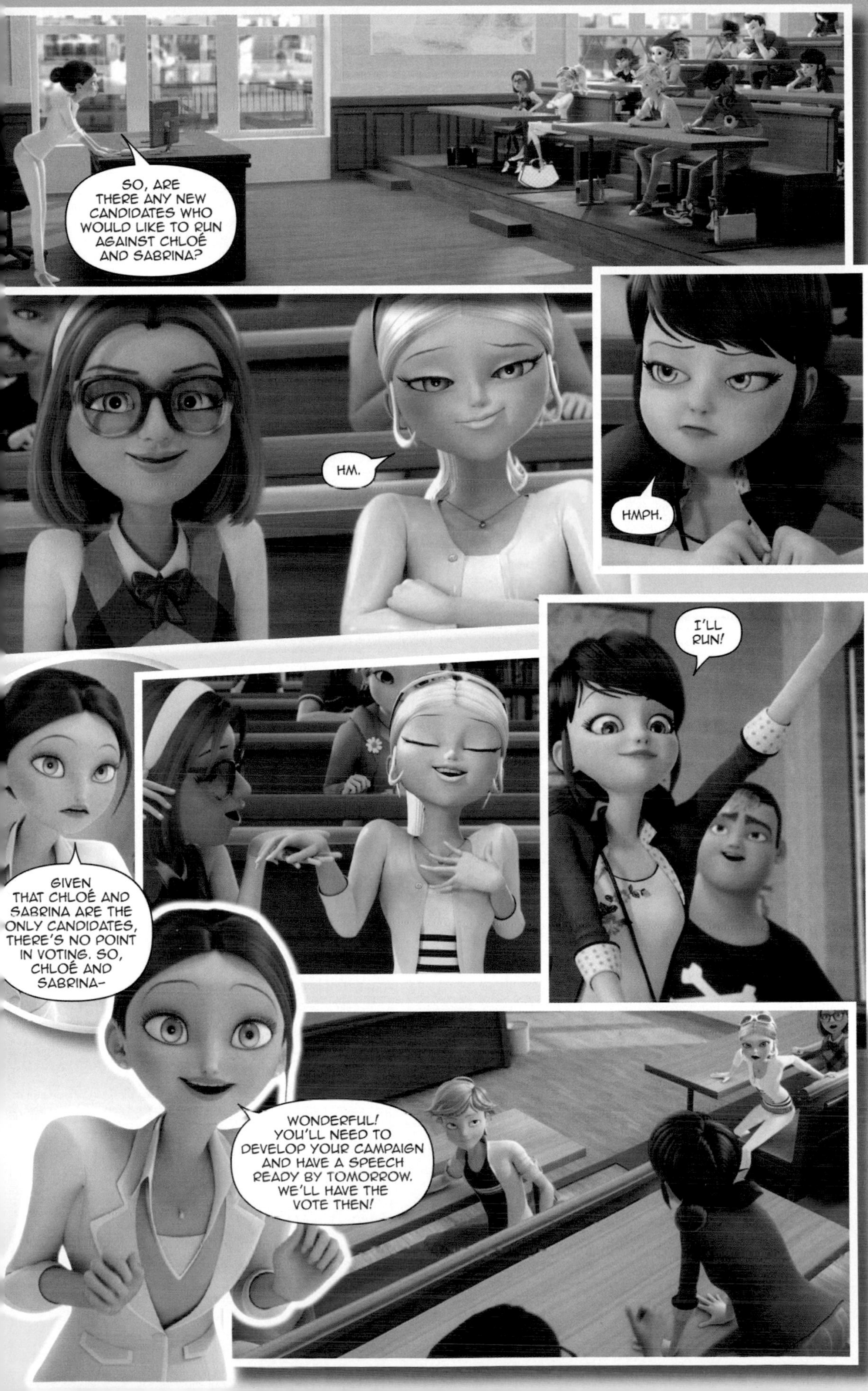
SO, ARE THERE ANY NEW CANDIDATES WHO WOULD LIKE TO RUN AGAINST CHLOÉ AND SABRINA?
HM.
HMPH.
GIVEN THAT CHLOÉ AND SABRINA ARE THE ONLY CANDIDATES, THERE'S NO POINT IN VOTING. SO, CHLOÉ AND SABRINA-
I'LL RUN!
WONDERFUL! YOU'LL NEED TO DEVELOP YOUR CAMPAIGN AND HAVE A SPEECH READY BY TOMORROW. WE'LL HAVE THE VOTE THEN!

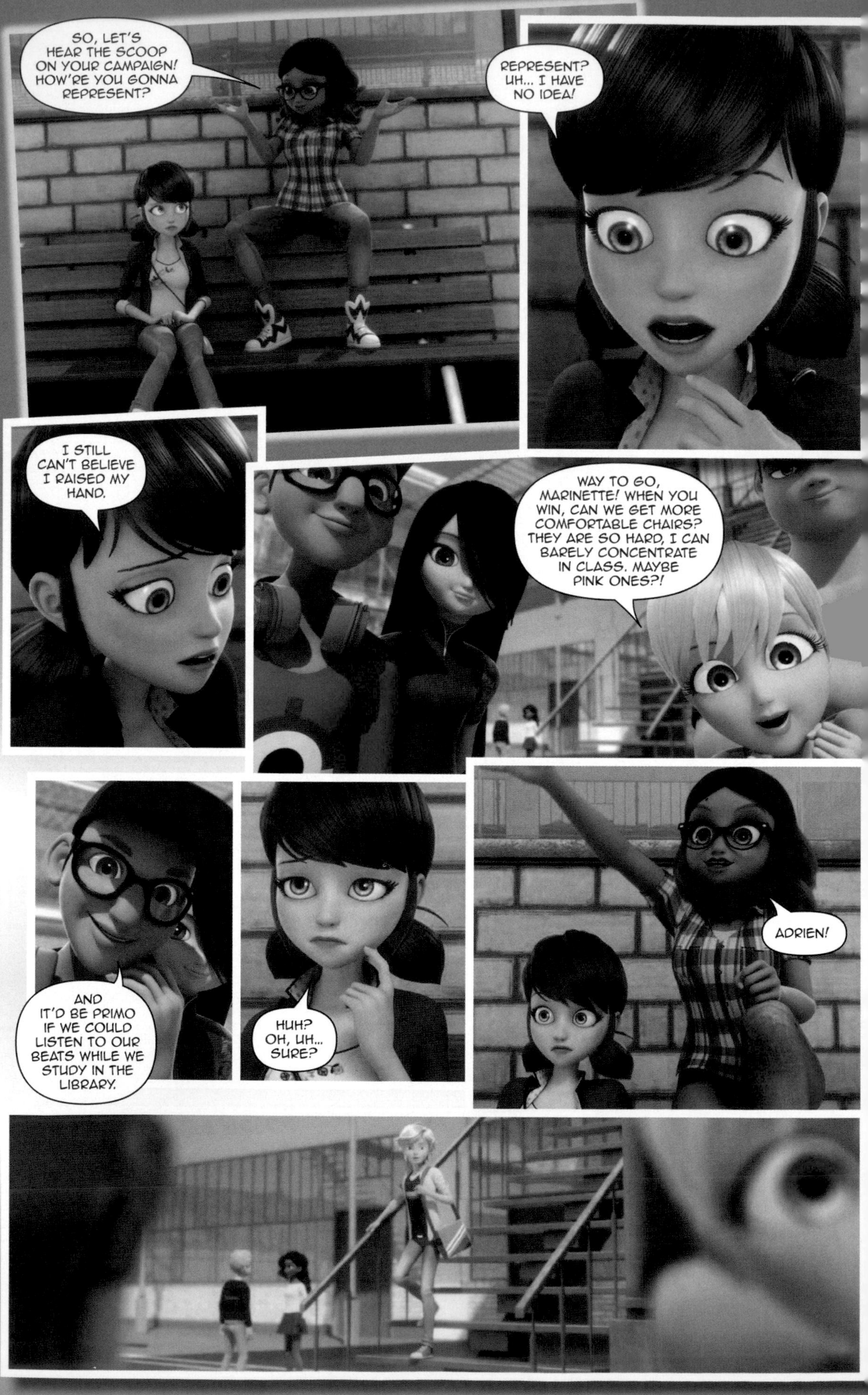
SO, LET'S HEAR THE SCOOP ON YOUR CAMPAIGN! HOW'RE YOU GONNA REPRESENT?
REPRESENT? UH... I HAVE NO IDEA!
I STILL CAN'T BELIEVE I RAISED MY HAND.
WAY TO GO, MARINETTE! WHEN YOU WIN, CAN WE GET MORE COMFORTABLE CHAIRS? THEY ARE SO HARD, I CAN BARELY CONCENTRATE IN CLASS. MAYBE PINK ONES?!
AND IT'D BE PRIMO IF WE COULD LISTEN TO OUR BEATS WHILE WE STUDY IN THE LIBRARY.
HUH? OH, UH... SURE?
ADRIEN!

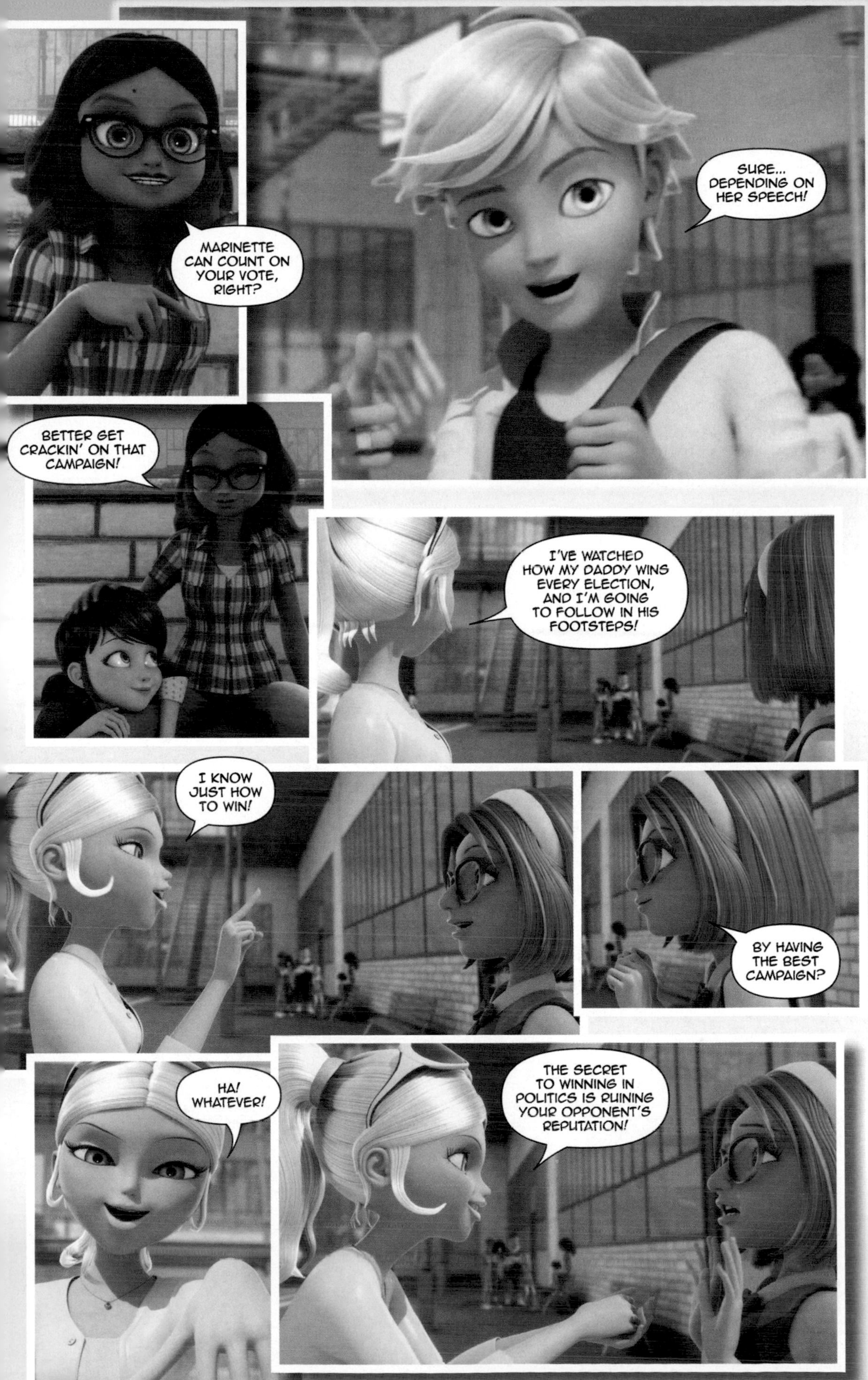
MARINETTE CAN COUNT ON YOUR VOTE, RIGHT?
SURE... DEPENDING ON HER SPEECH!
BETTER GET CRACKIN' ON THAT CAMPAIGN!
I'VE WATCHED HOW MY DADDY WINS EVERY ELECTION, AND I'M GOING TO FOLLOW IN HIS FOOTSTEPS!
I KNOW JUST HOW TO WIN!
BY HAVING THE BEST CAMPAIGN?
HA! WHATEVER!
THE SECRET TO WINNING IN POLITICS IS RUINING YOUR OPPONENT'S REPUTATION!

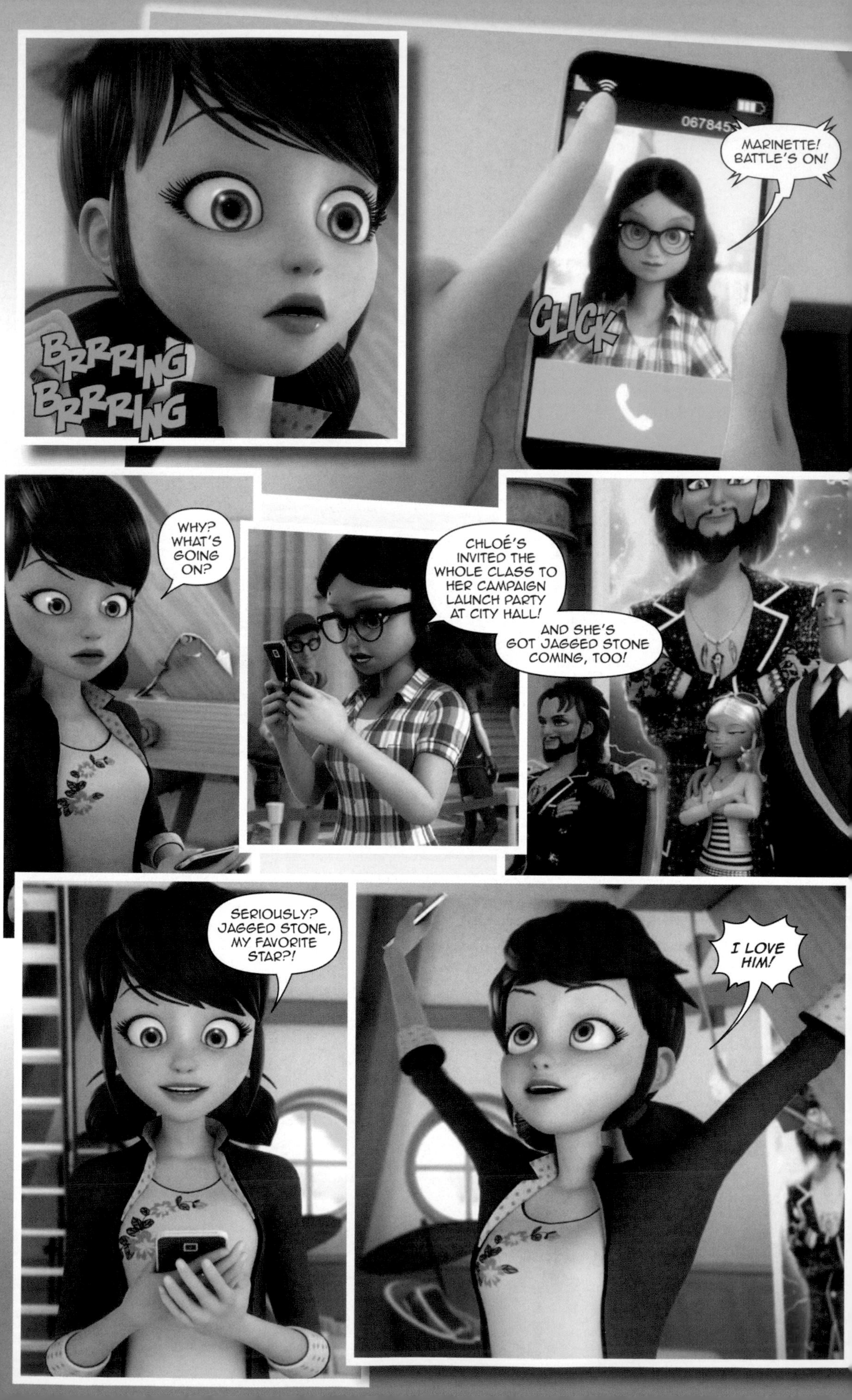
BRRRING
BRRRING
CLICK
067845
MARINETTE! BATTLE'S ON!
WHY? WHAT'S GOING ON?
CHLOÉ'S INVITED THE WHOLE CLASS TO HER CAMPAIGN LAUNCH PARTY AT CITY HALL!
AND SHE'S GOT JAGGED STONE COMING, TOO!
SERIOUSLY? JAGGED STONE, MY FAVORITE STAR?!
I LOVE HIM!

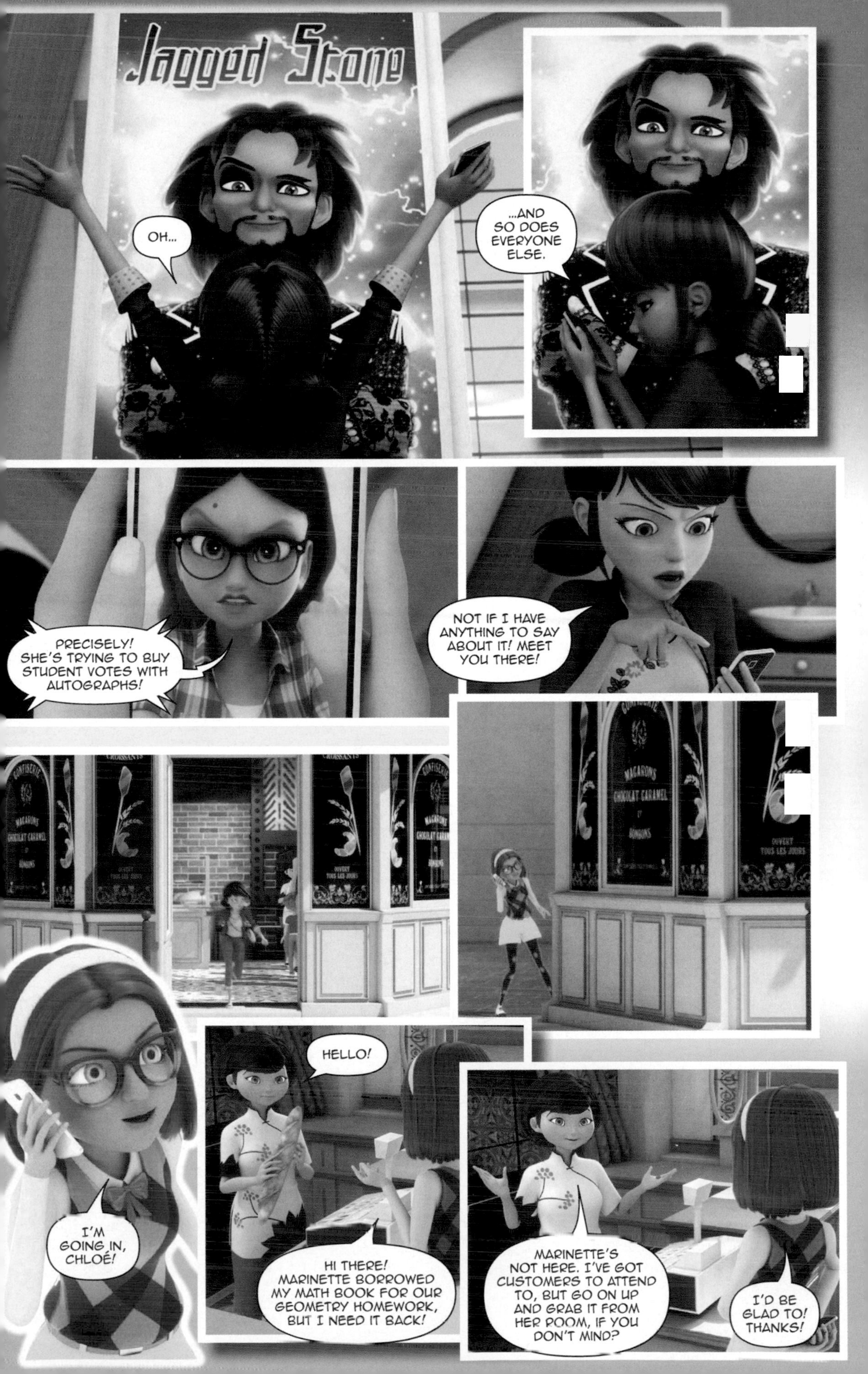

Jagged Stone
OH...
...AND SO DOES EVERYONE ELSE.
PRECISELY! SHE'S TRYING TO BUY STUDENT VOTES WITH AUTOGRAPHS!
NOT IF I HAVE ANYTHING TO SAY ABOUT IT! MEET YOU THERE!
I'M GOING IN, CHLOÉ!
HELLO!
HI THERE! MARINETTE BORROWED MY MATH BOOK FOR OUR GEOMETRY HOMEWORK, BUT I NEED IT BACK!
MARINETTE'S NOT HERE. I'VE GOT CUSTOMERS TO ATTEND TO, BUT GO ON UP AND GRAB IT FROM HER ROOM, IF YOU DON'T MIND?
I'D BE GLAD TO! THANKS!

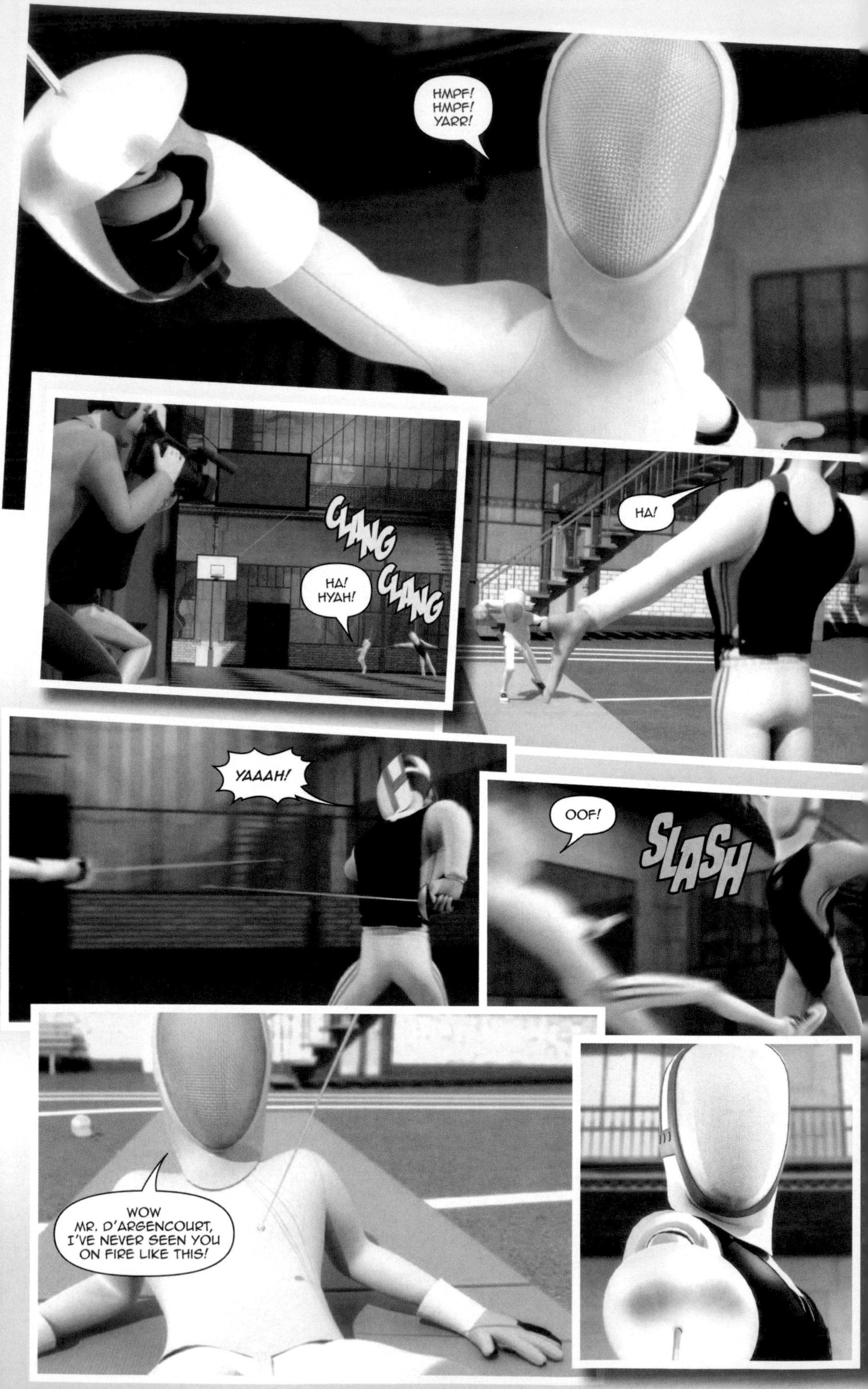
HMPF! HMPF! YARR!
CLANG CLANG
HA! HYAH!
HA!
YAAAH!
OOF!
SLASH
WOW MR. D'ARGENCOURT, I'VE NEVER SEEN YOU ON FIRE LIKE THIS!

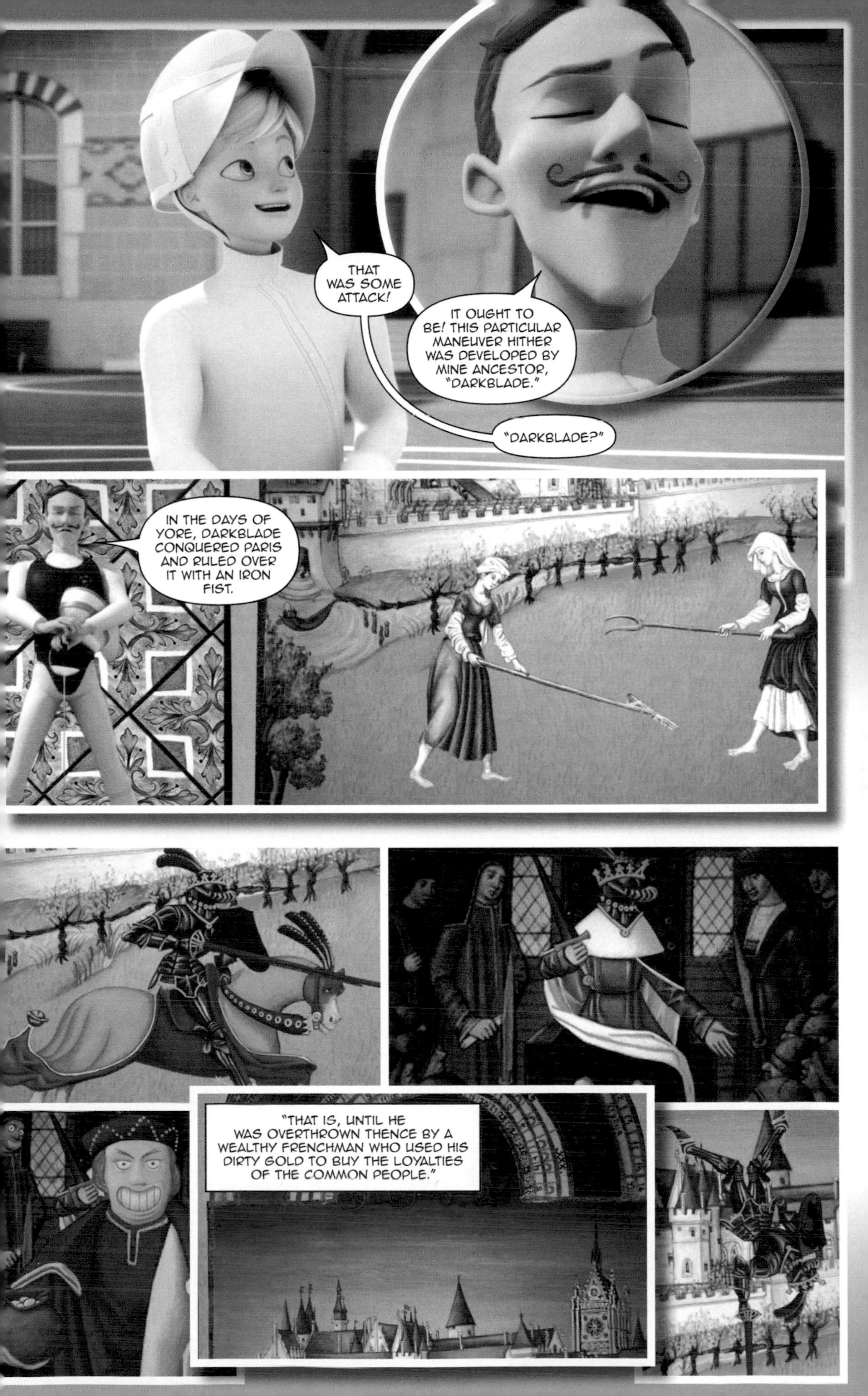
THAT WAS SOME ATTACK!
IT OUGHT TO BE! THIS PARTICULAR MANEUVER HITHER WAS DEVELOPED BY MINE ANCESTOR, "DARKBLADE."
"DARKBLADE?"
IN THE DAYS OF YORE, DARKBLADE CONQUERED PARIS AND RULED OVER IT WITH AN IRON FIST.
"THAT IS, UNTIL HE WAS OVERTHROWN THENCE BY A WEALTHY FRENCHMAN WHO USED HIS DIRTY GOLD TO BUY THE LOYALTIES OF THE COMMON PEOPLE."

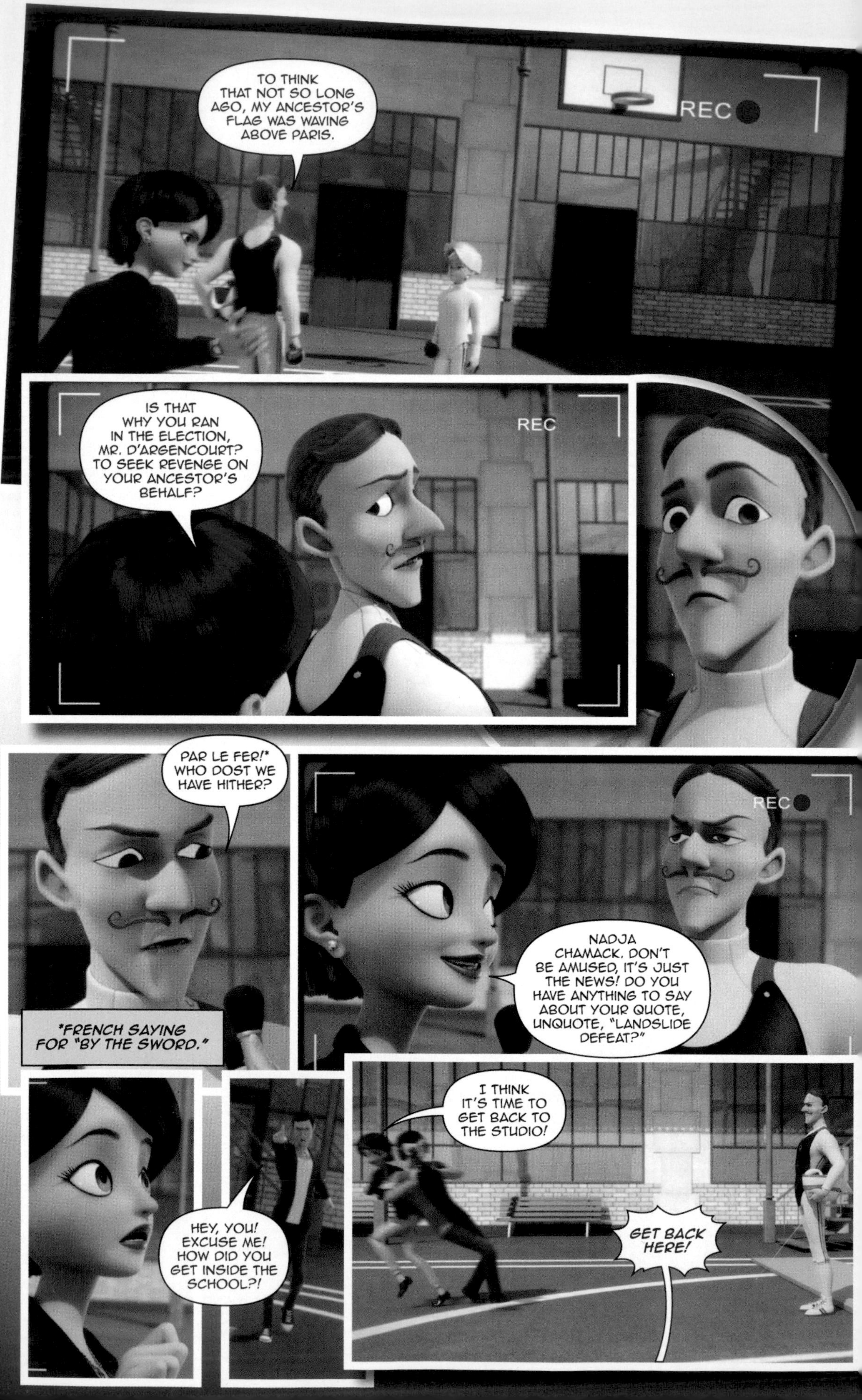
REC
TO THINK THAT NOT SO LONG AGO, MY ANCESTOR'S FLAG WAS WAVING ABOVE PARIS.
REC
IS THAT WHY YOU RAN IN THE ELECTION, MR. D'ARGENCOURT? TO SEEK REVENGE ON YOUR ANCESTOR'S BEHALF?
PAR LE FER!* WHO DOST WE HAVE HITHER?
*FRENCH SAYING FOR "BY THE SWORD."
REC
NADJA CHAMACK. DON'T BE AMUSED, IT'S JUST THE NEWS! DO YOU HAVE ANYTHING TO SAY ABOUT YOUR QUOTE, UNQUOTE, "LANDSLIDE DEFEAT?"
HEY, YOU! EXCUSE ME! HOW DID YOU GET INSIDE THE SCHOOL?!
I THINK IT'S TIME TO GET BACK TO THE STUDIO!
GET BACK HERE!

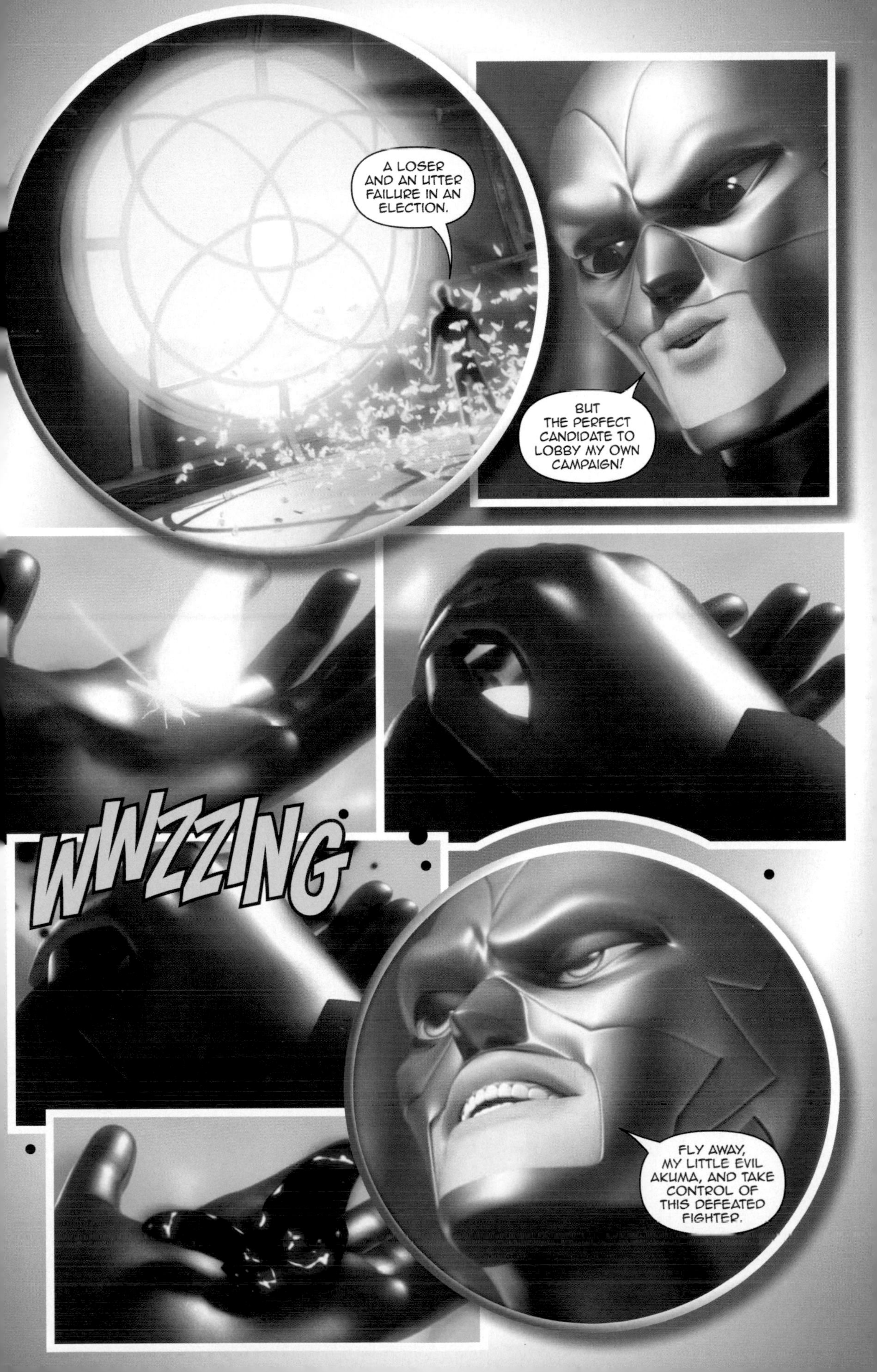
A LOSER AND AN UTTER FAILURE IN AN ELECTION.
BUT THE PERFECT CANDIDATE TO LOBBY MY OWN CAMPAIGN!
WWZZING
FLY AWAY, MY LITTLE EVIL AKUMA, AND TAKE CONTROL OF THIS DEFEATED FIGHTER.

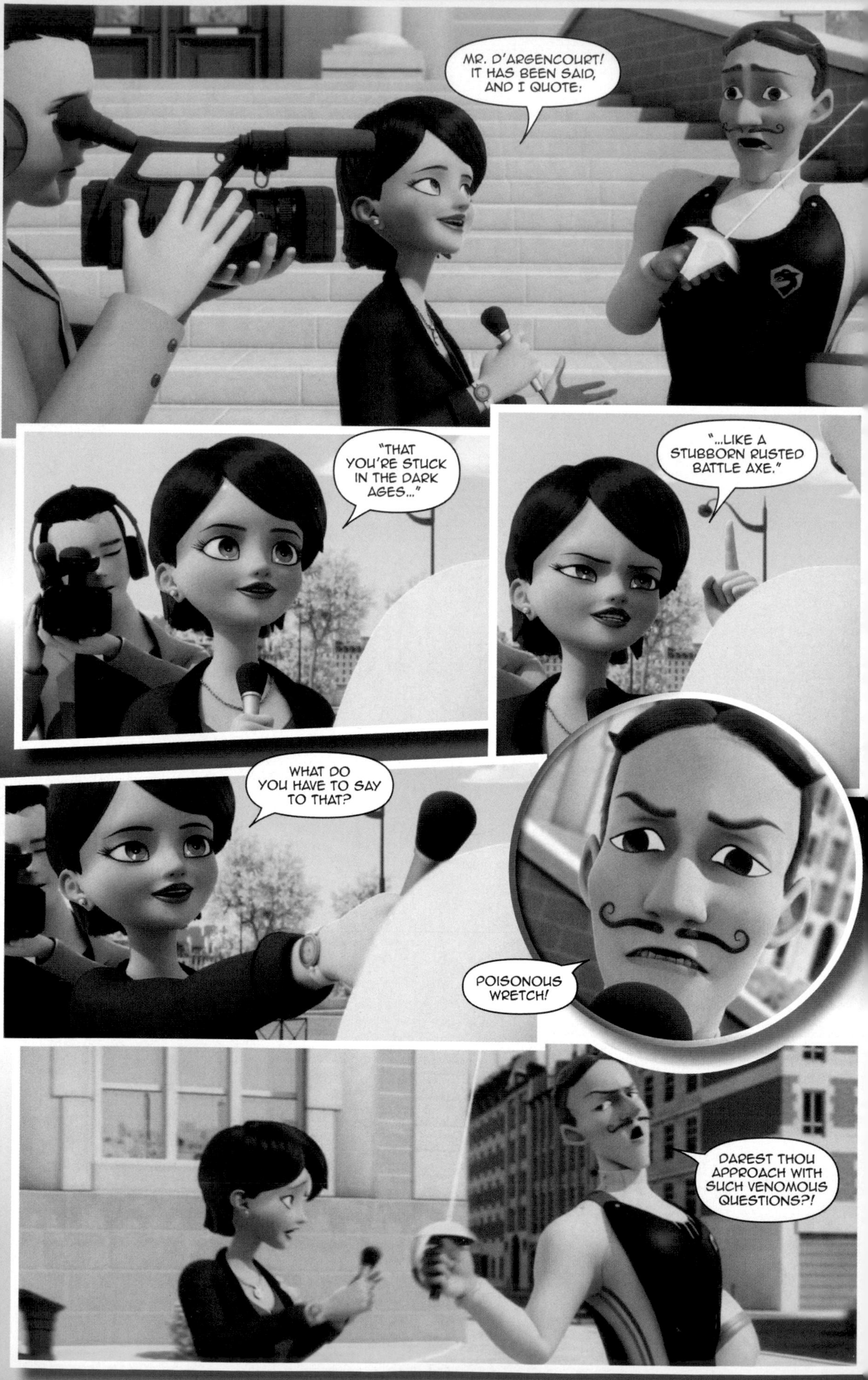
MR. D'ARGENCOURT! IT HAS BEEN SAID, AND I QUOTE:
"THAT YOU'RE STUCK IN THE DARK AGES..."
"...LIKE A STUBBORN RUSTED BATTLE AXE."
WHAT DO YOU HAVE TO SAY TO THAT?
POISONOUS WRETCH!
DAREST THOU APPROACH WITH SUCH VENOMOUS QUESTIONS?!

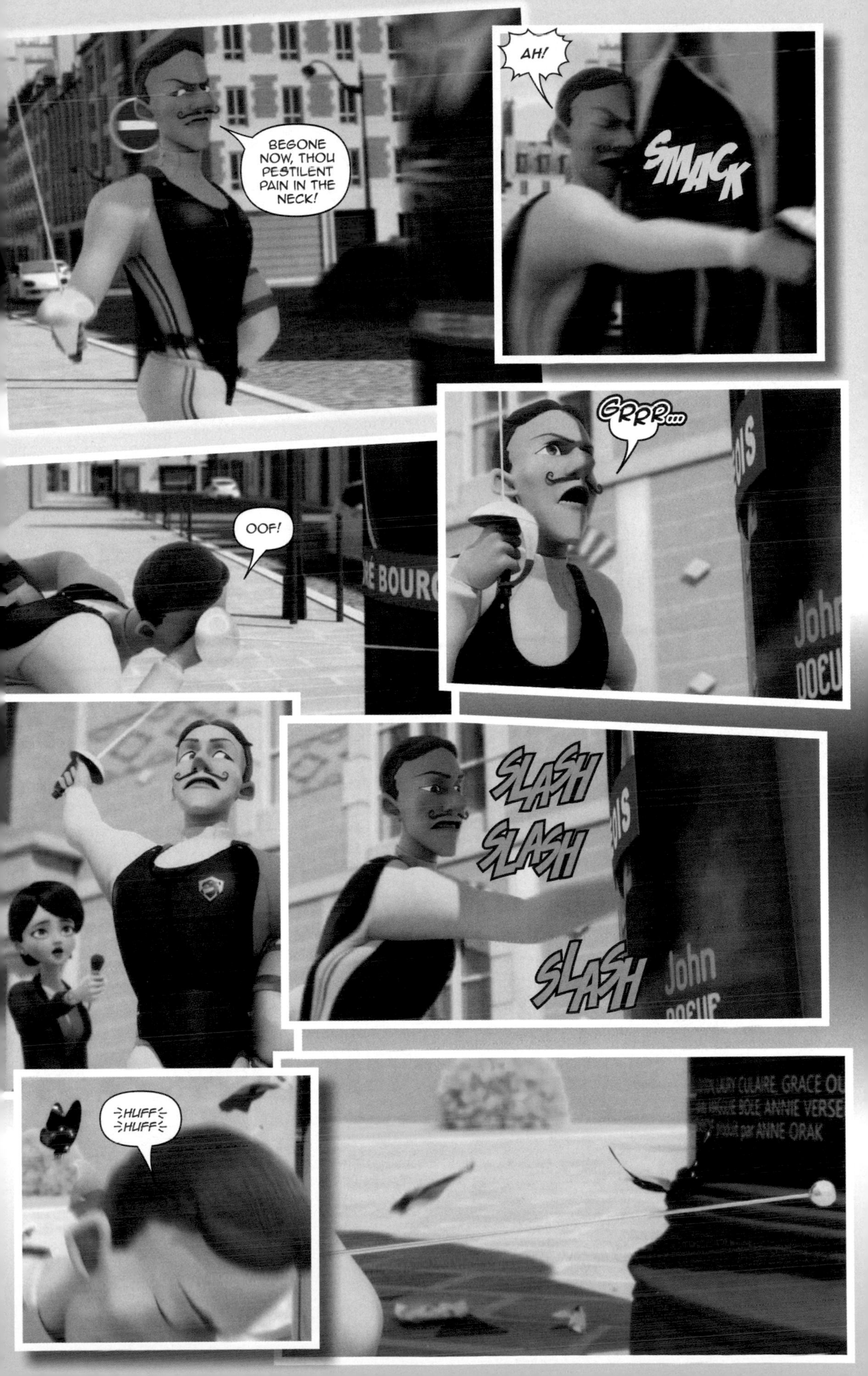
BEGONE NOW, THOU PESTILENT PAIN IN THE NECK!
AH!
SMACK
GRRR...
OOF!
SLASH
SLASH
SLASH
John
HUFF HUFF

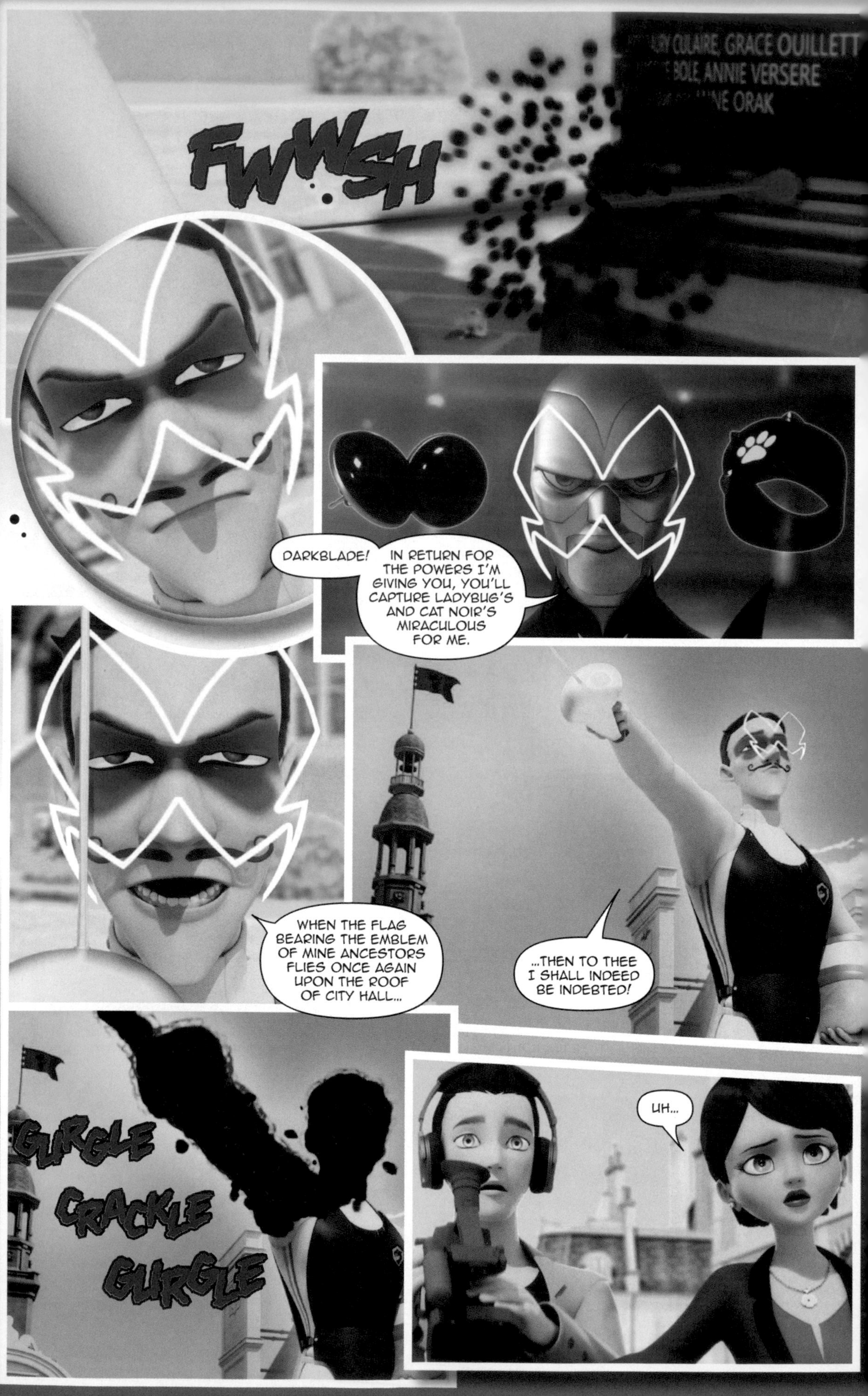
FWWSH
DARKBLADE!
IN RETURN FOR THE POWERS I'M GIVING YOU, YOU'LL CAPTURE LADYBUG'S AND CAT NOIR'S MIRACULOUS FOR ME.
WHEN THE FLAG BEARING THE EMBLEM OF MINE ANCESTORS FLIES ONCE AGAIN UPON THE ROOF OF CITY HALL...
...THEN TO THEE I SHALL INDEED BE INDEBTED!
GURGLE
CRACKLE
GURGLE
UH...

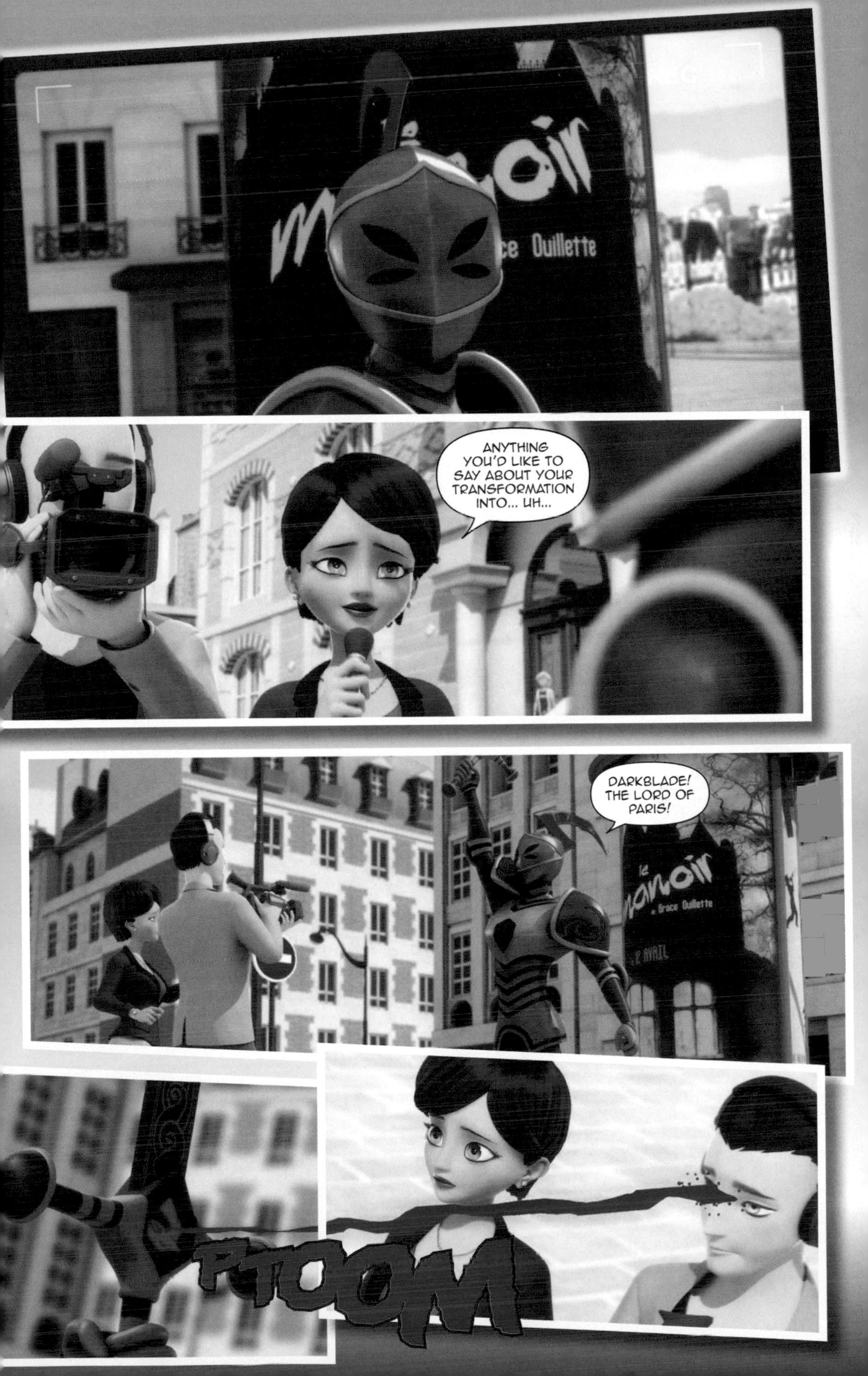
ANYTHING YOU'D LIKE TO SAY ABOUT YOUR TRANSFORMATION INTO... UH...
DARKBLADE! THE LORD OF PARIS!
PTOOM

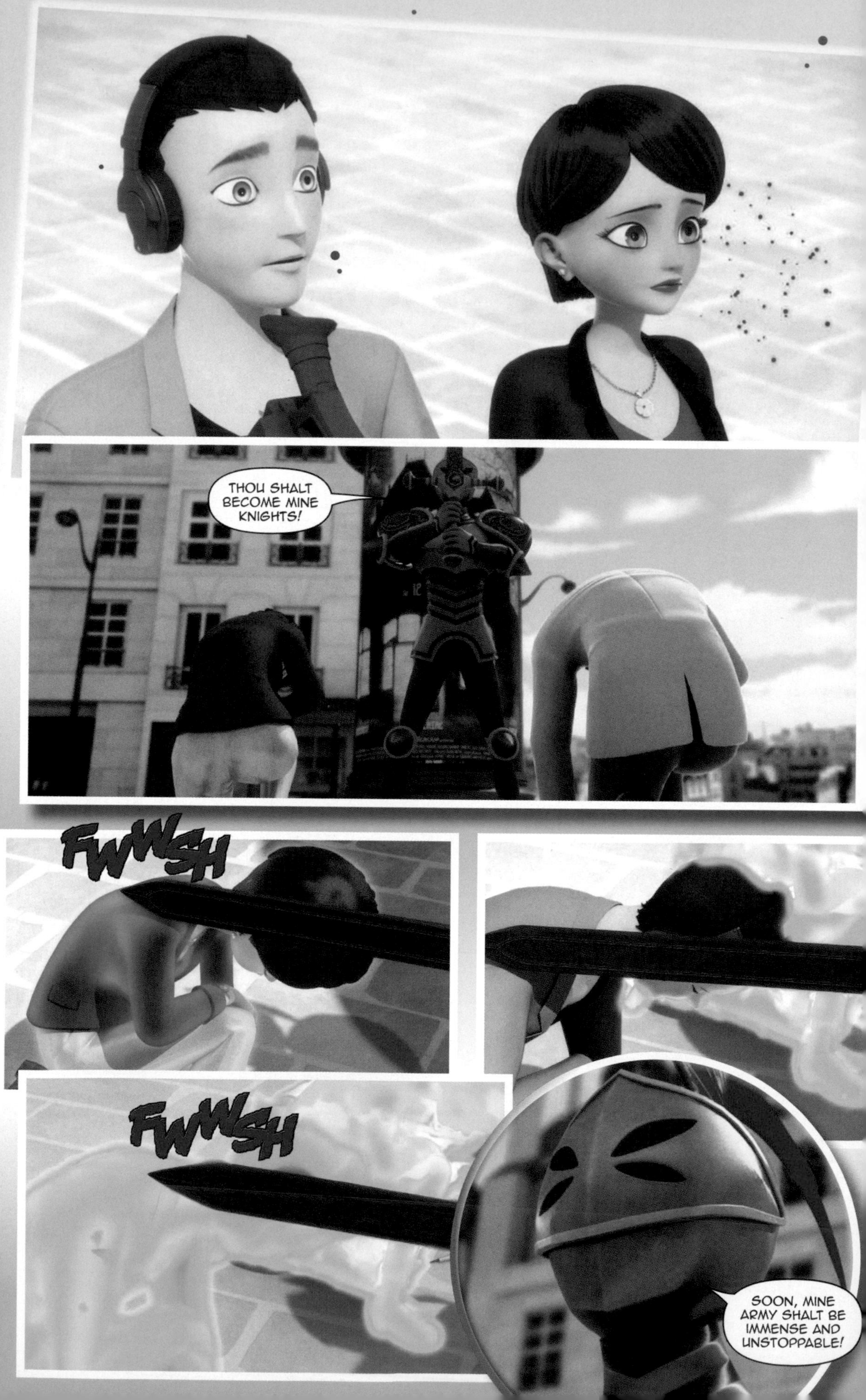
THOU SHALT BECOME MINE KNIGHTS!
FWWSH
FWWSH
SOON, MINE ARMY SHALT BE IMMENSE AND UNSTOPPABLE!

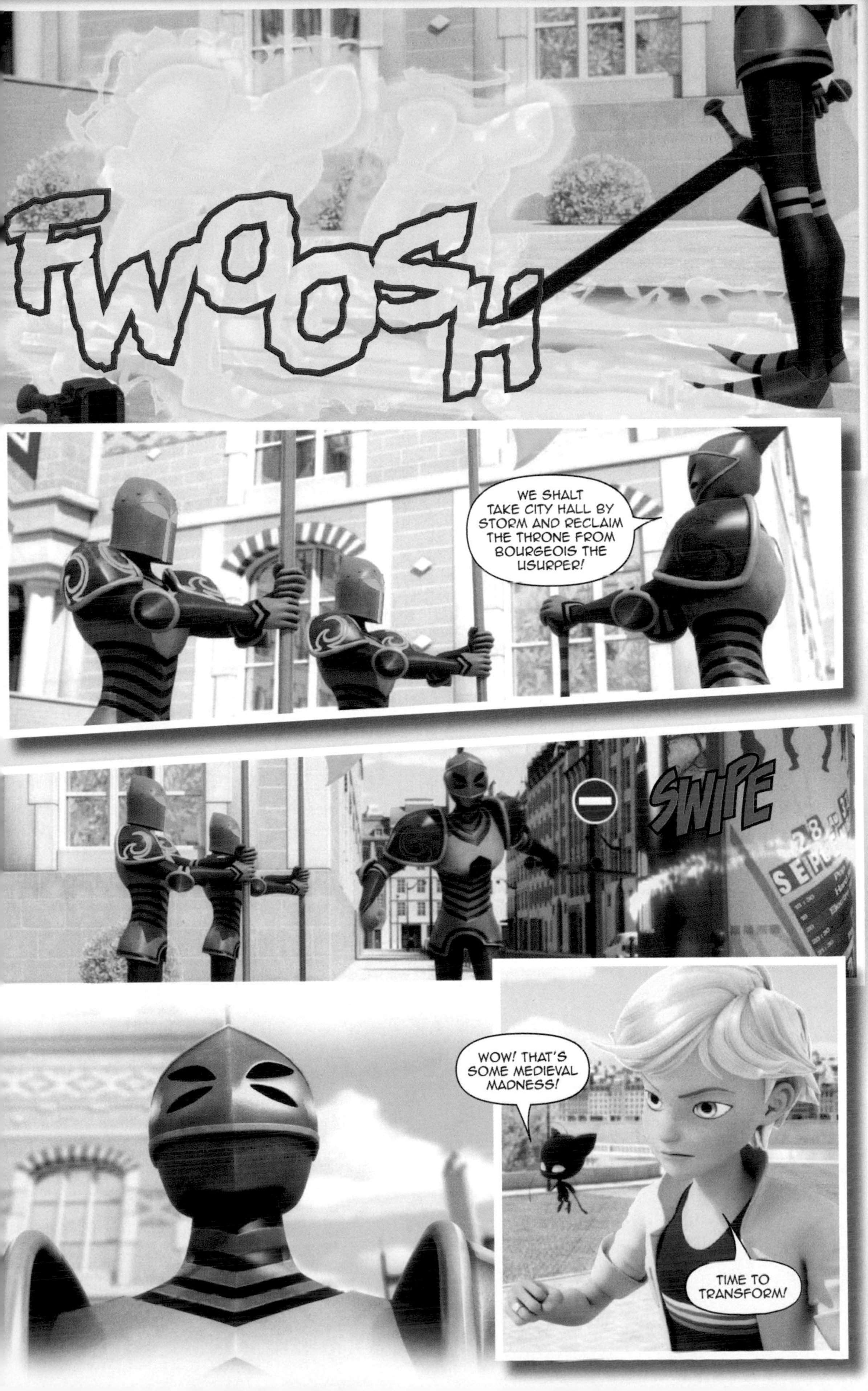
FWOOSH
WE SHALT TAKE CITY HALL BY STORM AND RECLAIM THE THRONE FROM BOURGEOIS THE USURPER!
SWIPE
WOW! THAT'S SOME MEDIEVAL MADNESS!
TIME TO TRANSFORM!

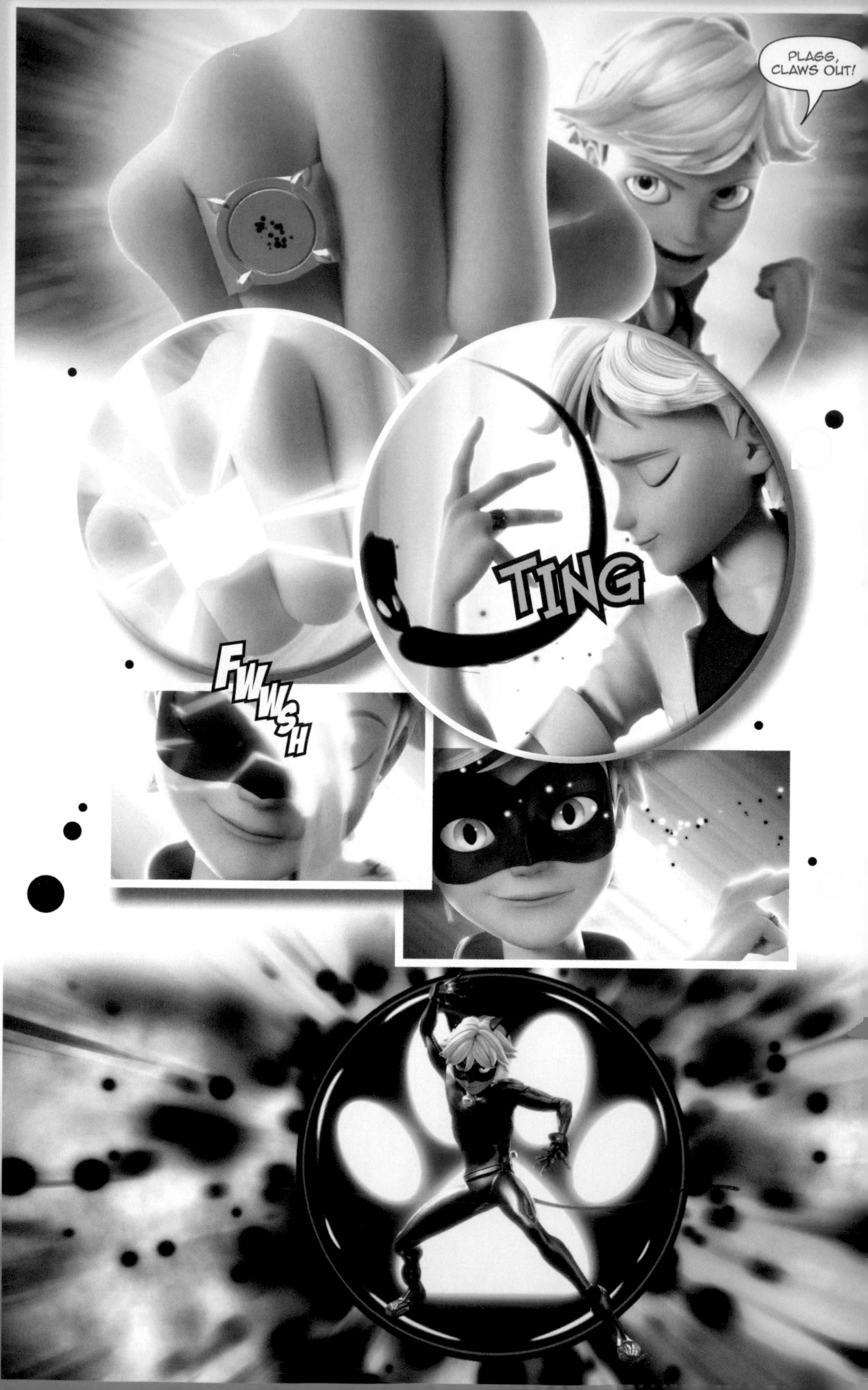
PLAGG, CLAWS OUT!
TING
FWWSH

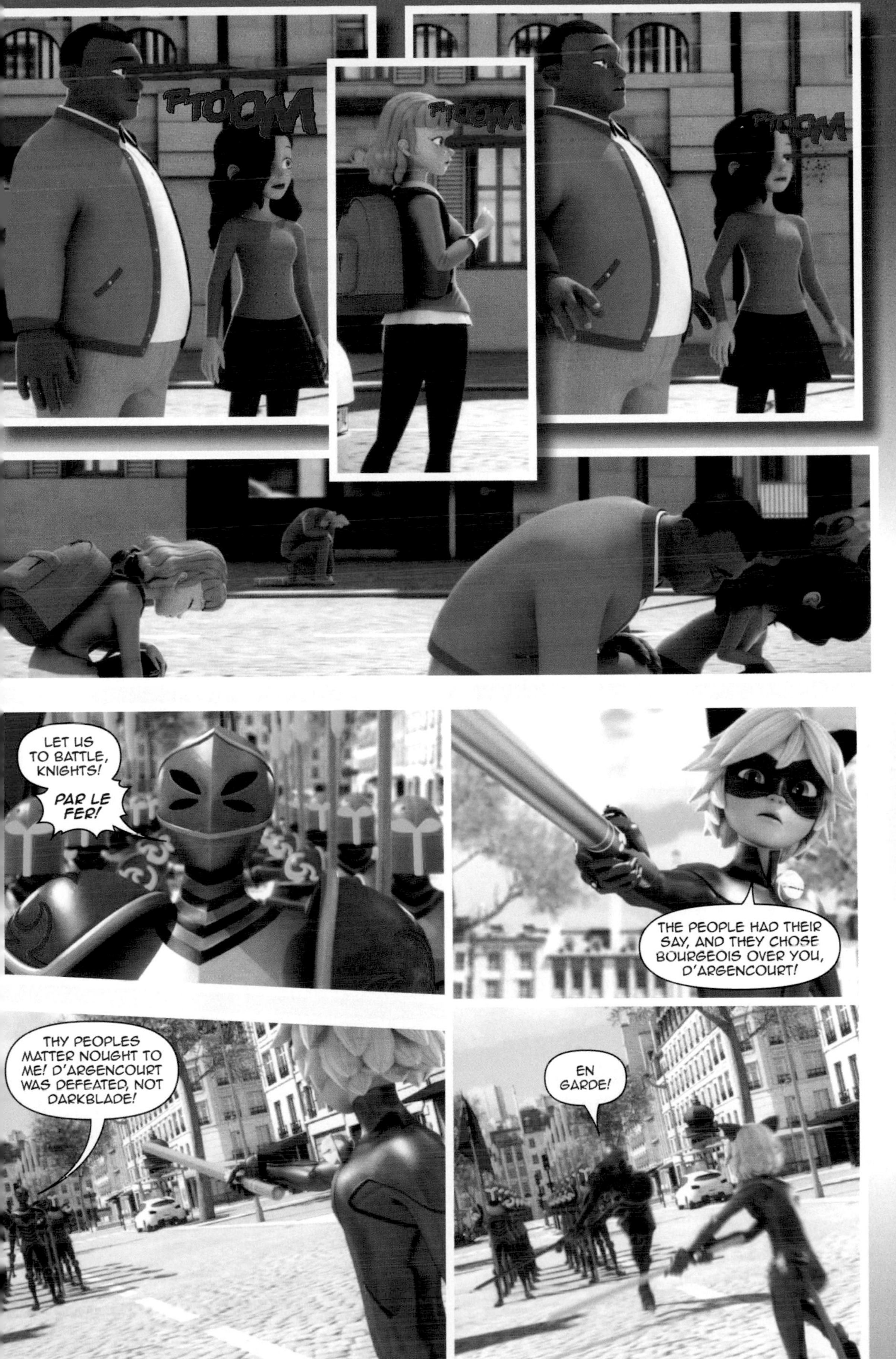
PTOOM
PTOOM
PTOOM
LET US TO BATTLE, KNIGHTS!
PAR LE FER!
THE PEOPLE HAD THEIR SAY, AND THEY CHOSE BOURGEOIS OVER YOU, D'ARGENCOURT!
THY PEOPLES MATTER NOUGHT TO ME! D'ARGENCOURT WAS DEFEATED, NOT DARKBLADE!
EN GARDE!

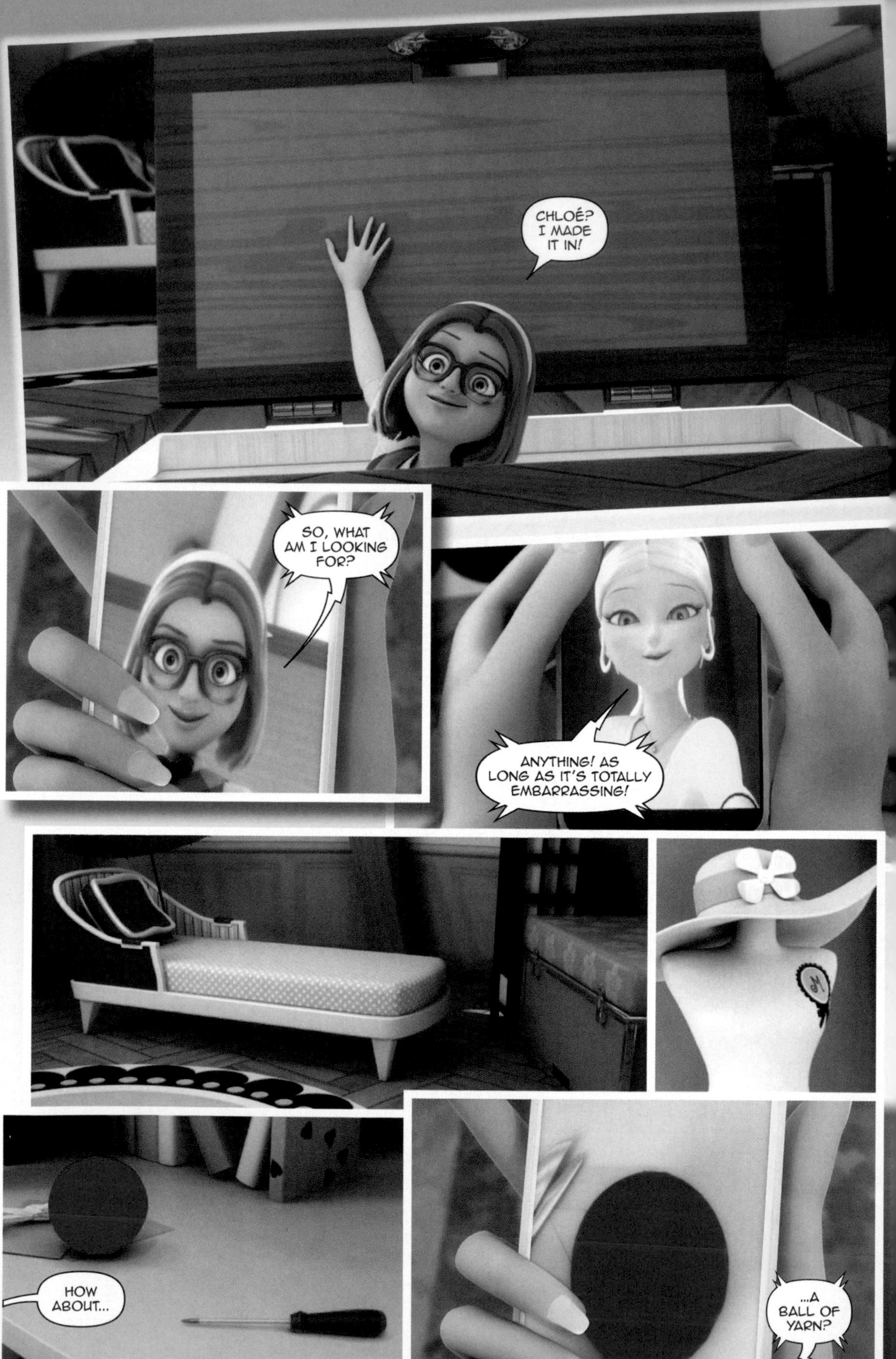
CHLOÉ? I MADE IT IN!
SO, WHAT AM I LOOKING FOR?
ANYTHING! AS LONG AS IT'S TOTALLY EMBARRASSING!
HOW ABOUT...
...A BALL OF YARN?

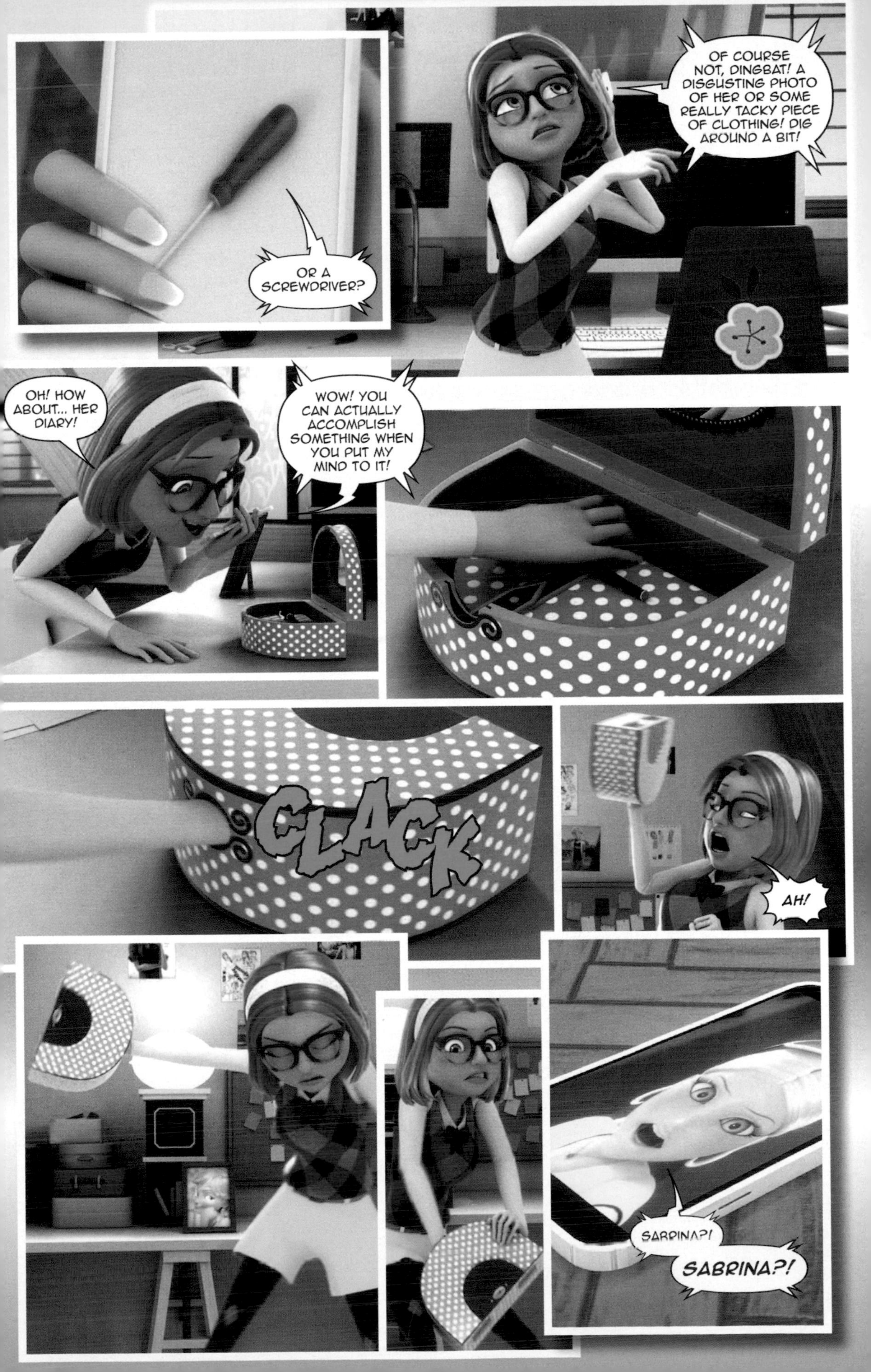
OR A SCREWDRIVER?
OF COURSE NOT, DINGBAT! A DISGUSTING PHOTO OF HER OR SOME REALLY TACKY PIECE OF CLOTHING! DIG AROUND A BIT!
OH! HOW ABOUT... HER DIARY!
WOW! YOU CAN ACTUALLY ACCOMPLISH SOMETHING WHEN YOU PUT MY MIND TO IT!
CLACK
AH!
SABRINA?!
SABRINA?!

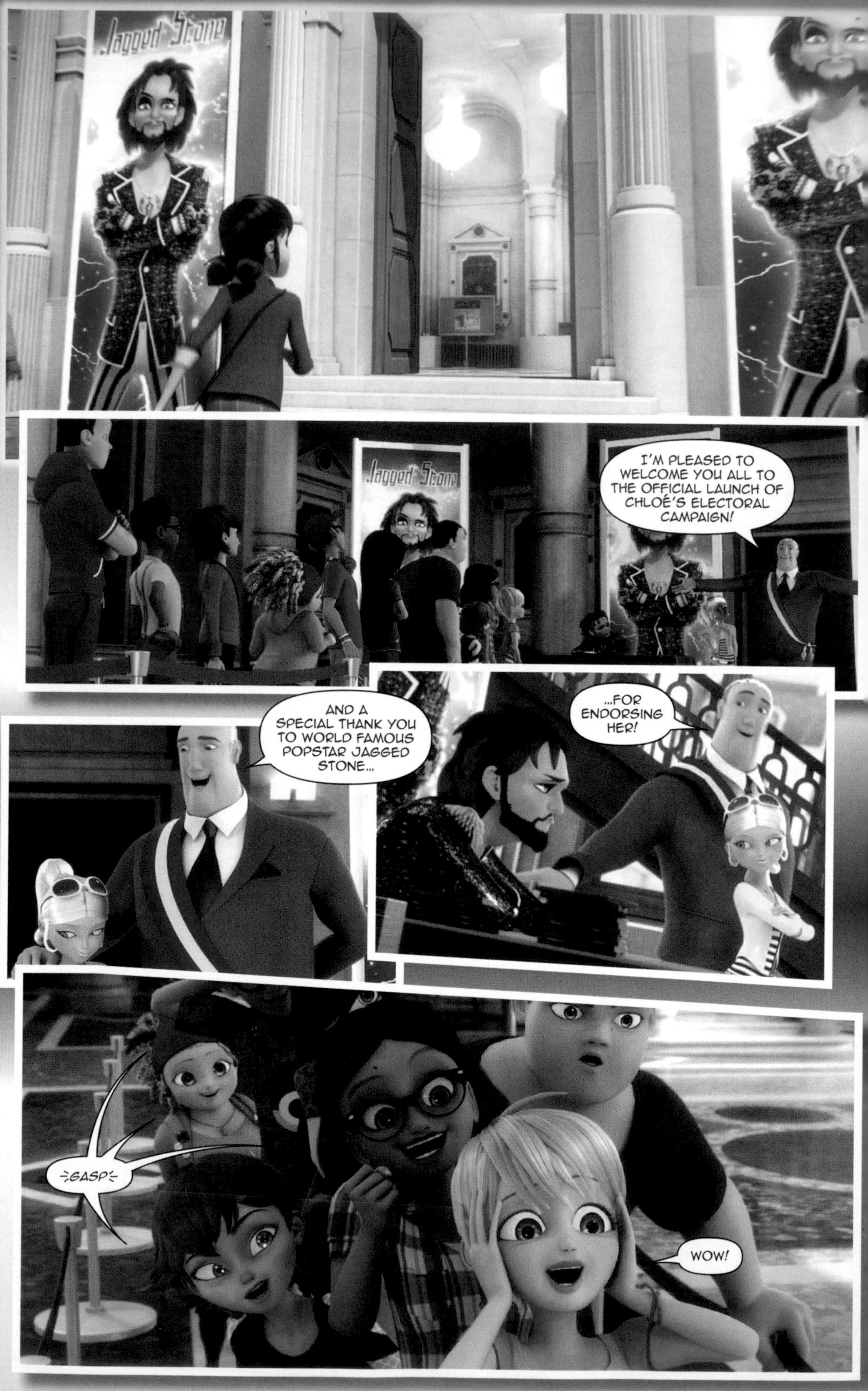
Jagged Stone
Jagged Stone
I'M PLEASED TO WELCOME YOU ALL TO THE OFFICIAL LAUNCH OF CHLOÉ'S ELECTORAL CAMPAIGN!
AND A SPECIAL THANK YOU TO WORLD FAMOUS POPSTAR JAGGED STONE...
...FOR ENDORSING HER!
GASP
WOW!

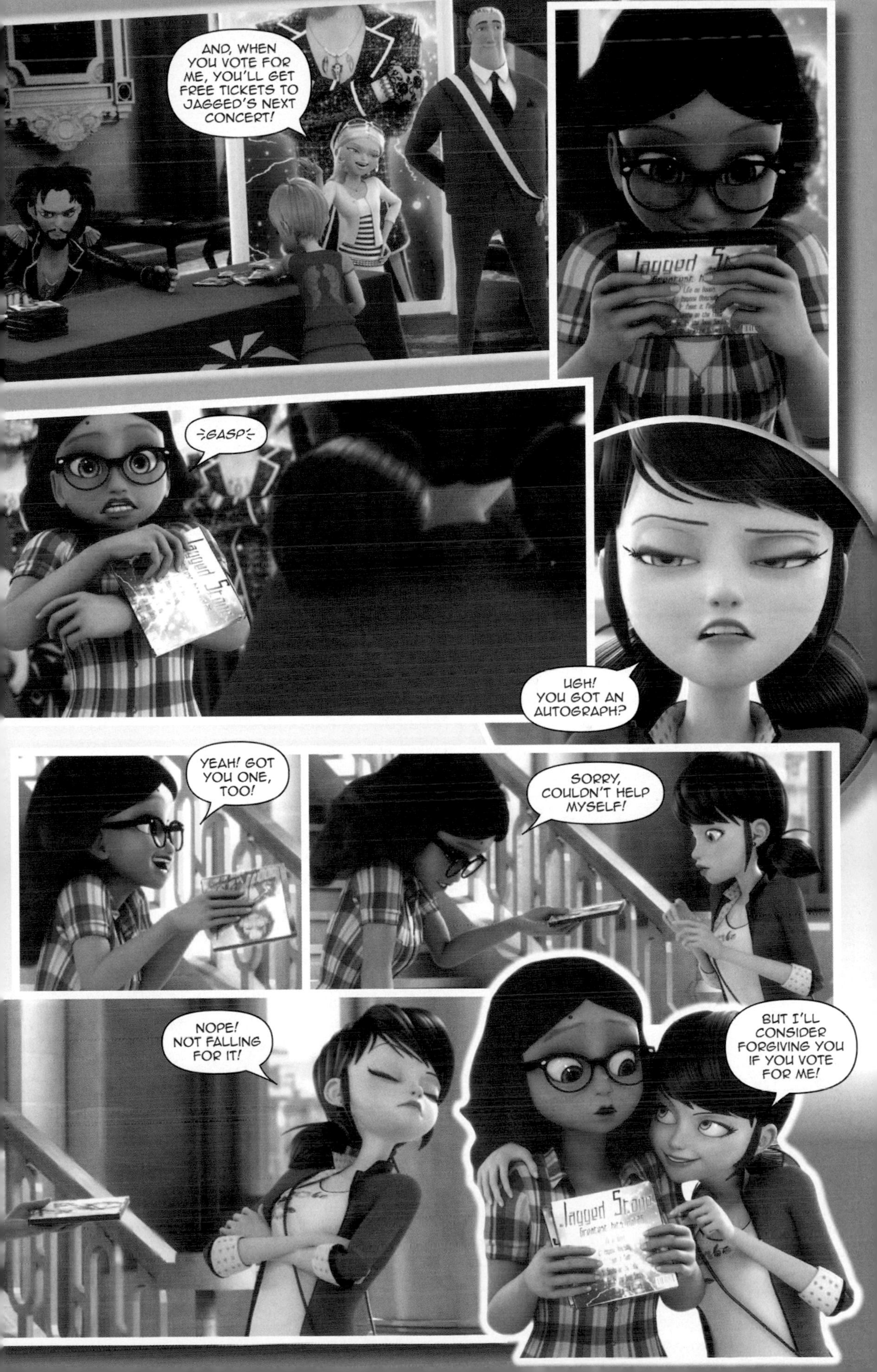

AND, WHEN YOU VOTE FOR ME, YOU'LL GET FREE TICKETS TO JAGGED'S NEXT CONCERT!
Jagged Stone
GASP
UGH! YOU GOT AN AUTOGRAPH?
YEAH! GOT YOU ONE, TOO!
SORRY, COULDN'T HELP MYSELF!
NOPE! NOT FALLING FOR IT!
BUT I'LL CONSIDER FORGIVING YOU IF YOU VOTE FOR ME!

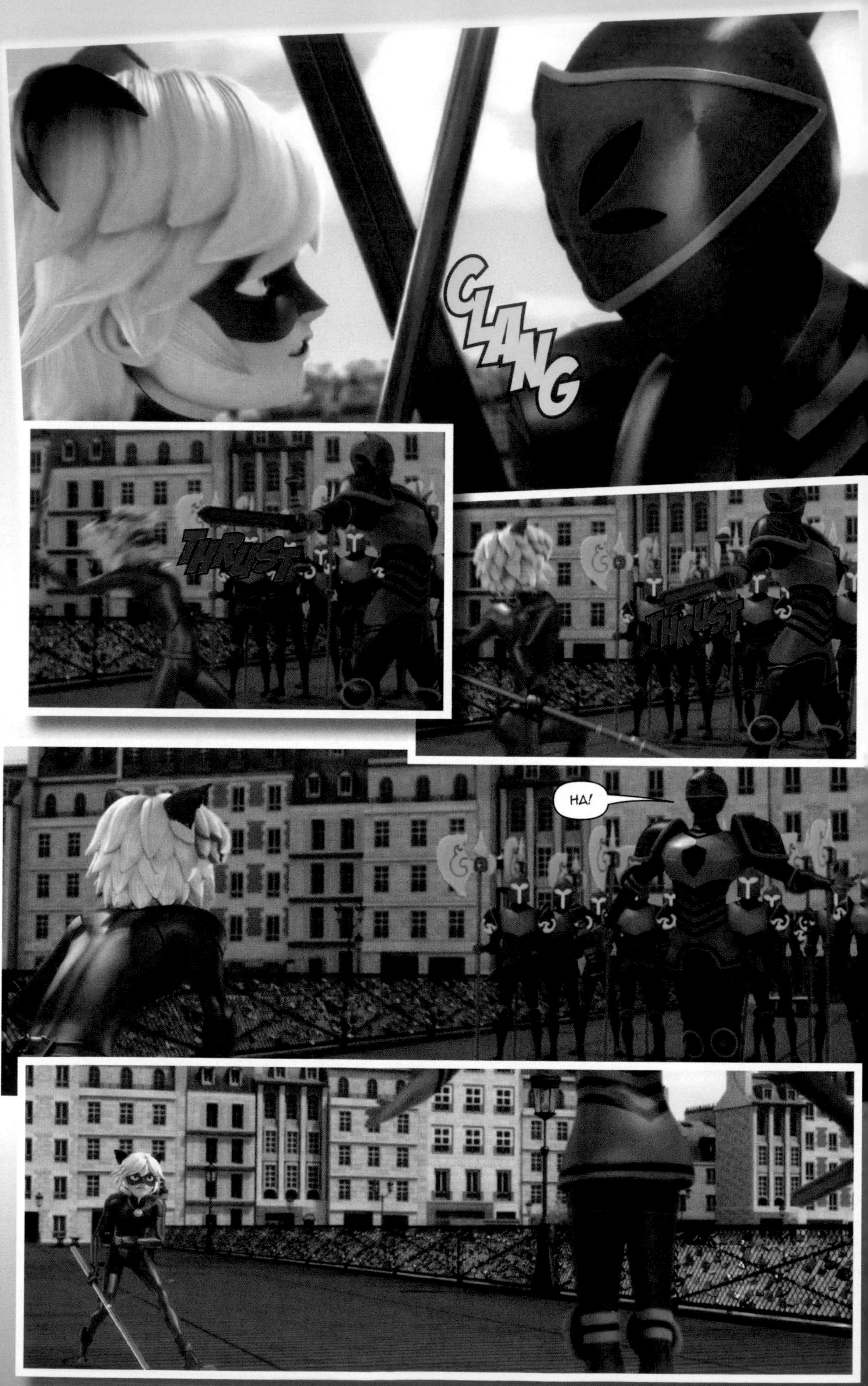
CLANG
THRUST
THRUST
HA!

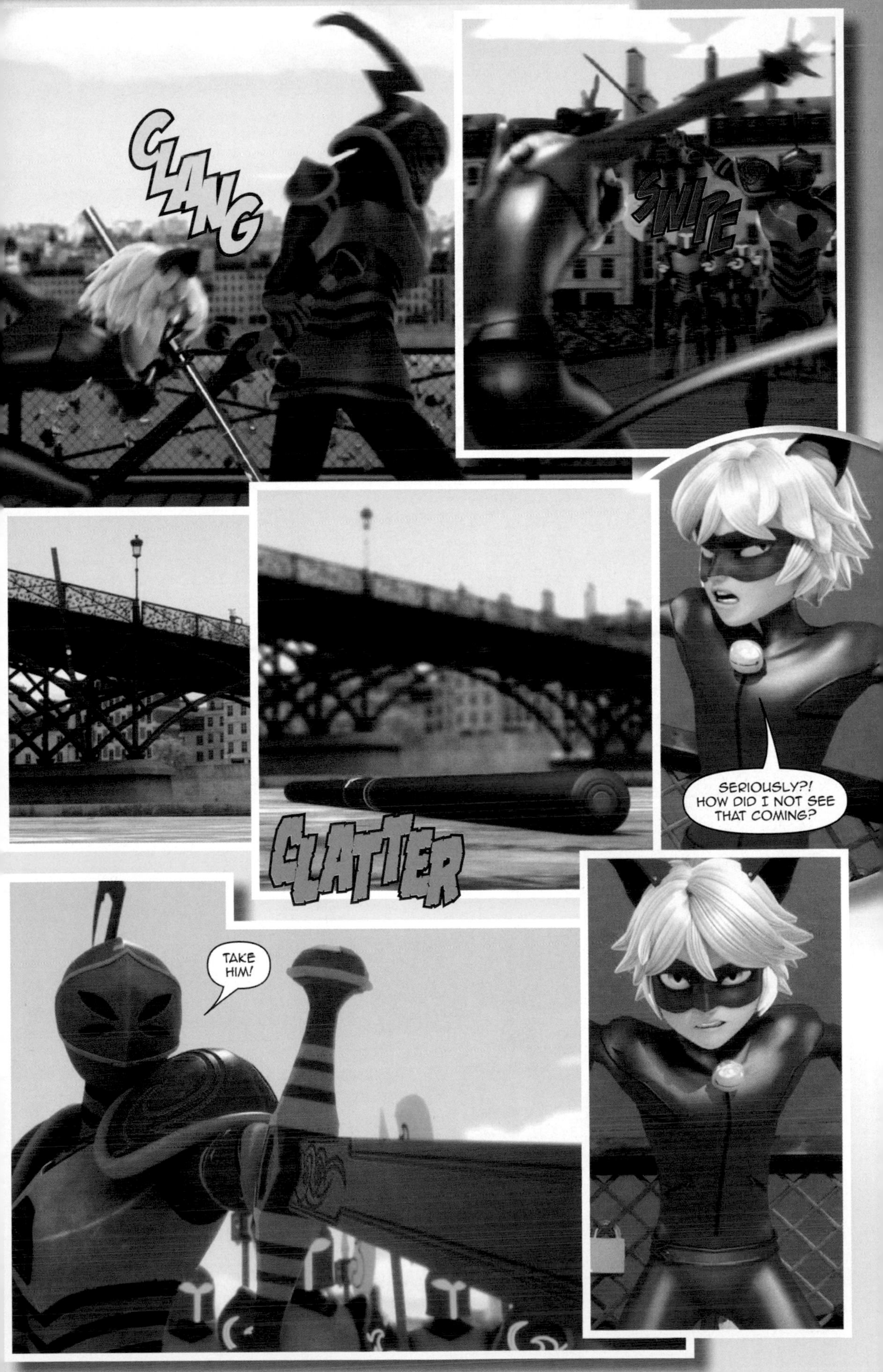
CLANG
SWIPE
CLATTER
SERIOUSLY?! HOW DID I NOT SEE THAT COMING?
TAKE HIM!

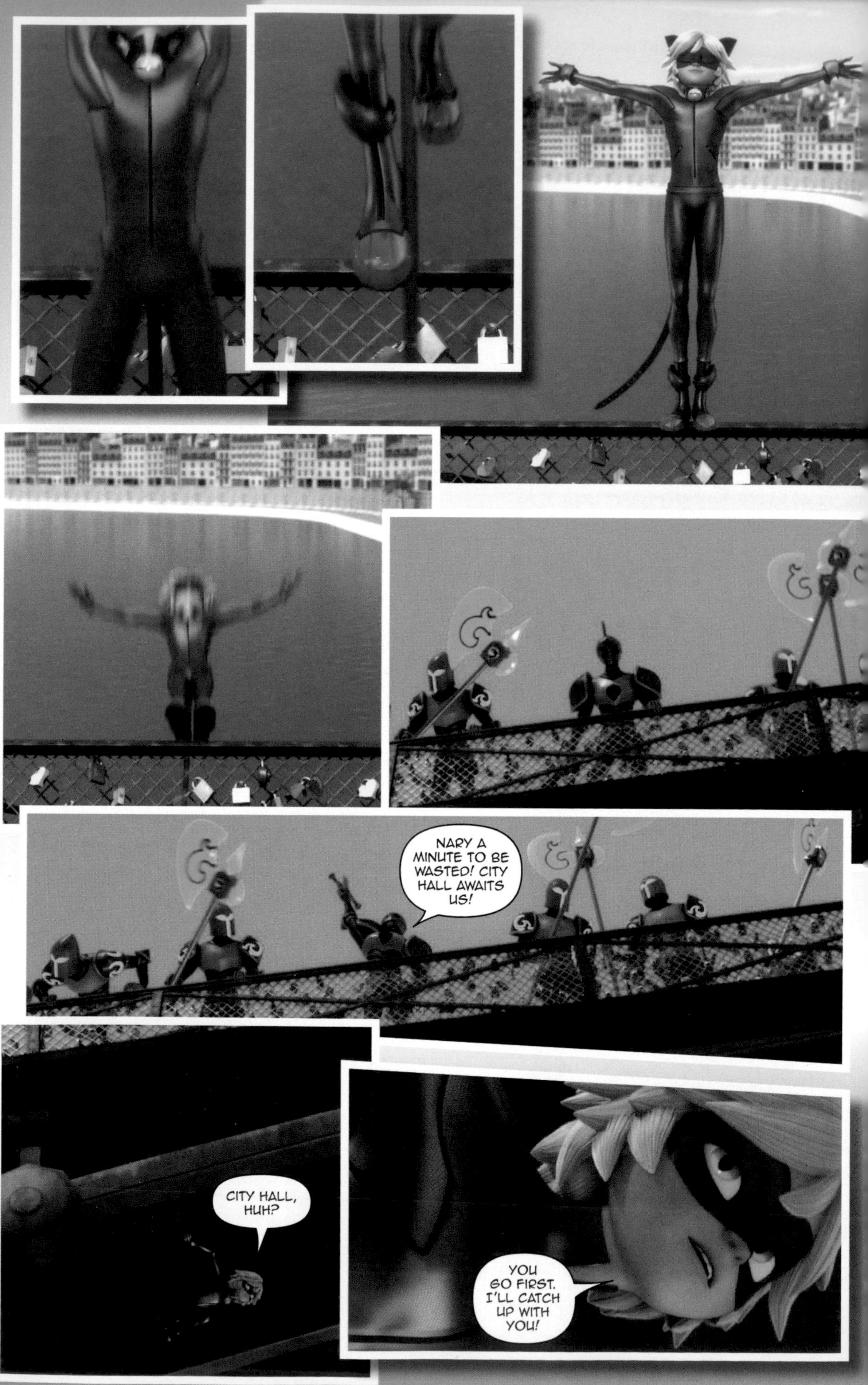
NARY A MINUTE TO BE WASTED! CITY HALL AWAITS US!
CITY HALL, HUH?
YOU GO FIRST. I'LL CATCH UP WITH YOU!

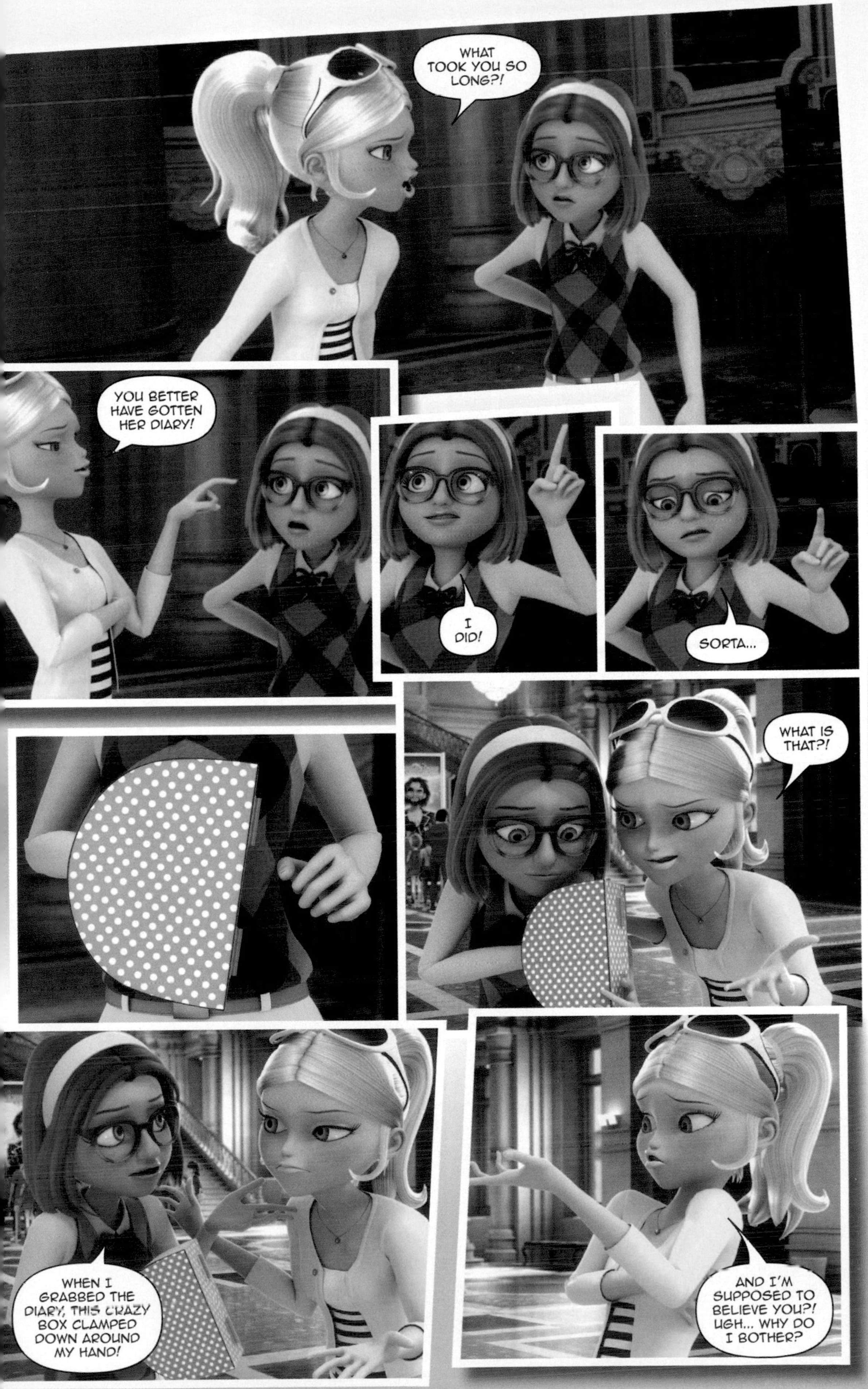
WHAT TOOK YOU SO LONG?!
YOU BETTER HAVE GOTTEN HER DIARY!
I DID!
SORTA...
WHAT IS THAT?!
WHEN I GRABBED THE DIARY, THIS CRAZY BOX CLAMPED DOWN AROUND MY HAND!
AND I'M SUPPOSED TO BELIEVE YOU?! UGH... WHY DO I BOTHER?

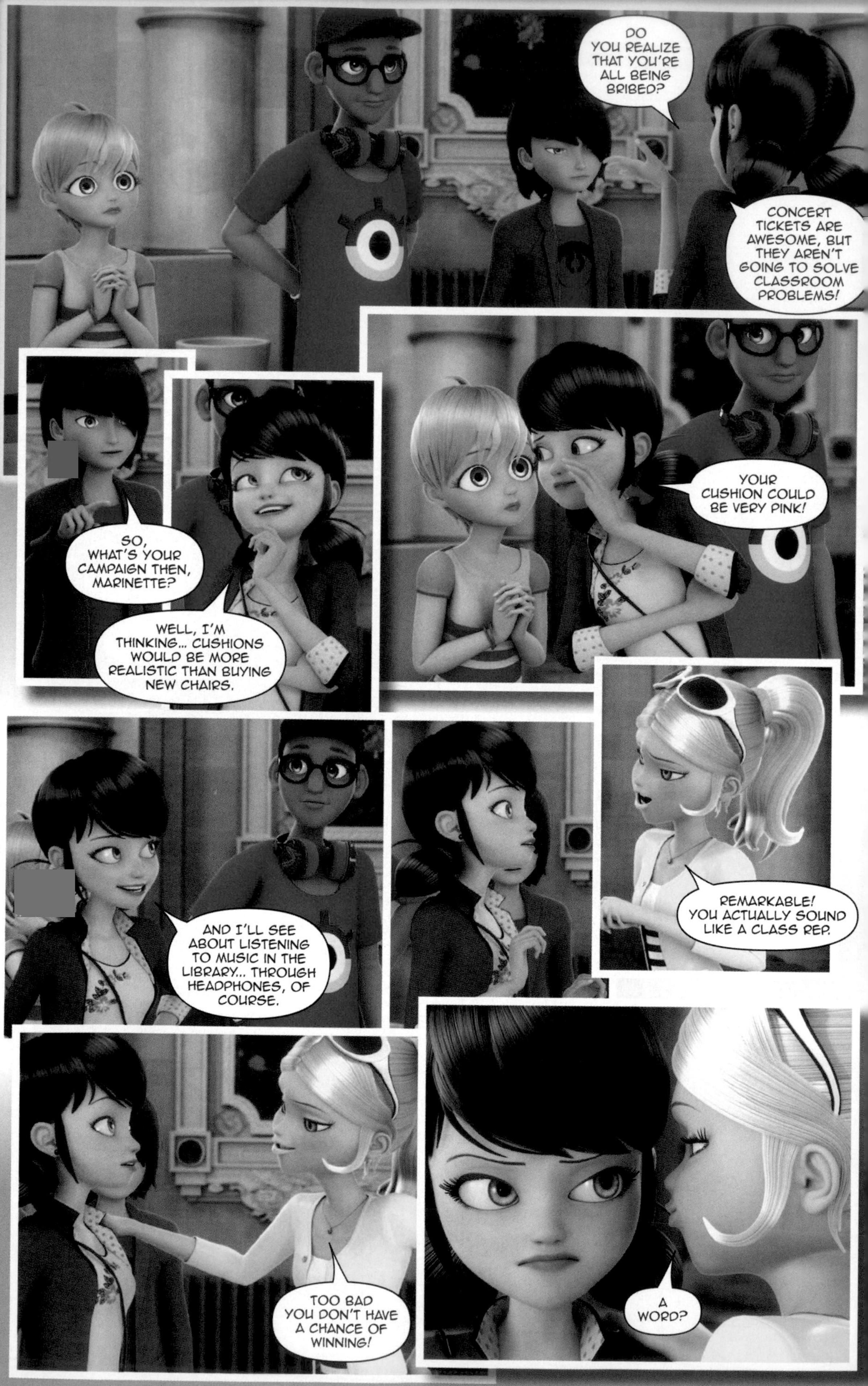
DO YOU REALIZE THAT YOU'RE ALL BEING BRIBED?
CONCERT TICKETS ARE AWESOME, BUT THEY AREN'T GOING TO SOLVE CLASSROOM PROBLEMS!
SO, WHAT'S YOUR CAMPAIGN THEN, MARINETTE?
WELL, I'M THINKING... CUSHIONS WOULD BE MORE REALISTIC THAN BUYING NEW CHAIRS.
YOUR CUSHION COULD BE VERY PINK!
AND I'LL SEE ABOUT LISTENING TO MUSIC IN THE LIBRARY... THROUGH HEADPHONES, OF COURSE.
REMARKABLE! YOU ACTUALLY SOUND LIKE A CLASS REP.
TOO BAD YOU DON'T HAVE A CHANCE OF WINNING!
A WORD?

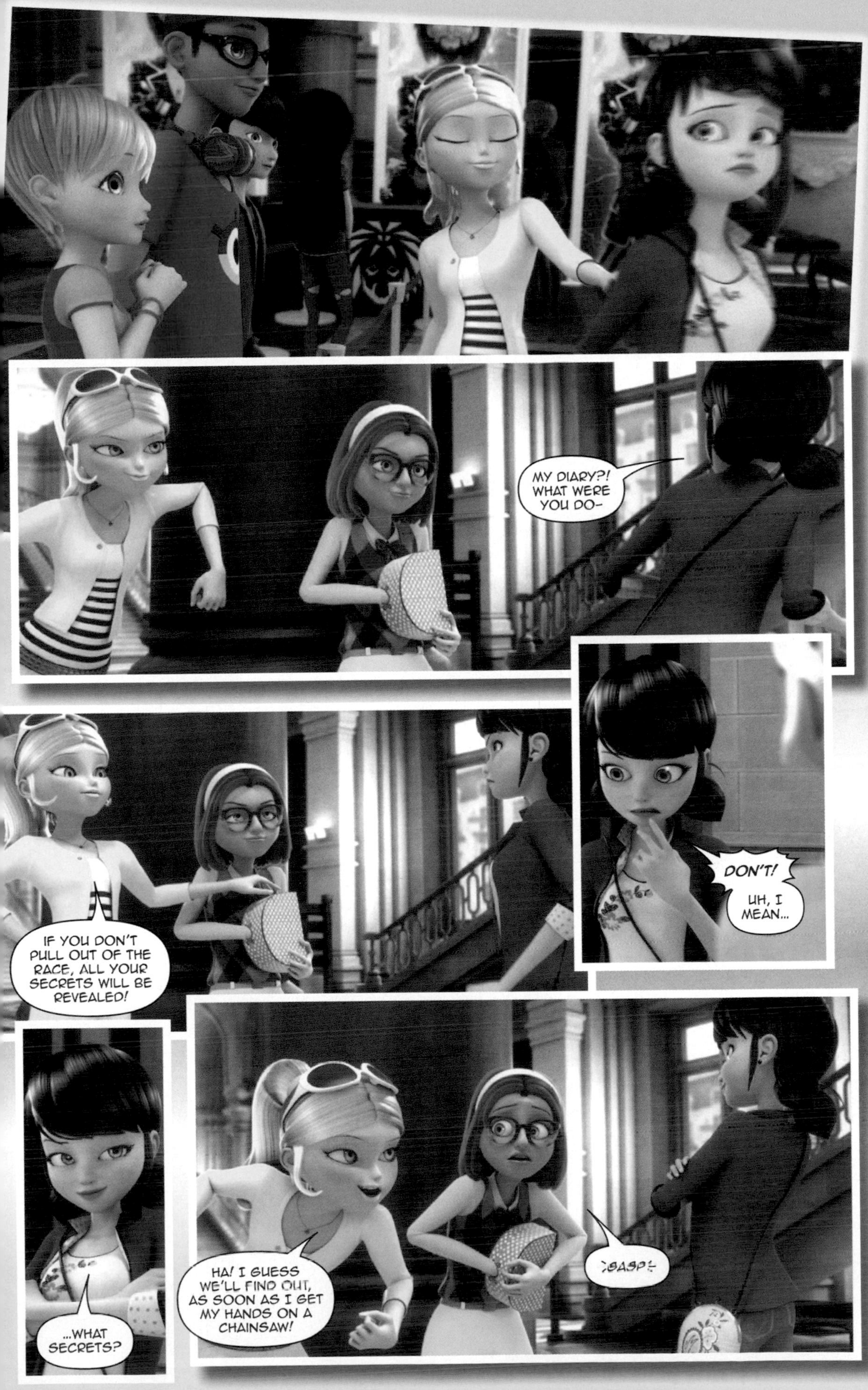
MY DIARY?! WHAT WERE YOU DO-
IF YOU DON'T PULL OUT OF THE RACE, ALL YOUR SECRETS WILL BE REVEALED!
DON'T!
UH, I MEAN...
...WHAT SECRETS?
HA! I GUESS WE'LL FIND OUT, AS SOON AS I GET MY HANDS ON A CHAINSAW!
>GASP<

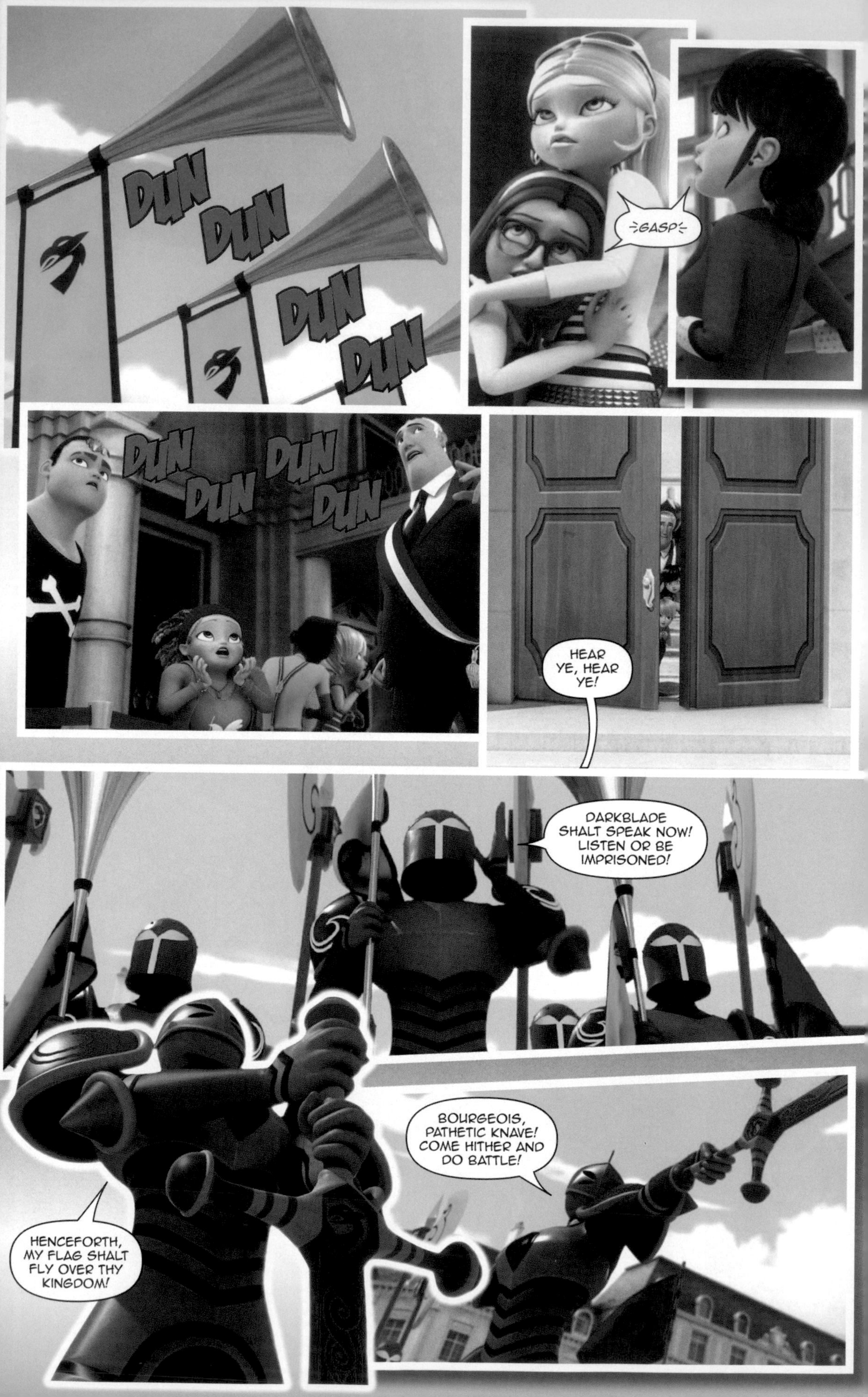
DUN
DUN
DUN
DUN
GASP
DUN
DUN
DUN
DUN
HEAR YE, HEAR YE!
DARKBLADE SHALT SPEAK NOW! LISTEN OR BE IMPRISONED!
BOURGEOIS, PATHETIC KNAVE! COME HITHER AND DO BATTLE!
HENCEFORTH, MY FLAG SHALT FLY OVER THY KINGDOM!

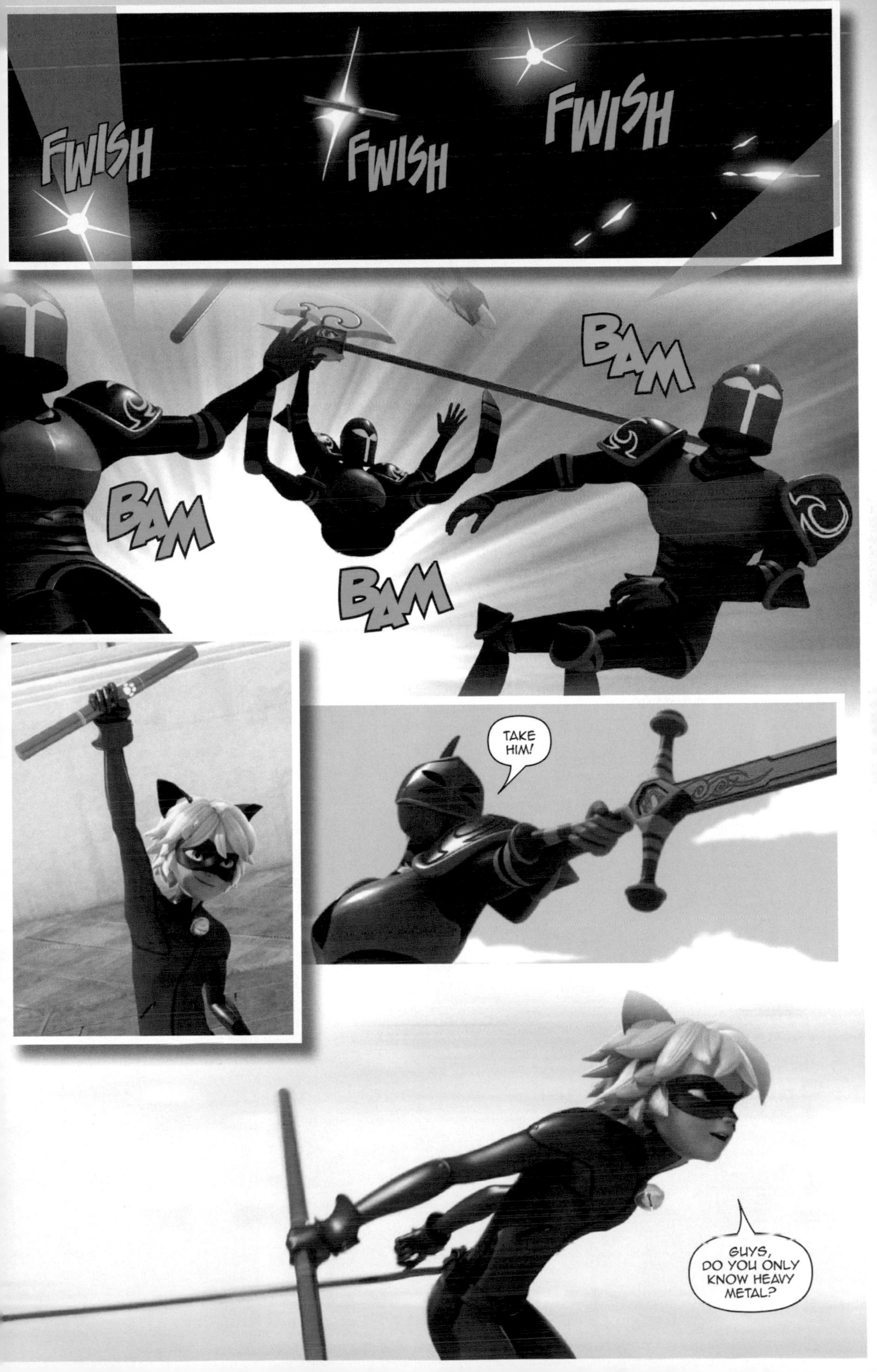
FWISH
FWISH
FWISH
BAM
BAM
BAM
TAKE HIM!
GUYS, DO YOU ONLY KNOW HEAVY METAL?

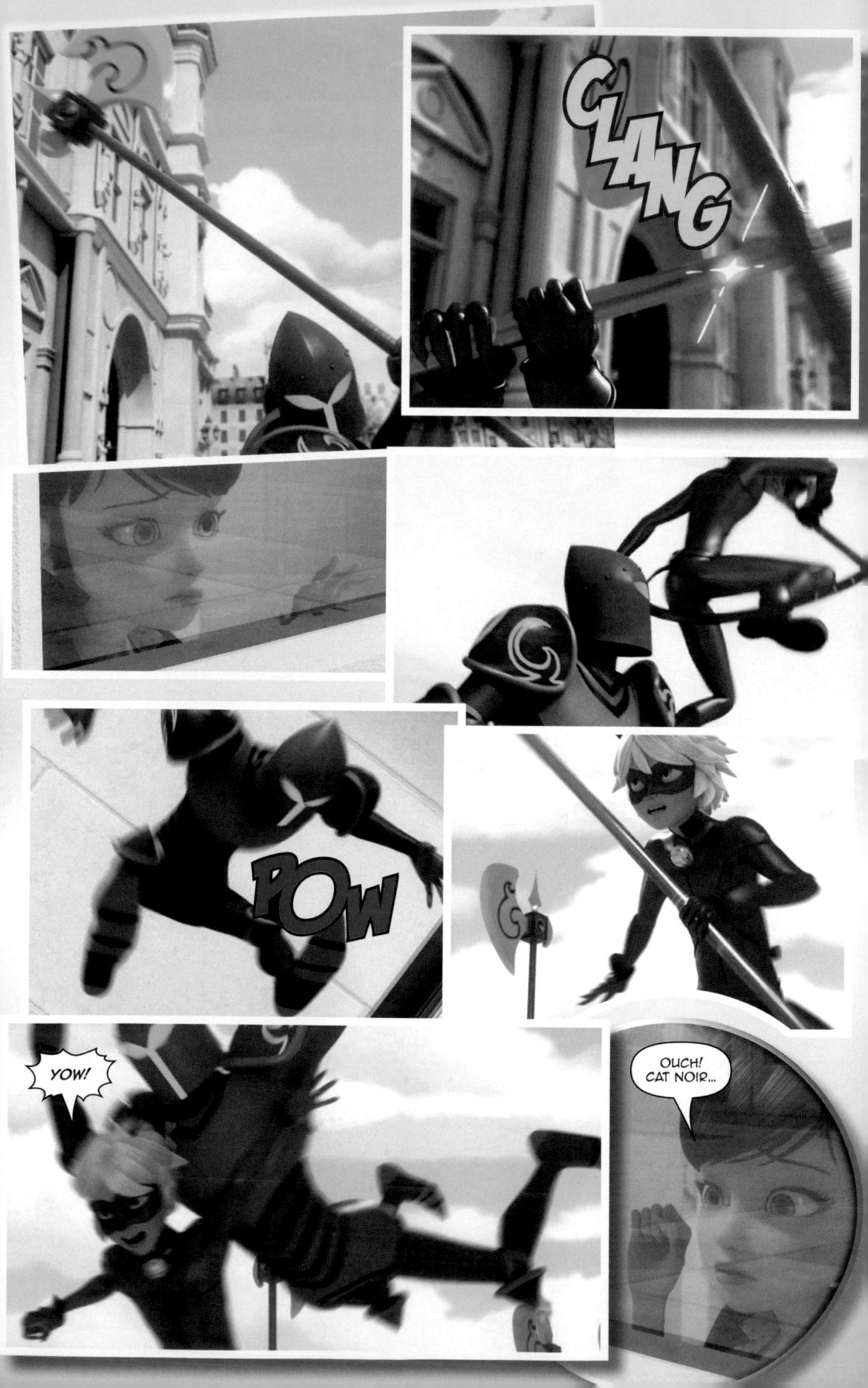
CLANG
POW
YOW!
OUCH! CAT NOIR...

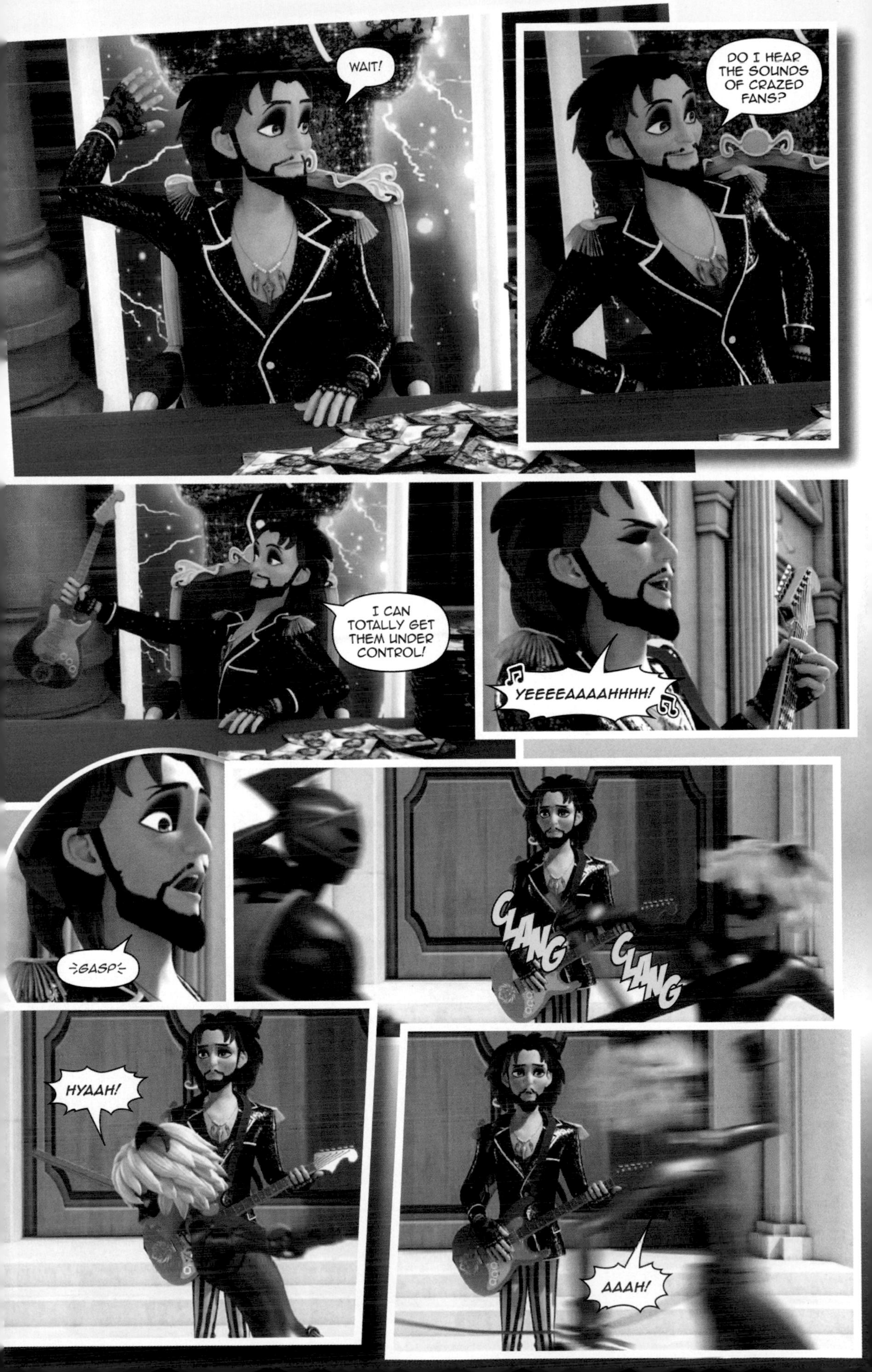
WAIT!
DO I HEAR THE SOUNDS OF CRAZED FANS?
I CAN TOTALLY GET THEM UNDER CONTROL!
YEEEEAAAAHHHH!
GASP
CLANG
CLANG
HYAAH!
AAAH!

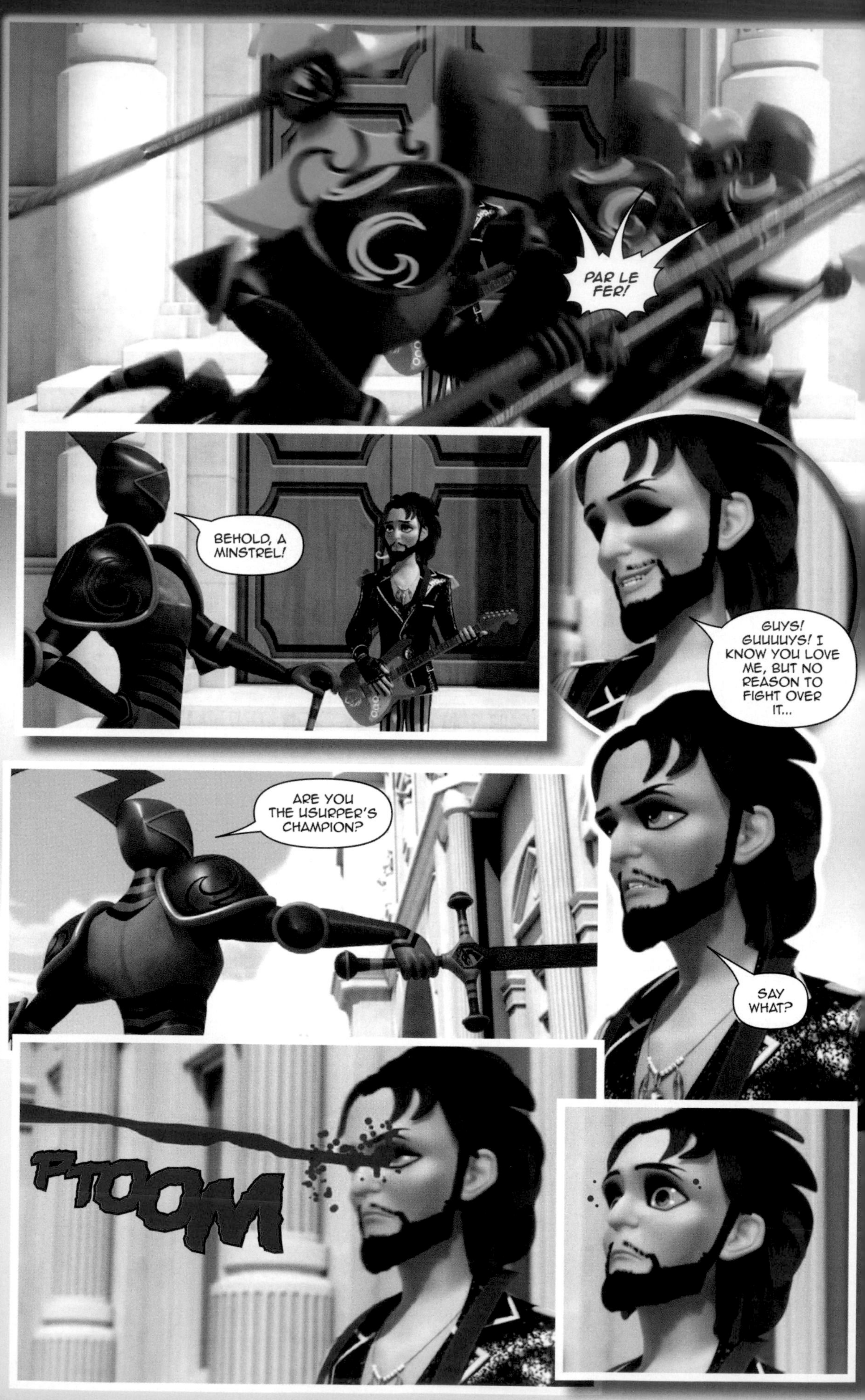
PAR LE FER!
BEHOLD, A MINSTREL!
GUYS! GUUUUYS! I KNOW YOU LOVE ME, BUT NO REASON TO FIGHT OVER IT...
ARE YOU THE USURPER'S CHAMPION?
SAY WHAT?
PTOOM

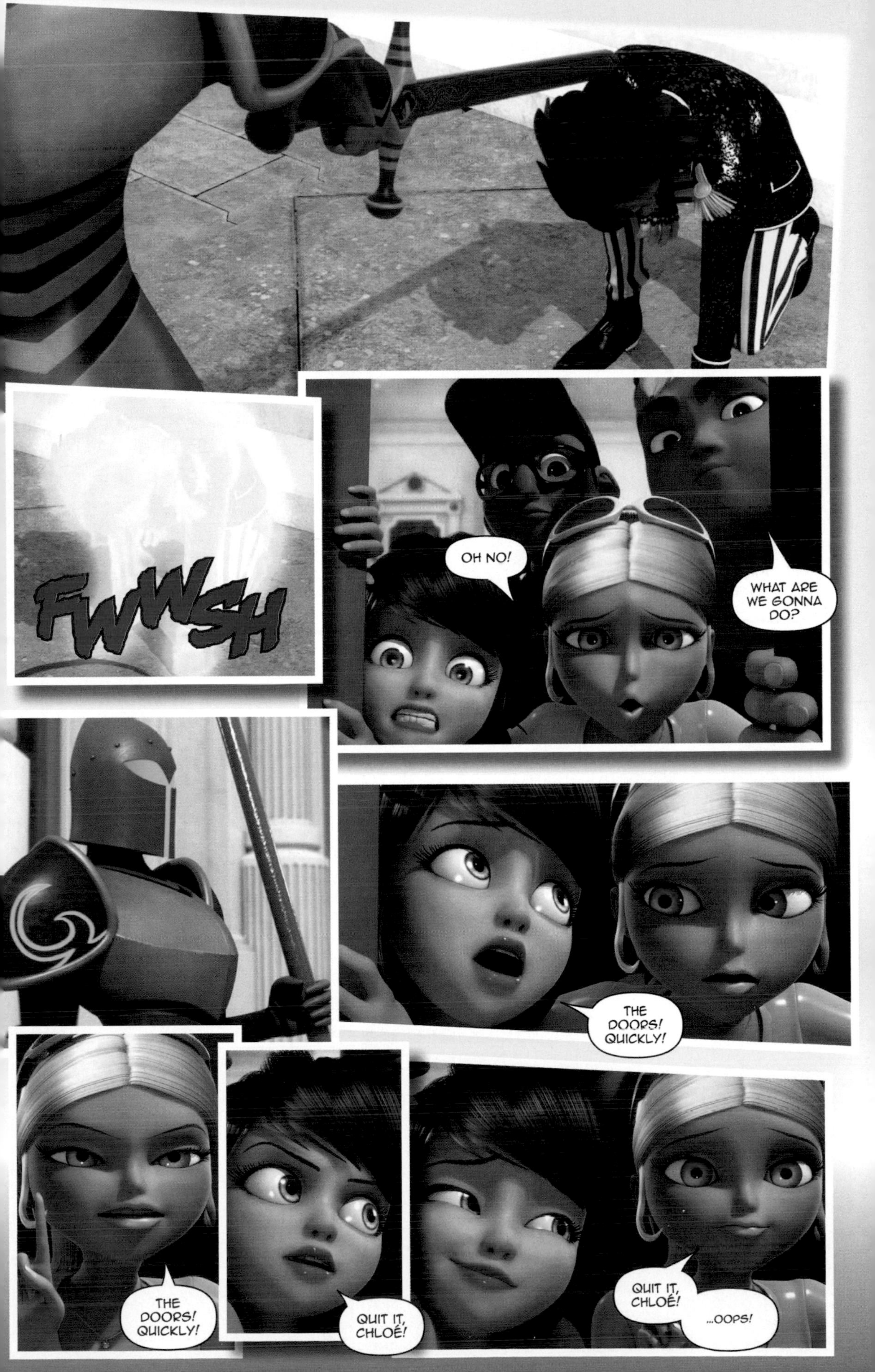
FWWSH
OH NO!
WHAT ARE WE GONNA DO?
THE DOORS! QUICKLY!
THE DOORS! QUICKLY!
QUIT IT, CHLOÉ!
QUIT IT, CHLOÉ!
...OOPS!

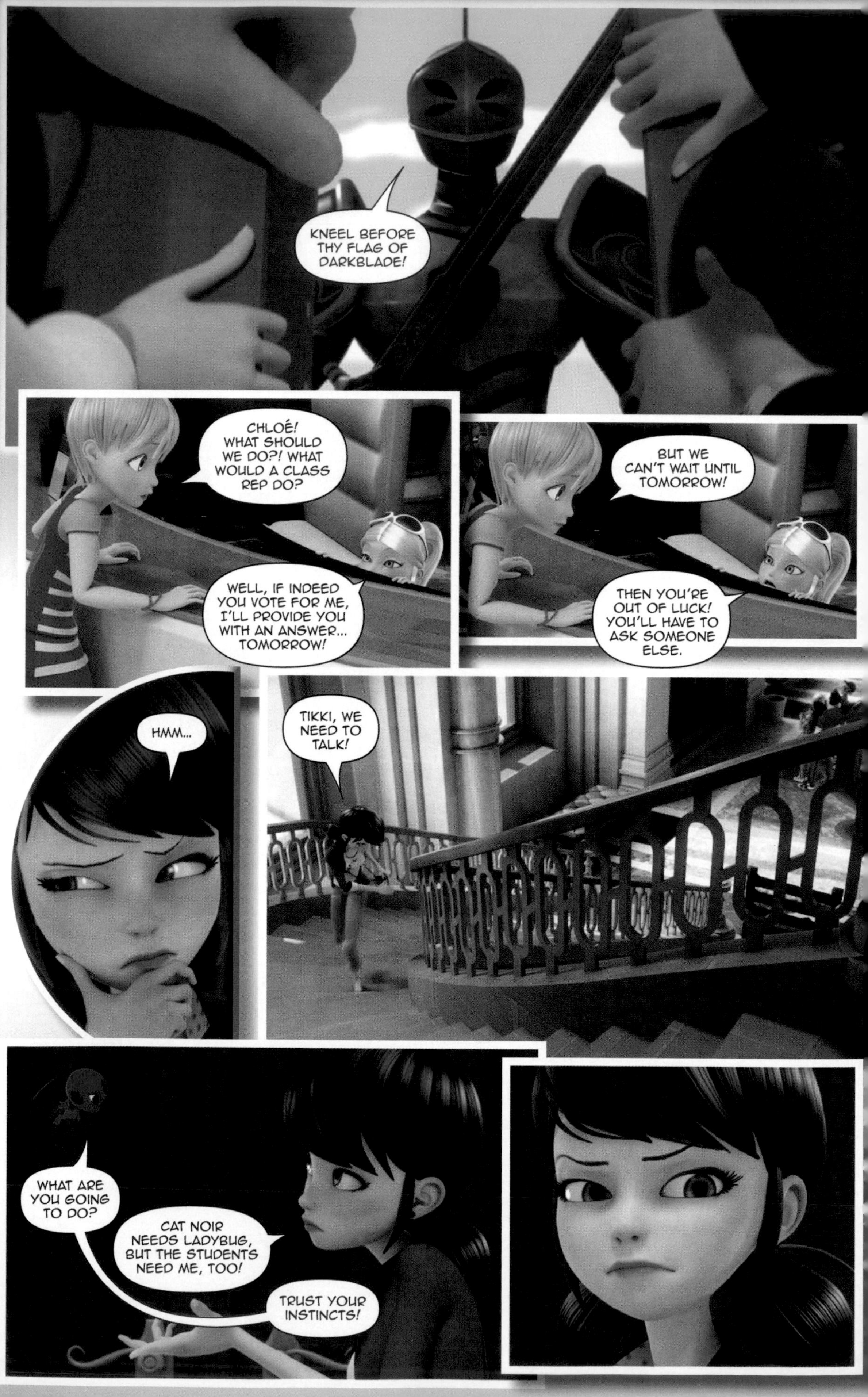

KNEEL BEFORE THY FLAG OF DARKBLADE!
CHLOÉ! WHAT SHOULD WE DO?! WHAT WOULD A CLASS REP DO?
WELL, IF INDEED YOU VOTE FOR ME, I'LL PROVIDE YOU WITH AN ANSWER... TOMORROW!
BUT WE CAN'T WAIT UNTIL TOMORROW!
THEN YOU'RE OUT OF LUCK! YOU'LL HAVE TO ASK SOMEONE ELSE.
HMM...
TIKKI, WE NEED TO TALK!
WHAT ARE YOU GOING TO DO?
CAT NOIR NEEDS LADYBUG, BUT THE STUDENTS NEED ME, TOO!
TRUST YOUR INSTINCTS!

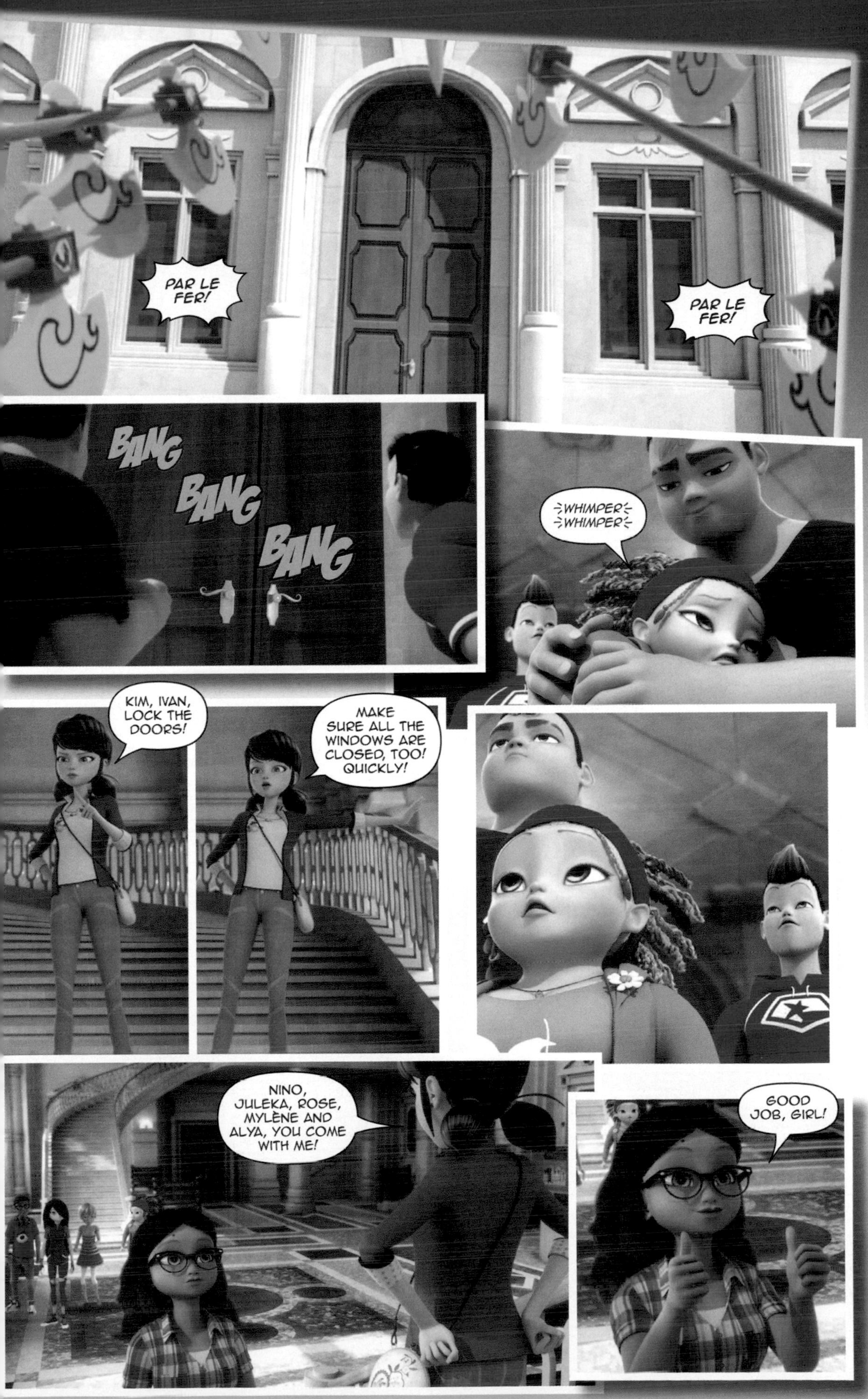
PAR LE FER!
PAR LE FER!
BANG BANG BANG
WHIMPER WHIMPER
KIM, IVAN, LOCK THE DOORS!
MAKE SURE ALL THE WINDOWS ARE CLOSED, TOO! QUICKLY!
NINO, JULEKA, ROSE, MYLÈNE AND ALYA, YOU COME WITH ME!
GOOD JOB, GIRL!

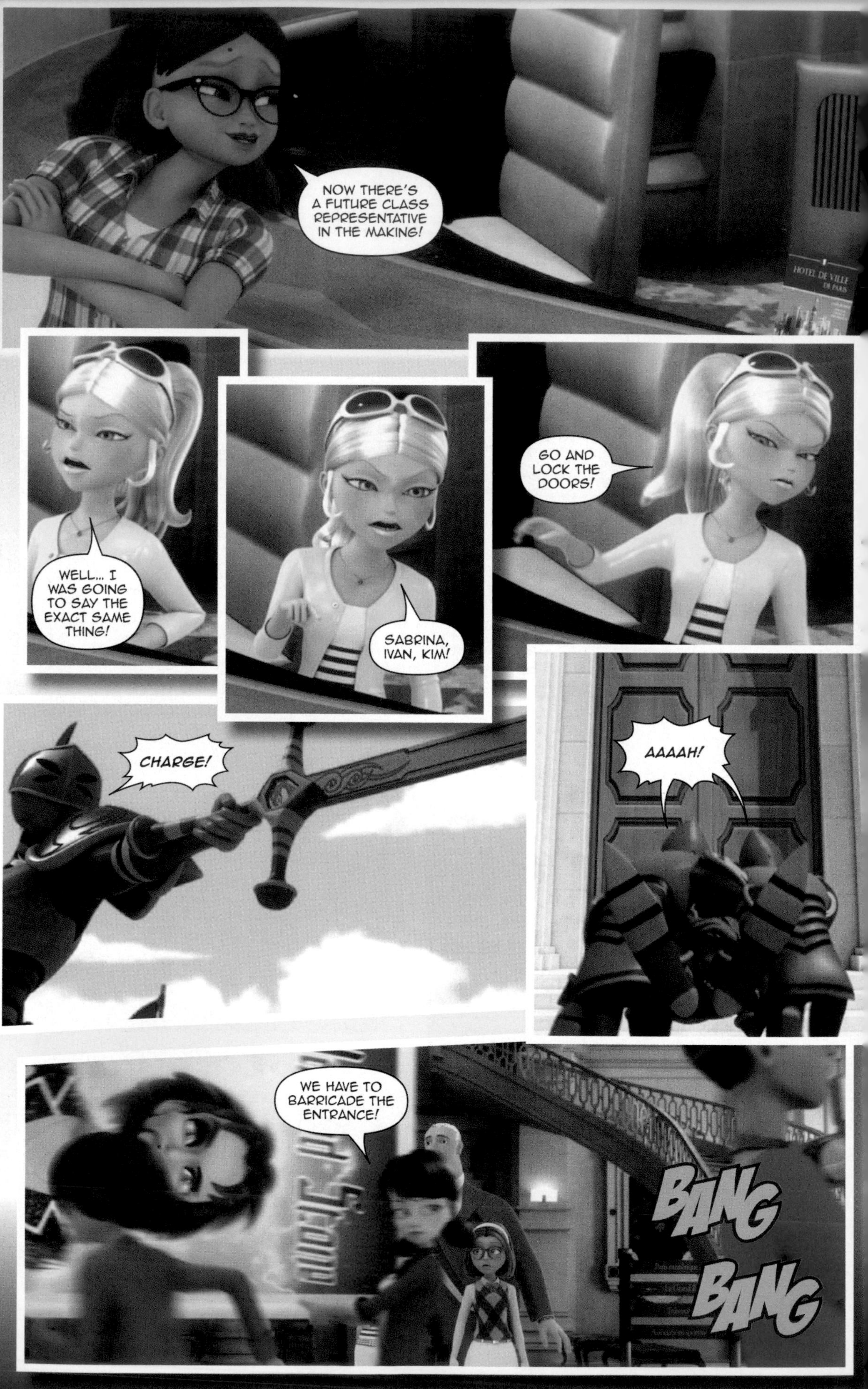
NOW THERE'S A FUTURE CLASS REPRESENTATIVE IN THE MAKING!
HOTEL DE VILLE DE PARIS
WELL... I WAS GOING TO SAY THE EXACT SAME THING!
SABRINA, IVAN, KIM!
GO AND LOCK THE DOORS!
CHARGE!
AAAAH!
WE HAVE TO BARRICADE THE ENTRANCE!
BANG
BANG

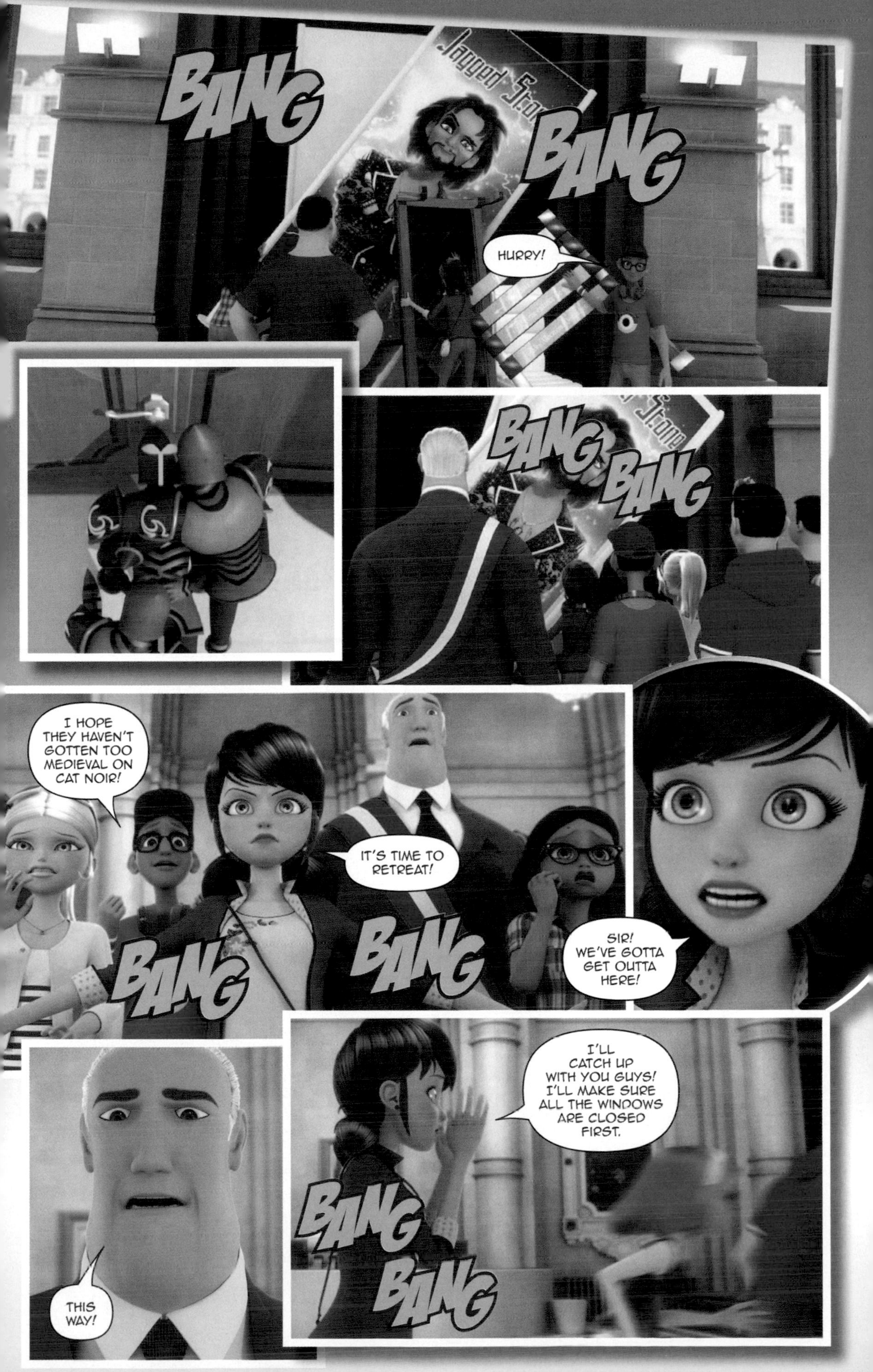
BANG
BANG
HURRY!
BANG
BANG
I HOPE THEY HAVEN'T GOTTEN TOO MEDIEVAL ON CAT NOIR!
IT'S TIME TO RETREAT!
BANG
BANG
SIR! WE'VE GOTTA GET OUTTA HERE!
THIS WAY!
I'LL CATCH UP WITH YOU GUYS! I'LL MAKE SURE ALL THE WINDOWS ARE CLOSED FIRST.
BANG
BANG

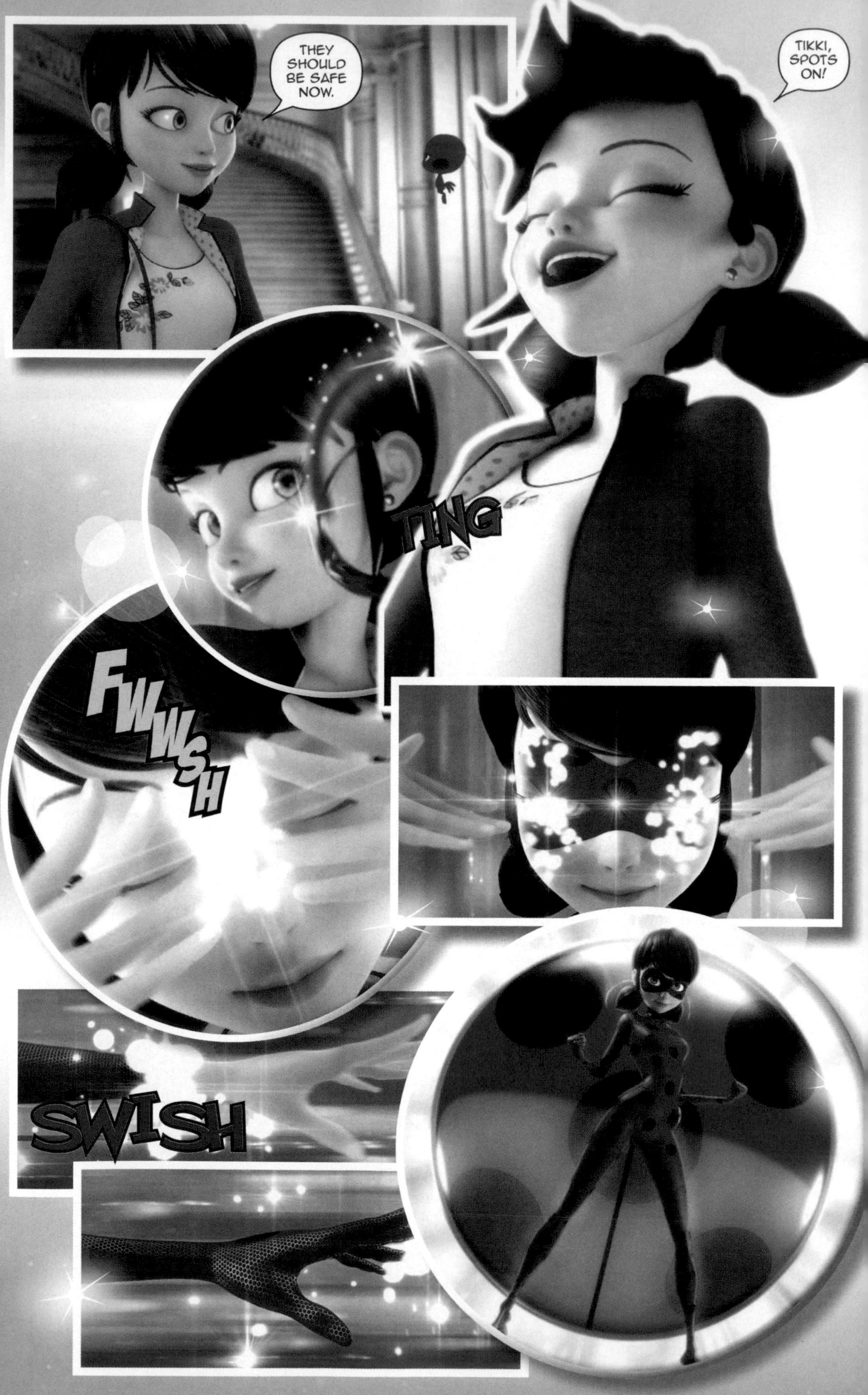
THEY SHOULD BE SAFE NOW.
TIKKI, SPOTS ON!
TING
FWWSH
SWISH

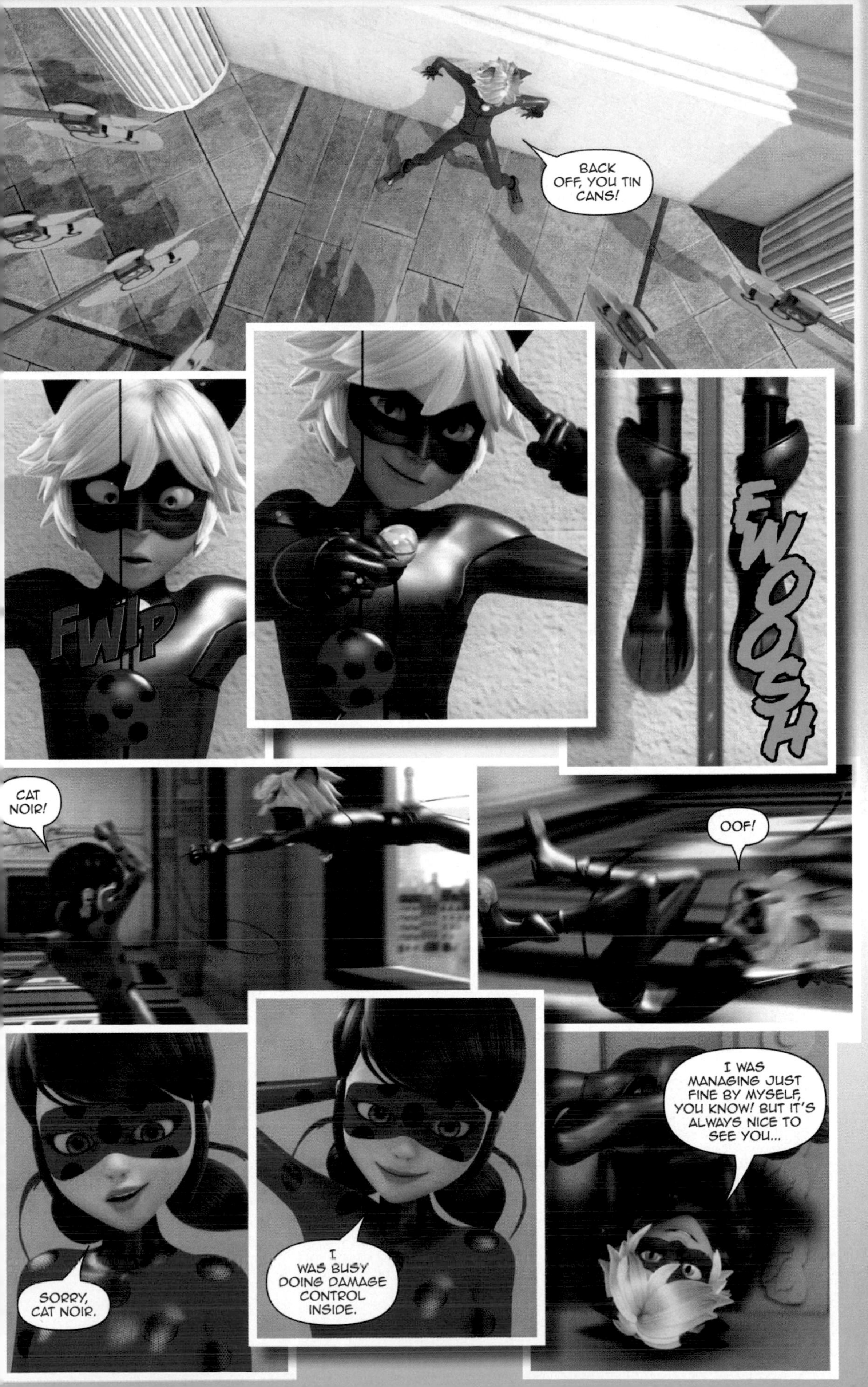
BACK OFF, YOU TIN CANS!
FWIP
FWOOSH
CAT NOIR!
OOF!
SORRY, CAT NOIR.
I WAS BUSY DOING DAMAGE CONTROL INSIDE.
I WAS MANAGING JUST FINE BY MYSELF, YOU KNOW! BUT IT'S ALWAYS NICE TO SEE YOU...

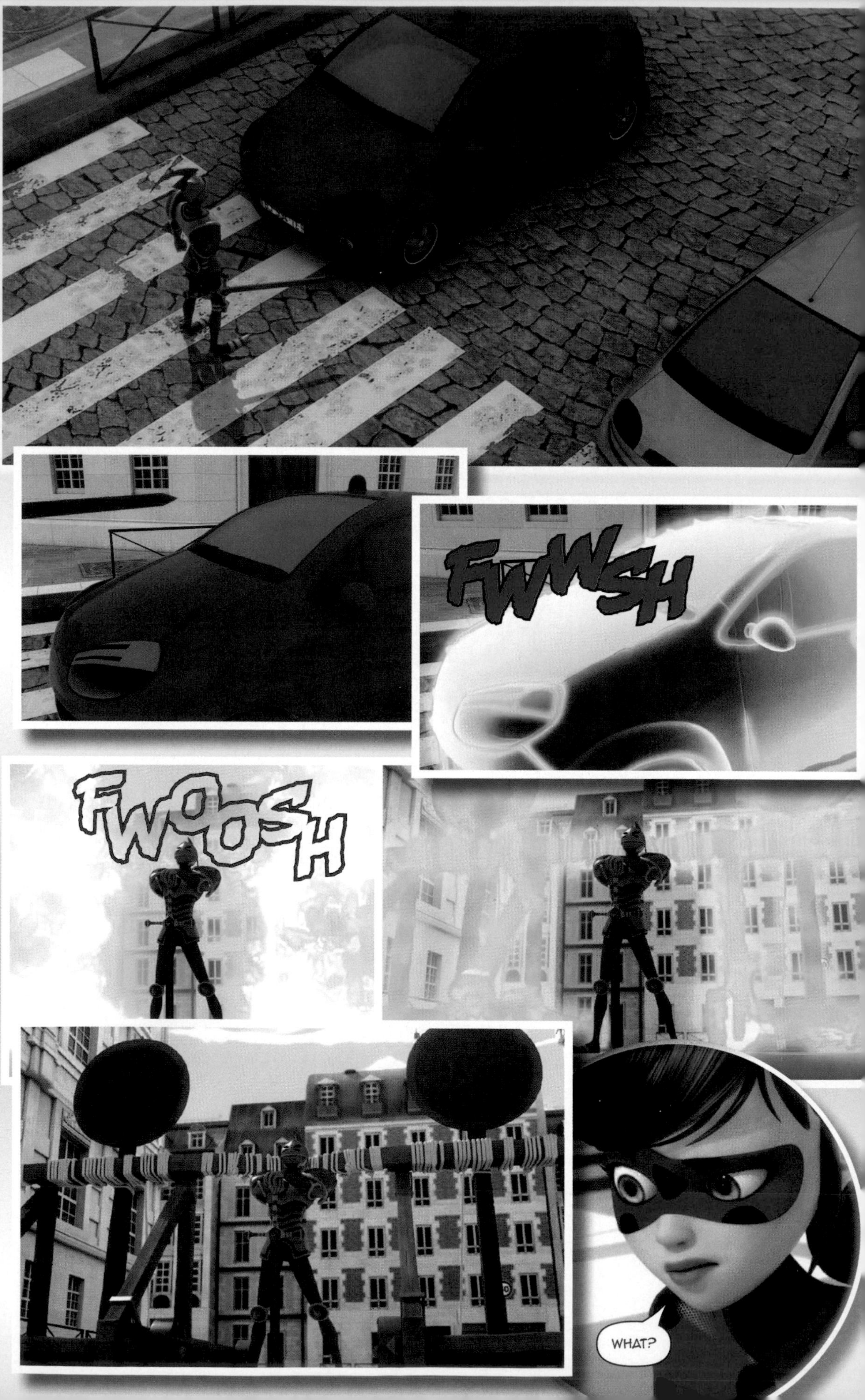
FWWSH
FWOOSH
WHAT?

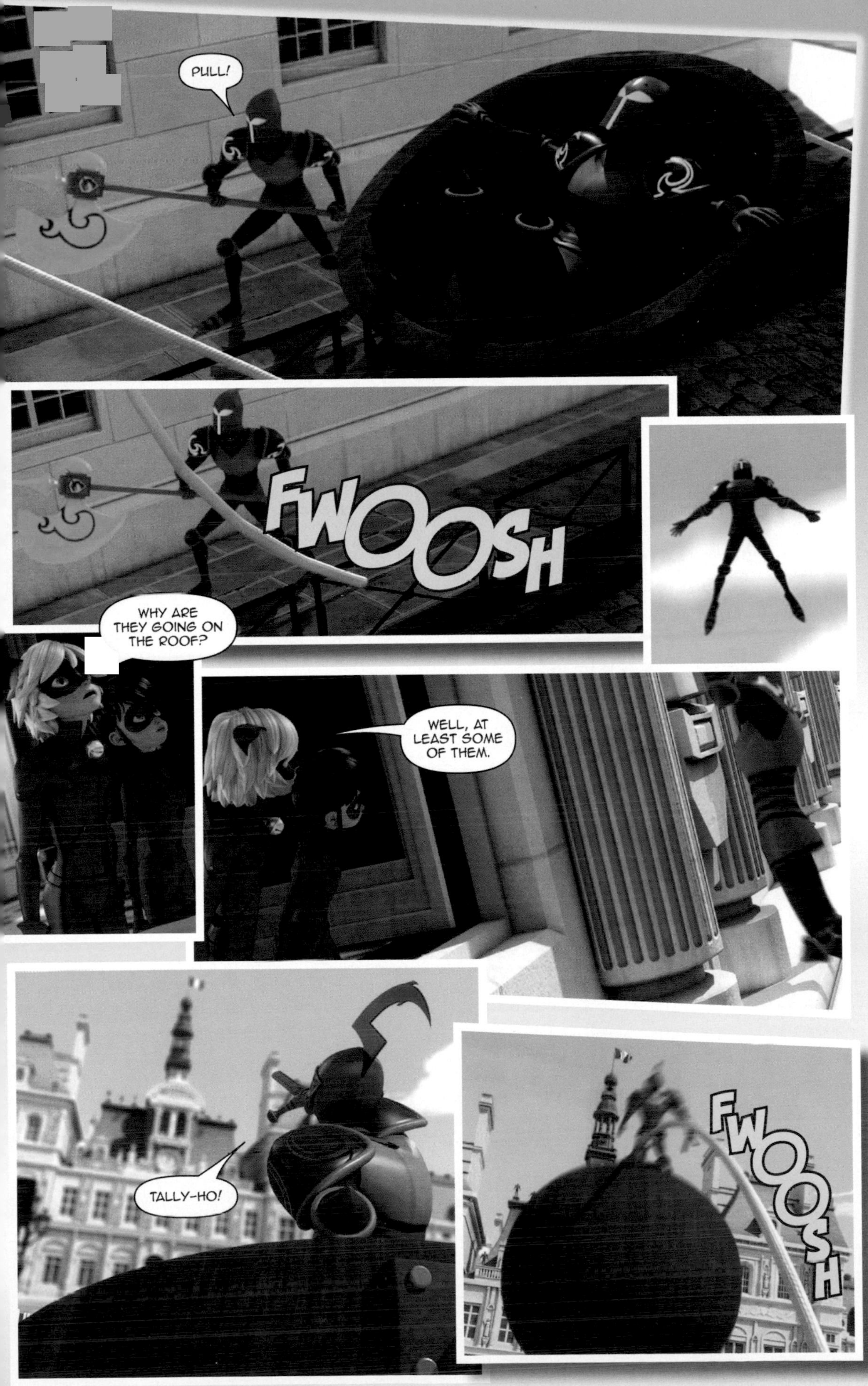
PULL!
FWOOSH
WHY ARE THEY GOING ON THE ROOF?
WELL, AT LEAST SOME OF THEM.
TALLY-HO!
FWOOSH

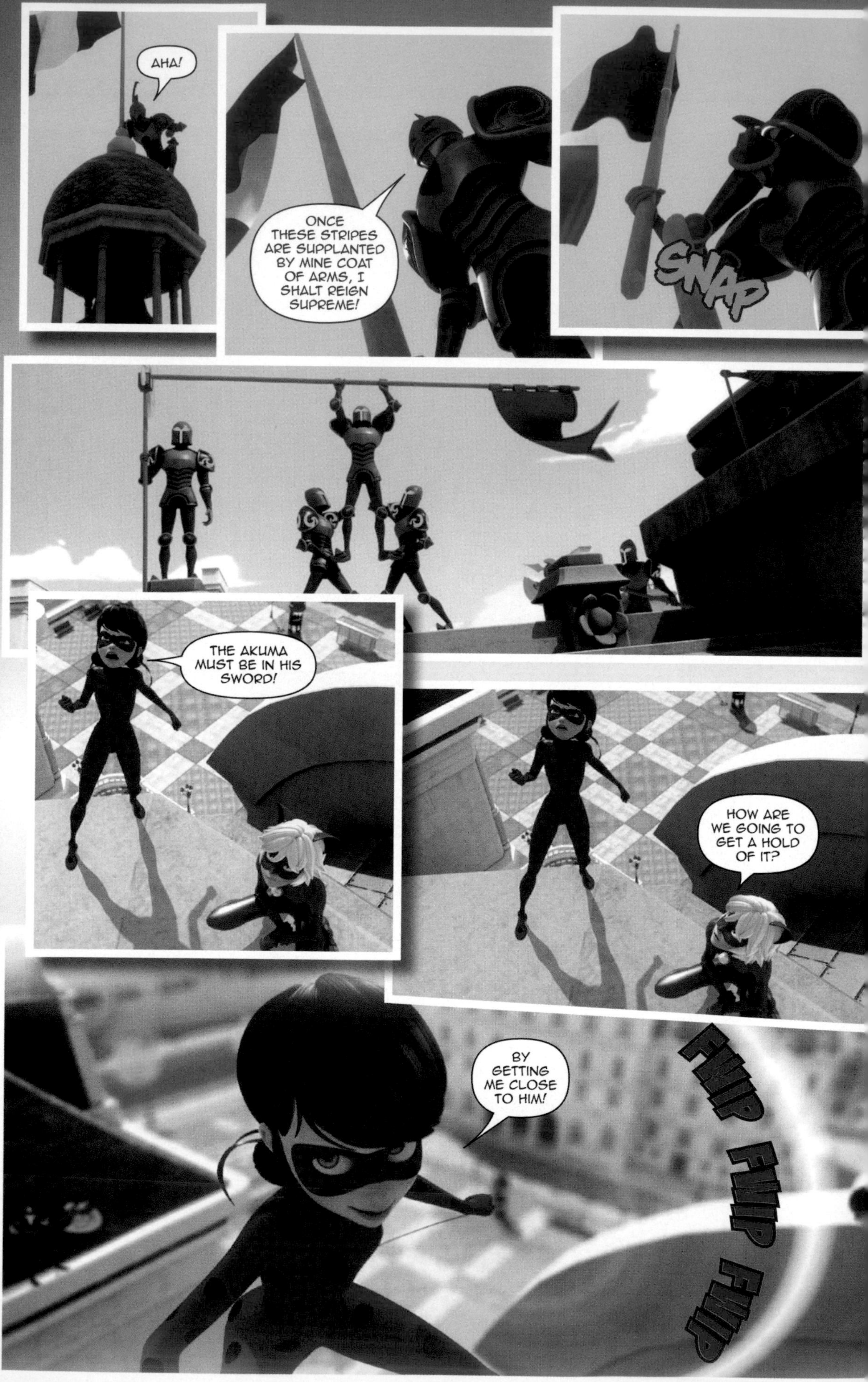
AHA!
ONCE THESE STRIPES ARE SUPPLANTED BY MINE COAT OF ARMS, I SHALT REIGN SUPREME!
SNAP
THE AKUMA MUST BE IN HIS SWORD!
HOW ARE WE GOING TO GET A HOLD OF IT?
BY GETTING ME CLOSE TO HIM!
FWIP FWIP FWIP

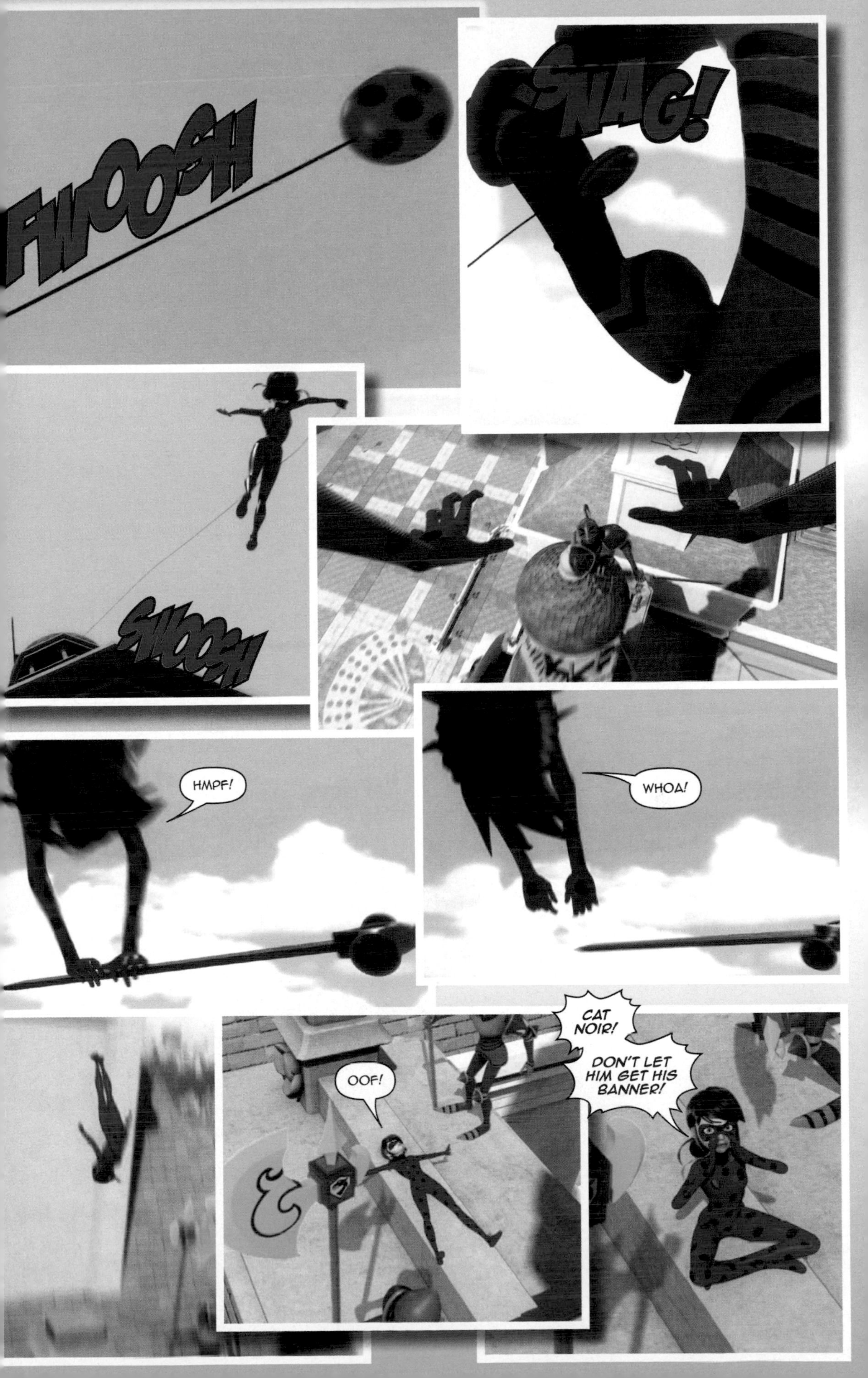
FWOOSH
SNAG!
SWOOSH
HMPF!
WHOA!
OOF!
CAT NOIR!
DON'T LET HIM GET HIS BANNER!

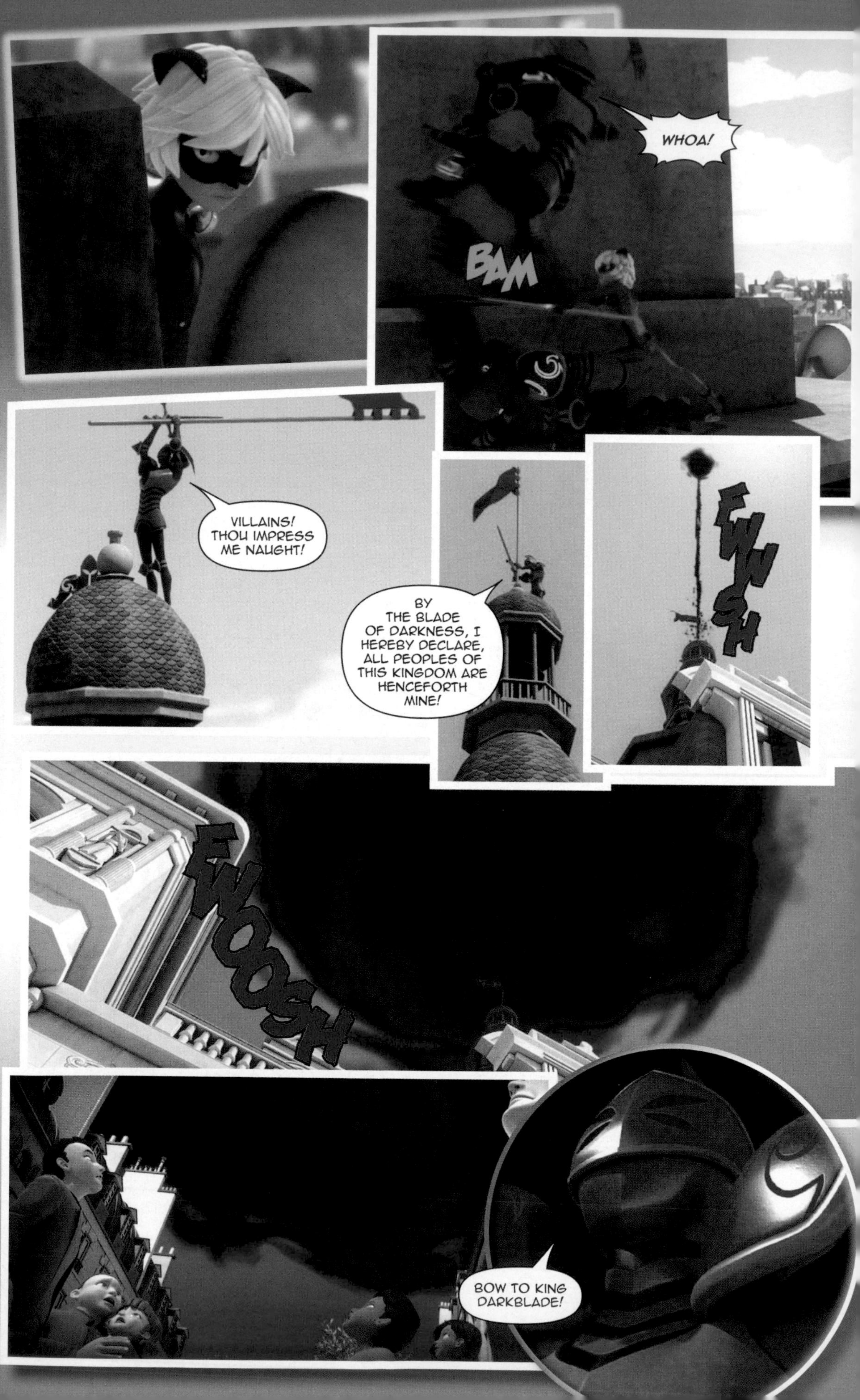
WHOA!
BAM
VILLAINS! THOU IMPRESS ME NAUGHT!
BY THE BLADE OF DARKNESS, I HEREBY DECLARE, ALL PEOPLES OF THIS KINGDOM ARE HENCEFORTH MINE!
FWWSH
FWOOSH
BOW TO KING DARKBLADE!

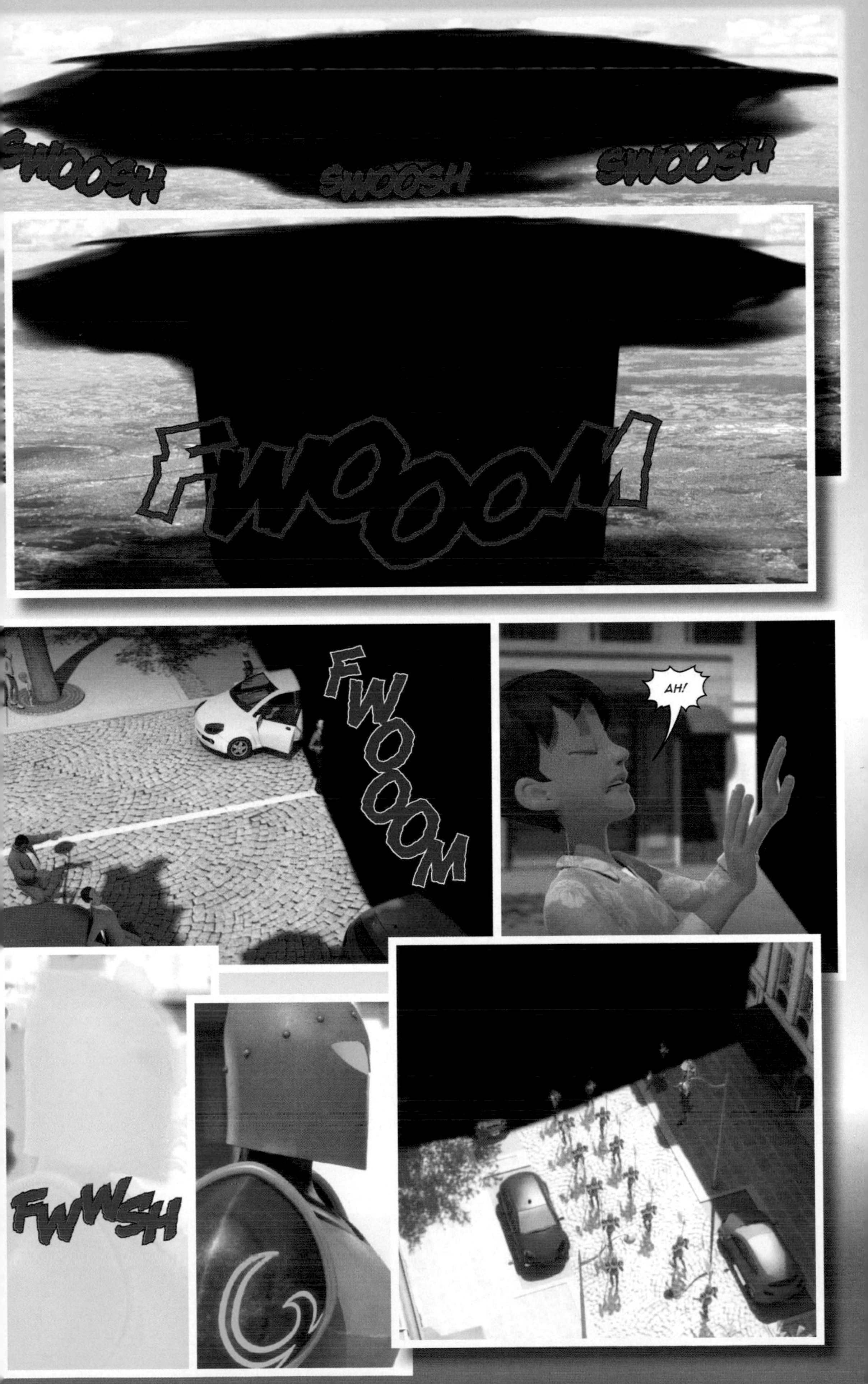
SWOOSH
SWOOSH
SWOOSH
FWOOOM
FWOOOOM
AH!
FWWSH

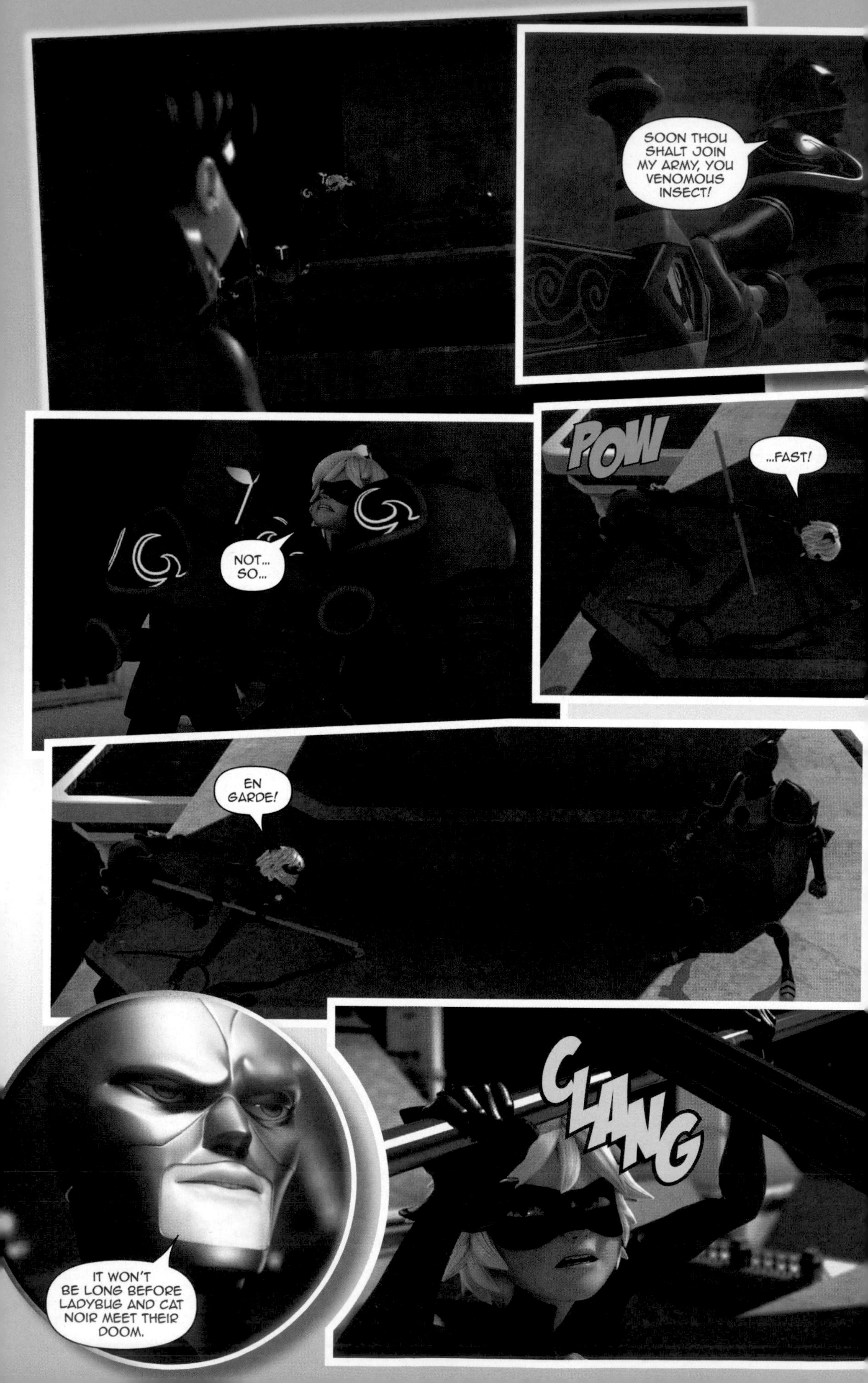

SOON THOU SHALT JOIN MY ARMY, YOU VENOMOUS INSECT!
NOT... SO...
POW
...FAST!
EN GARDE!
IT WON'T BE LONG BEFORE LADYBUG AND CAT NOIR MEET THEIR DOOM.
CLANG

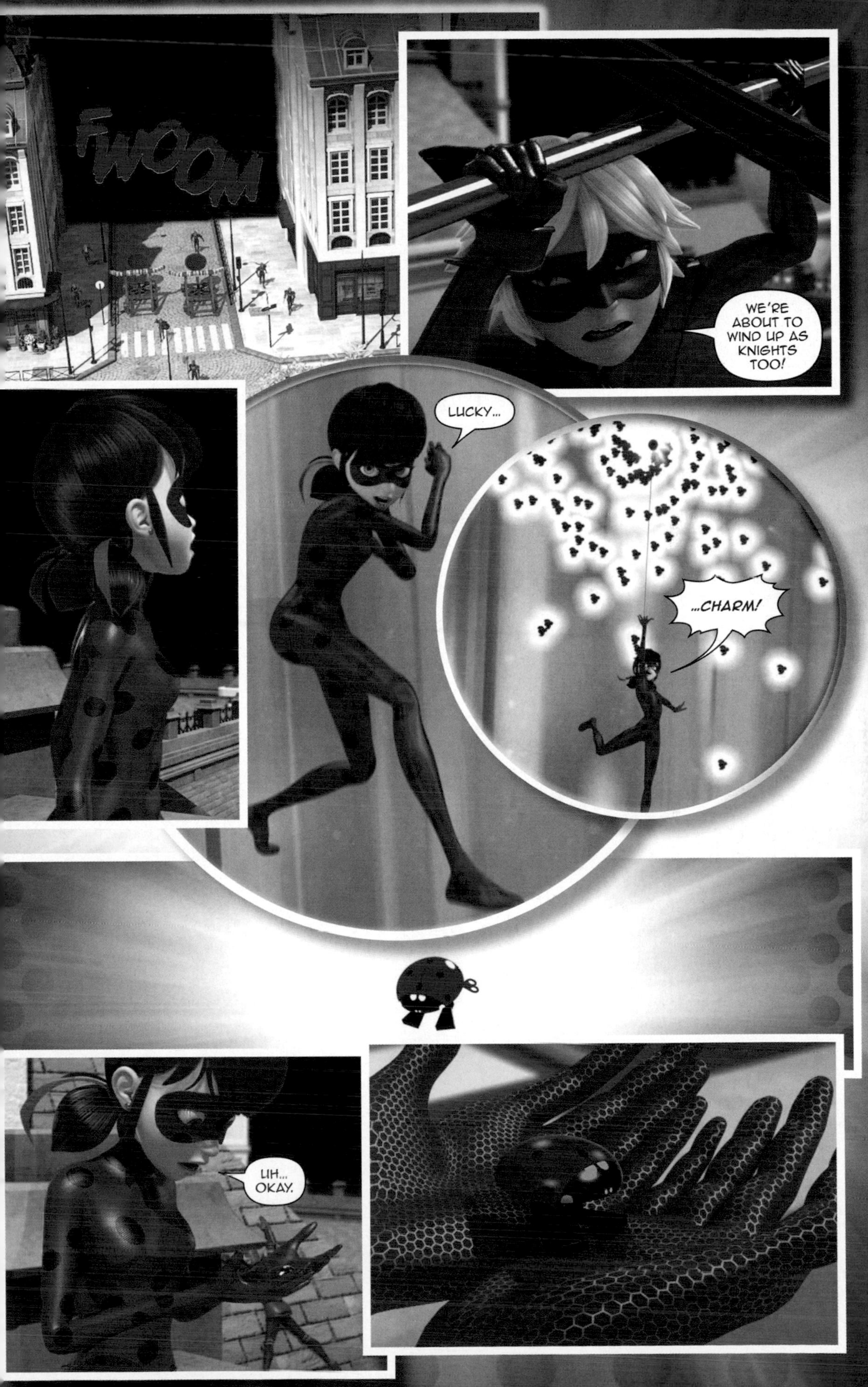
FWOOM
WE'RE ABOUT TO WIND UP AS KNIGHTS TOO!
LUCKY...
...CHARM!
UH... OKAY.

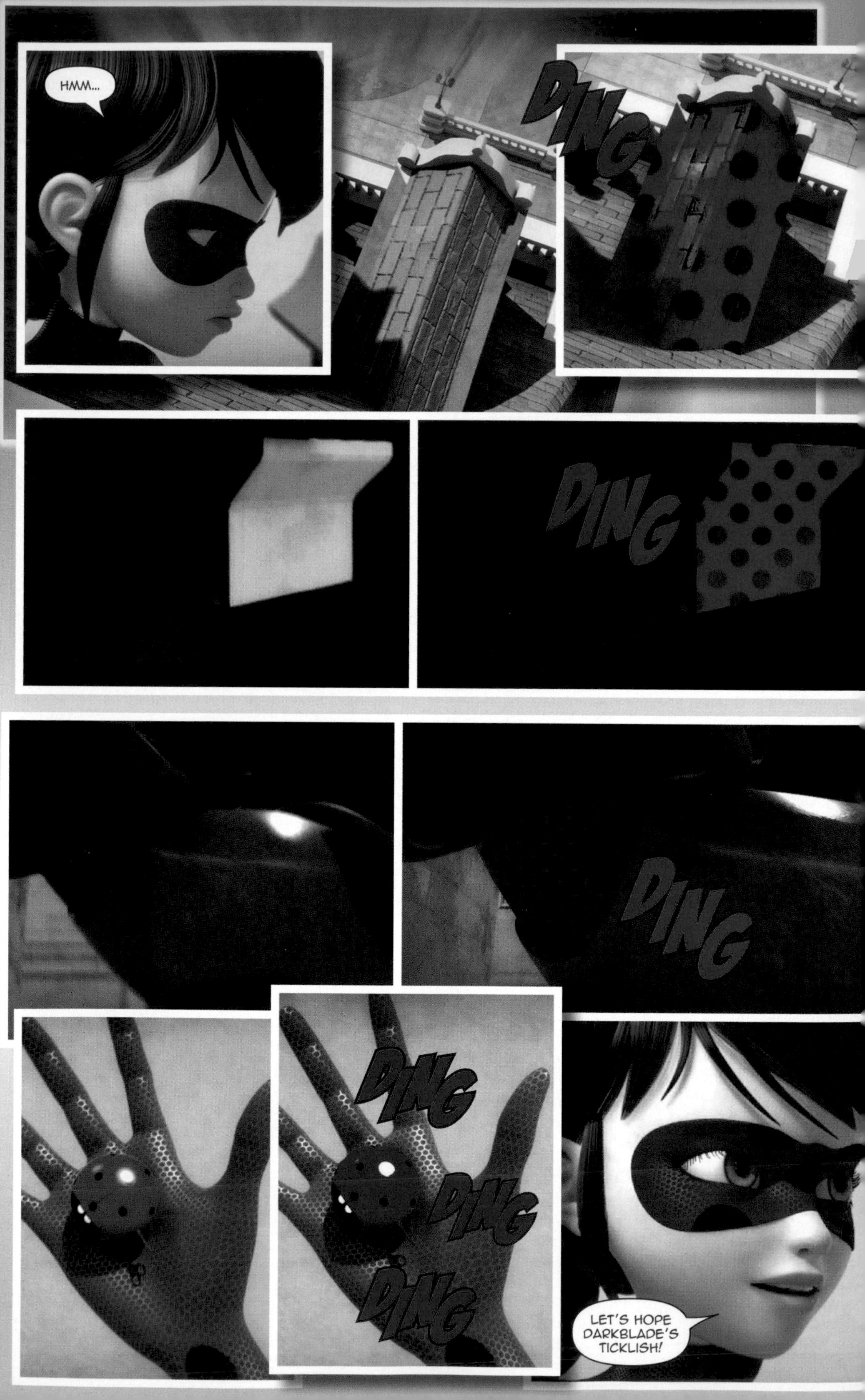
HMM...
DING
DING
DING
DING
DING
DING
LET'S HOPE DARKBLADE'S TICKLISH!

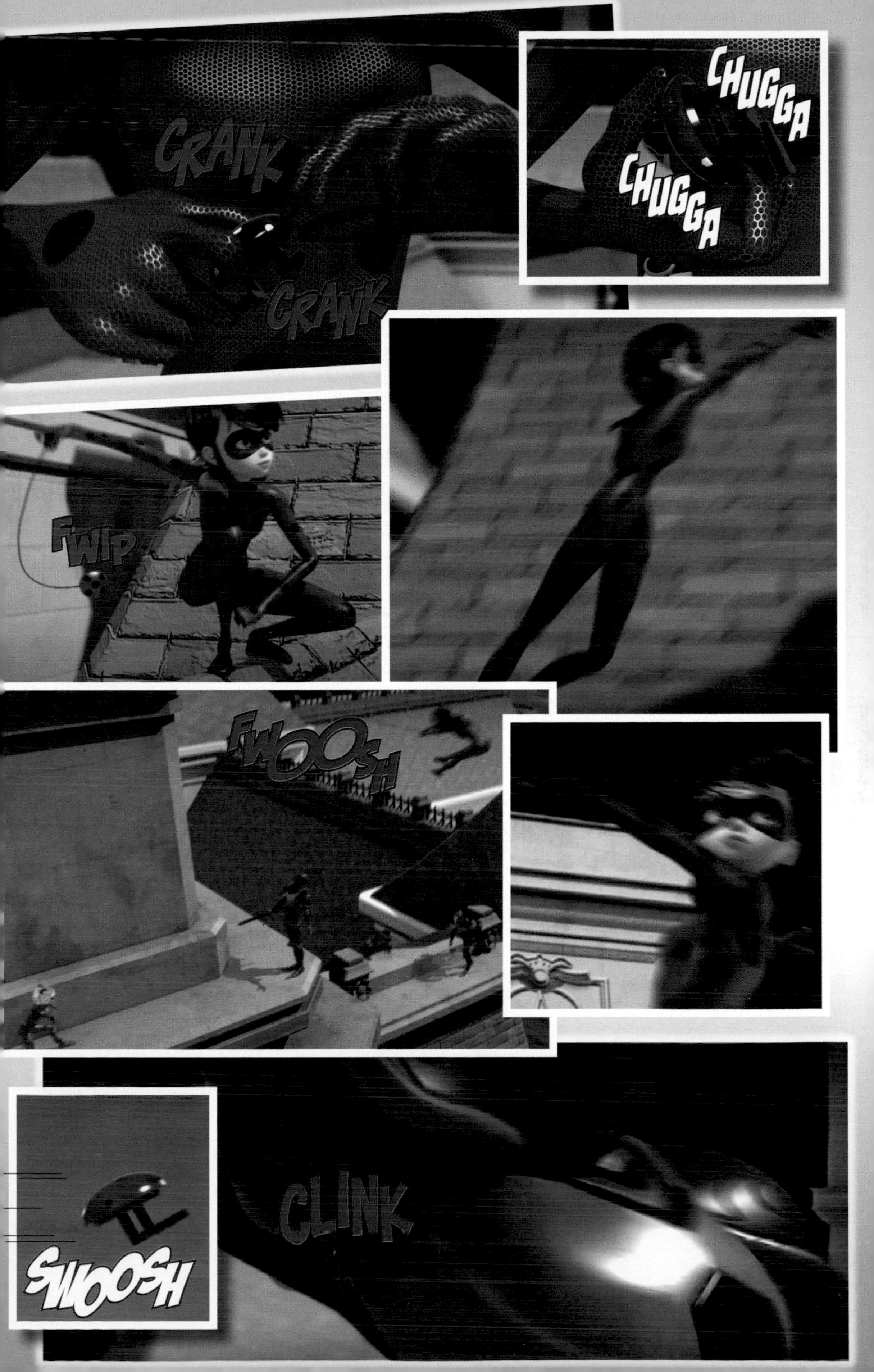
CRANK
CRANK
CHUGGA
CHUGGA
FWIP
FWOOSH
SWOOSH
CLINK

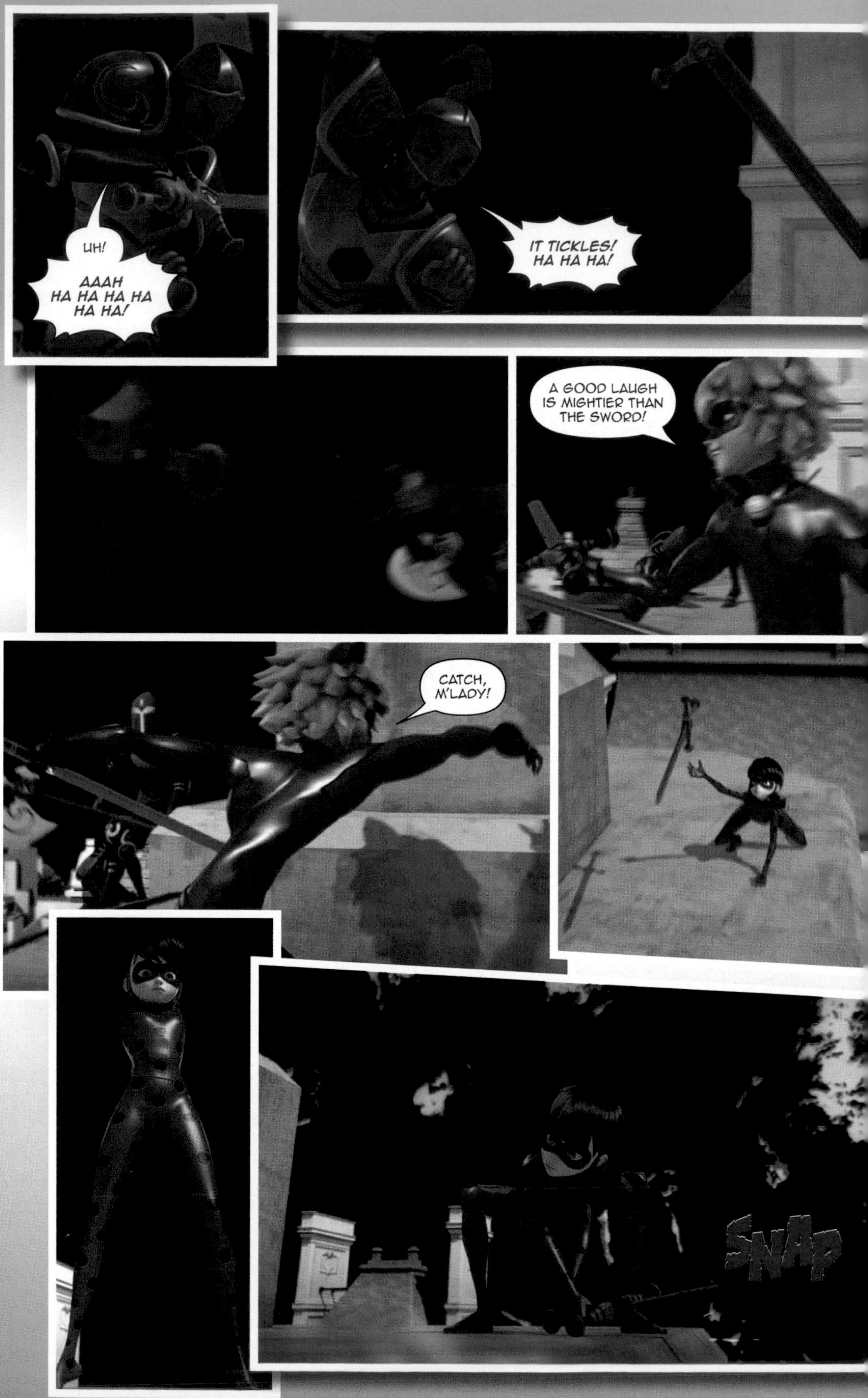
UH!
AAAH HA HA HA HA HA HA!
IT TICKLES! HA HA HA!
A GOOD LAUGH IS MIGHTIER THAN THE SWORD!
CATCH, M'LADY!
SNAP

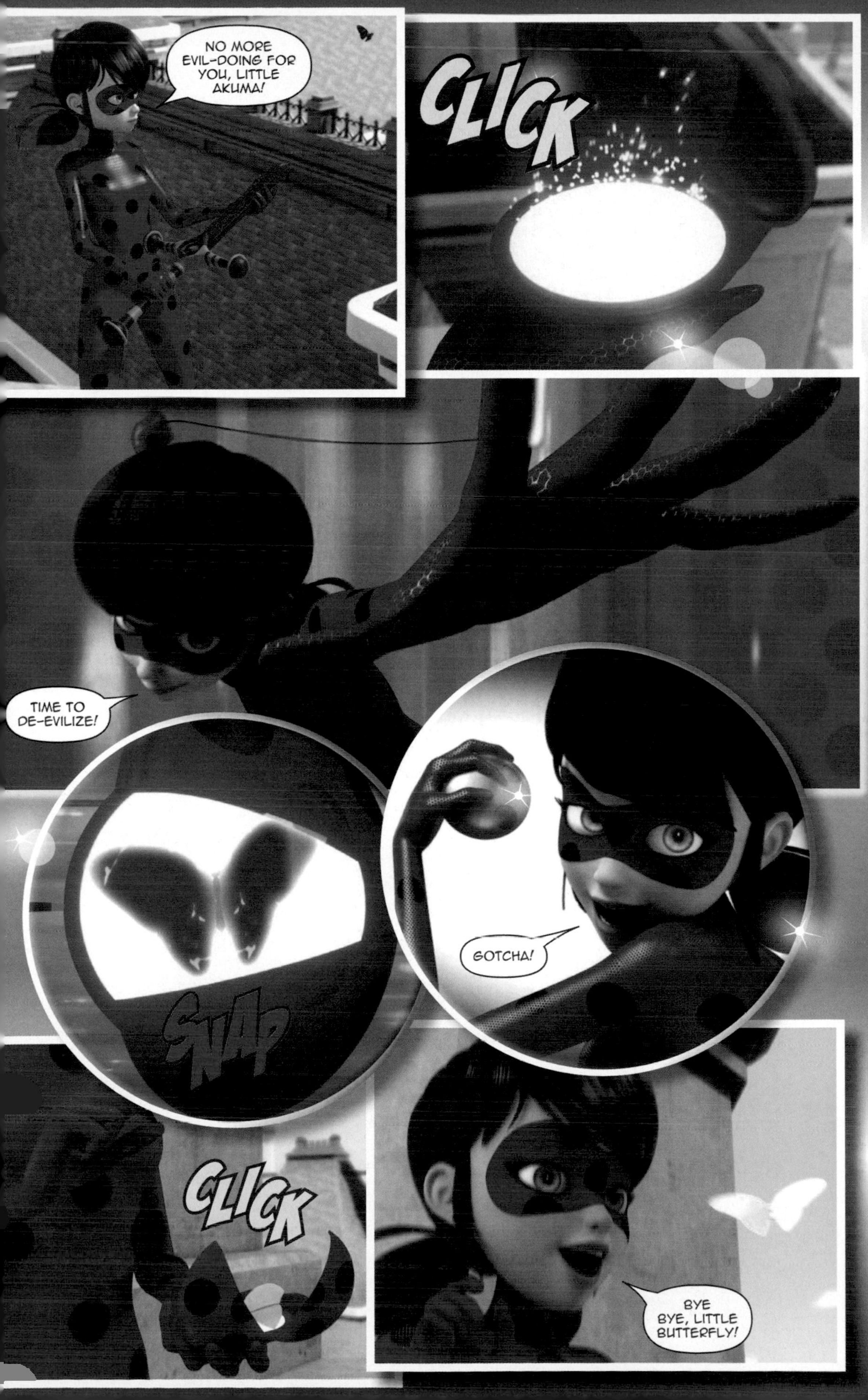
NO MORE EVIL-DOING FOR YOU, LITTLE AKUMA!
CLICK
TIME TO DE-EVILIZE!
SNAP
GOTCHA!
CLICK
BYE BYE, LITTLE BUTTERFLY!

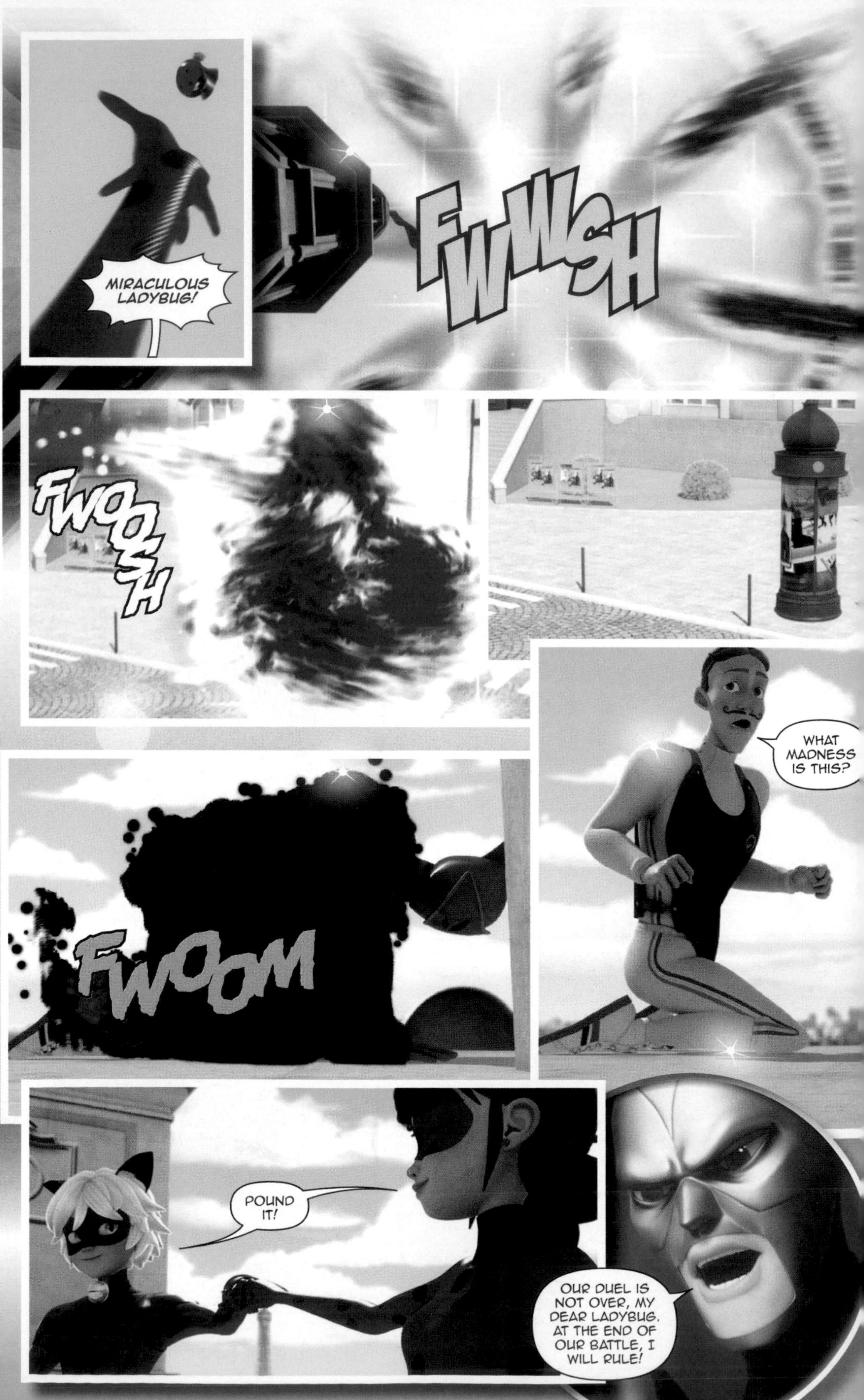
MIRACULOUS LADYBUG!
FWWSH
FWOOSH
WHAT MADNESS IS THIS?
FWOOM
POUND IT!
OUR DUEL IS NOT OVER, MY DEAR LADYBUG. AT THE END OF OUR BATTLE, I WILL RULE!

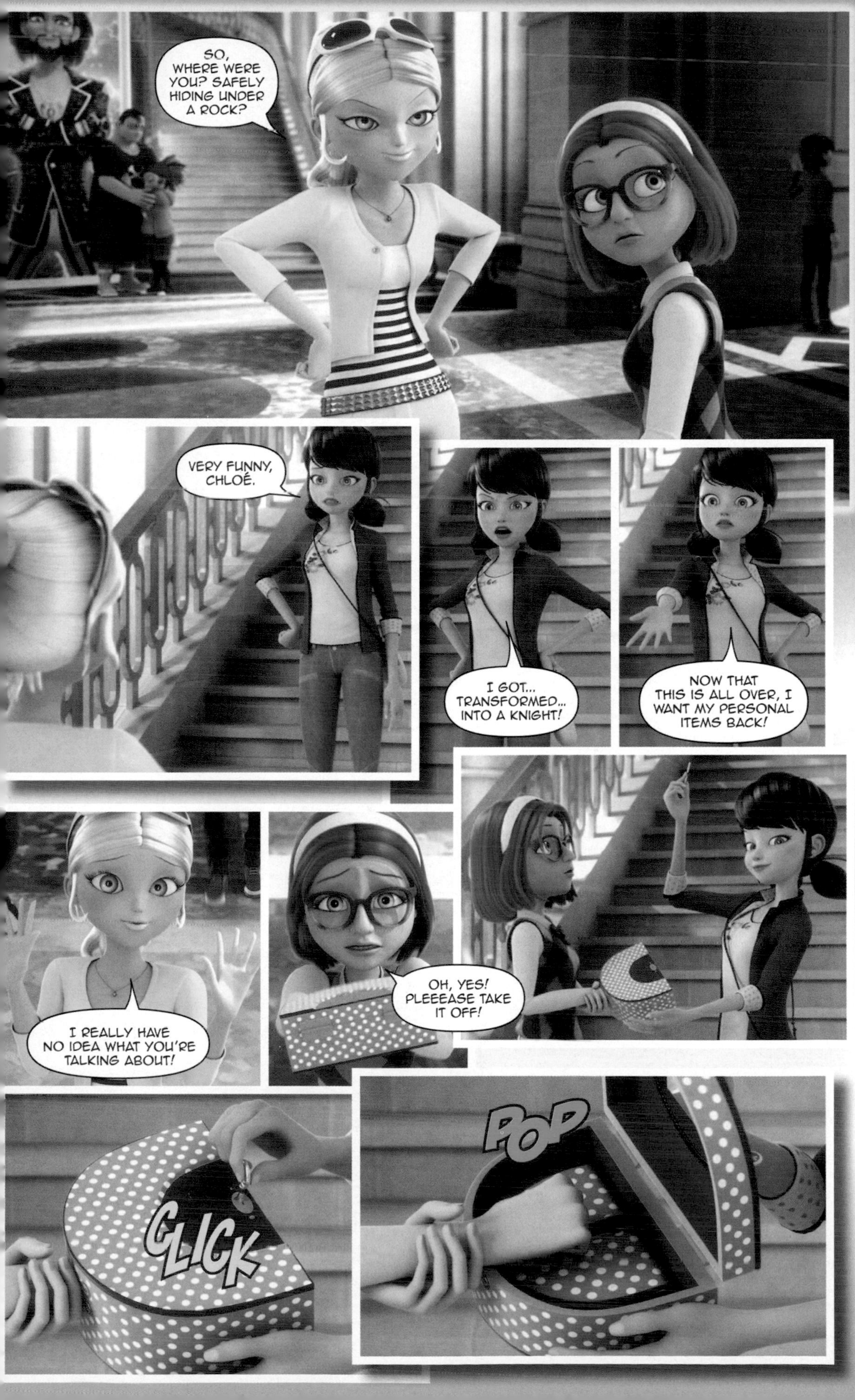
SO, WHERE WERE YOU? SAFELY HIDING UNDER A ROCK?
VERY FUNNY, CHLOÉ.
I GOT... TRANSFORMED... INTO A KNIGHT!
NOW THAT THIS IS ALL OVER, I WANT MY PERSONAL ITEMS BACK!
I REALLY HAVE NO IDEA WHAT YOU'RE TALKING ABOUT!
OH, YES! PLEEEASE TAKE IT OFF!
CLICK
POP

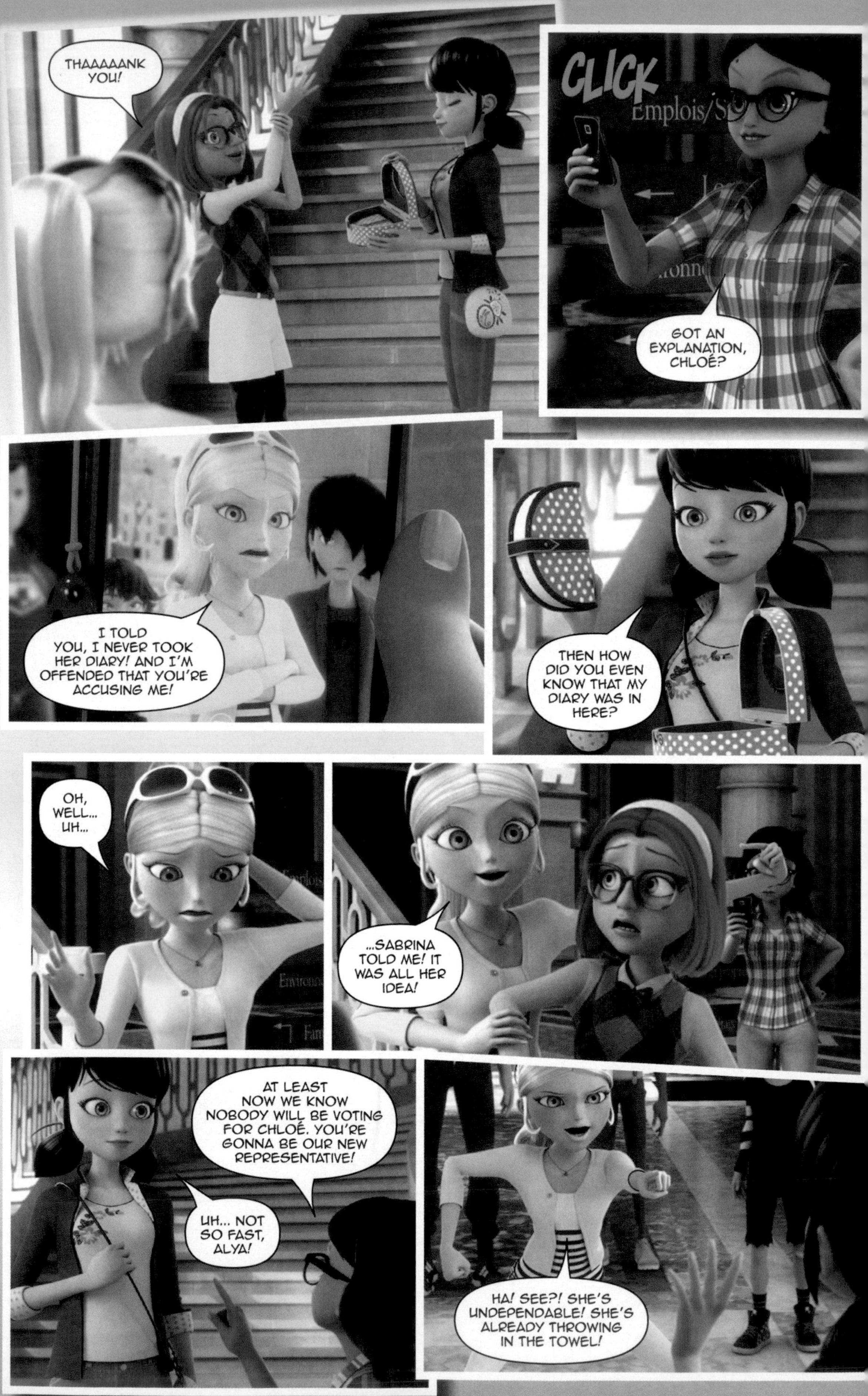
THAAAAANK YOU!
CLICK
Emplois/S
GOT AN EXPLANATION, CHLOÉ?
I TOLD YOU, I NEVER TOOK HER DIARY! AND I'M OFFENDED THAT YOU'RE ACCUSING ME!
THEN HOW DID YOU EVEN KNOW THAT MY DIARY WAS IN HERE?
OH, WELL... UH...
...SABRINA TOLD ME! IT WAS ALL HER IDEA!
AT LEAST NOW WE KNOW NOBODY WILL BE VOTING FOR CHLOÉ. YOU'RE GONNA BE OUR NEW REPRESENTATIVE!
UH... NOT SO FAST, ALYA!
HA! SEE?! SHE'S UNDEPENDABLE! SHE'S ALREADY THROWING IN THE TOWEL!

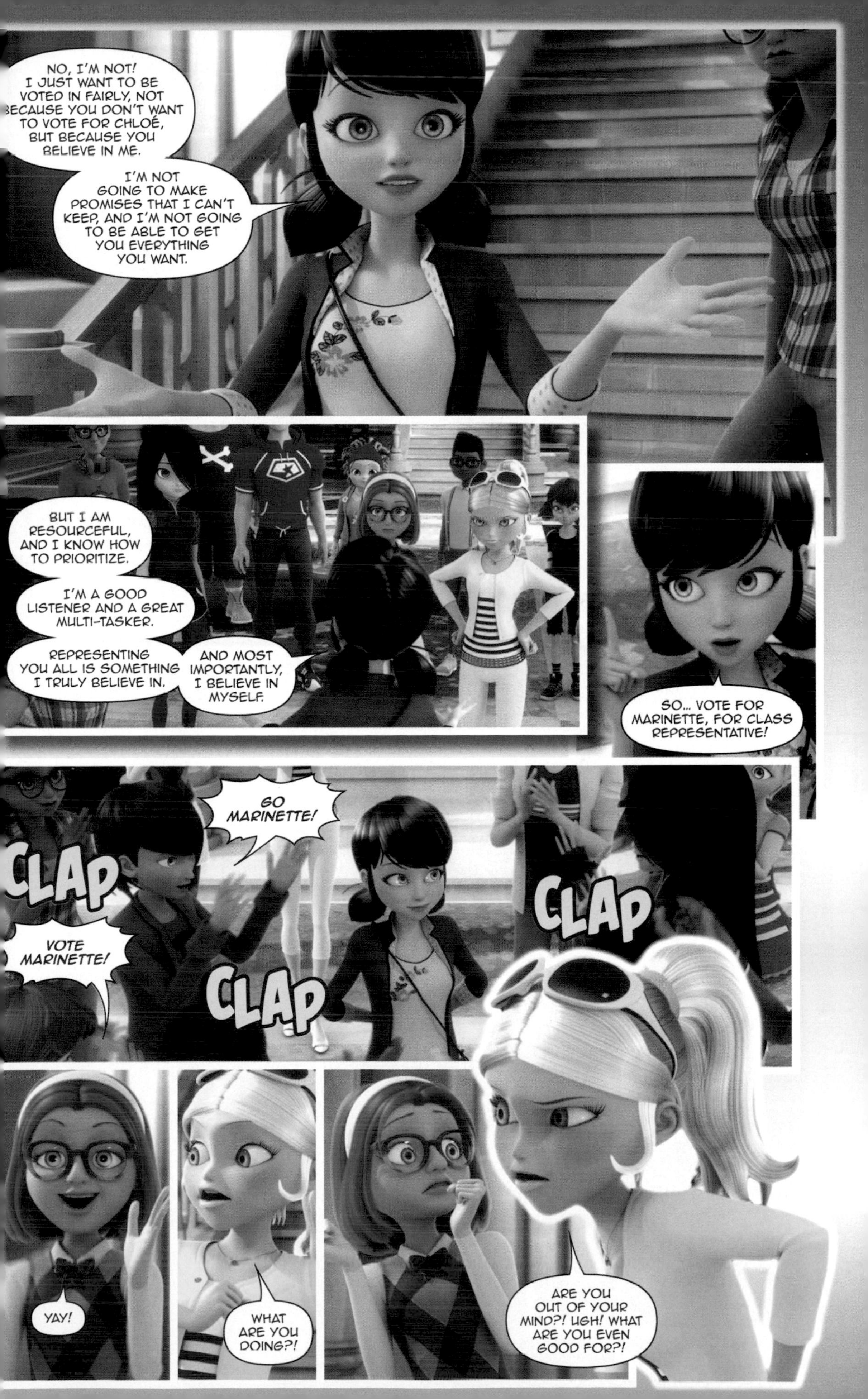

NO, I'M NOT! I JUST WANT TO BE VOTED IN FAIRLY, NOT BECAUSE YOU DON'T WANT TO VOTE FOR CHLOÉ, BUT BECAUSE YOU BELIEVE IN ME.
I'M NOT GOING TO MAKE PROMISES THAT I CAN'T KEEP, AND I'M NOT GOING TO BE ABLE TO GET YOU EVERYTHING YOU WANT.
BUT I AM RESOURCEFUL, AND I KNOW HOW TO PRIORITIZE.
I'M A GOOD LISTENER AND A GREAT MULTI-TASKER.
REPRESENTING YOU ALL IS SOMETHING I TRULY BELIEVE IN.
AND MOST IMPORTANTLY, I BELIEVE IN MYSELF.
SO... VOTE FOR MARINETTE, FOR CLASS REPRESENTATIVE!
CLAP
GO MARINETTE!
VOTE MARINETTE!
CLAP
CLAP
YAY!
WHAT ARE YOU DOING?!
ARE YOU OUT OF YOUR MIND?! UGH! WHAT ARE YOU EVEN GOOD FOR?!

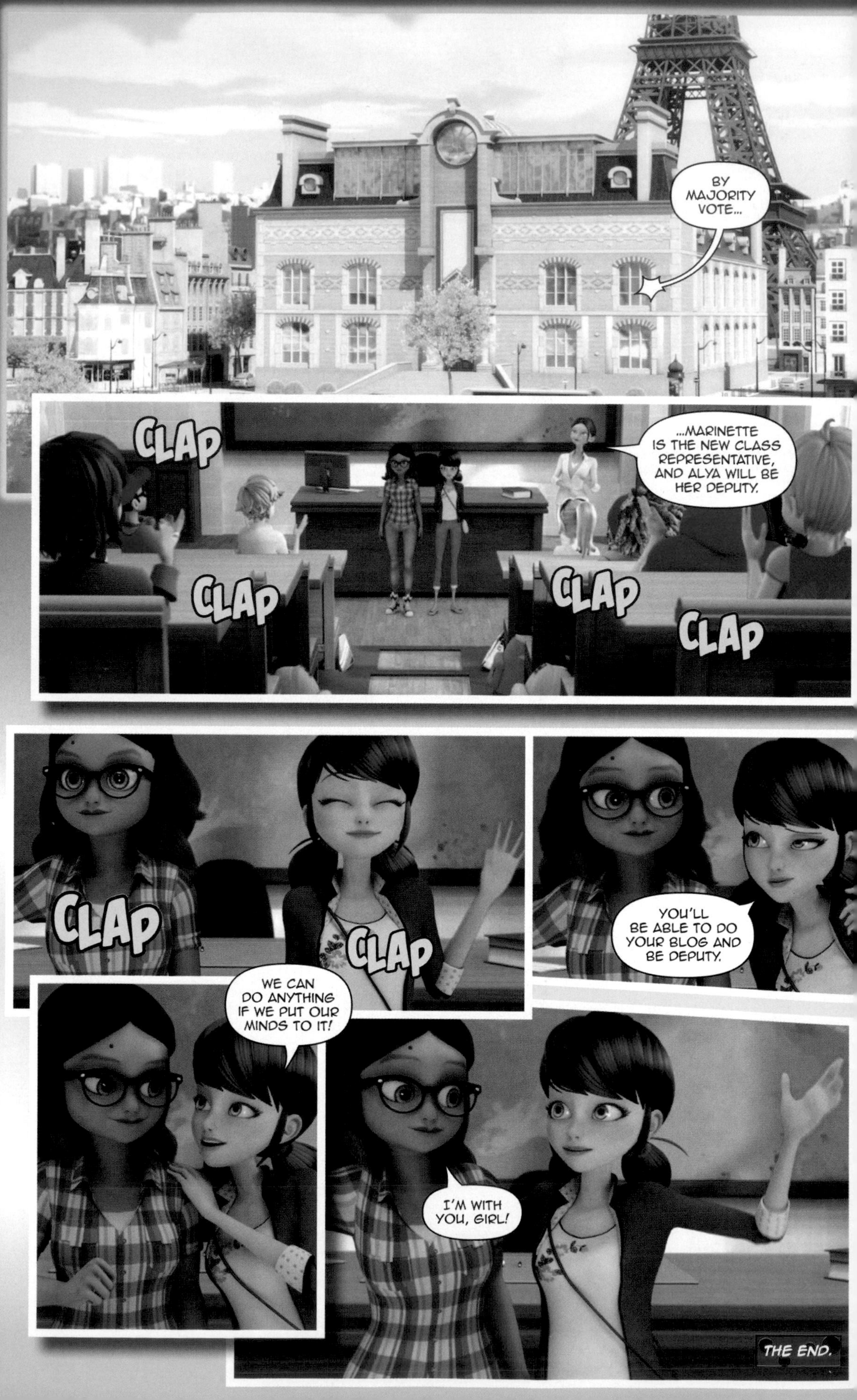
BY MAJORITY VOTE...
CLAP
...MARINETTE IS THE NEW CLASS REPRESENTATIVE, AND ALYA WILL BE HER DEPUTY.
CLAP
CLAP
CLAP
CLAP
CLAP
YOU'LL BE ABLE TO DO YOUR BLOG AND BE DEPUTY.
WE CAN DO ANYTHING IF WE PUT OUR MINDS TO IT!
I'M WITH YOU, GIRL!
THE END.

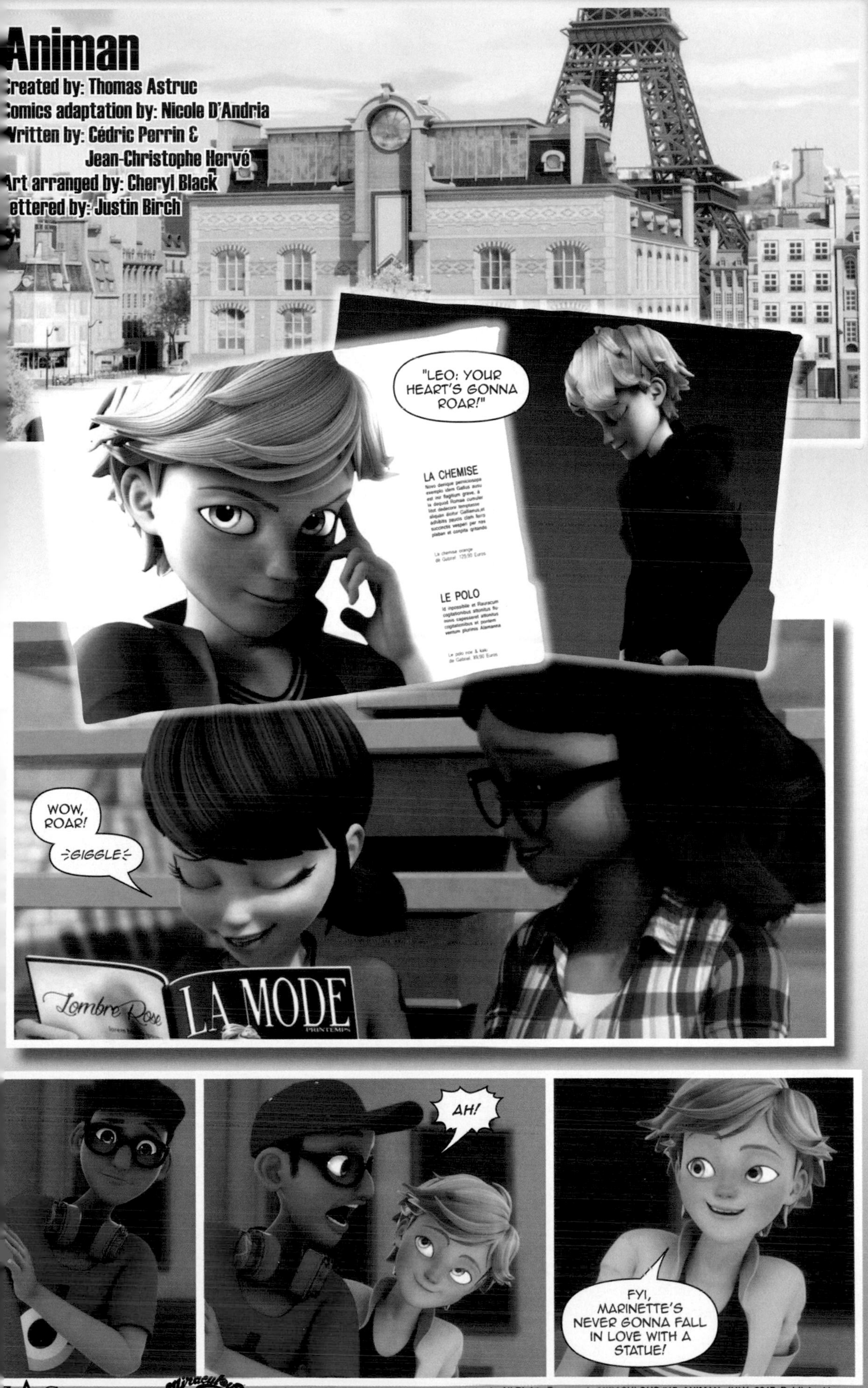
Animan
reated by: Thomas Astruc
omics adaptation by: Nicole D'Andria
ritten by: Cédric Perrin &
Jean-Christophe Hervé
rt arranged by: Cheryl Black
ettered by: Justin Birch
"LEO: YOUR HEART'S GONNA ROAR!"
LA CHEMISE
LE POLO
WOW, ROAR!
GIGGLE
LA MODE
PRINTEMPS
AH!
FYI, MARINETTE'S NEVER GONNA FALL IN LOVE WITH A STATUE!

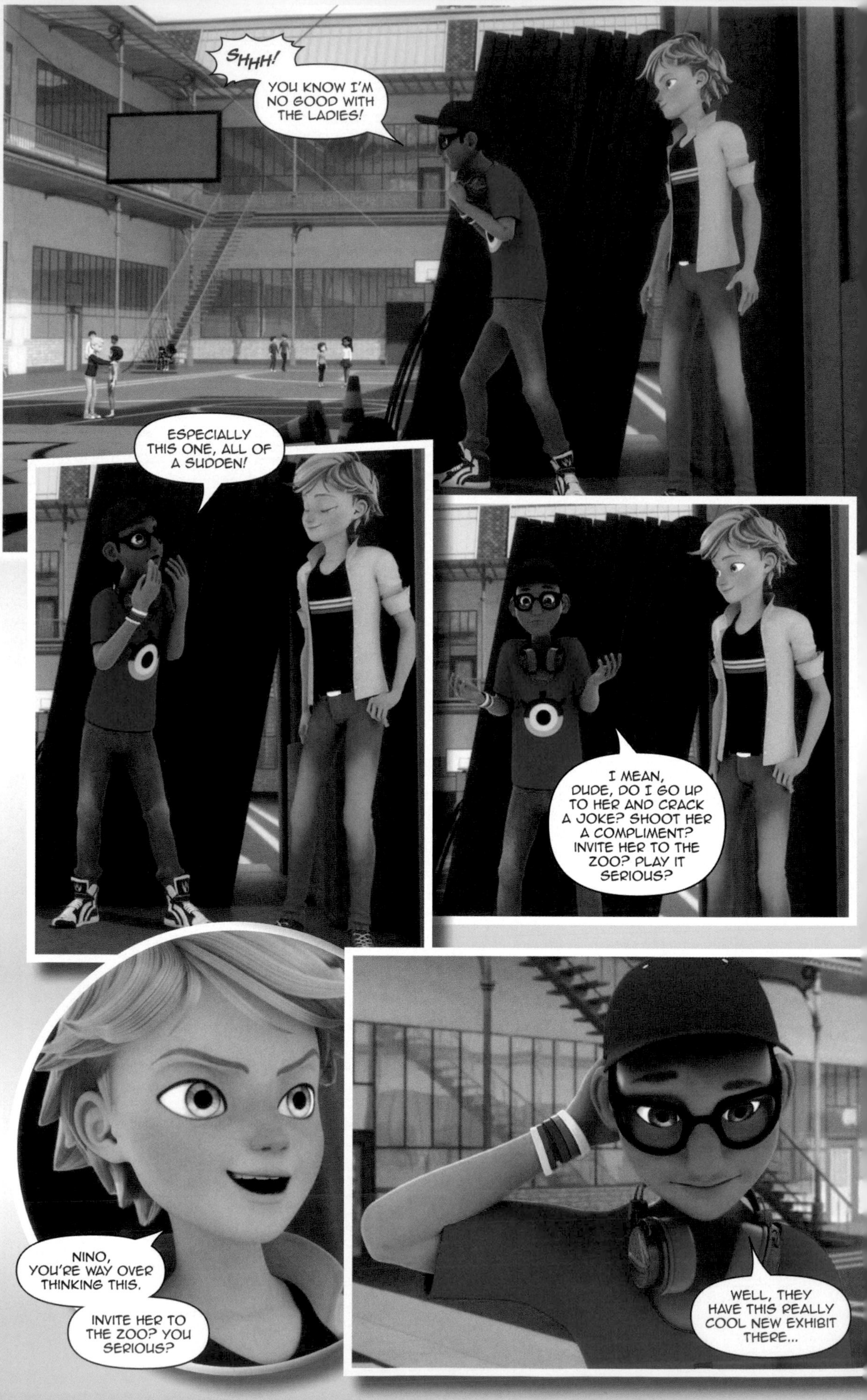
SHHH!
YOU KNOW I'M NO GOOD WITH THE LADIES!
ESPECIALLY THIS ONE, ALL OF A SUDDEN!
I MEAN, DUDE, DO I GO UP TO HER AND CRACK A JOKE? SHOOT HER A COMPLIMENT? INVITE HER TO THE ZOO? PLAY IT SERIOUS?
NINO, YOU'RE WAY OVER THINKING THIS.
INVITE HER TO THE ZOO? YOU SERIOUS?
WELL, THEY HAVE THIS REALLY COOL NEW EXHIBIT THERE...

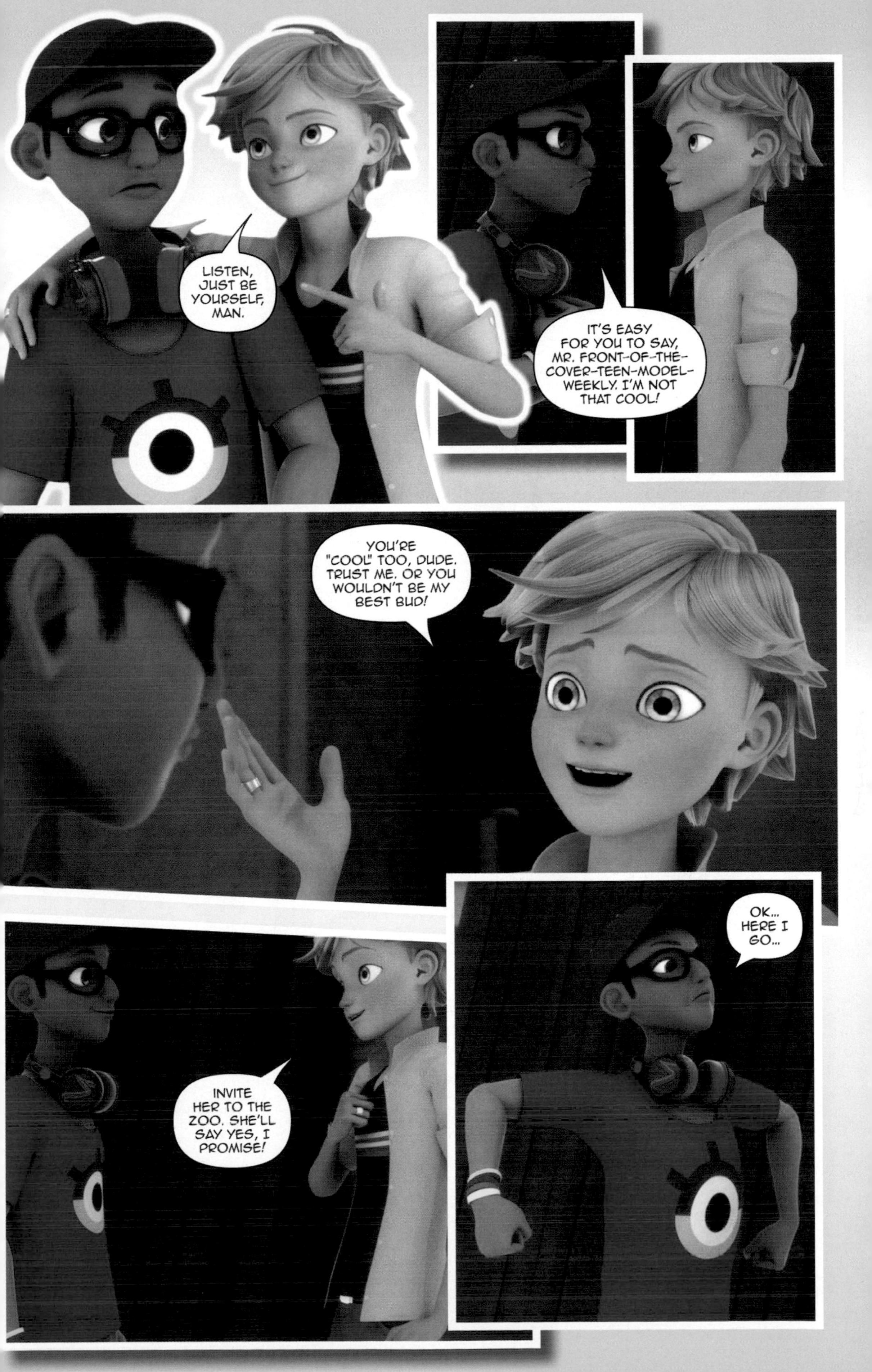
LISTEN, JUST BE YOURSELF, MAN.
IT'S EASY FOR YOU TO SAY, MR. FRONT-OF-THE-COVER-TEEN-MODEL-WEEKLY. I'M NOT THAT COOL!
YOU'RE "COOL" TOO, DUDE. TRUST ME. OR YOU WOULDN'T BE MY BEST BUD!
INVITE HER TO THE ZOO. SHE'LL SAY YES, I PROMISE!
OK... HERE I GO...

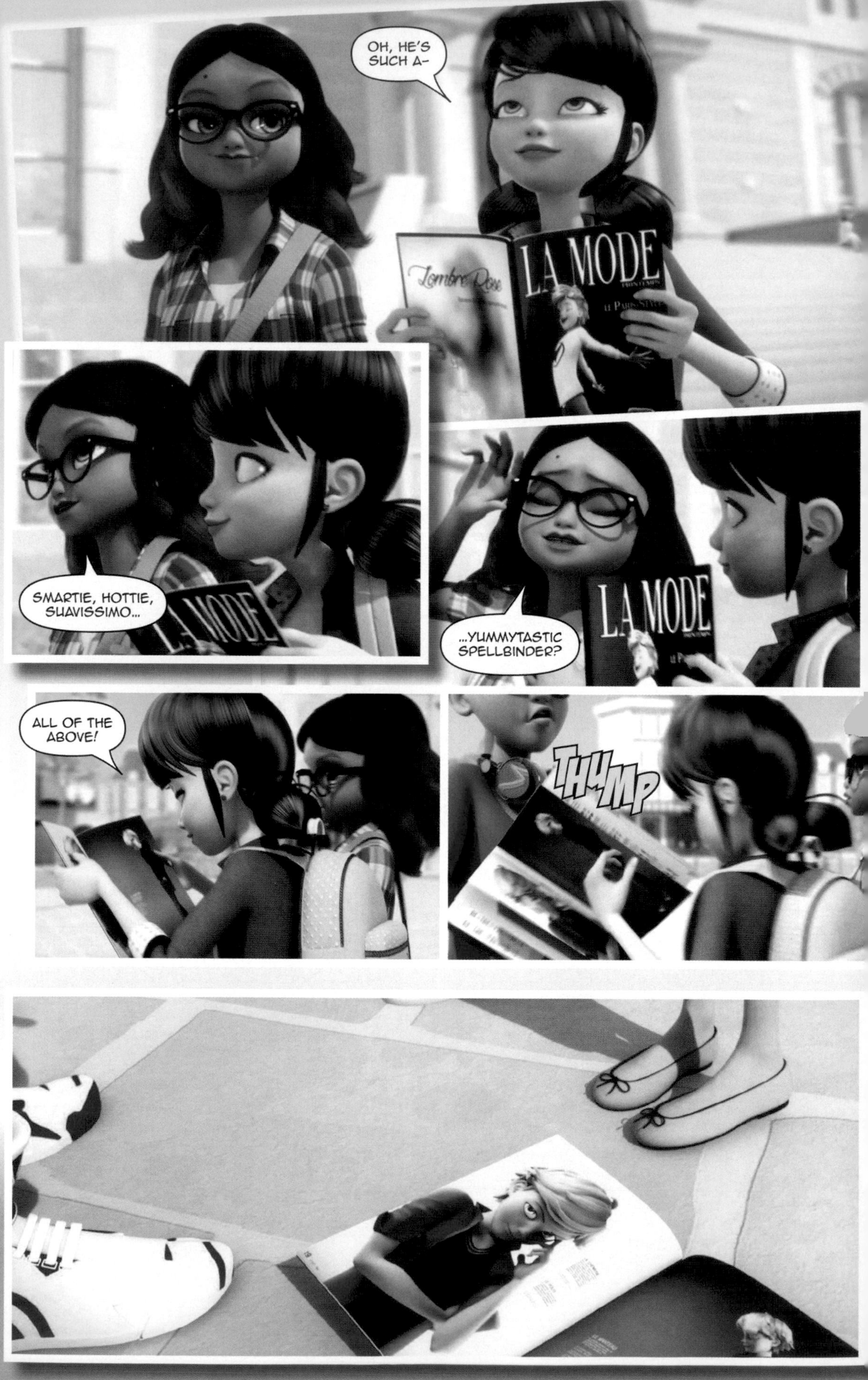
OH, HE'S SUCH A-
LA MODE
SMARTIE, HOTTIE, SUAVISSIMO...
...YUMMYTASTIC SPELLBINDER?
LA MODE
ALL OF THE ABOVE!
THUMP

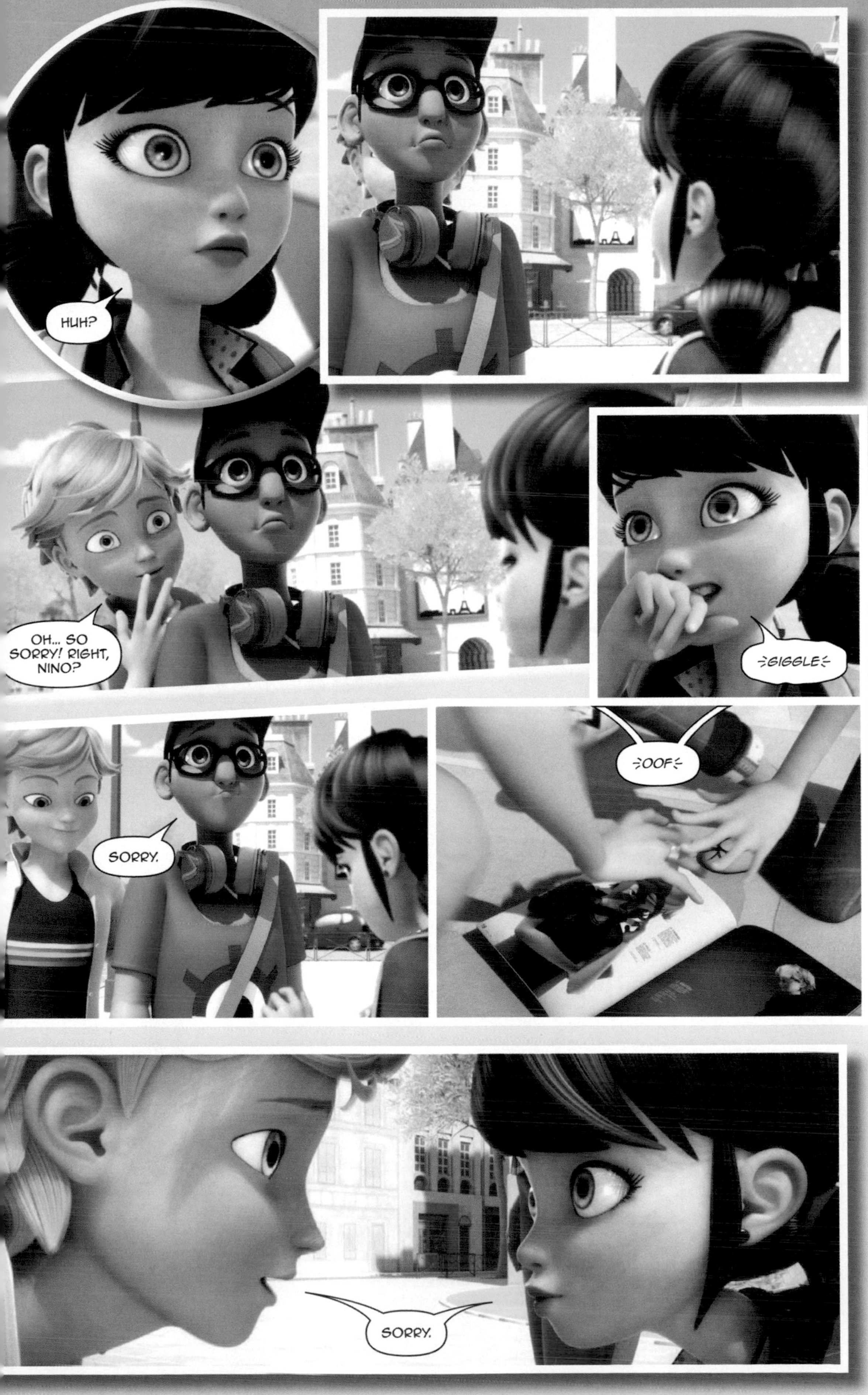
HUH?
OH... SO SORRY! RIGHT, NINO?
GIGGLE
SORRY.
OOF
SORRY.

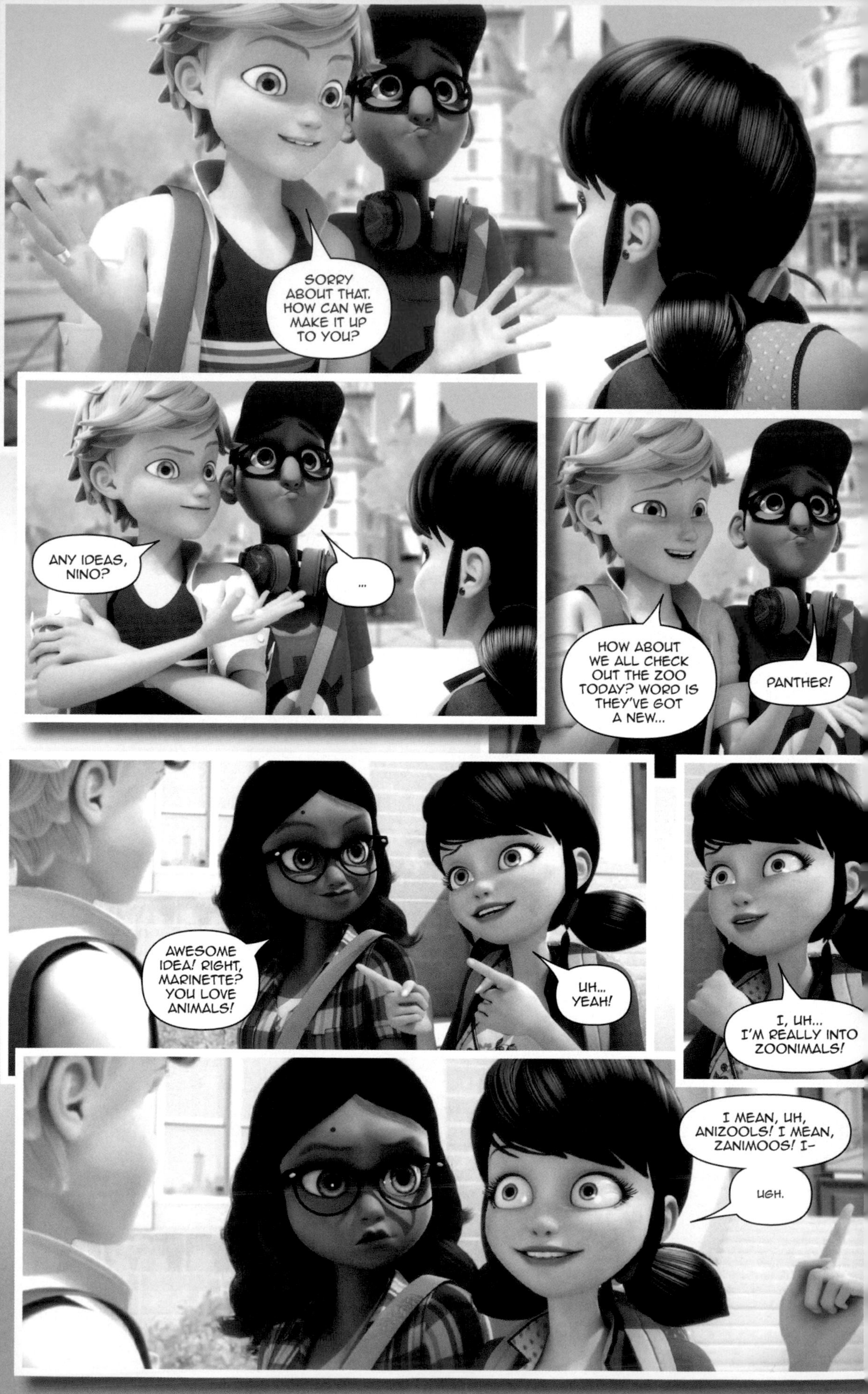
SORRY ABOUT THAT. HOW CAN WE MAKE IT UP TO YOU?
ANY IDEAS, NINO?
...
HOW ABOUT WE ALL CHECK OUT THE ZOO TODAY? WORD IS THEY'VE GOT A NEW...
PANTHER!
AWESOME IDEA! RIGHT, MARINETTE? YOU LOVE ANIMALS!
UH... YEAH!
I, UH... I'M REALLY INTO ZOONIMALS!
I MEAN, UH, ANIZOOLS! I MEAN, ZANIMOOS! I-
UGH.

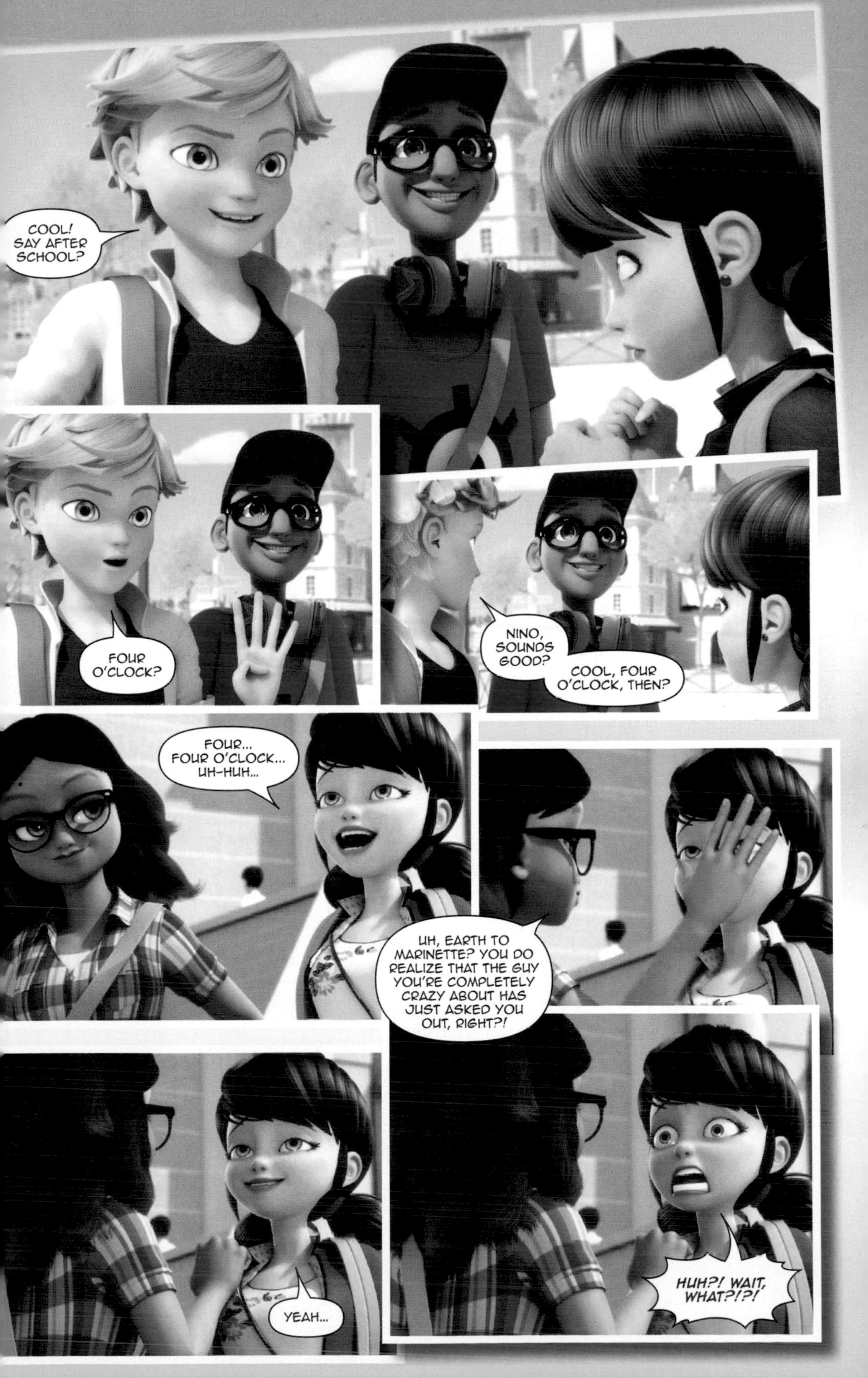
COOL! SAY AFTER SCHOOL?
FOUR O'CLOCK?
NINO, SOUNDS GOOD?
COOL, FOUR O'CLOCK, THEN?
FOUR... FOUR O'CLOCK... UH-HUH...
UH, EARTH TO MARINETTE? YOU DO REALIZE THAT THE GUY YOU'RE COMPLETELY CRAZY ABOUT HAS JUST ASKED YOU OUT, RIGHT?!
YEAH...
HUH?! WAIT, WHAT?!?!

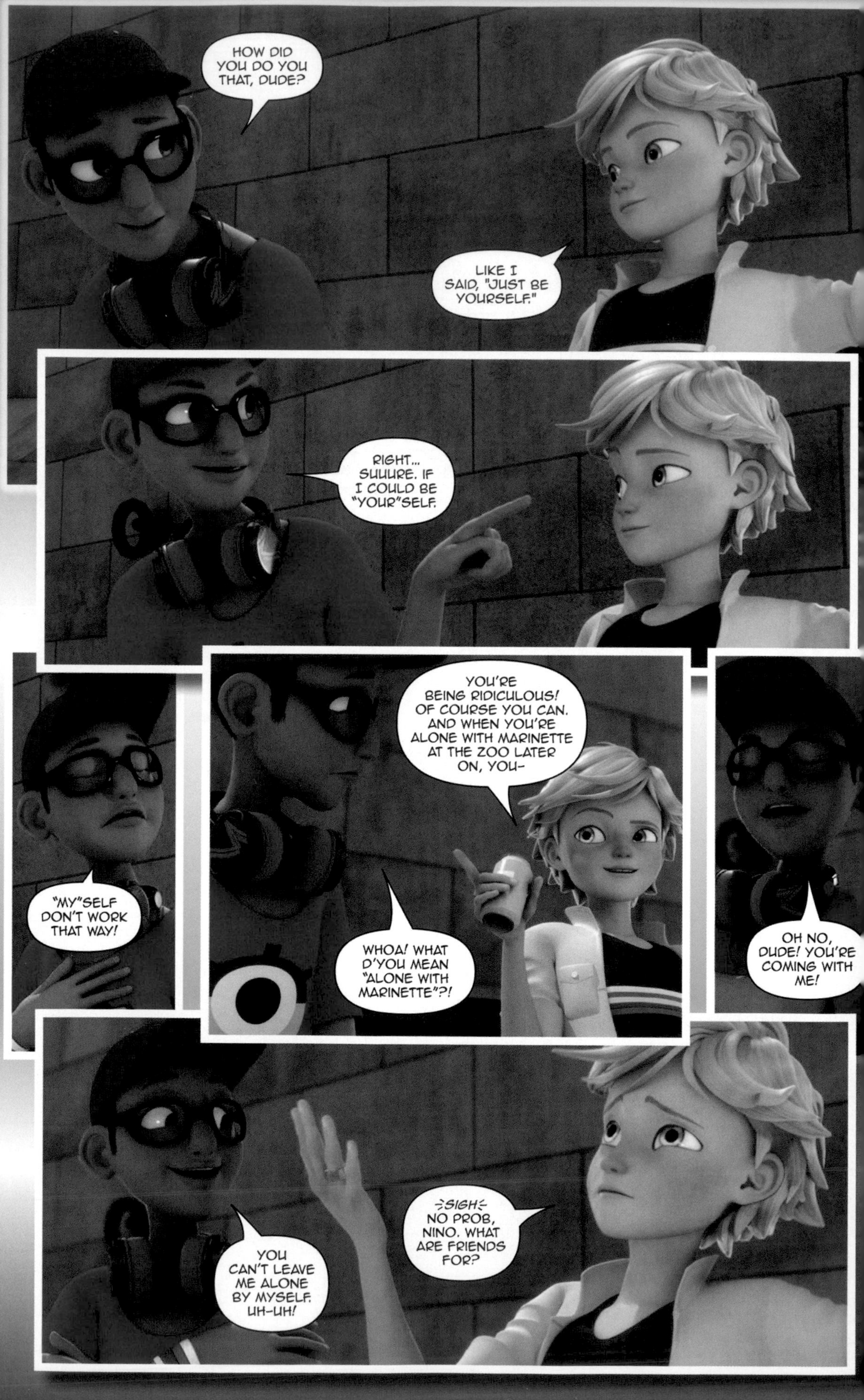
HOW DID YOU DO YOU THAT, DUDE?
LIKE I SAID, "JUST BE YOURSELF."
RIGHT... SUUURE. IF I COULD BE "YOUR"SELF.
"MY"SELF DON'T WORK THAT WAY!
YOU'RE BEING RIDICULOUS! OF COURSE YOU CAN. AND WHEN YOU'RE ALONE WITH MARINETTE AT THE ZOO LATER ON, YOU-
WHOA! WHAT D'YOU MEAN "ALONE WITH MARINETTE"?!
OH NO, DUDE! YOU'RE COMING WITH ME!
YOU CAN'T LEAVE ME ALONE BY MYSELF. UH-UH!
SIGH NO PROB, NINO. WHAT ARE FRIENDS FOR?

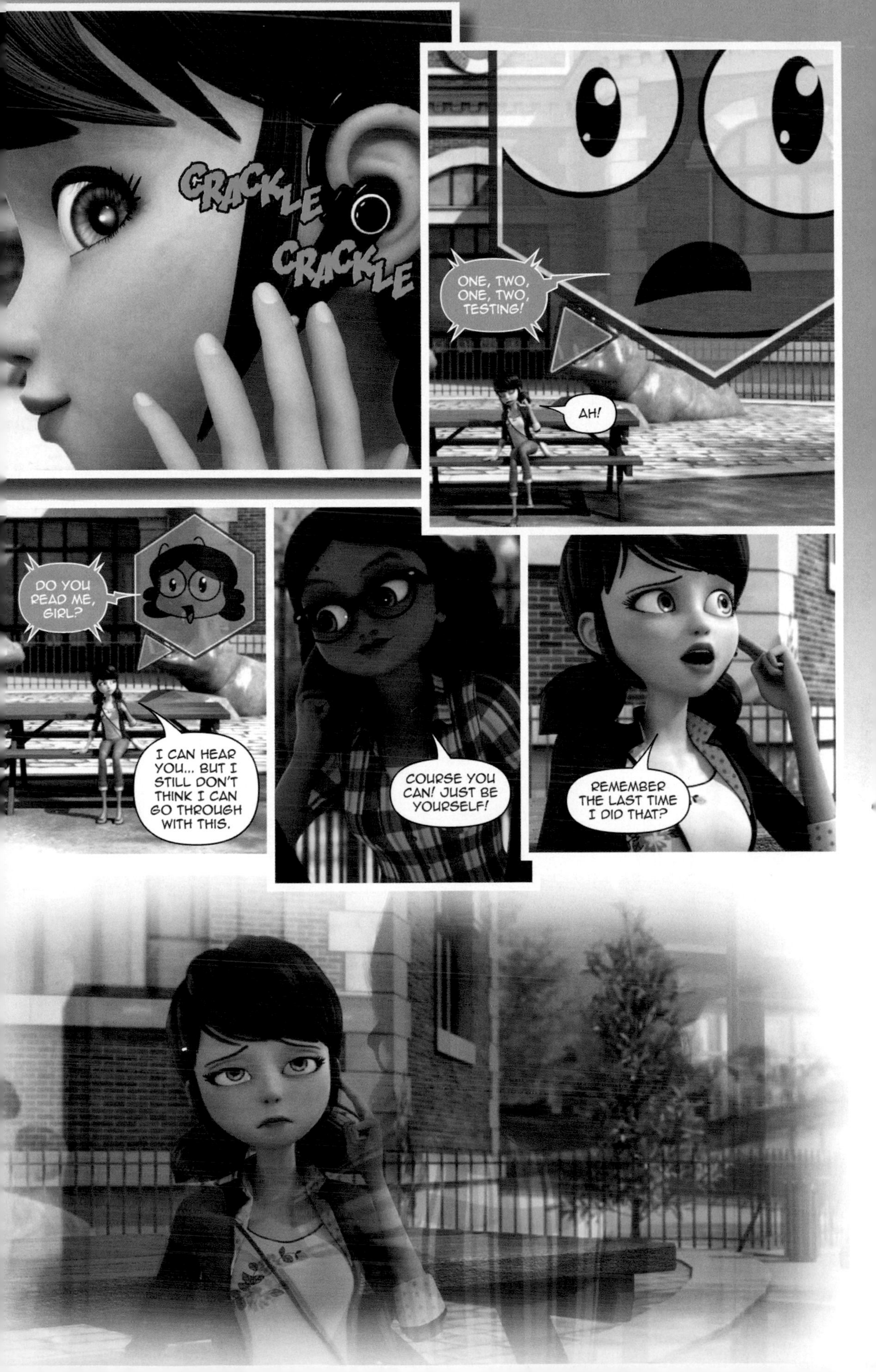
CRACKLE
CRACKLE
ONE, TWO, ONE, TWO, TESTING!
AH!
DO YOU READ ME, GIRL?
I CAN HEAR YOU... BUT I STILL DON'T THINK I CAN GO THROUGH WITH THIS.
COURSE YOU CAN! JUST BE YOURSELF!
REMEMBER THE LAST TIME I DID THAT?

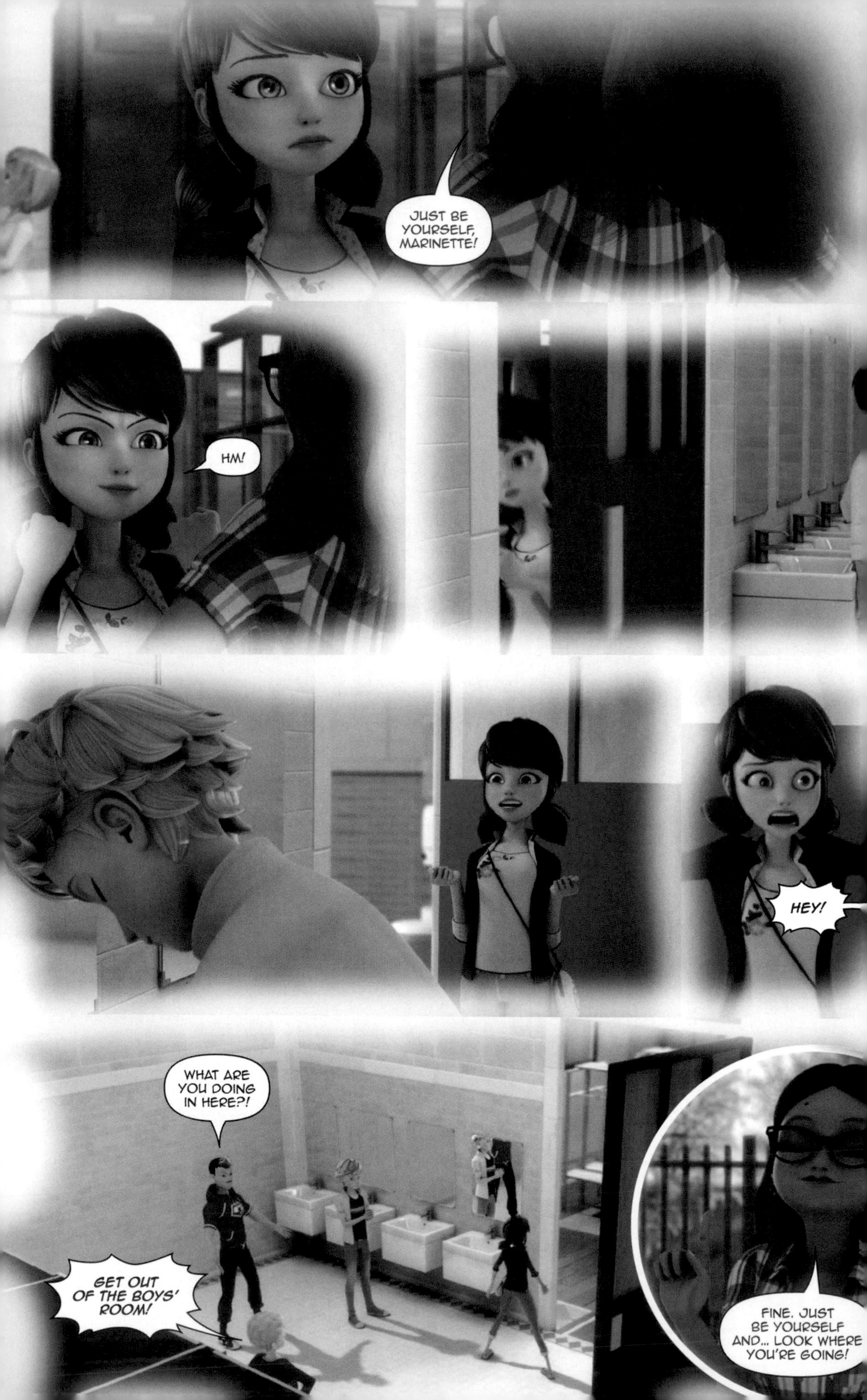
JUST BE YOURSELF, MARINETTE!
HM!
HEY!
WHAT ARE YOU DOING IN HERE?!
GET OUT OF THE BOYS' ROOM!
FINE. JUST BE YOURSELF AND... LOOK WHERE YOU'RE GOING!

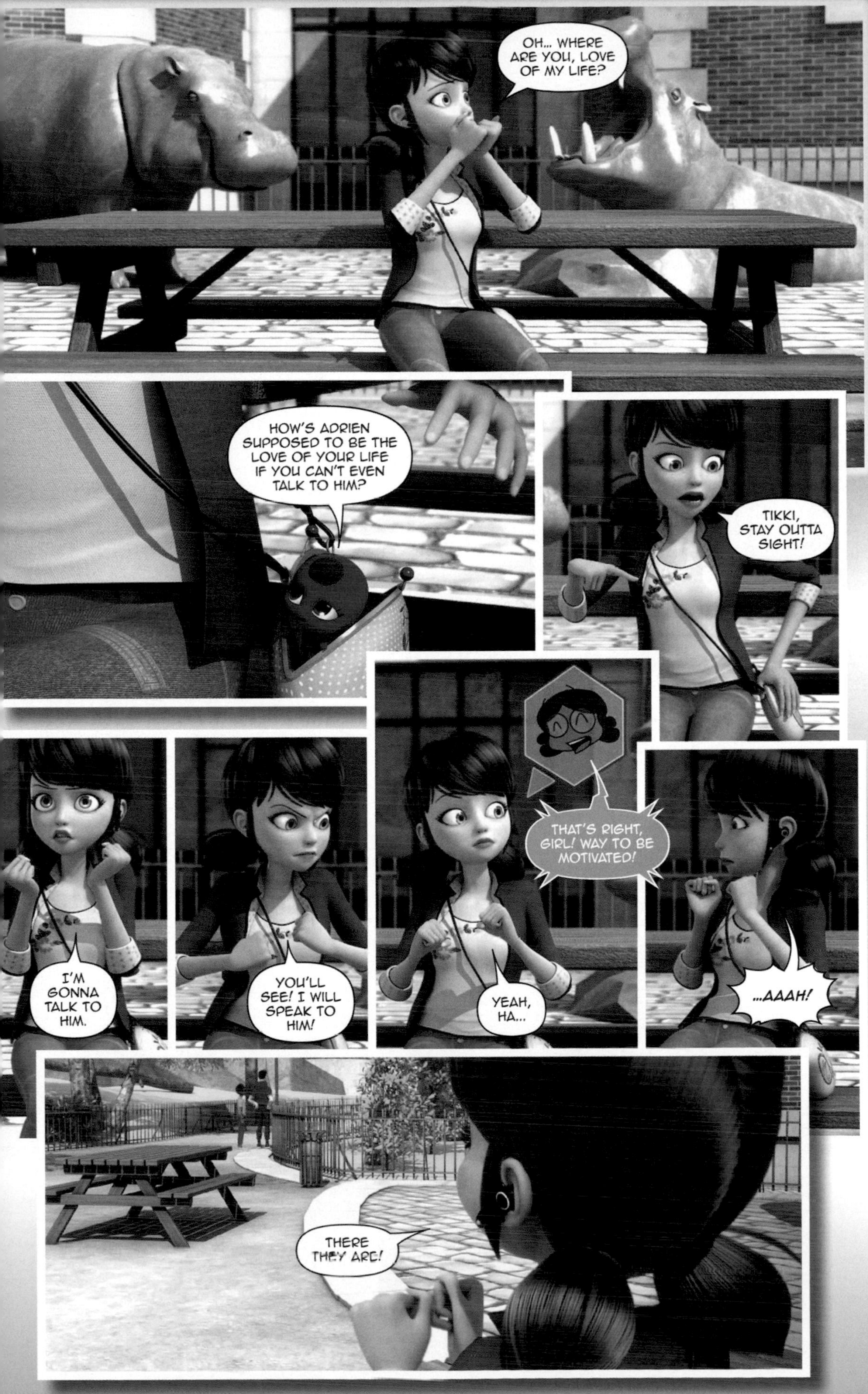
OH... WHERE ARE YOU, LOVE OF MY LIFE?
HOW'S ADRIEN SUPPOSED TO BE THE LOVE OF YOUR LIFE IF YOU CAN'T EVEN TALK TO HIM?
TIKKI, STAY OUTTA SIGHT!
I'M GONNA TALK TO HIM.
YOU'LL SEE! I WILL SPEAK TO HIM!
YEAH, HA...
THAT'S RIGHT, GIRL! WAY TO BE MOTIVATED!
...AAAH!
THERE THEY ARE!

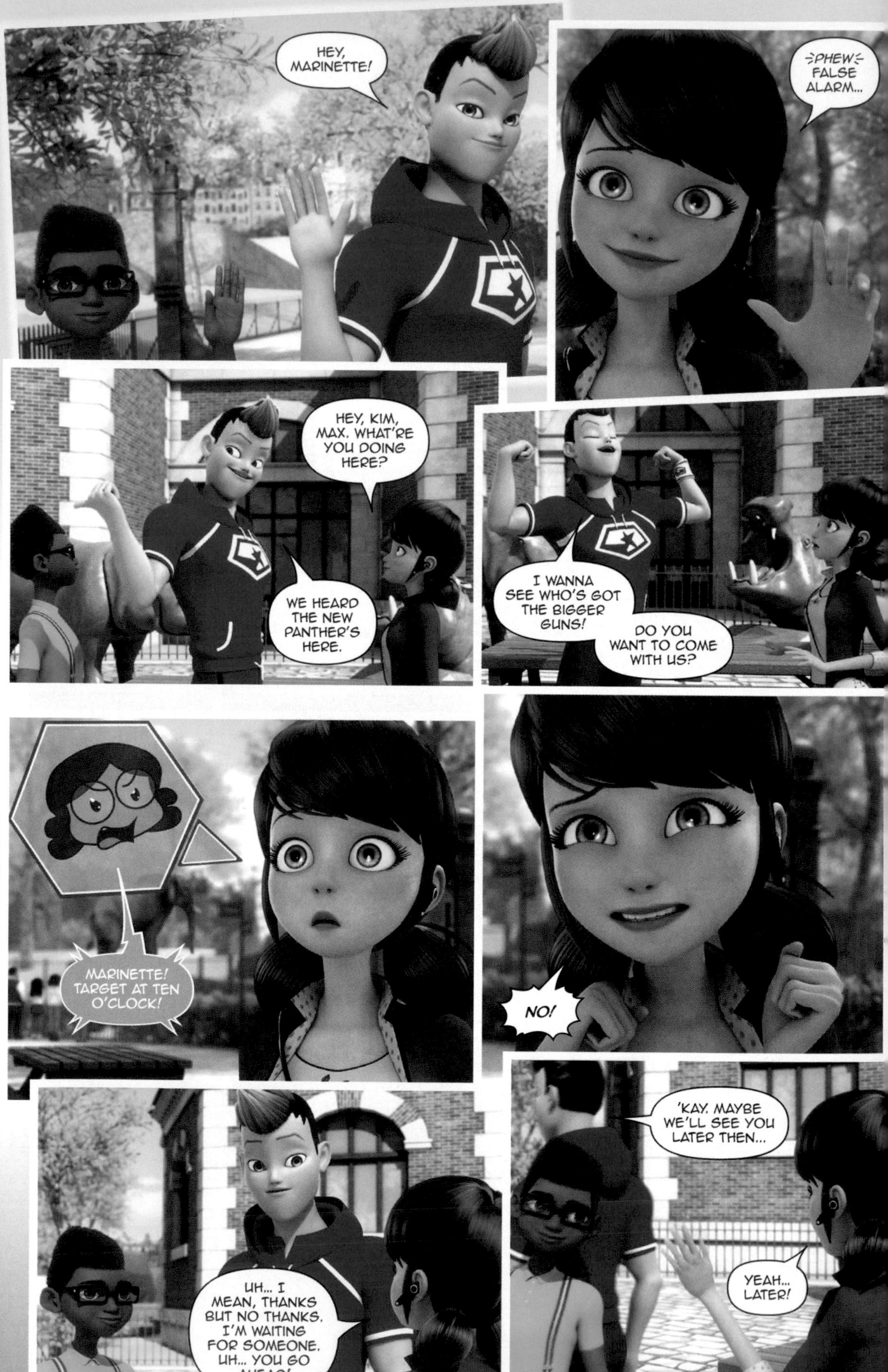
HEY, MARINETTE!
PHEW FALSE ALARM...
HEY, KIM, MAX. WHAT'RE YOU DOING HERE?
WE HEARD THE NEW PANTHER'S HERE.
I WANNA SEE WHO'S GOT THE BIGGER GUNS!
DO YOU WANT TO COME WITH US?
MARINETTE! TARGET AT TEN O'CLOCK!
NO!
UH... I MEAN, THANKS BUT NO THANKS. I'M WAITING FOR SOMEONE. UH... YOU GO AHEAD!
'KAY. MAYBE WE'LL SEE YOU LATER THEN...
YEAH... LATER!

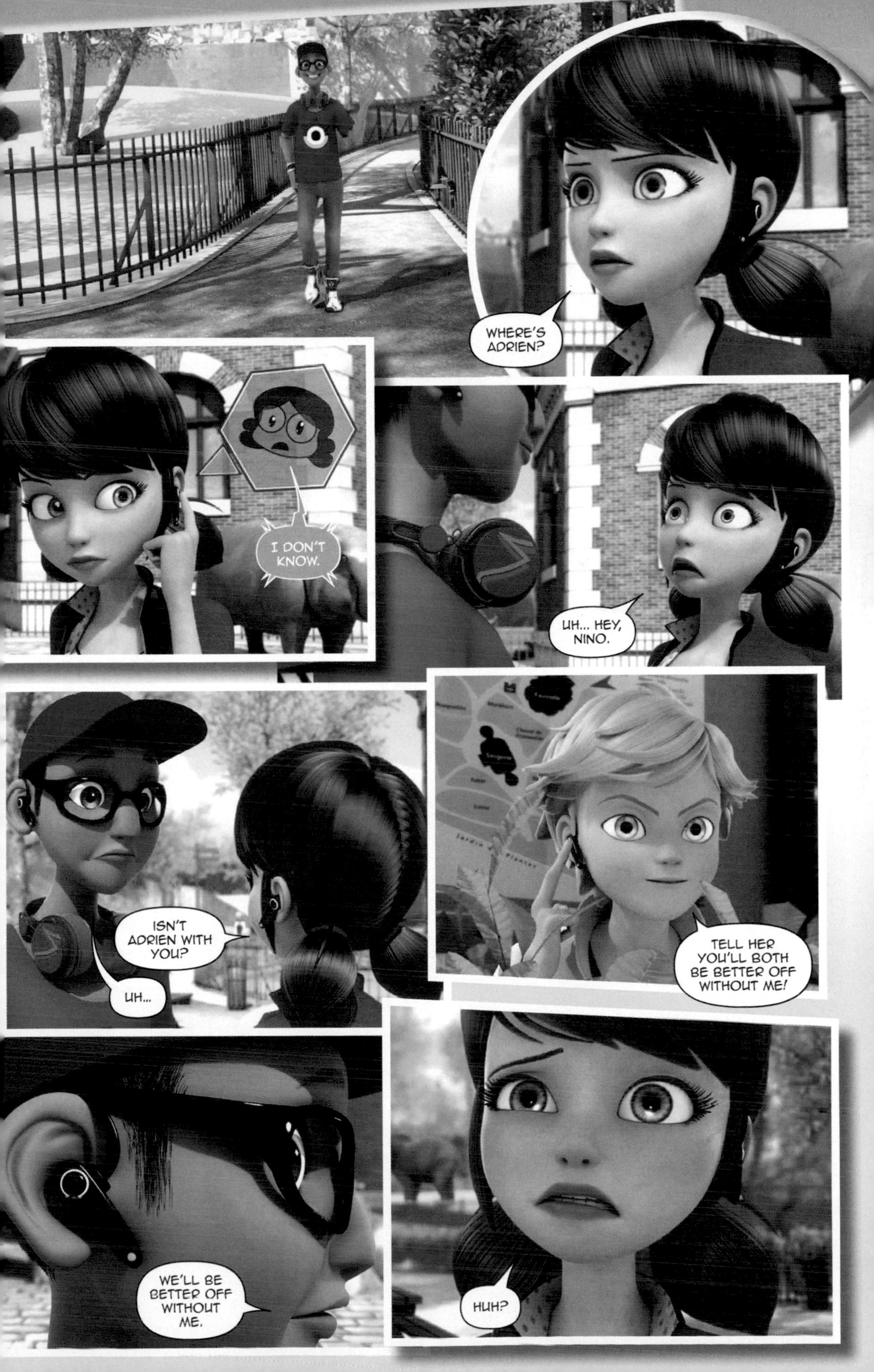
WHERE'S ADRIEN?
I DON'T KNOW.
UH... HEY, NINO.
ISN'T ADRIEN WITH YOU?
UH...
TELL HER YOU'LL BOTH BE BETTER OFF WITHOUT ME!
WE'LL BE BETTER OFF WITHOUT ME.
HUH?

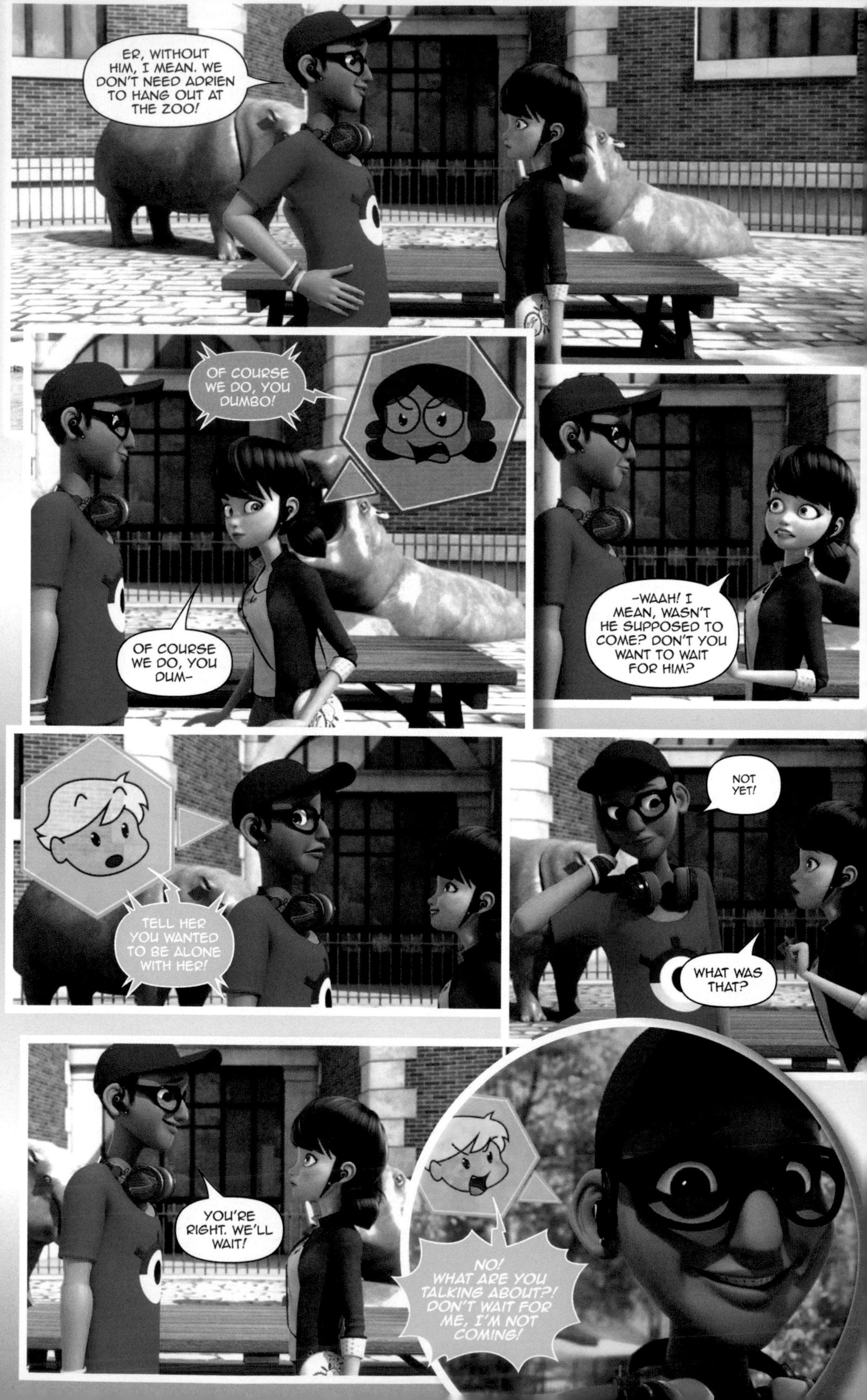
ER, WITHOUT HIM, I MEAN. WE DON'T NEED ADRIEN TO HANG OUT AT THE ZOO!
OF COURSE WE DO, YOU DUMBO!
OF COURSE WE DO, YOU DUM-
-WAAH! I MEAN, WASN'T HE SUPPOSED TO COME? DON'T YOU WANT TO WAIT FOR HIM?
TELL HER YOU WANTED TO BE ALONE WITH HER!
NOT YET!
WHAT WAS THAT?
YOU'RE RIGHT. WE'LL WAIT!
NO! WHAT ARE YOU TALKING ABOUT?! DON'T WAIT FOR ME, I'M NOT COMING!

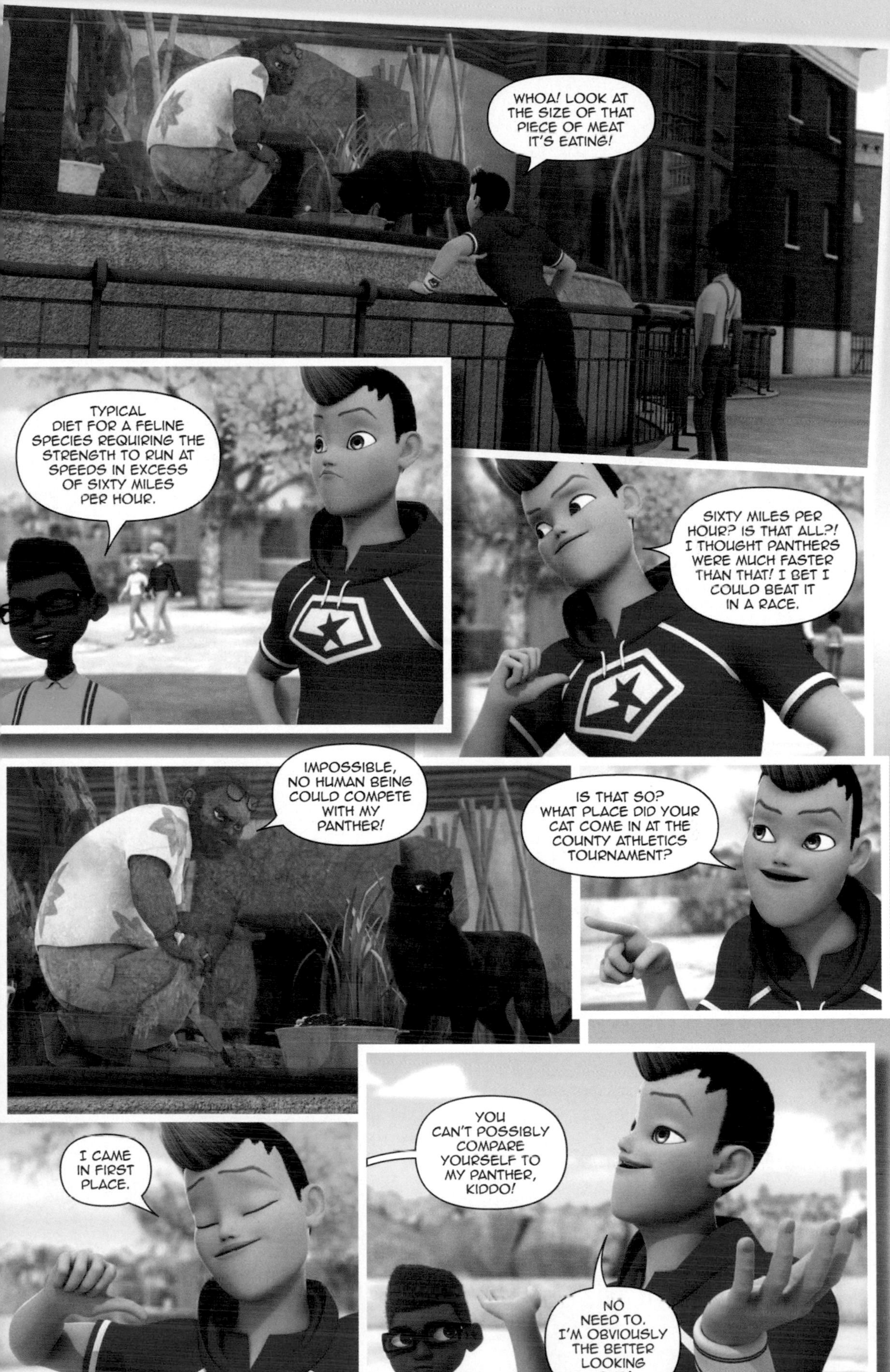

WHOA! LOOK AT THE SIZE OF THAT PIECE OF MEAT IT'S EATING!
TYPICAL DIET FOR A FELINE SPECIES REQUIRING THE STRENGTH TO RUN AT SPEEDS IN EXCESS OF SIXTY MILES PER HOUR.
SIXTY MILES PER HOUR? IS THAT ALL?! I THOUGHT PANTHERS WERE MUCH FASTER THAN THAT! I BET I COULD BEAT IT IN A RACE.
IMPOSSIBLE, NO HUMAN BEING COULD COMPETE WITH MY PANTHER!
IS THAT SO? WHAT PLACE DID YOUR CAT COME IN AT THE COUNTY ATHLETICS TOURNAMENT?
I CAME IN FIRST PLACE.
YOU CAN'T POSSIBLY COMPARE YOURSELF TO MY PANTHER, KIDDO!
NO NEED TO. I'M OBVIOUSLY THE BETTER LOOKING ONE!

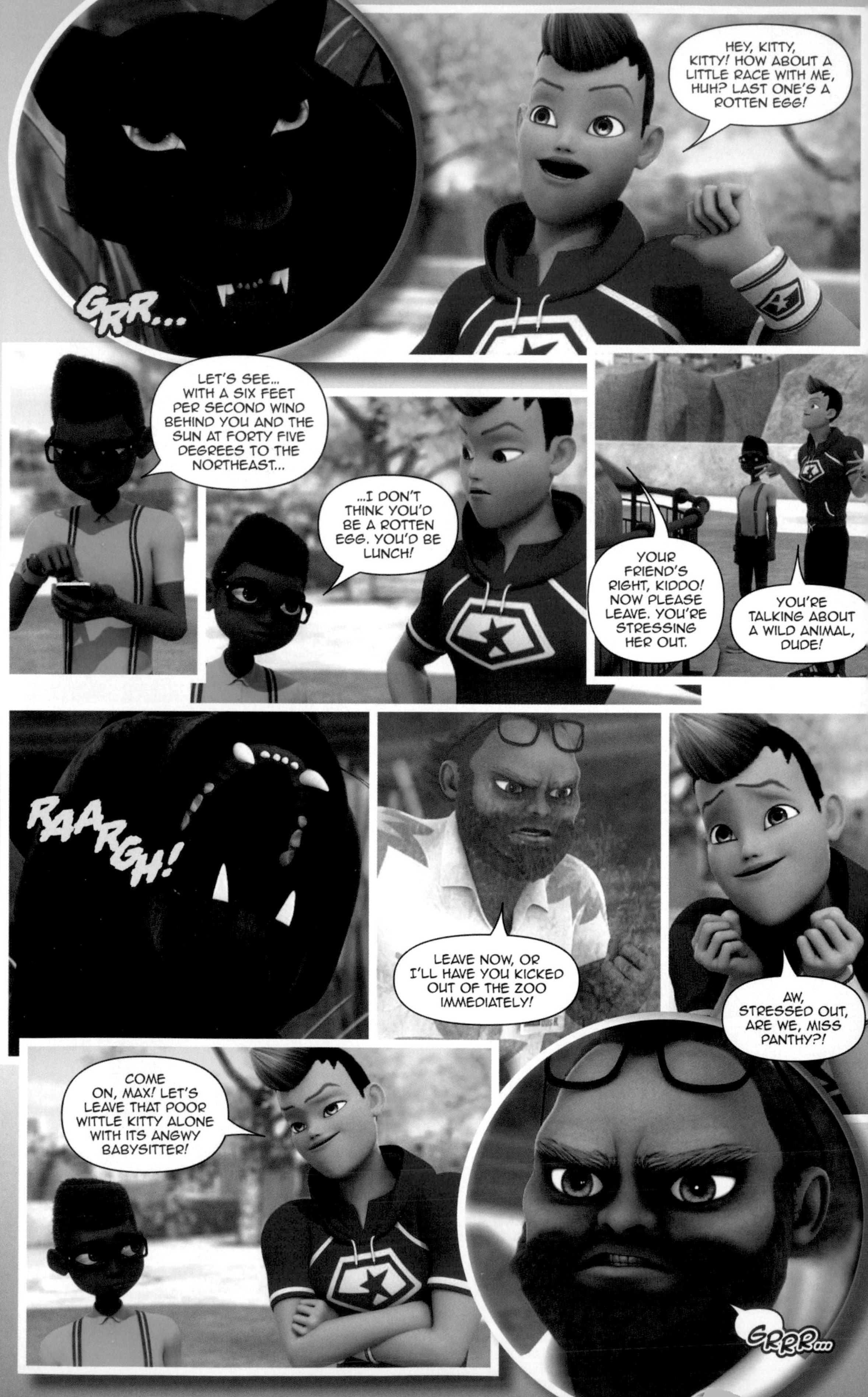

GRR...
HEY, KITTY, KITTY! HOW ABOUT A LITTLE RACE WITH ME, HUH? LAST ONE'S A ROTTEN EGG!
LET'S SEE... WITH A SIX FEET PER SECOND WIND BEHIND YOU AND THE SUN AT FORTY FIVE DEGREES TO THE NORTHEAST...
...I DON'T THINK YOU'D BE A ROTTEN EGG. YOU'D BE LUNCH!
YOUR FRIEND'S RIGHT, KIDDO! NOW PLEASE LEAVE. YOU'RE STRESSING HER OUT.
YOU'RE TALKING ABOUT A WILD ANIMAL, DUDE!
RAARGH!
LEAVE NOW, OR I'LL HAVE YOU KICKED OUT OF THE ZOO IMMEDIATELY!
AW, STRESSED OUT, ARE WE, MISS PANTHY?!
COME ON, MAX! LET'S LEAVE THAT POOR WITTLE KITTY ALONE WITH ITS ANGWY BABYSITTER!
GRRR...

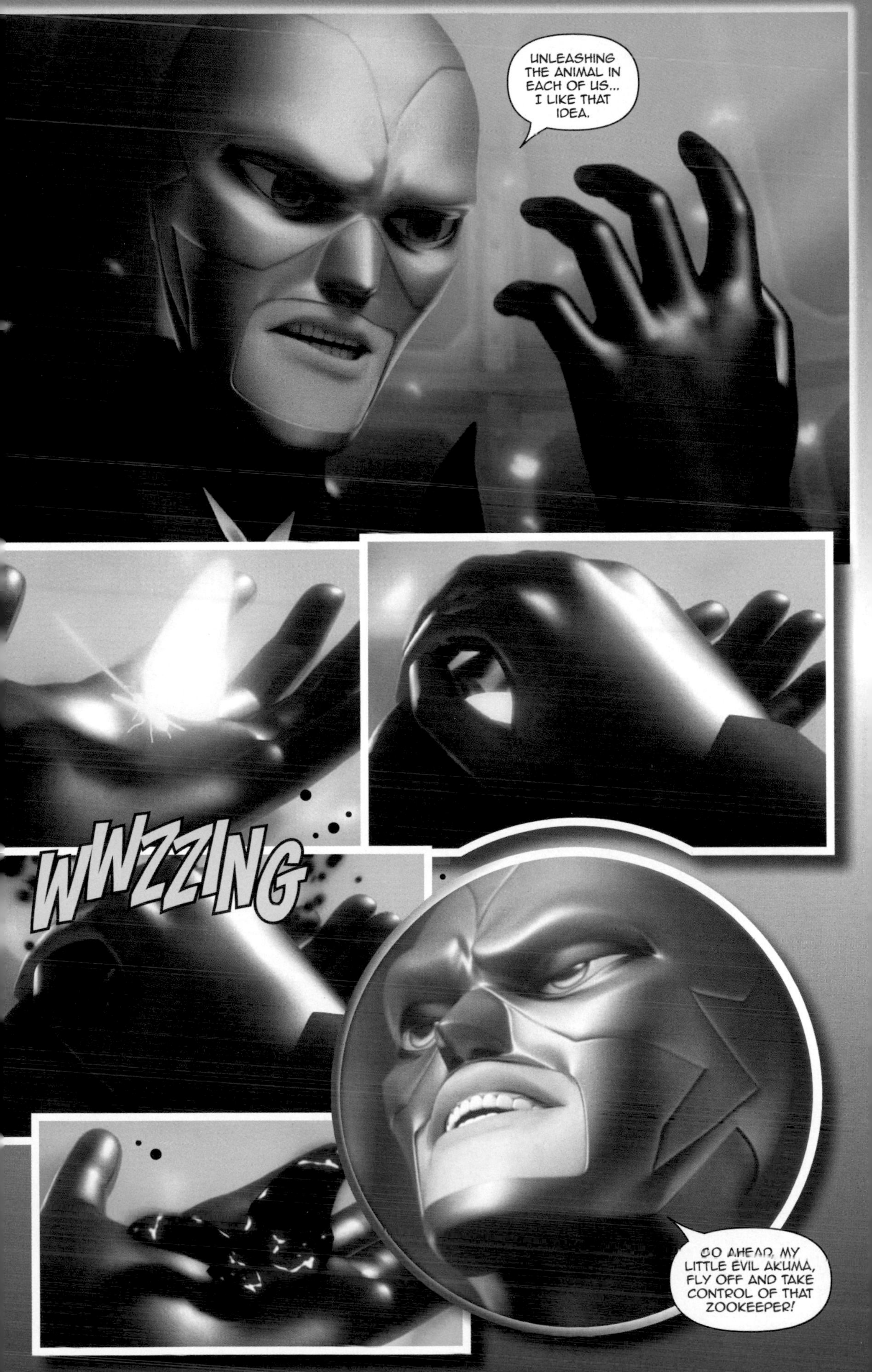
UNLEASHING THE ANIMAL IN EACH OF US... I LIKE THAT IDEA.
WWZZING
GO AHEAD, MY LITTLE EVIL AKUMA, FLY OFF AND TAKE CONTROL OF THAT ZOOKEEPER!

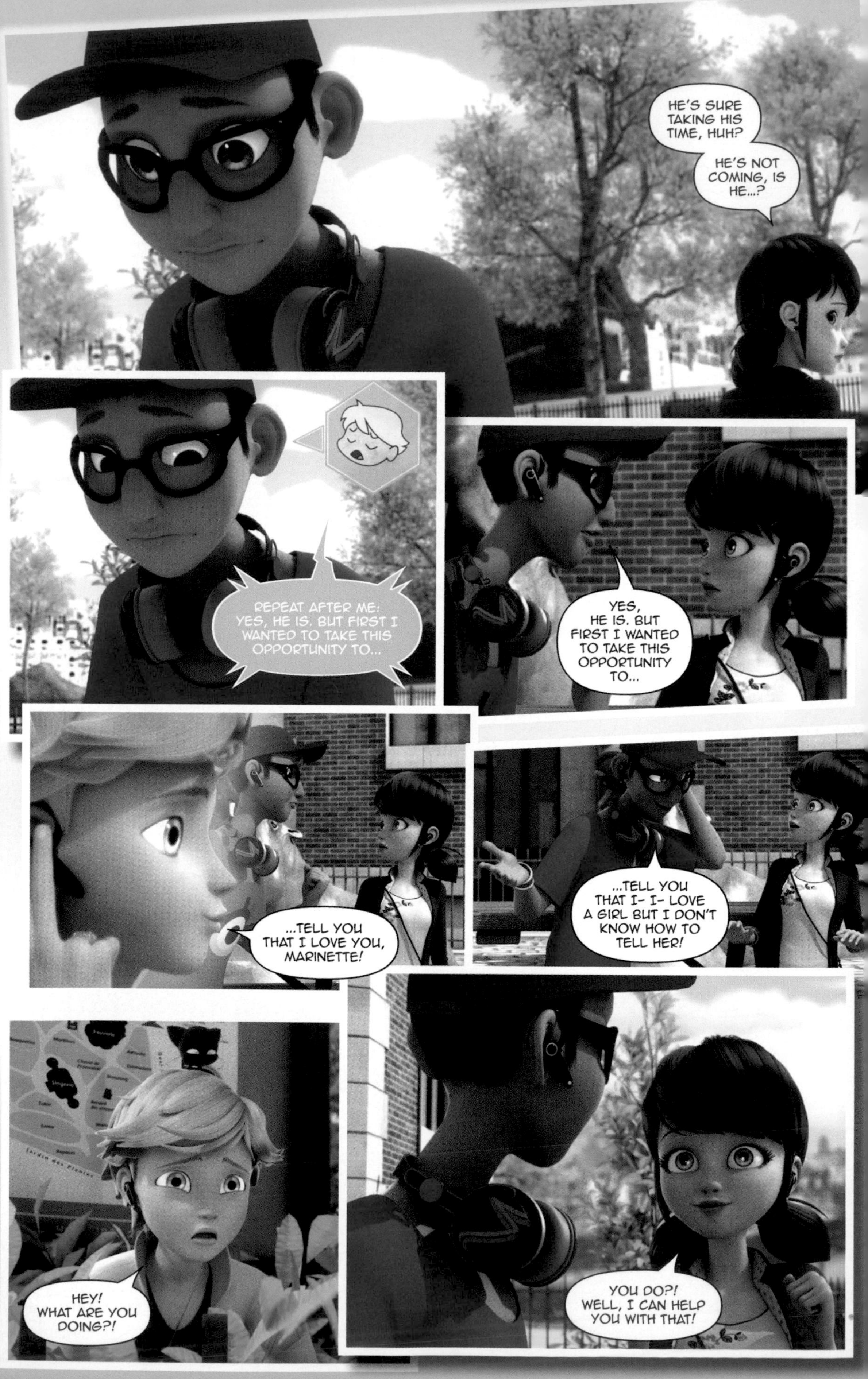
HE'S SURE TAKING HIS TIME, HUH?
HE'S NOT COMING, IS HE...?
REPEAT AFTER ME: YES, HE IS. BUT FIRST I WANTED TO TAKE THIS OPPORTUNITY TO...
YES, HE IS. BUT FIRST I WANTED TO TAKE THIS OPPORTUNITY TO...
...TELL YOU THAT I LOVE YOU, MARINETTE!
...TELL YOU THAT I- I- LOVE A GIRL BUT I DON'T KNOW HOW TO TELL HER!
HEY! WHAT ARE YOU DOING?!
YOU DO?! WELL, I CAN HELP YOU WITH THAT!

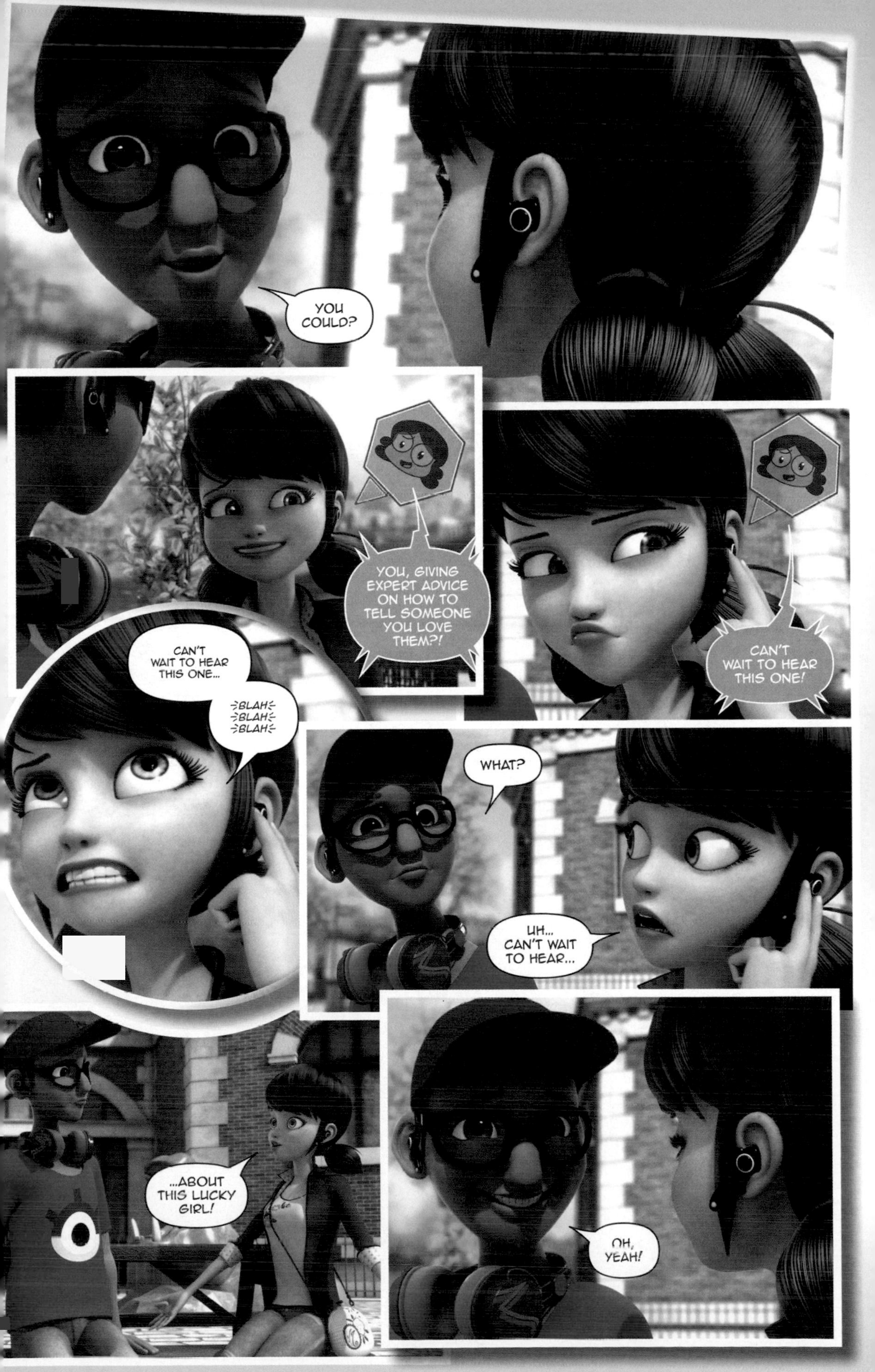
YOU COULD?
YOU, GIVING EXPERT ADVICE ON HOW TO TELL SOMEONE YOU LOVE THEM?!
CAN'T WAIT TO HEAR THIS ONE!
CAN'T WAIT TO HEAR THIS ONE...
BLAH BLAH BLAH
WHAT?
UH... CAN'T WAIT TO HEAR...
...ABOUT THIS LUCKY GIRL!
OH, YEAH!

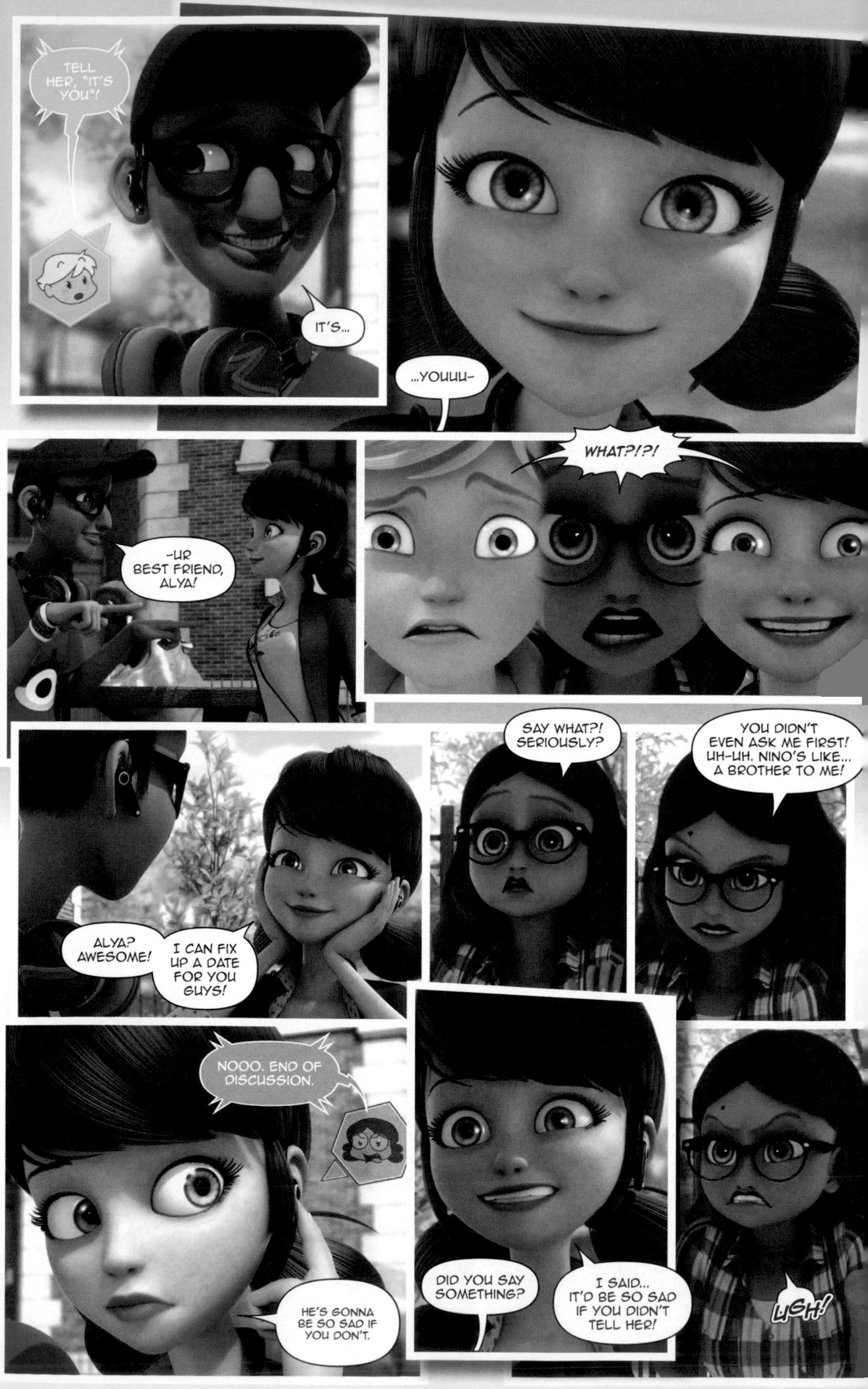
TELL HER, "IT'S YOU"!
IT'S...
...YOUUU-
-UR BEST FRIEND, ALYA!
WHAT?!?!
ALYA? AWESOME!
I CAN FIX UP A DATE FOR YOU GUYS!
SAY WHAT?! SERIOUSLY?
YOU DIDN'T EVEN ASK ME FIRST! UH-UH. NINO'S LIKE... A BROTHER TO ME!
NOOO. END OF DISCUSSION.
HE'S GONNA BE SO SAD IF YOU DON'T.
DID YOU SAY SOMETHING?
I SAID... IT'D BE SO SAD IF YOU DIDN'T TELL HER!
UGH!

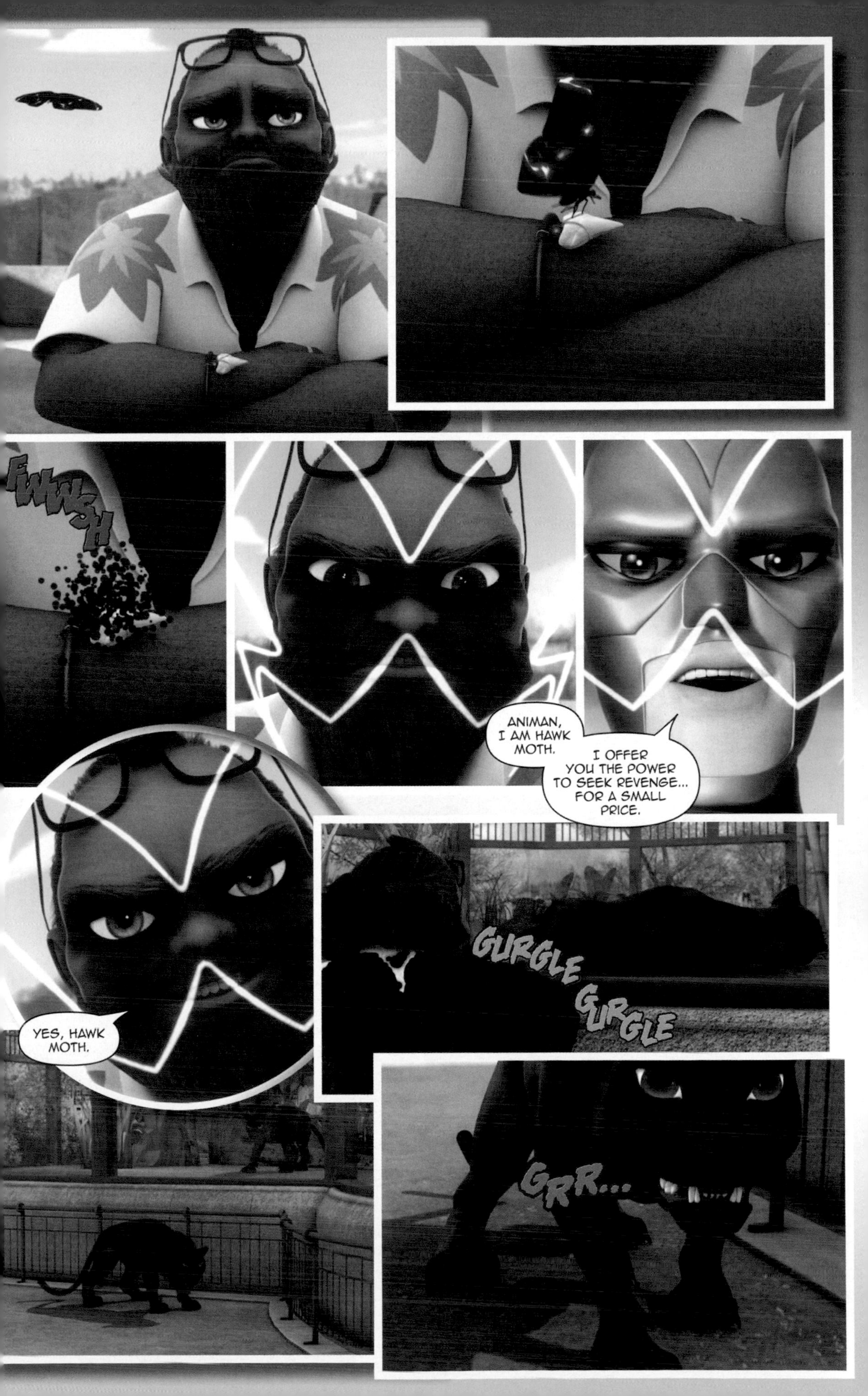
FWWSH
ANIMAN, I AM HAWK MOTH.
I OFFER YOU THE POWER TO SEEK REVENGE... FOR A SMALL PRICE.
YES, HAWK MOTH.
GURGLE GURGLE
GRR...

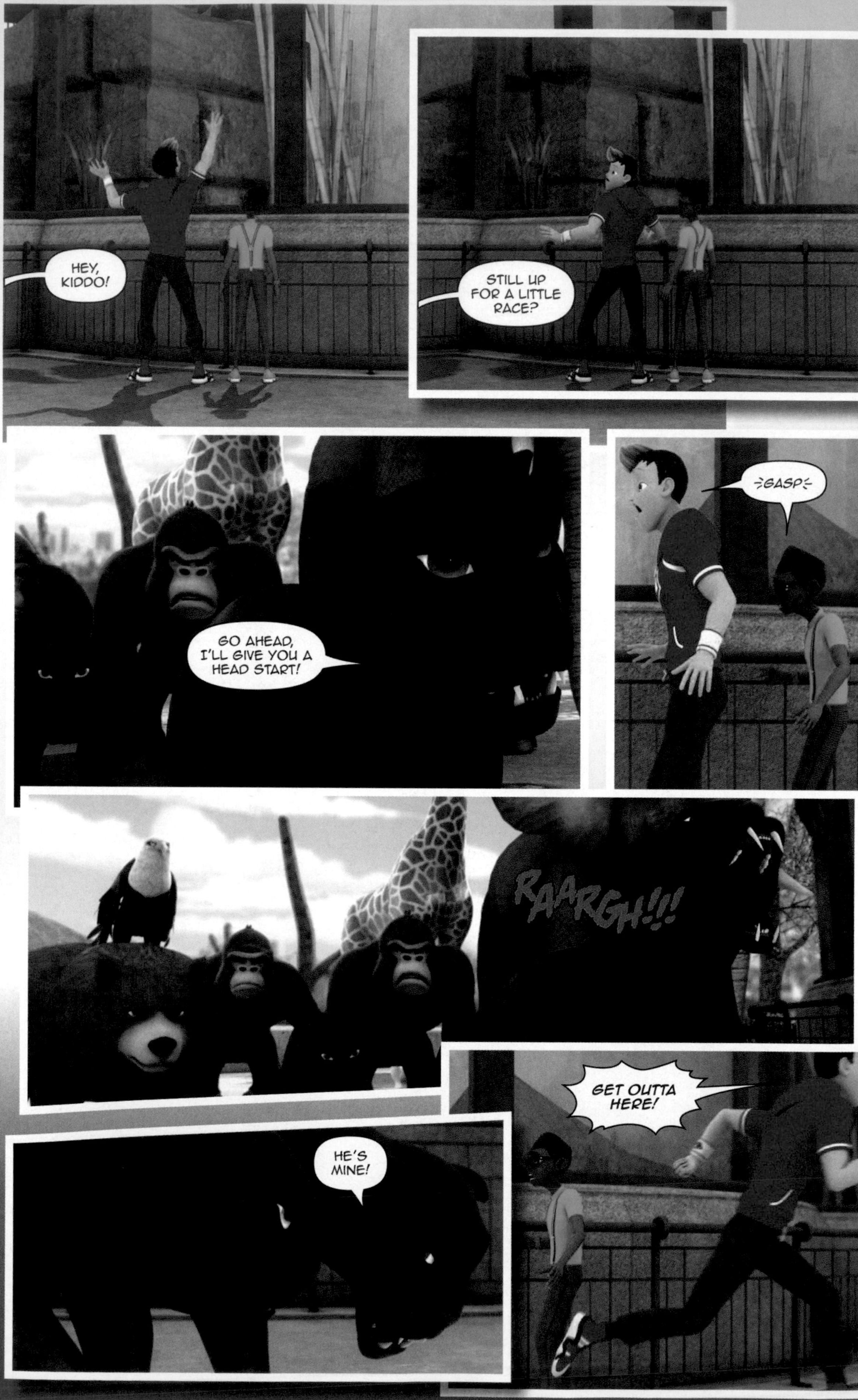
HEY, KIDDO!
STILL UP FOR A LITTLE RACE?
GO AHEAD, I'LL GIVE YOU A HEAD START!
GASP
RAARGH!!!
HE'S MINE!
GET OUTTA HERE!

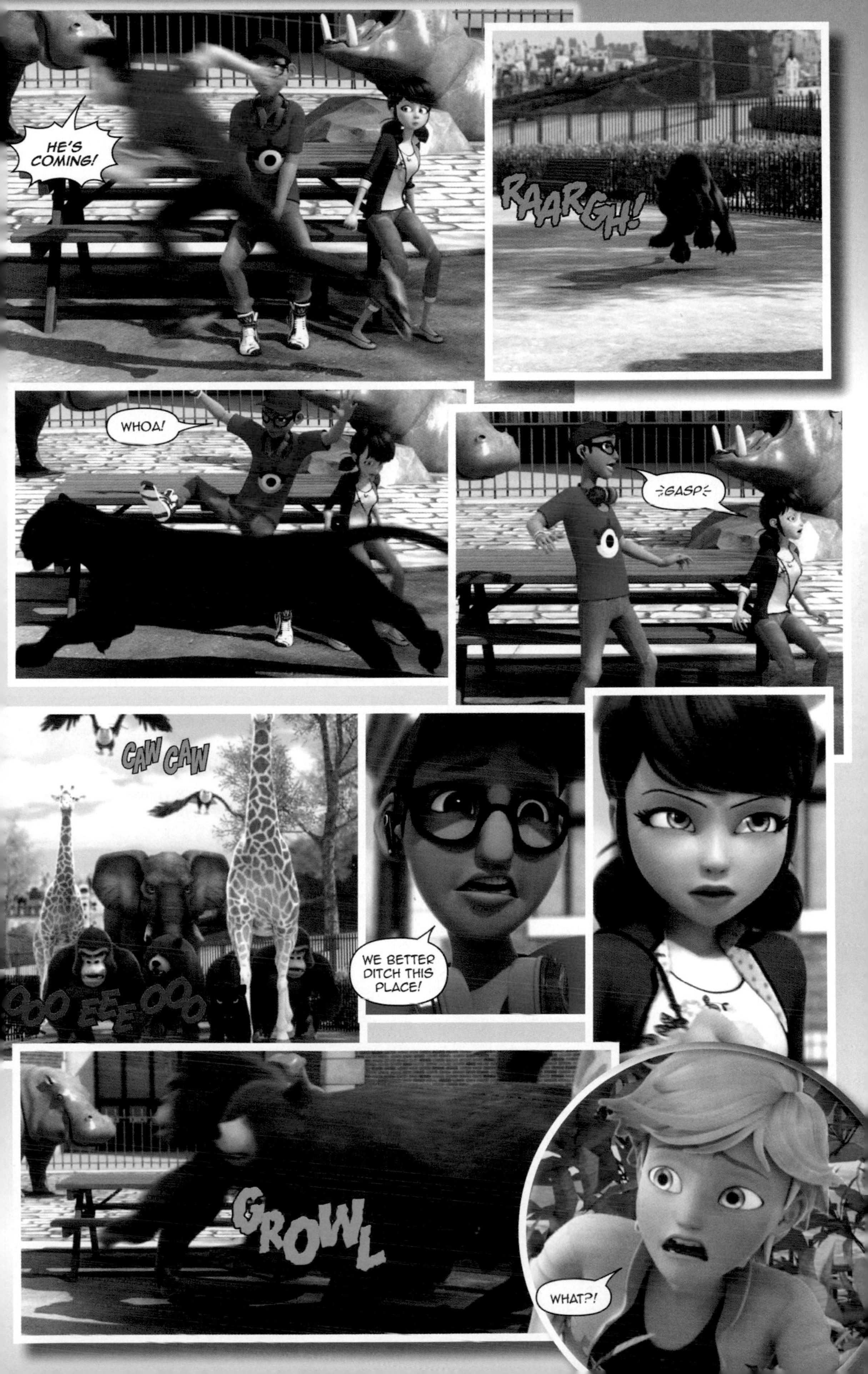
HE'S COMING!
RAARGH!
WHOA!
-GASP-
CAW CAW
OOO EEE OOO
WE BETTER DITCH THIS PLACE!
GROWL
WHAT?!

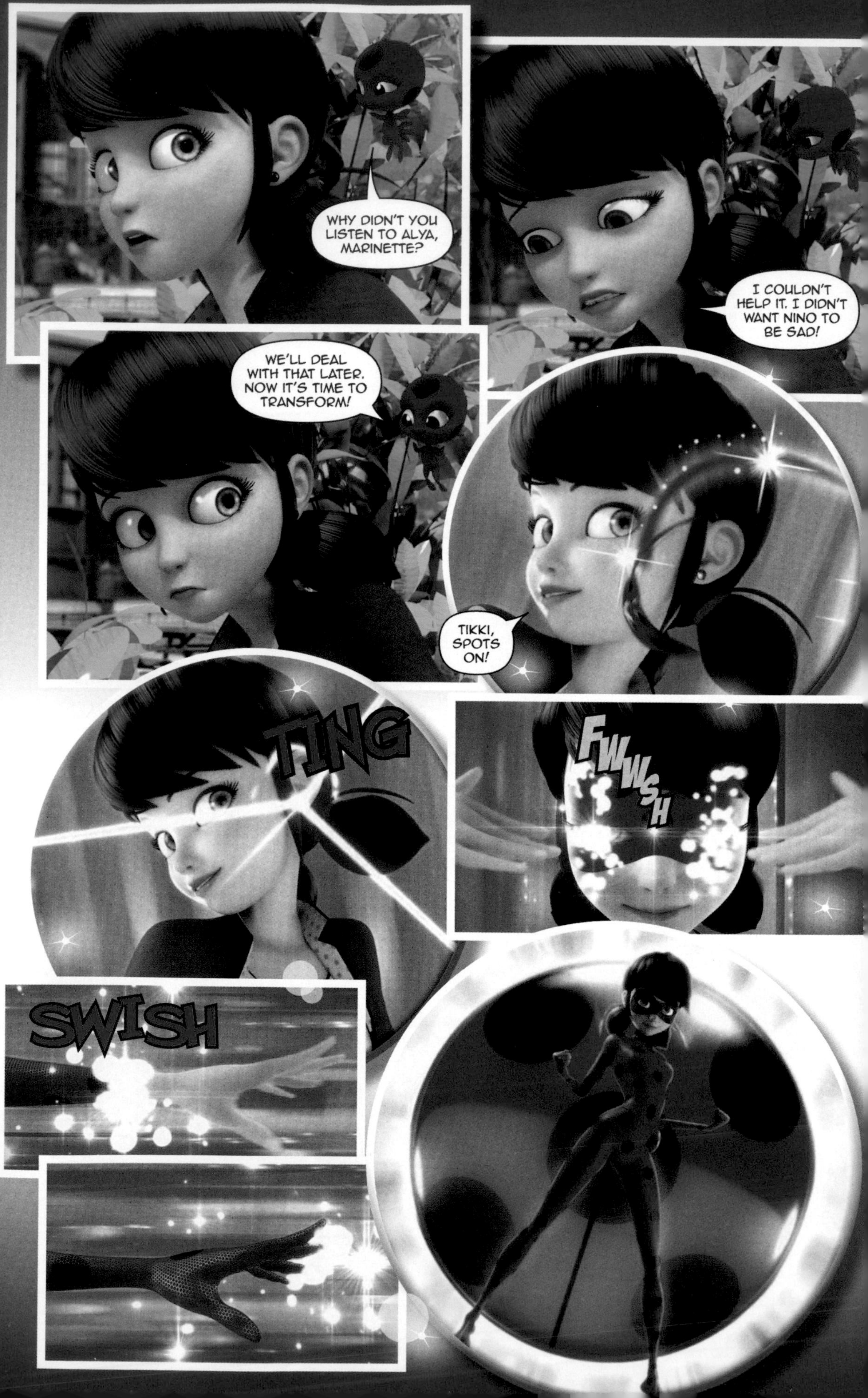
WHY DIDN'T YOU LISTEN TO ALYA, MARINETTE?
I COULDN'T HELP IT. I DIDN'T WANT NINO TO BE SAD!
WE'LL DEAL WITH THAT LATER. NOW IT'S TIME TO TRANSFORM!
TIKKI, SPOTS ON!
TING
FWWSH
SWISH

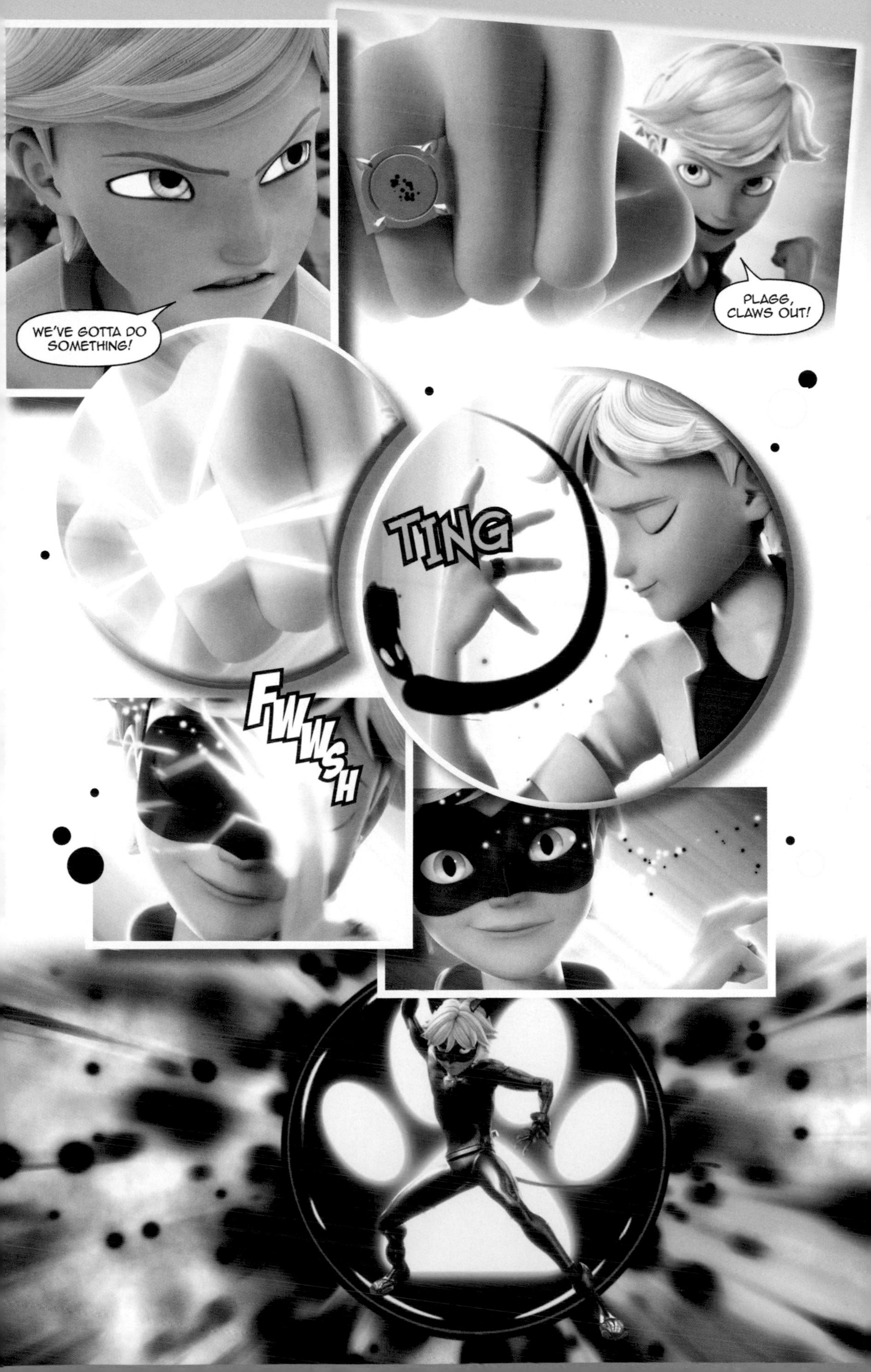
WE'VE GOTTA DO SOMETHING!
PLAGG, CLAWS OUT!
TING
FWWSH

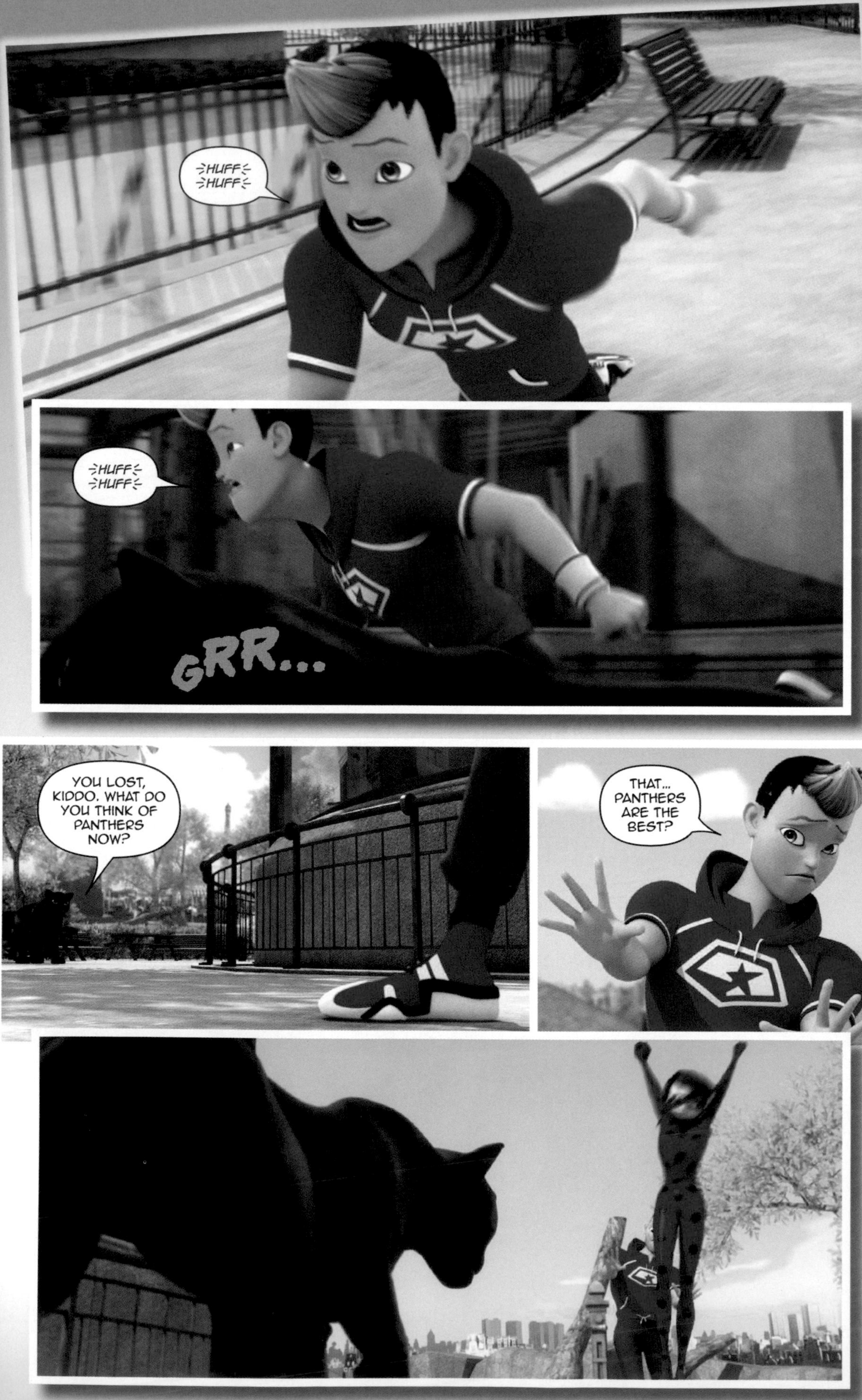
HUFF HUFF
HUFF HUFF
GRR...
YOU LOST, KIDDO. WHAT DO YOU THINK OF PANTHERS NOW?
THAT... PANTHERS ARE THE BEST?

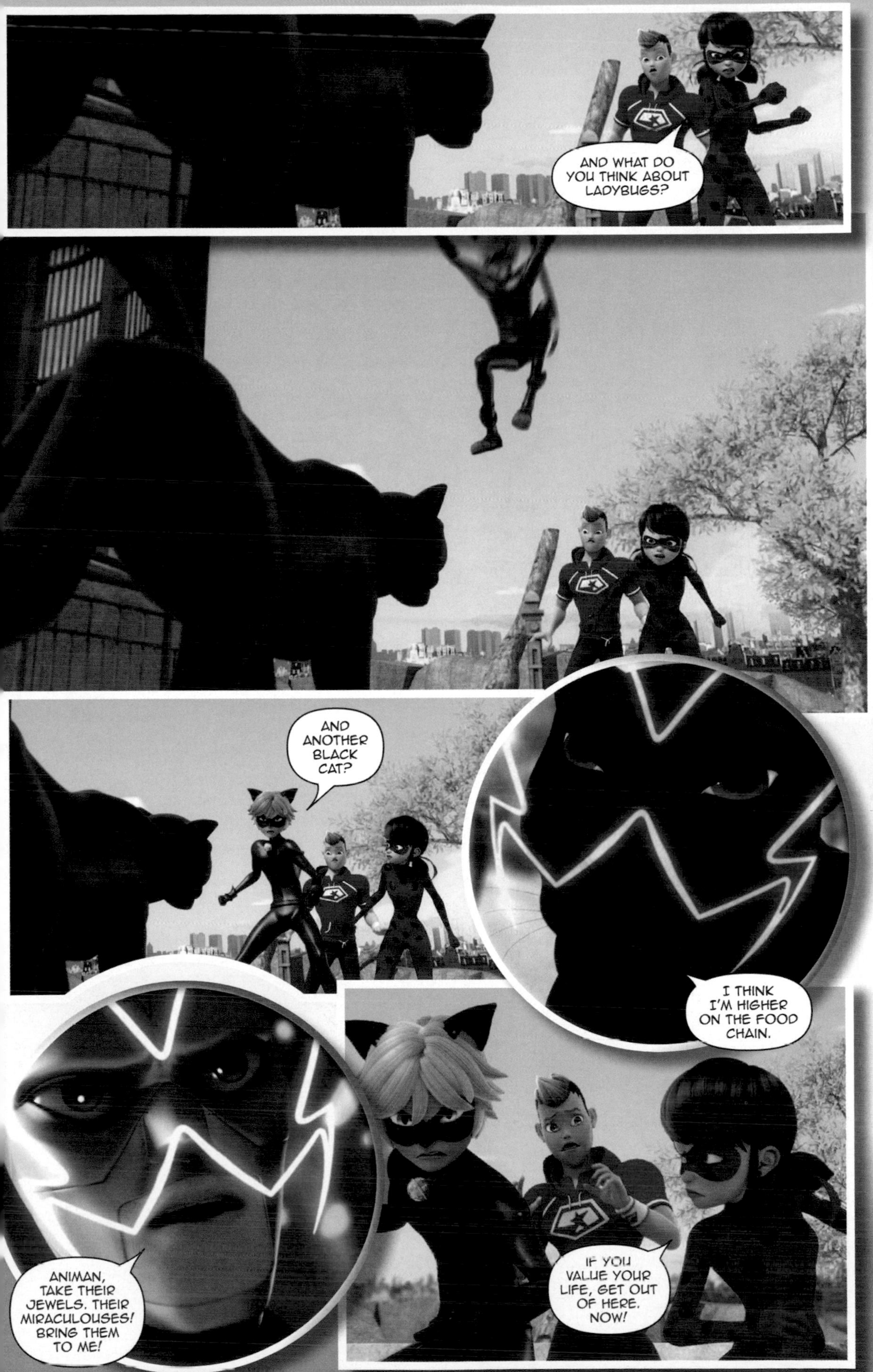
AND WHAT DO YOU THINK ABOUT LADYBUGS?
AND ANOTHER BLACK CAT?
I THINK I'M HIGHER ON THE FOOD CHAIN.
ANIMAN, TAKE THEIR JEWELS. THEIR MIRACULOUSES! BRING THEM TO ME!
IF YOU VALUE YOUR LIFE, GET OUT OF HERE. NOW!

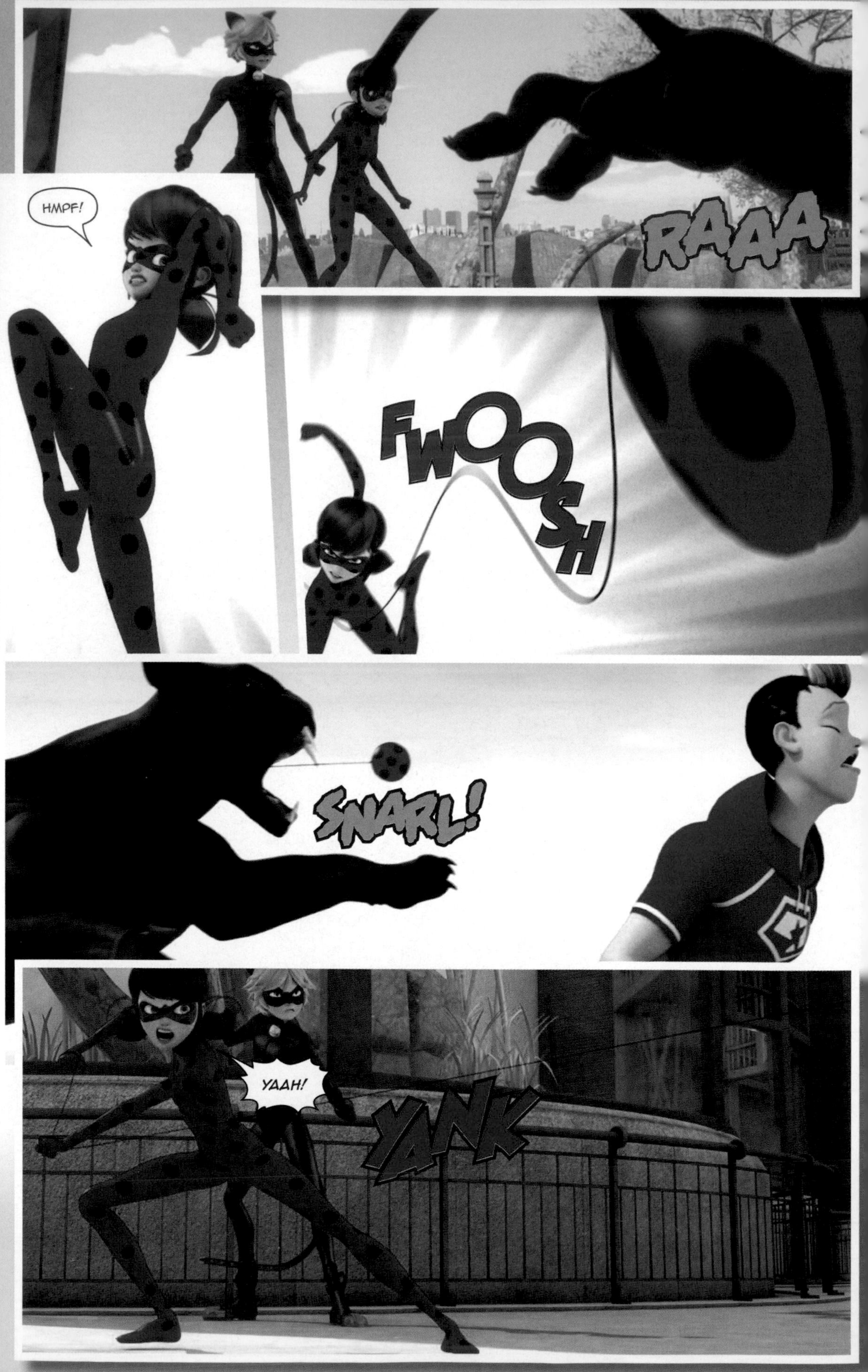
RAAA
HMPF!
FWOOSH
SNARL!
YAAH!
YANK

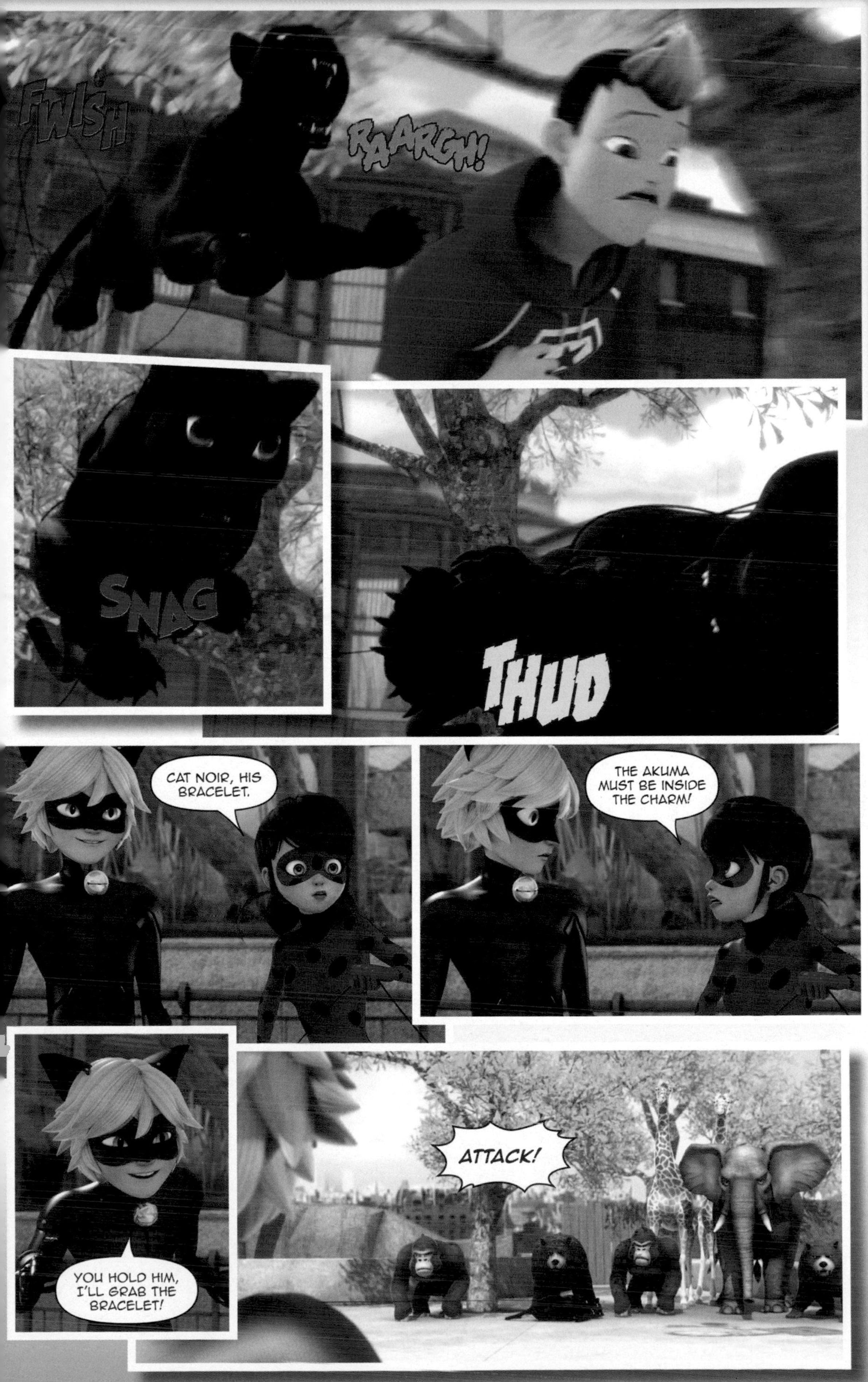
FWISH
RAARGH!
SNAG
THUD
CAT NOIR, HIS BRACELET.
THE AKUMA MUST BE INSIDE THE CHARM!
YOU HOLD HIM, I'LL GRAB THE BRACELET!
ATTACK!

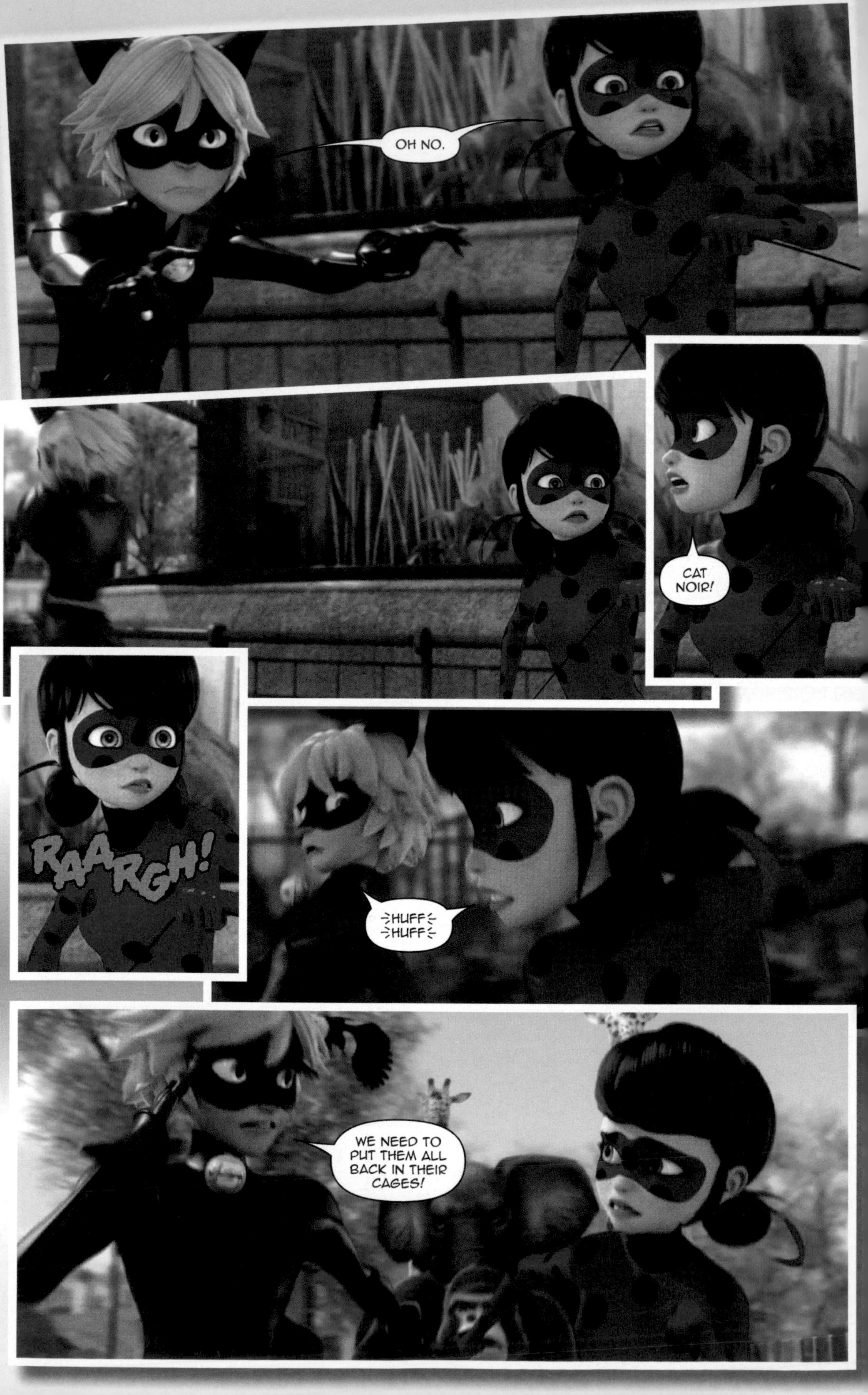
OH NO.
CAT NOIR!
RAARGH!
HUFF HUFF
WE NEED TO PUT THEM ALL BACK IN THEIR CAGES!

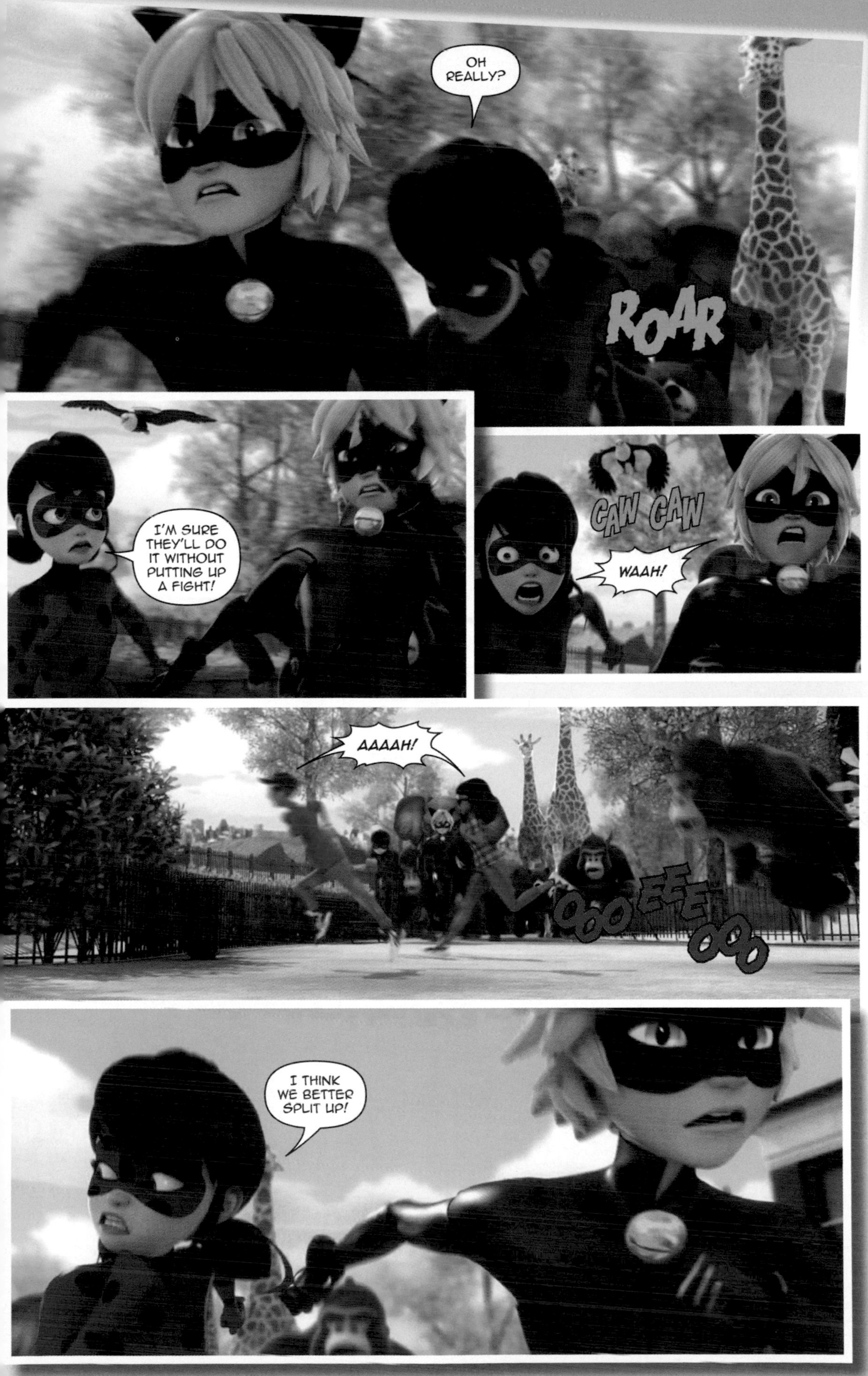
OH REALLY?
ROAR
I'M SURE THEY'LL DO IT WITHOUT PUTTING UP A FIGHT!
CAW CAW
WAAH!
AAAAH!
OOOEEEOOO
I THINK WE BETTER SPLIT UP!

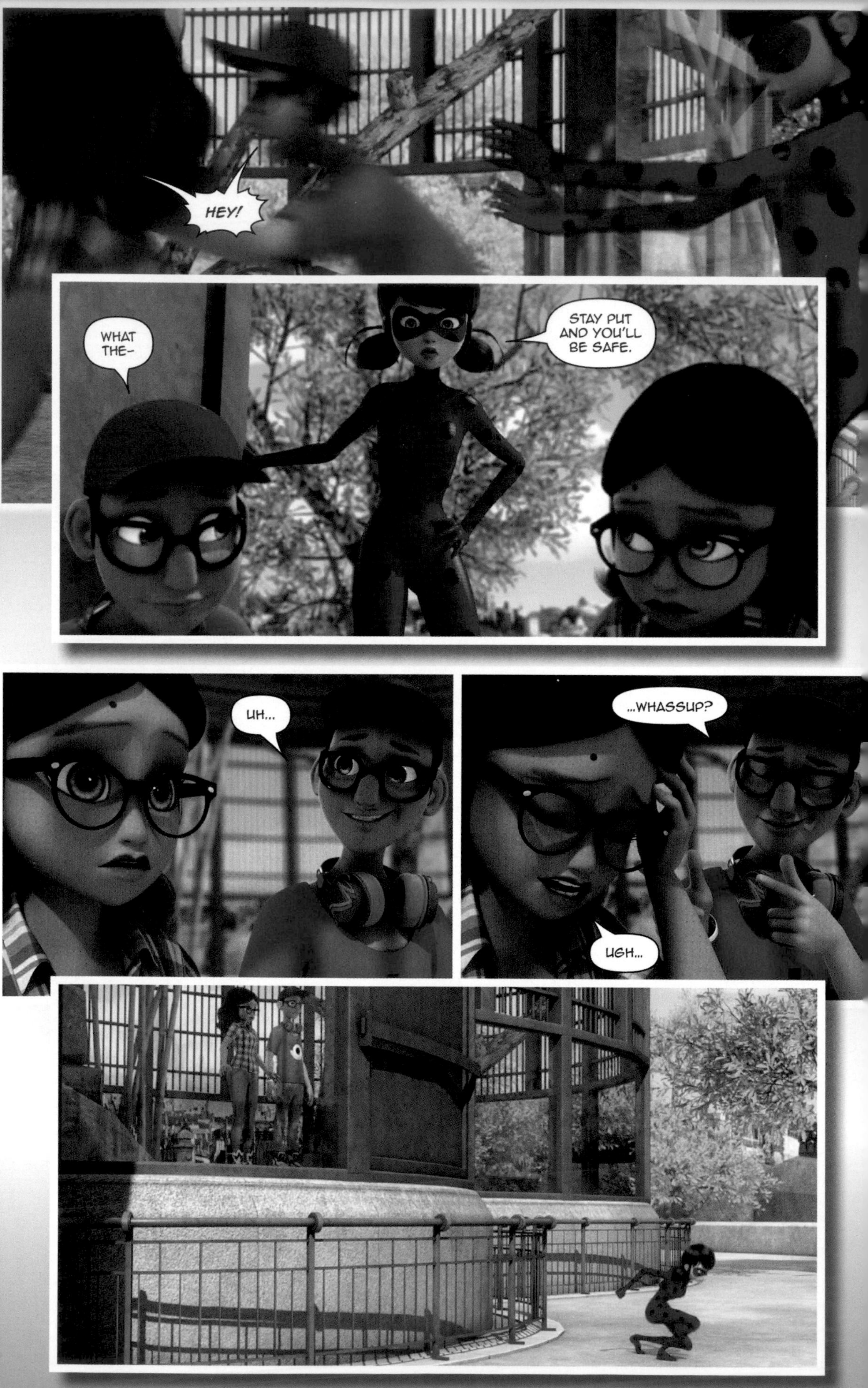
HEY!
WHAT THE-
STAY PUT AND YOU'LL BE SAFE.
UH...
...WHASSUP?
UGH...

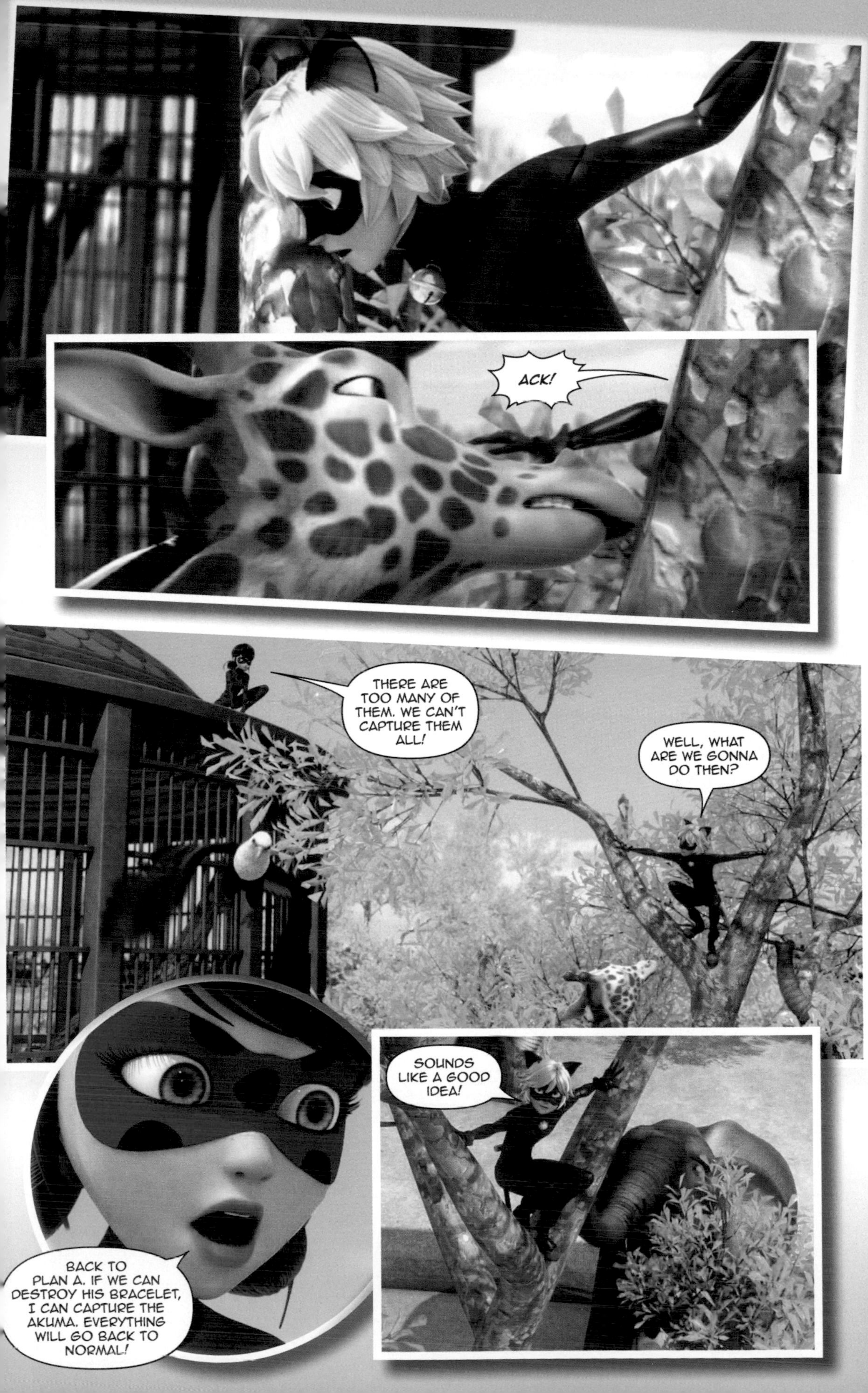
ACK!
THERE ARE TOO MANY OF THEM. WE CAN'T CAPTURE THEM ALL!
WELL, WHAT ARE WE GONNA DO THEN?
BACK TO PLAN A. IF WE CAN DESTROY HIS BRACELET, I CAN CAPTURE THE AKUMA. EVERYTHING WILL GO BACK TO NORMAL!
SOUNDS LIKE A GOOD IDEA!

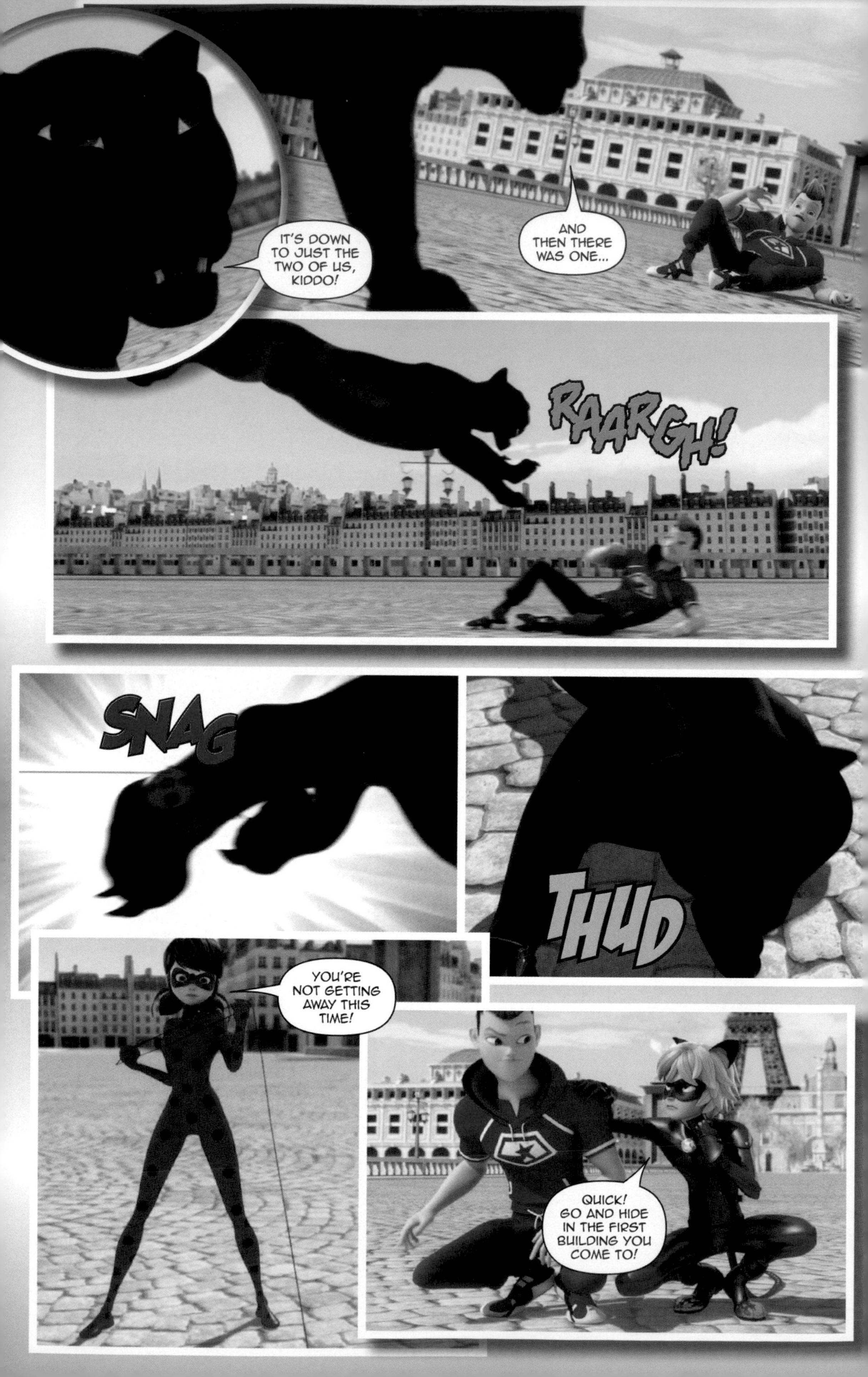
IT'S DOWN TO JUST THE TWO OF US, KIDDO!
AND THEN THERE WAS ONE...
RAARGH!
SNAG
THUD
YOU'RE NOT GETTING AWAY THIS TIME!
QUICK! GO AND HIDE IN THE FIRST BUILDING YOU COME TO!

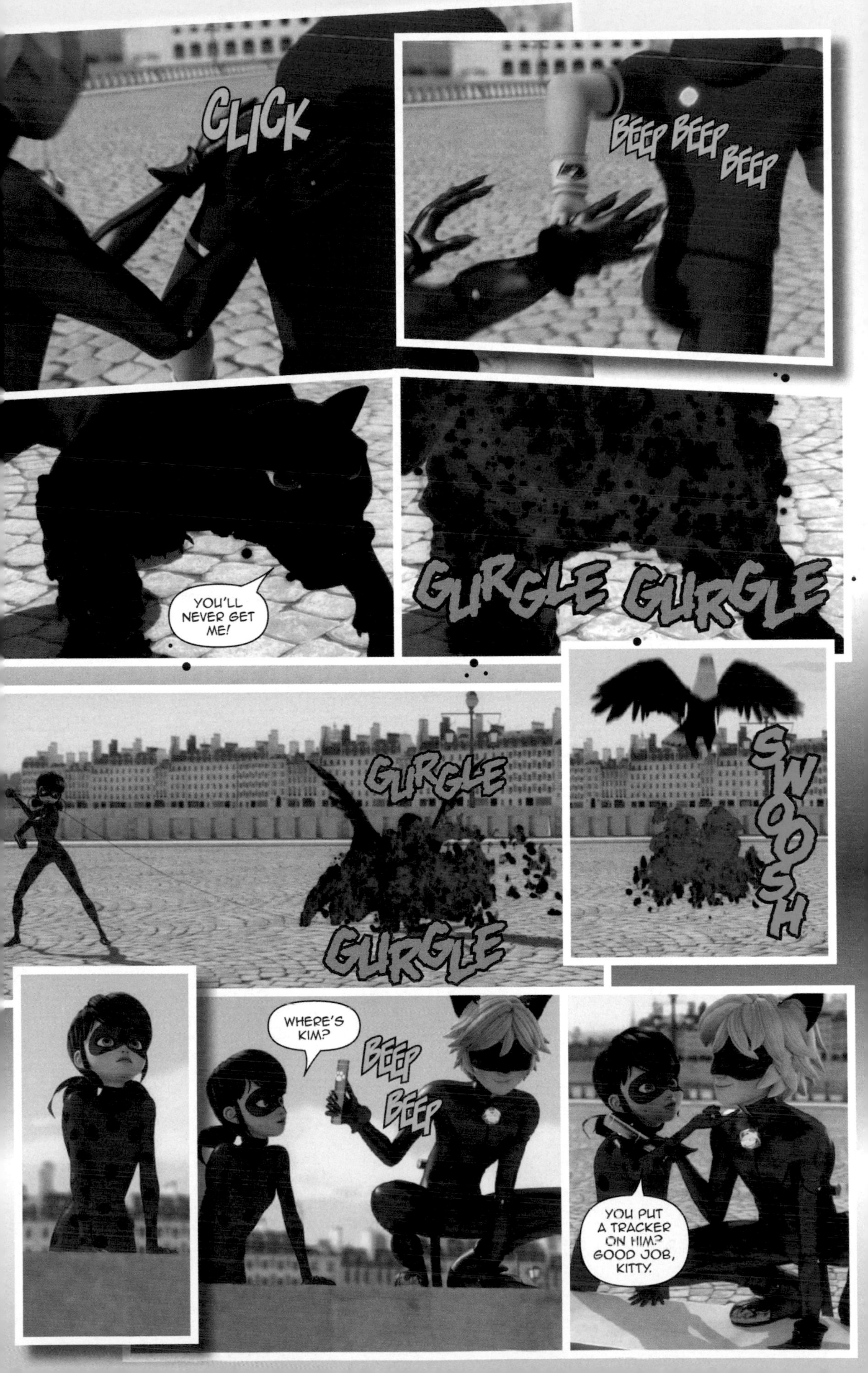
CLICK
BEEP BEEP BEEP
YOU'LL NEVER GET ME!
GURGLE GURGLE
GURGLE
GURGLE
SWOOSH
WHERE'S KIM?
BEEP BEEP
YOU PUT A TRACKER ON HIM? GOOD JOB, KITTY.

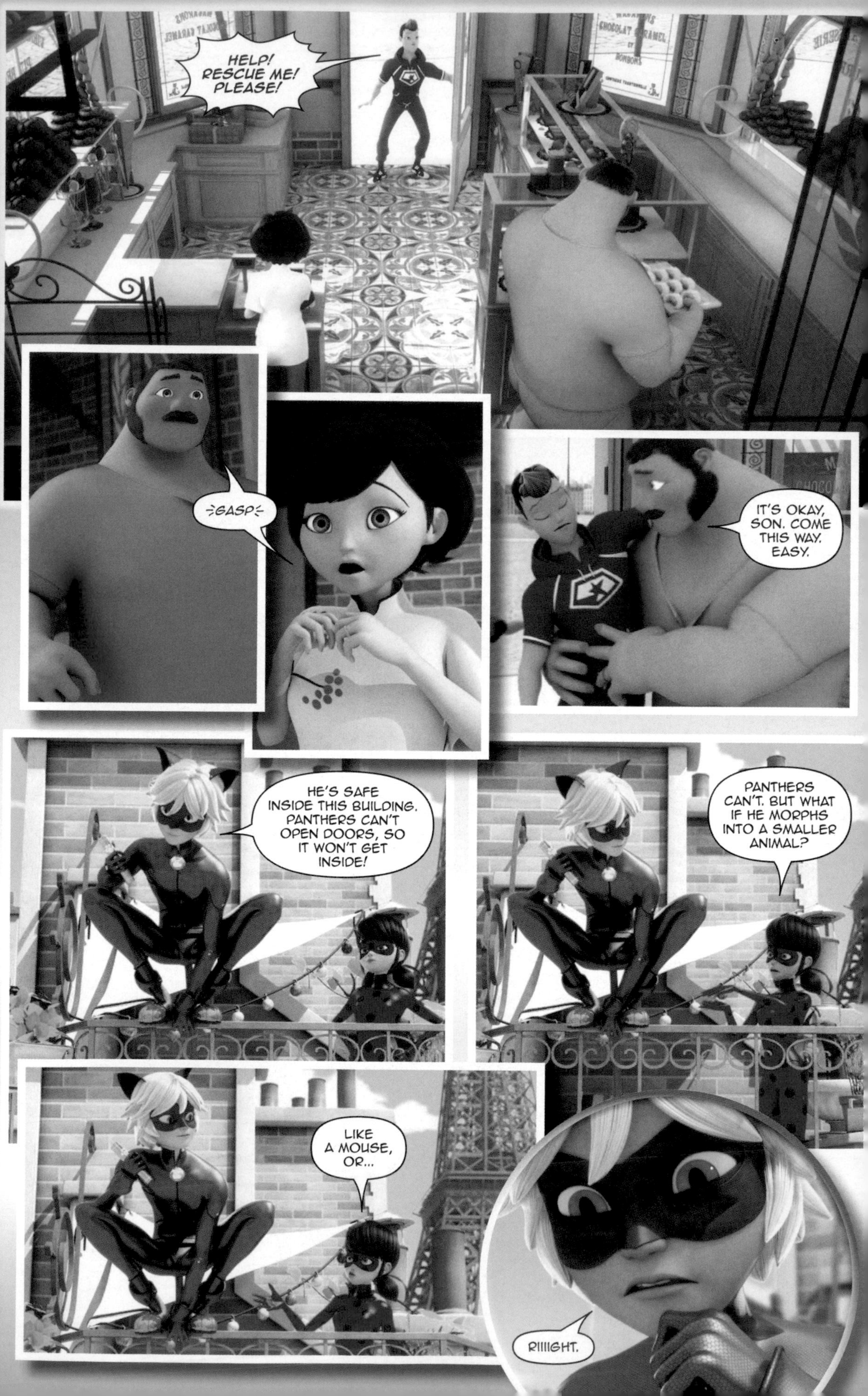
HELP! RESCUE ME! PLEASE!
GASP
IT'S OKAY, SON. COME THIS WAY. EASY.
HE'S SAFE INSIDE THIS BUILDING. PANTHERS CAN'T OPEN DOORS, SO IT WON'T GET INSIDE!
PANTHERS CAN'T. BUT WHAT IF HE MORPHS INTO A SMALLER ANIMAL?
LIKE A MOUSE, OR...
RIIIGHT.

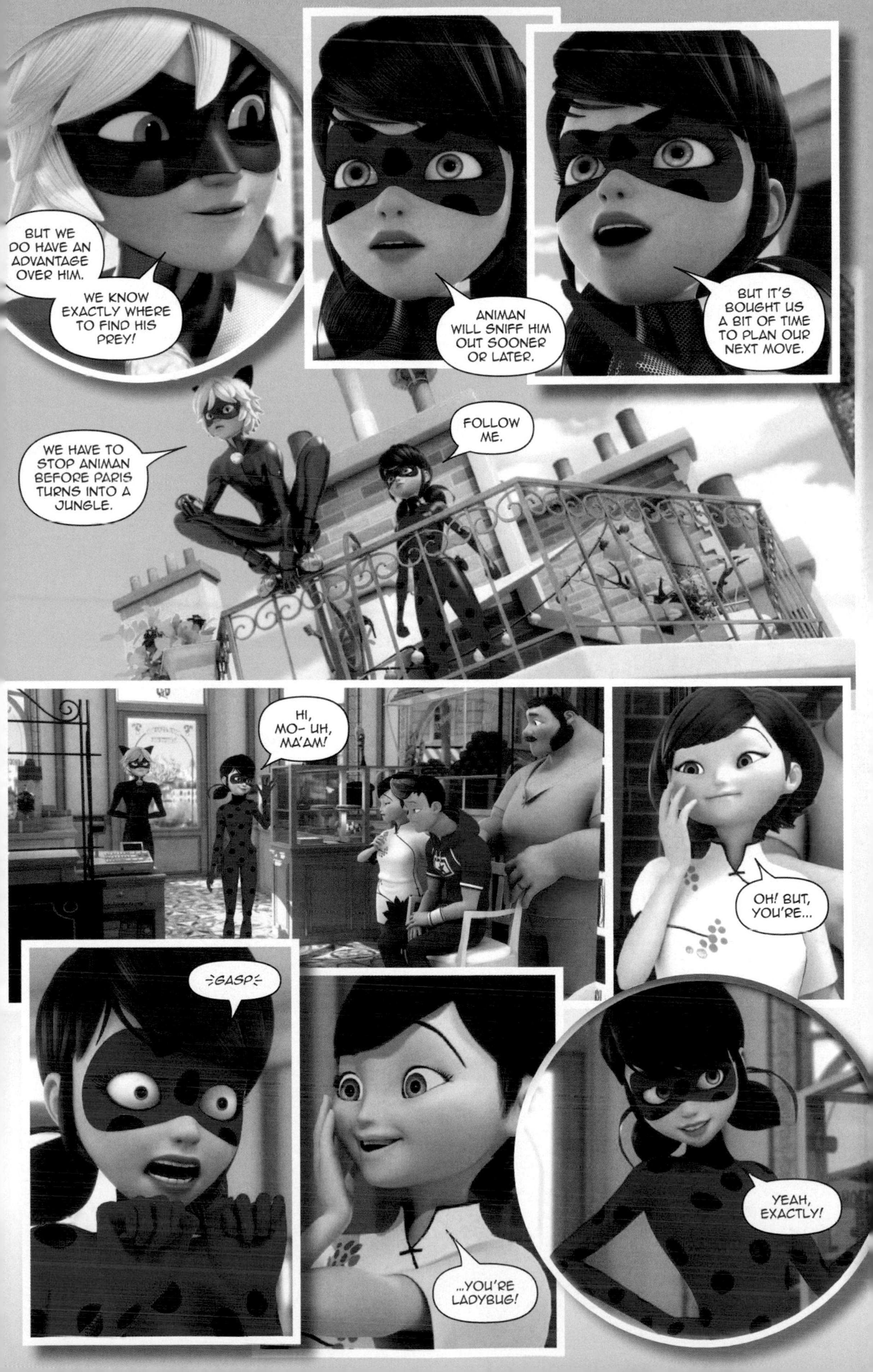
BUT WE DO HAVE AN ADVANTAGE OVER HIM.
WE KNOW EXACTLY WHERE TO FIND HIS PREY!
ANIMAN WILL SNIFF HIM OUT SOONER OR LATER.
BUT IT'S BOUGHT US A BIT OF TIME TO PLAN OUR NEXT MOVE.
WE HAVE TO STOP ANIMAN BEFORE PARIS TURNS INTO A JUNGLE.
FOLLOW ME.
HI, MO– UH, MA'AM!
OH! BUT, YOU'RE...
GASP
...YOU'RE LADYBUG!
YEAH, EXACTLY!

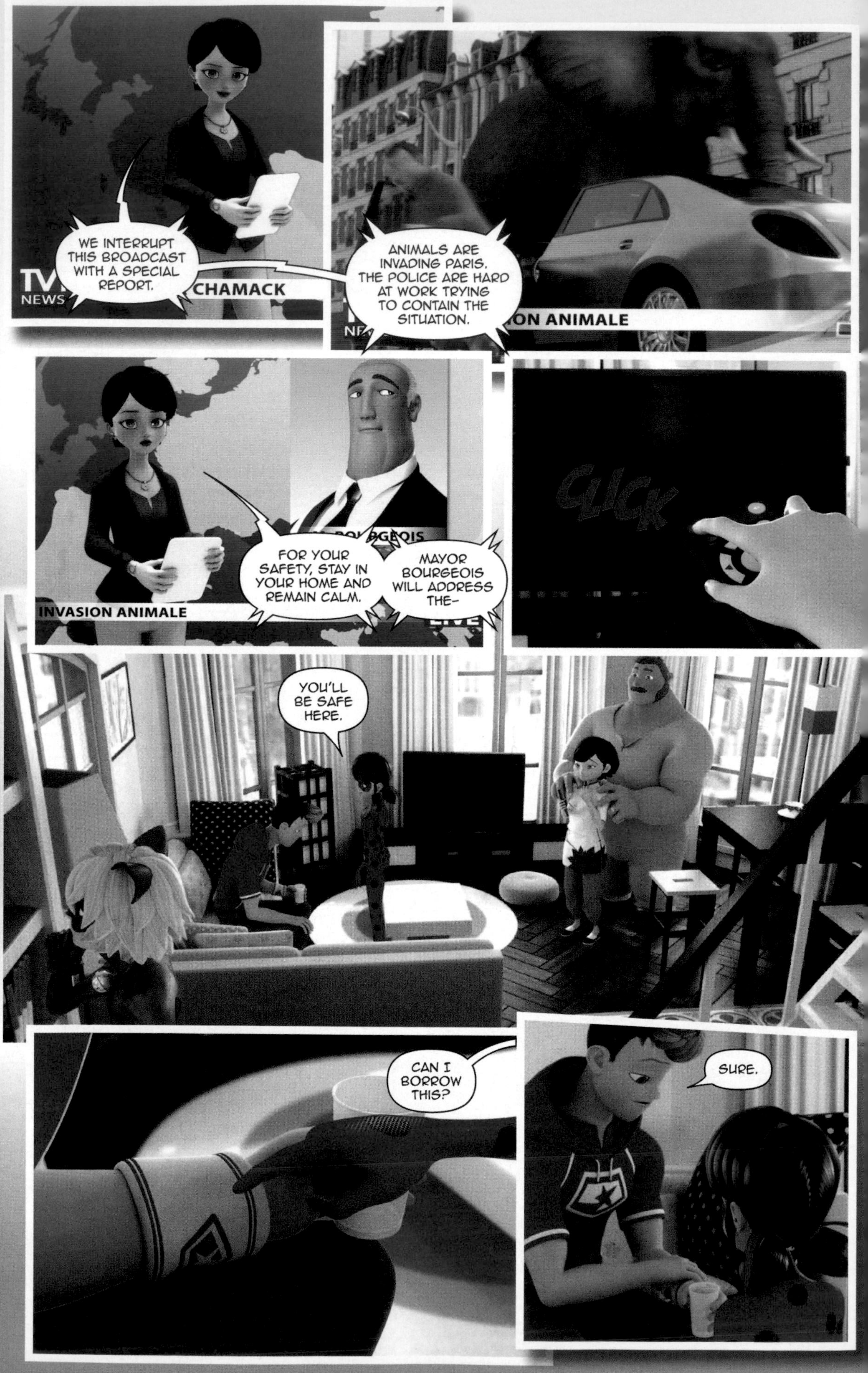
WE INTERRUPT THIS BROADCAST WITH A SPECIAL REPORT.
CHAMACK
NEWS
ANIMALS ARE INVADING PARIS. THE POLICE ARE HARD AT WORK TRYING TO CONTAIN THE SITUATION.
ON ANIMALE
FOR YOUR SAFETY, STAY IN YOUR HOME AND REMAIN CALM.
MAYOR BOURGEOIS WILL ADDRESS THE-
INVASION ANIMALE
CLICK
YOU'LL BE SAFE HERE.
CAN I BORROW THIS?
SURE.

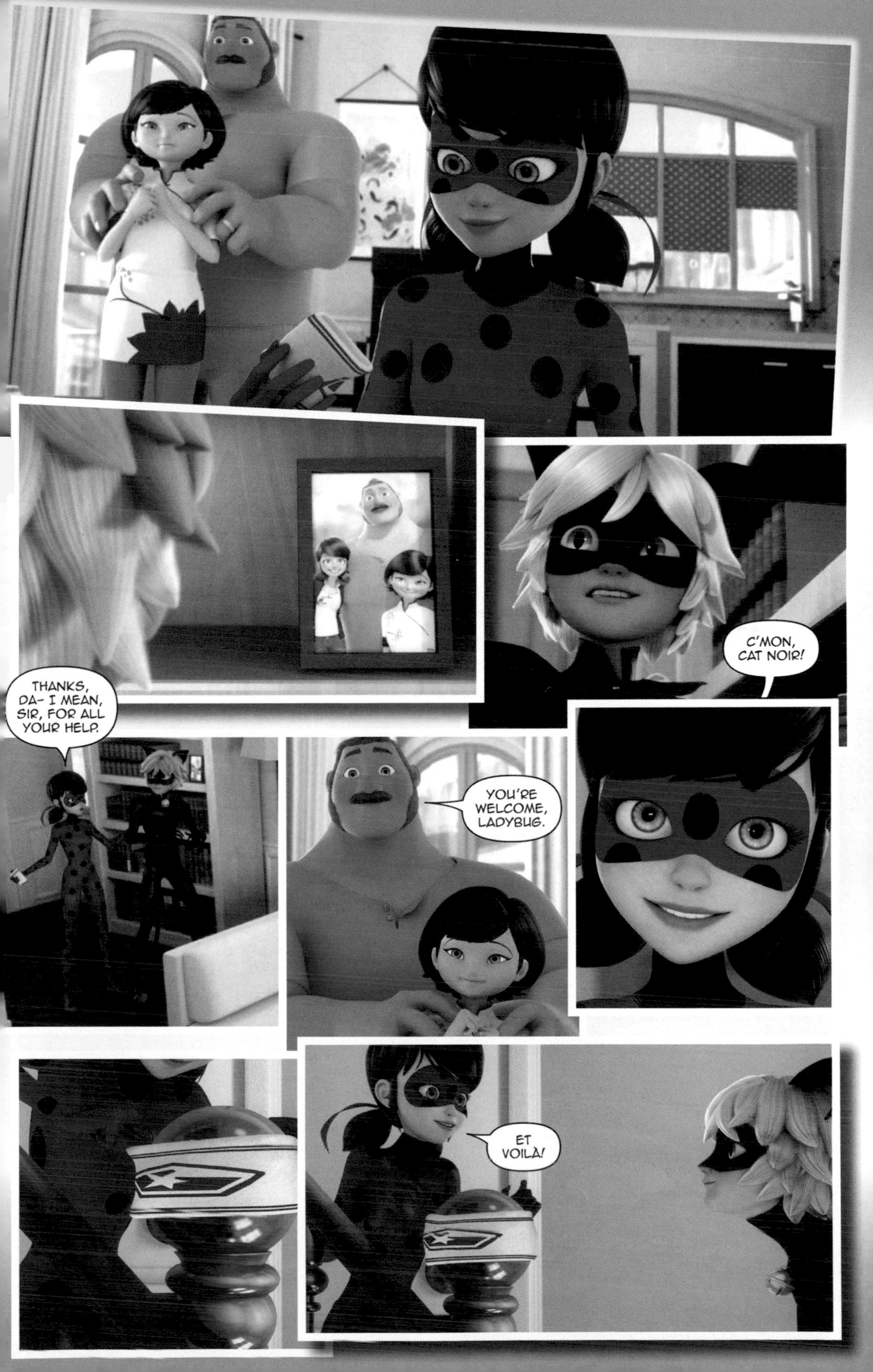
C'MON, CAT NOIR!
THANKS, DA– I MEAN, SIR, FOR ALL YOUR HELP.
YOU'RE WELCOME, LADYBUG.
ET VOILÀ!

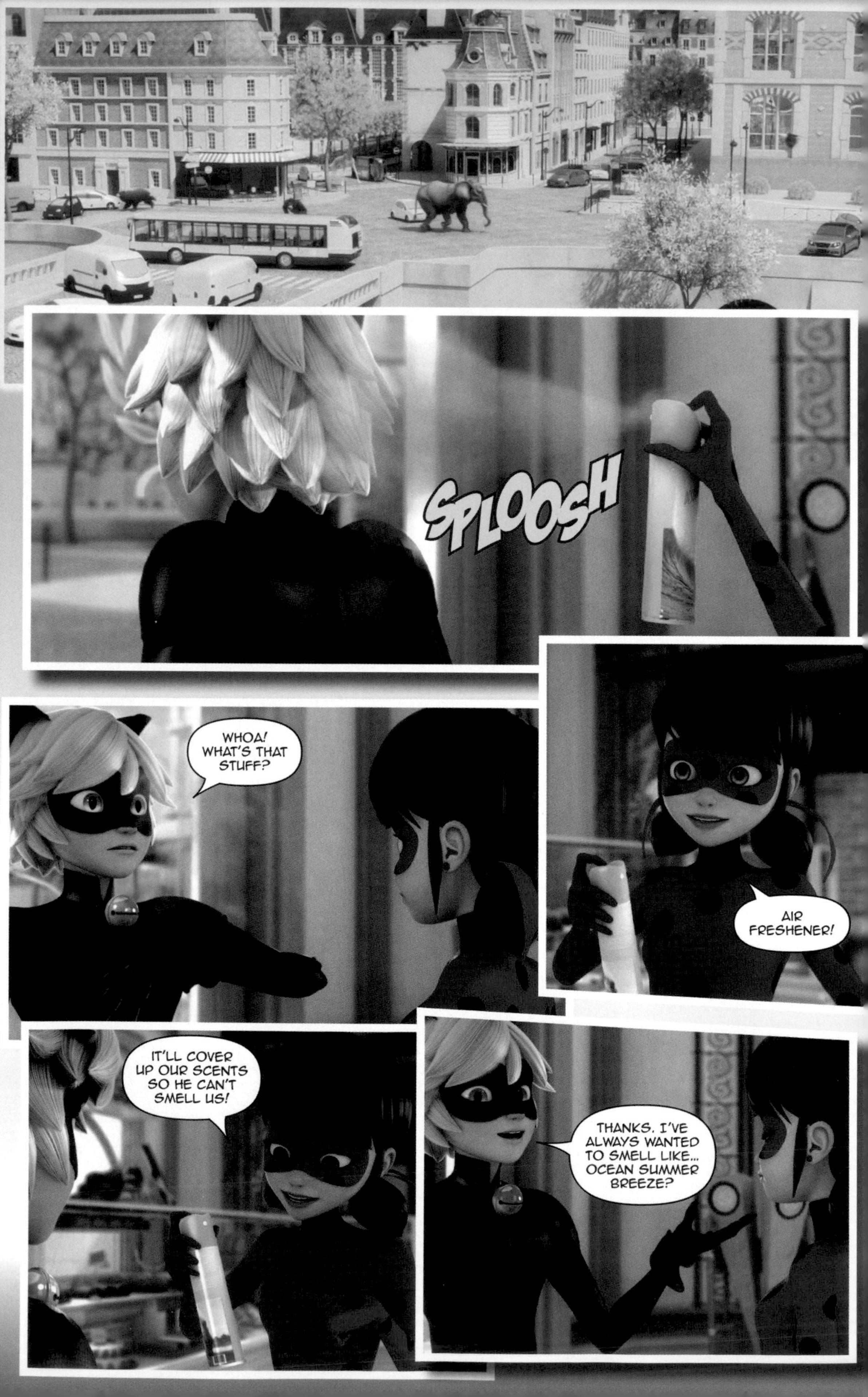
SPLOOSH
WHOA! WHAT'S THAT STUFF?
AIR FRESHENER!
IT'LL COVER UP OUR SCENTS SO HE CAN'T SMELL US!
THANKS. I'VE ALWAYS WANTED TO SMELL LIKE... OCEAN SUMMER BREEZE?

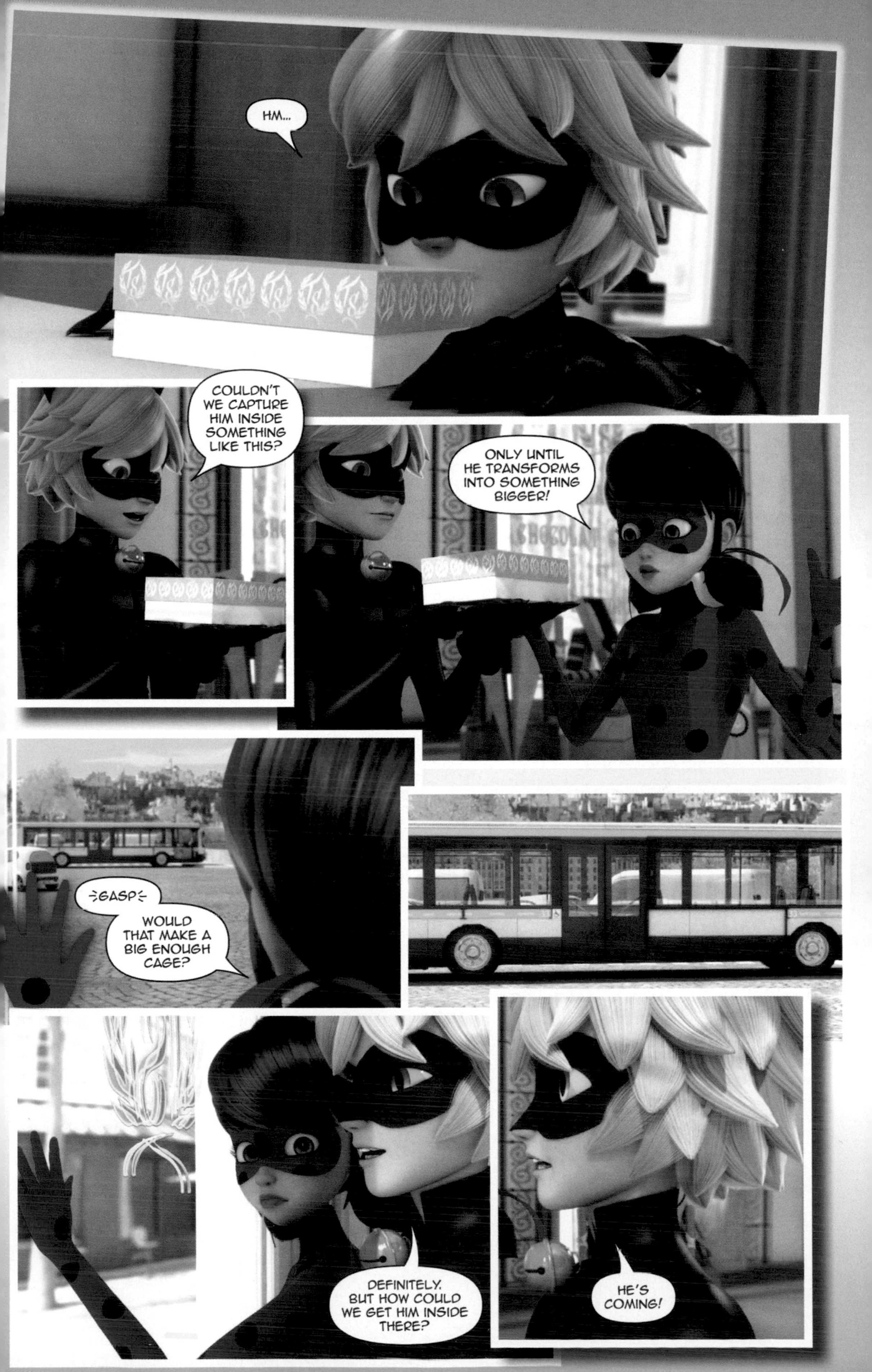
HM...
COULDN'T WE CAPTURE HIM INSIDE SOMETHING LIKE THIS?
ONLY UNTIL HE TRANSFORMS INTO SOMETHING BIGGER!
GASP
WOULD THAT MAKE A BIG ENOUGH CAGE?
DEFINITELY. BUT HOW COULD WE GET HIM INSIDE THERE?
HE'S COMING!

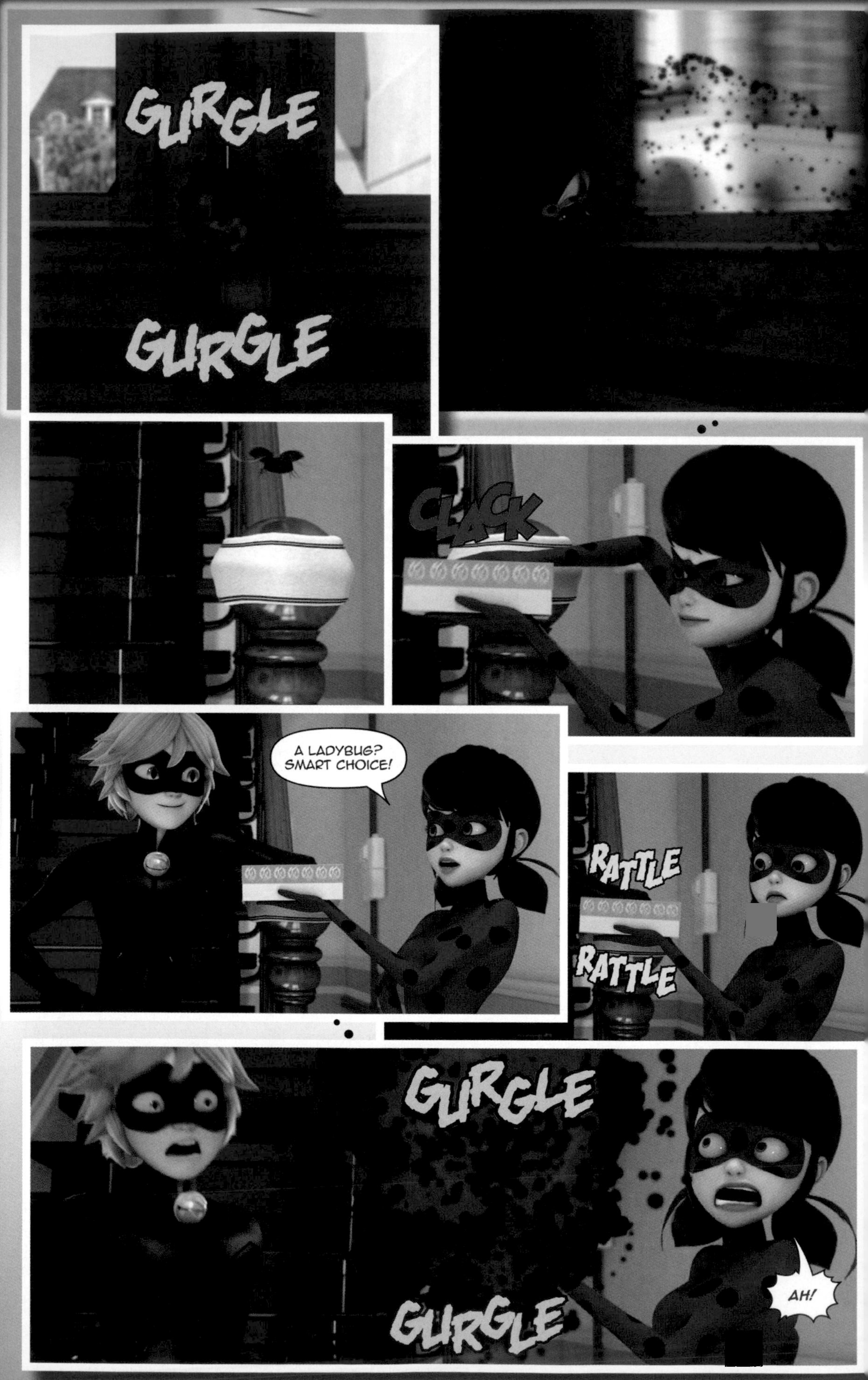
GURGLE
GURGLE
CLACK
A LADYBUG? SMART CHOICE!
RATTLE
RATTLE
GURGLE
AH!
GURGLE

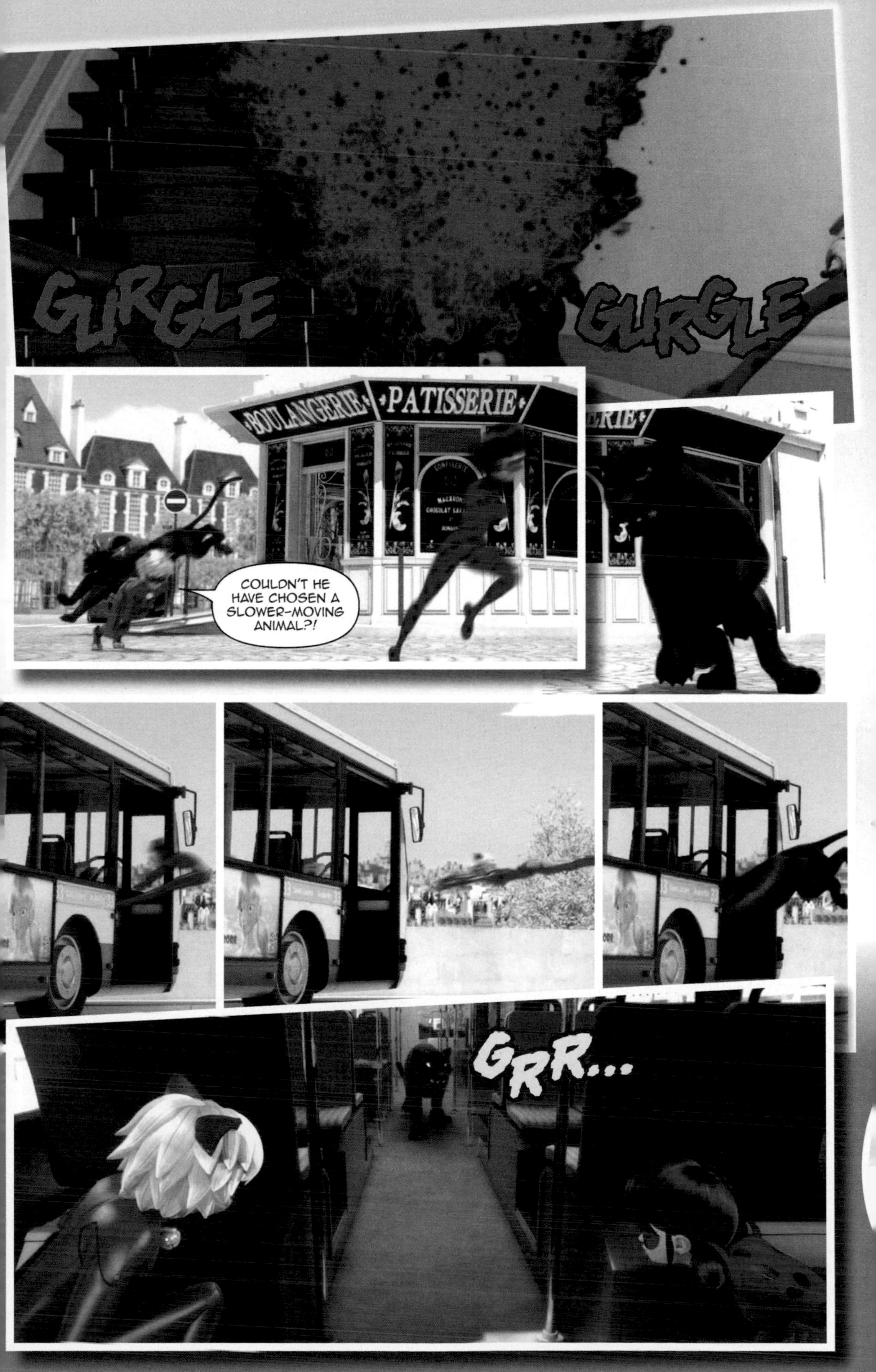
GURGLE
GURGLE
BOULANGERIE
PATISSERIE
CONFISERIE
MACARONS
CHOCOLAT
COULDN'T HE HAVE CHOSEN A SLOWER-MOVING ANIMAL?!
GRR...

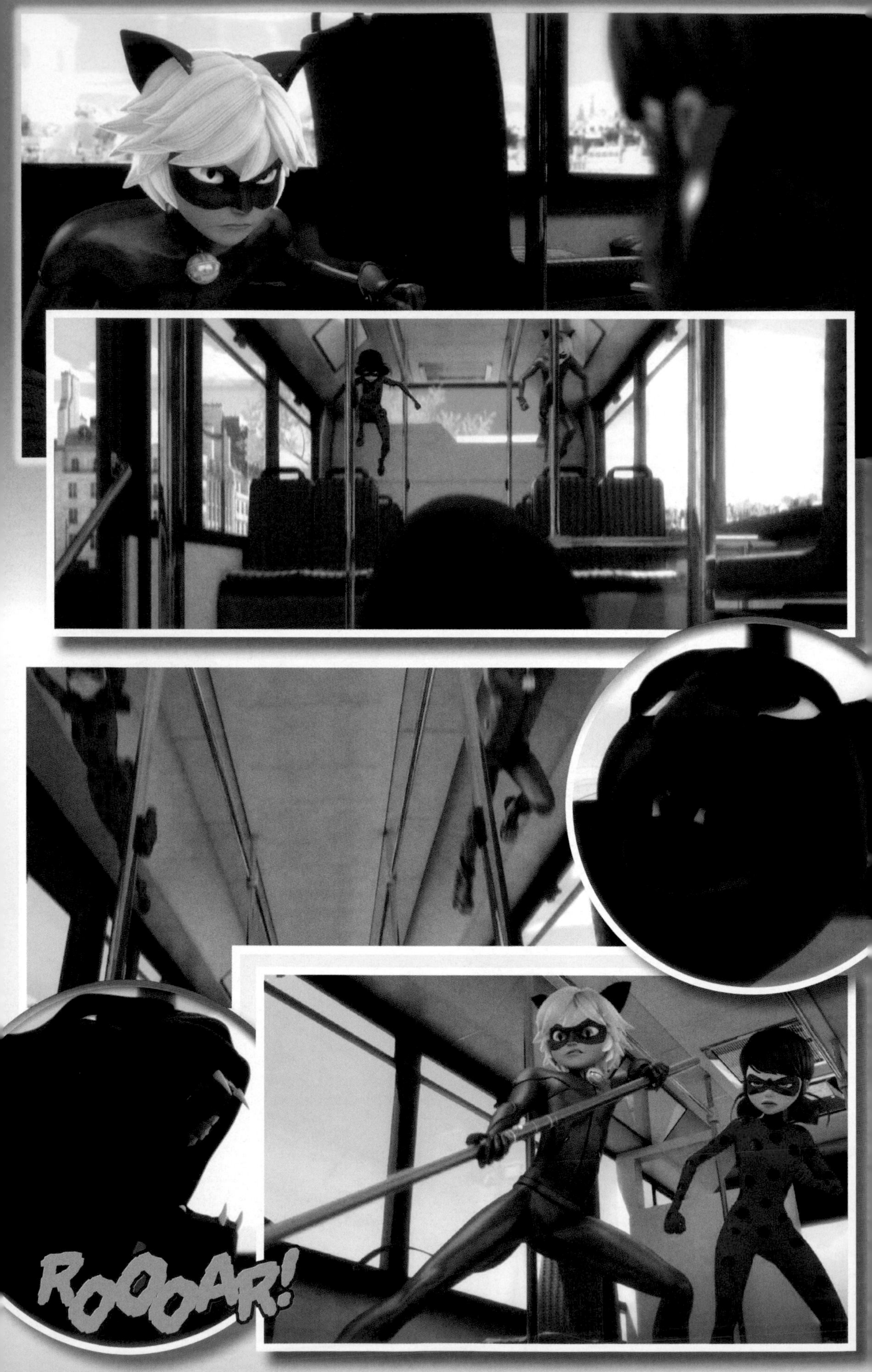
ROOOAR!

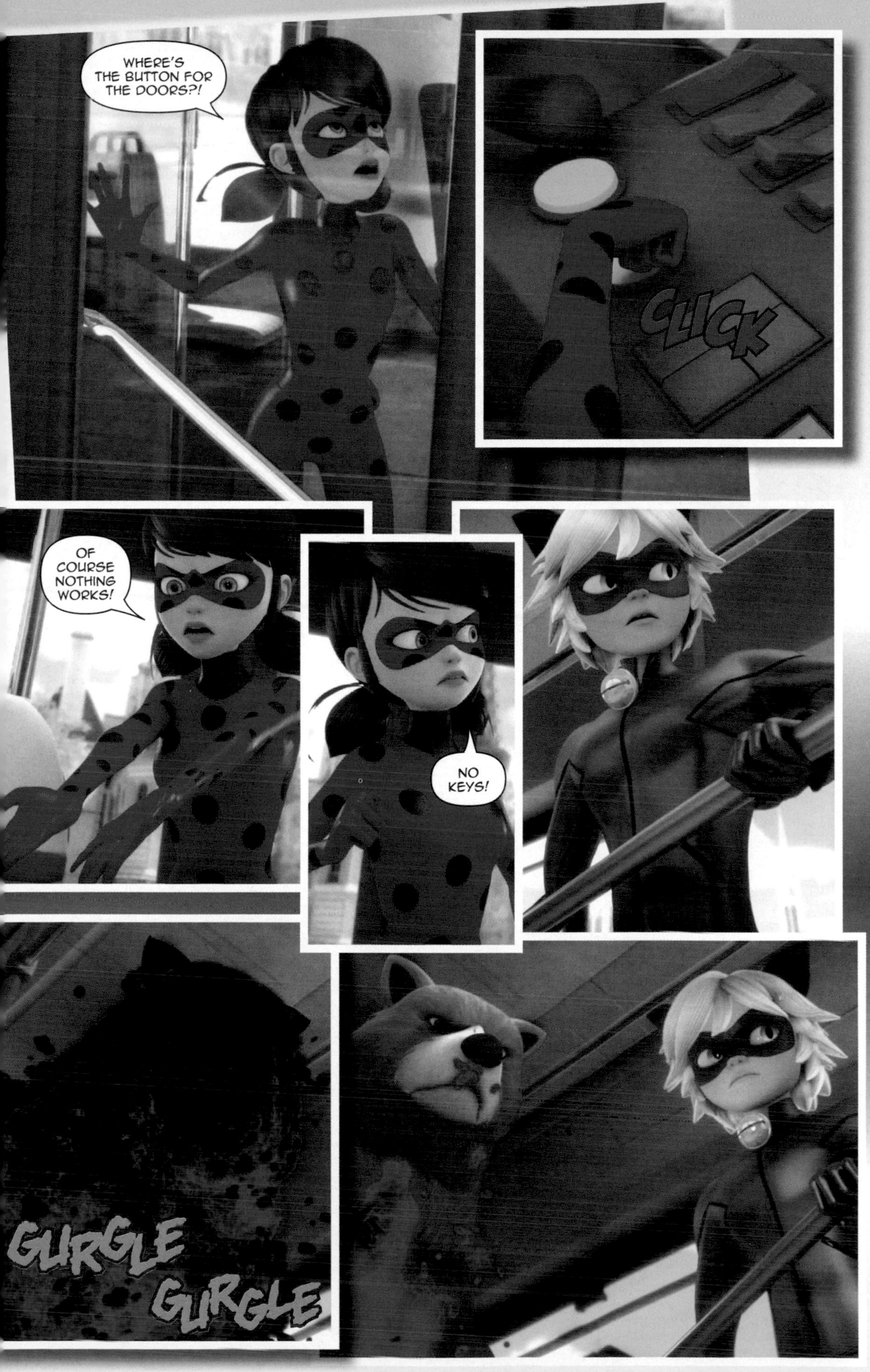

WHERE'S THE BUTTON FOR THE DOORS?!
CLICK
OF COURSE NOTHING WORKS!
NO KEYS!
GURGLE
GURGLE

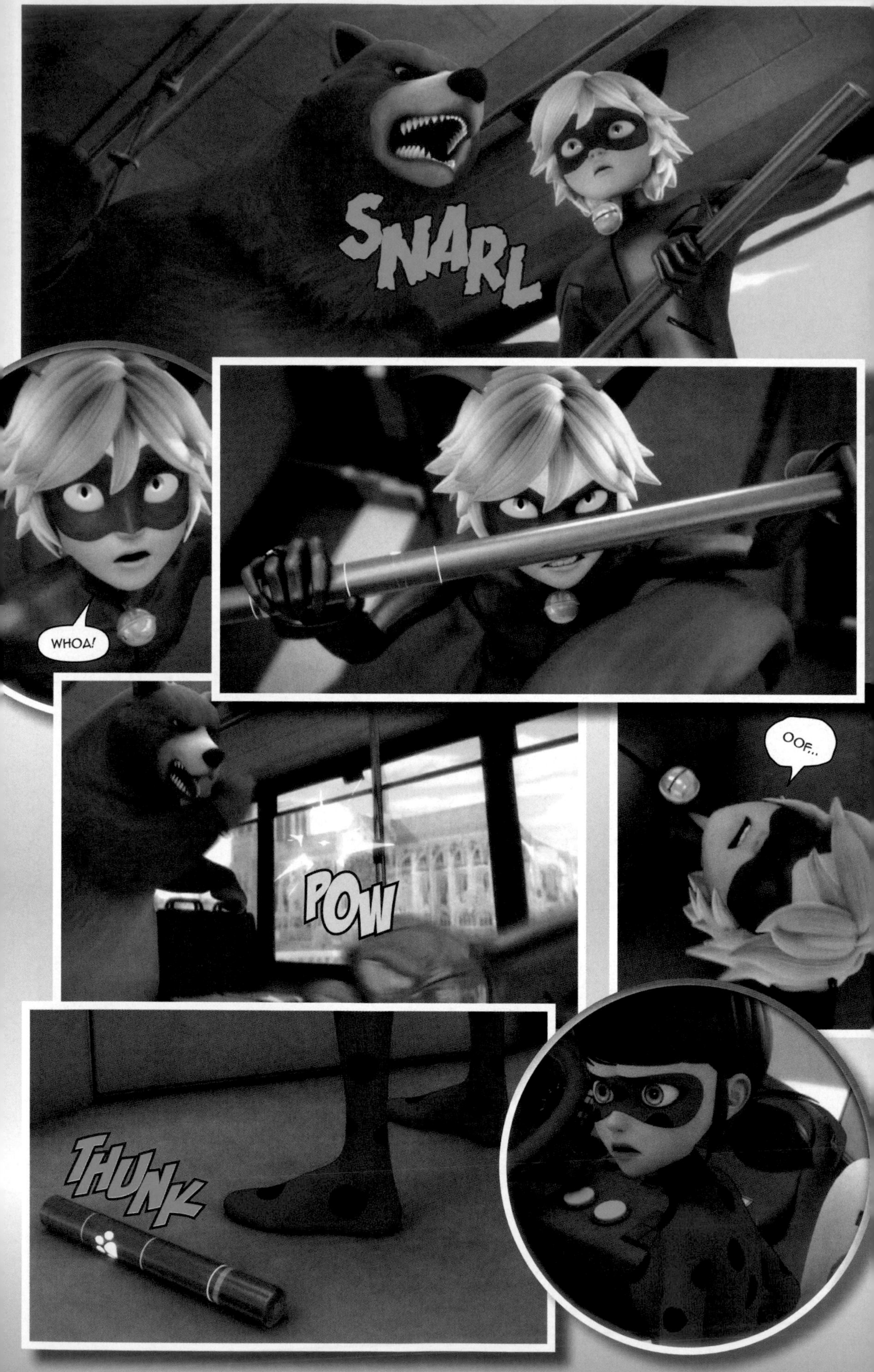
SNARL
WHOA!
POW
OOF...
THUNK

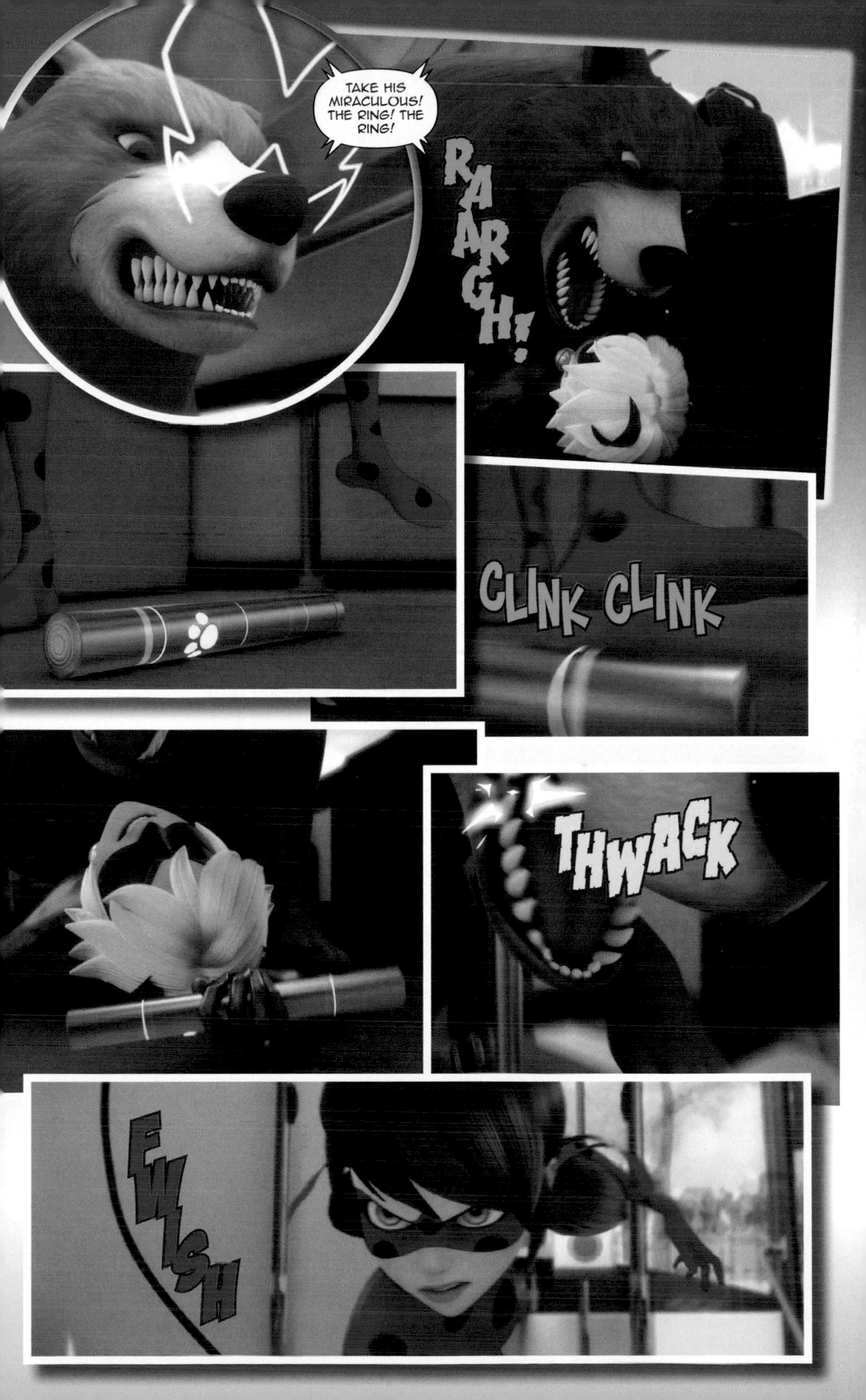
TAKE HIS MIRACULOUS! THE RING! THE RING!
RAARGH!
CLINK CLINK
THWACK
FWISH

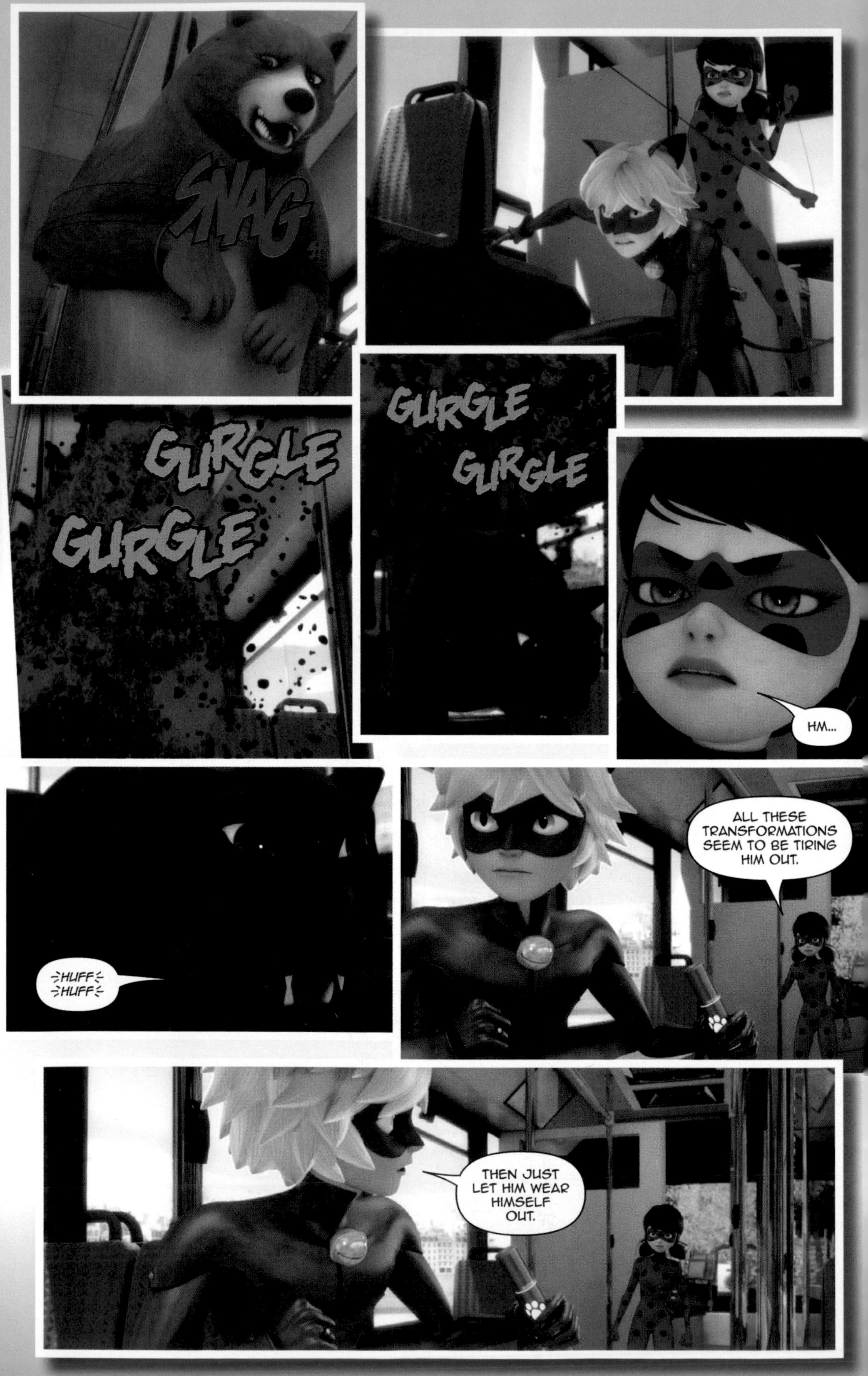
SNAG
GURGLE
GURGLE
GURGLE
GURGLE
HM...
HUFF
HUFF
ALL THESE TRANSFORMATIONS SEEM TO BE TIRING HIM OUT.
THEN JUST LET HIM WEAR HIMSELF OUT.

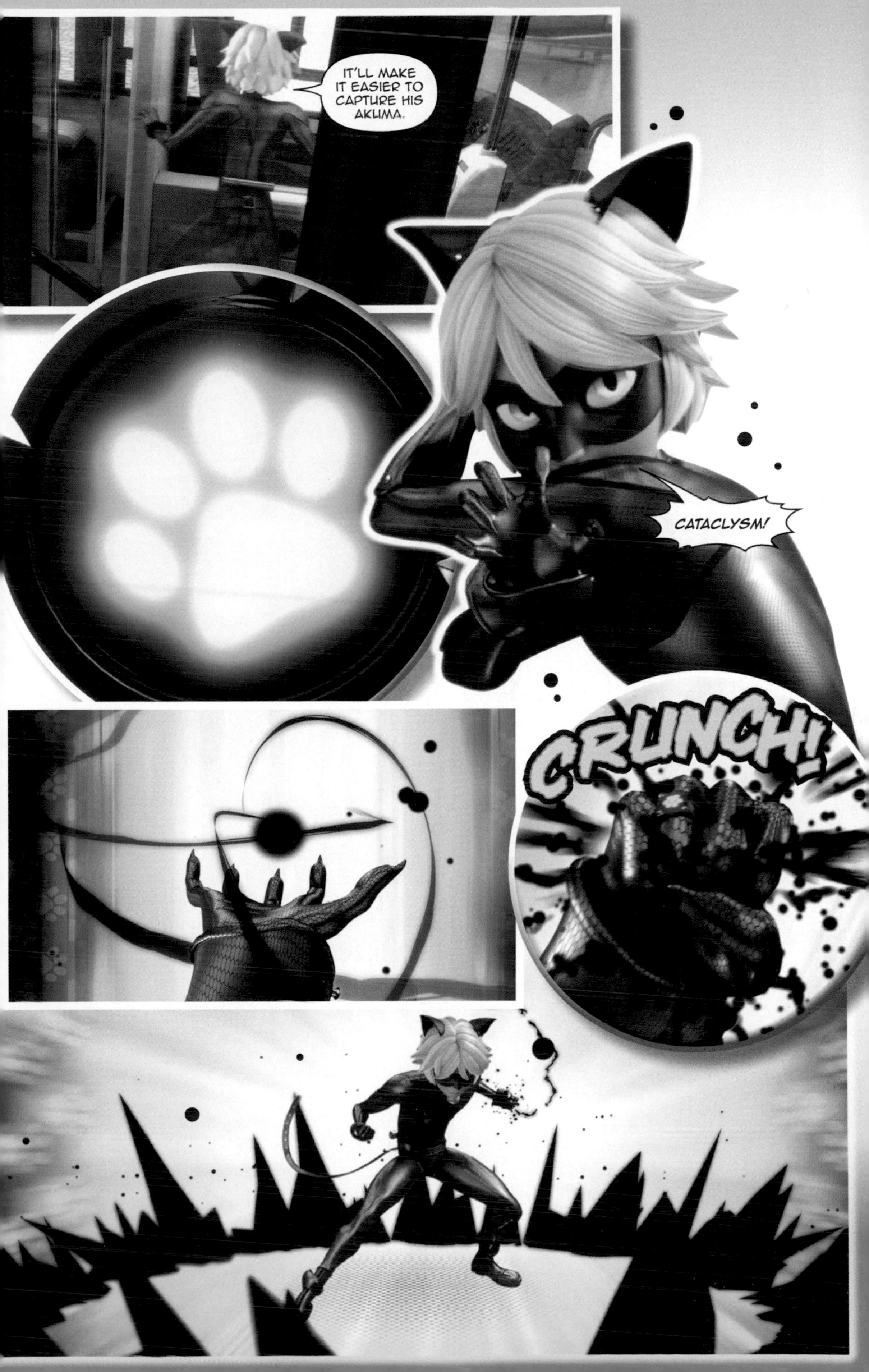
IT'LL MAKE IT EASIER TO CAPTURE HIS AKUMA.
CATACLYSM!
CRUNCH!

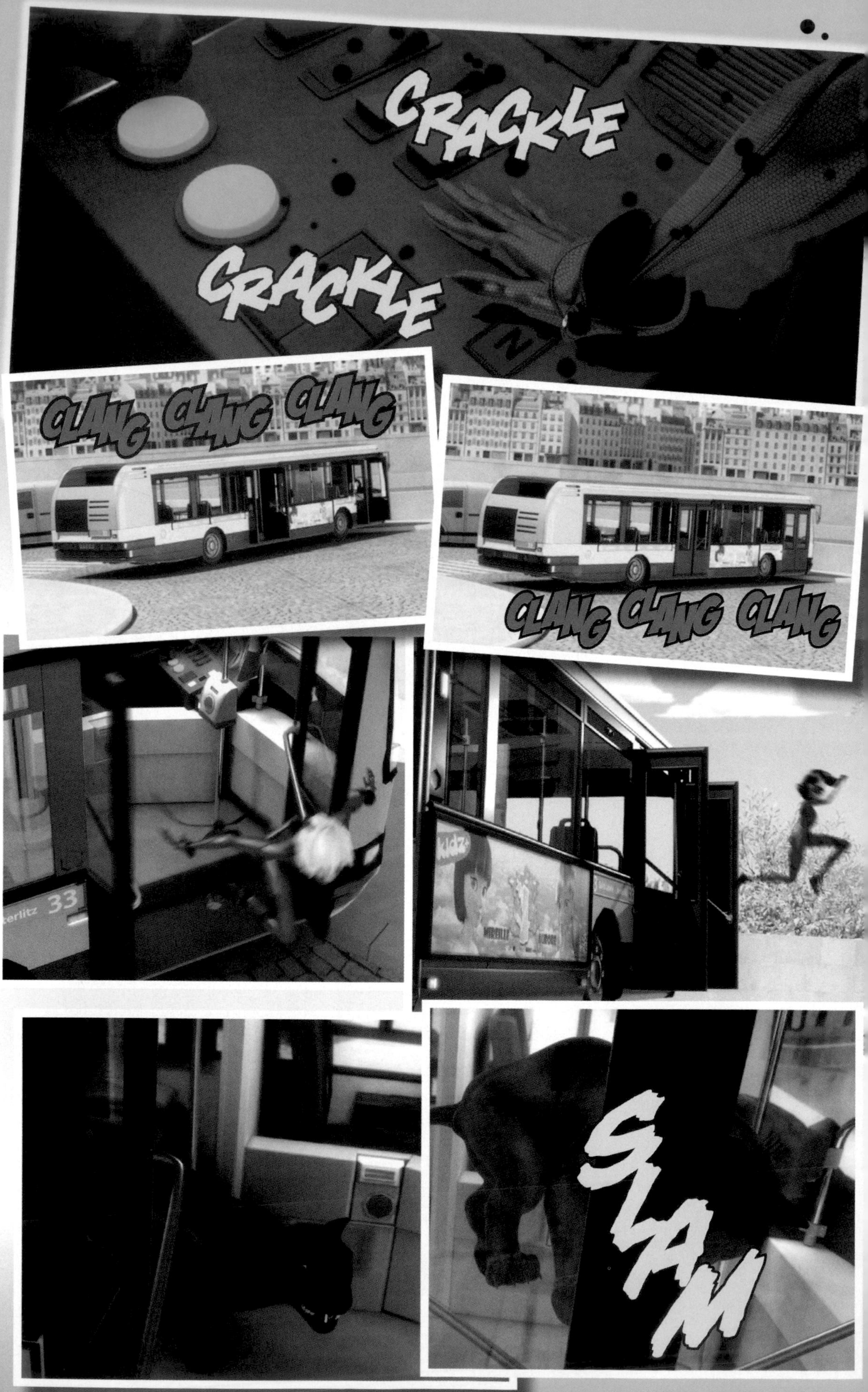
CRACKLE
CRACKLE
CLANG CLANG CLANG
CLANG CLANG CLANG
33
SLAM

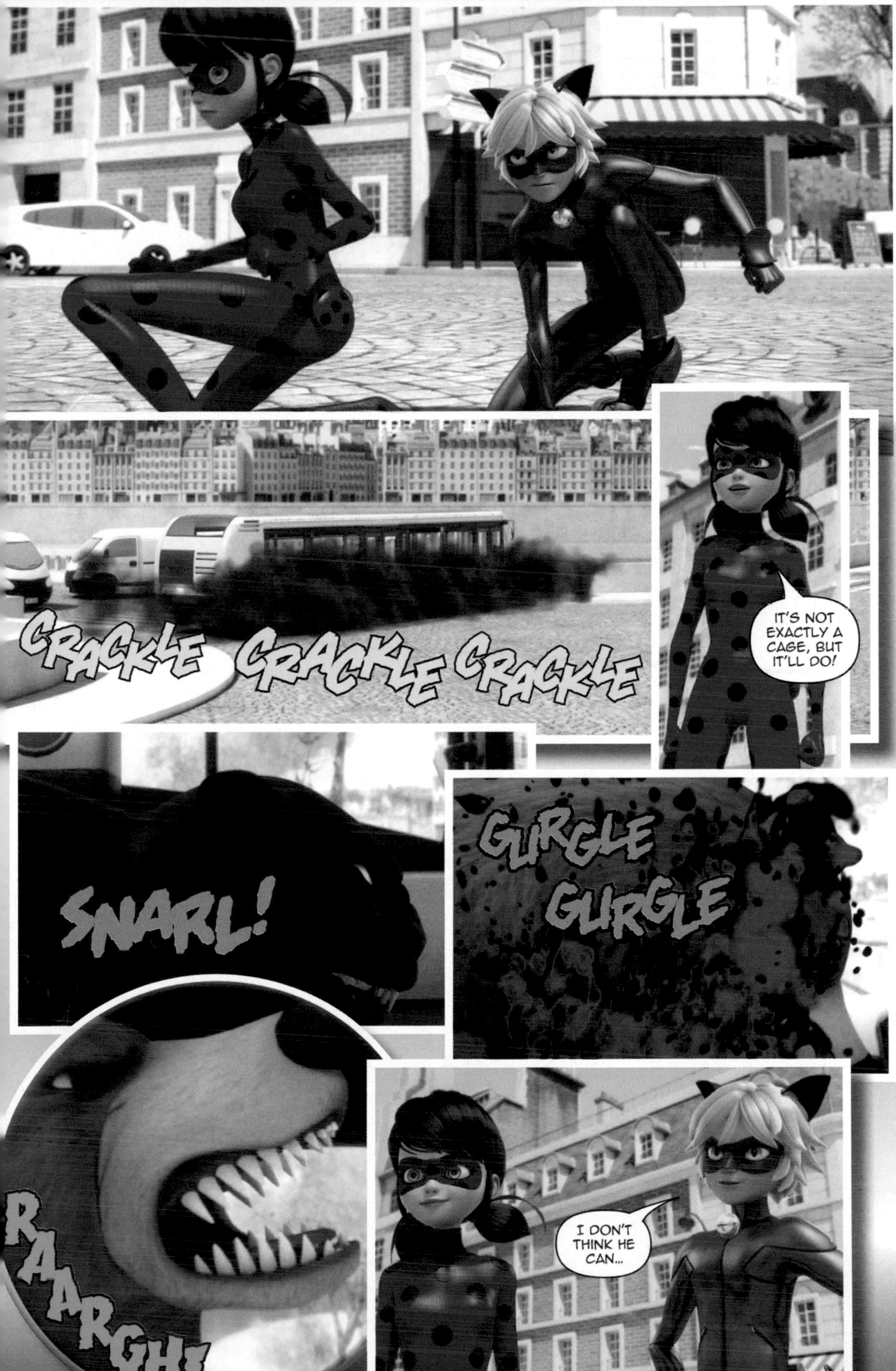
CRACKLE CRACKLE CRACKLE
IT'S NOT EXACTLY A CAGE, BUT IT'LL DO!
SNARL!
GURGLE GURGLE
RAARGH!
I DON'T THINK HE CAN...

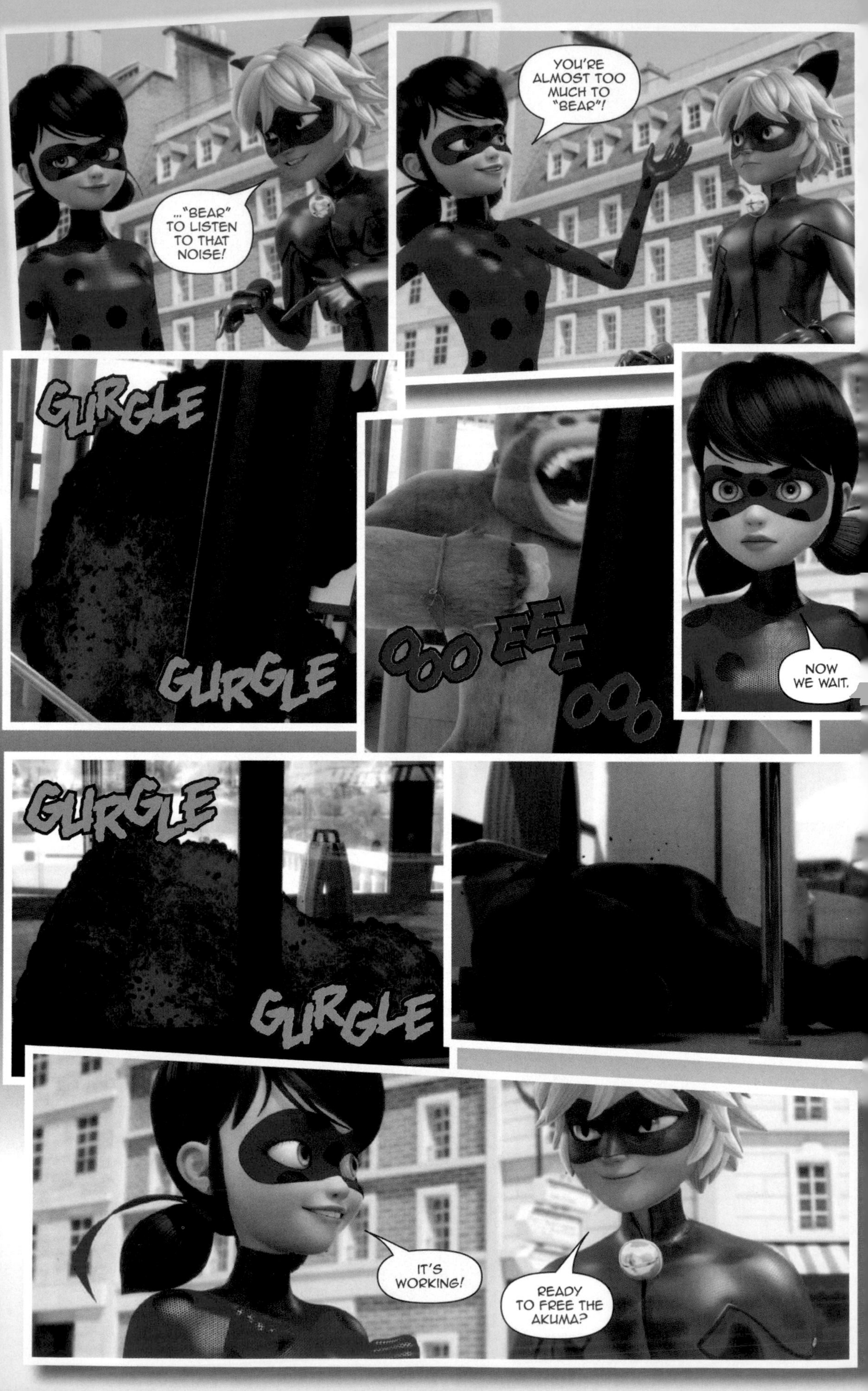
..."BEAR" TO LISTEN TO THAT NOISE!
YOU'RE ALMOST TOO MUCH TO "BEAR"!
GURGLE
GURGLE
OOO EEE OOO
NOW WE WAIT.
GURGLE
GURGLE
IT'S WORKING!
READY TO FREE THE AKUMA?

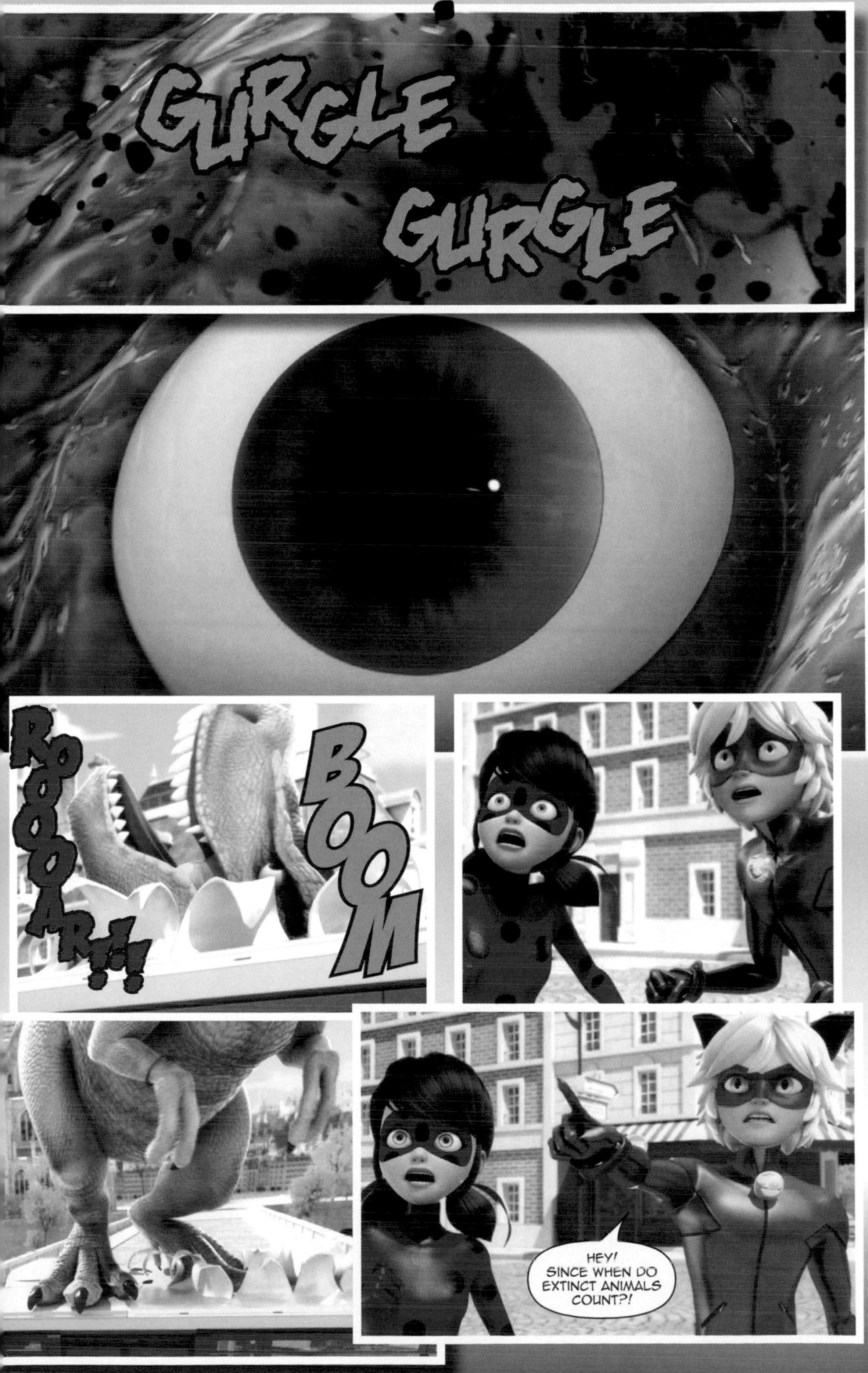
GURGLE
GURGLE
ROOOAR!!!
BOOOM
HEY! SINCE WHEN DO EXTINCT ANIMALS COUNT?!

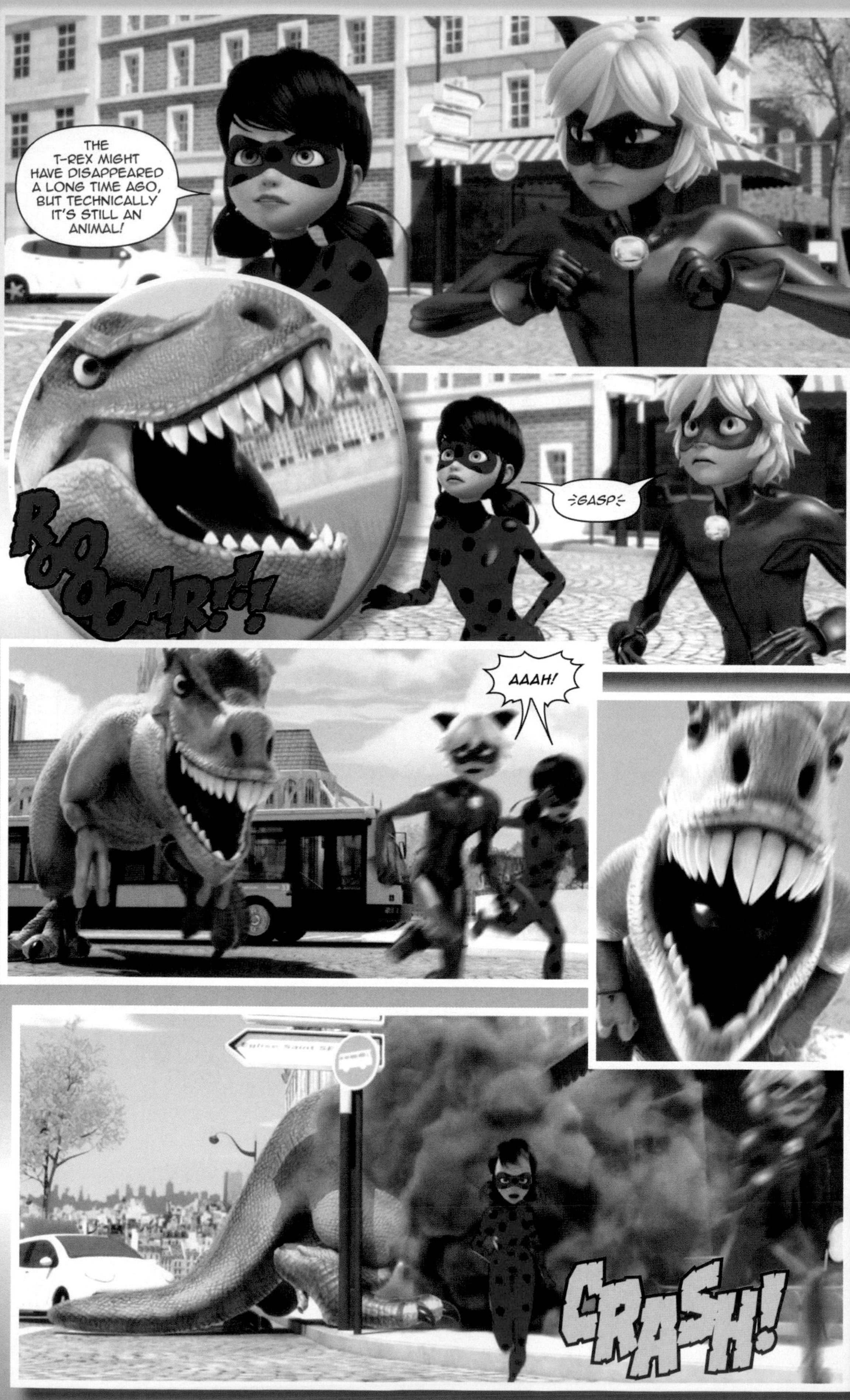
THE T-REX MIGHT HAVE DISAPPEARED A LONG TIME AGO, BUT TECHNICALLY IT'S STILL AN ANIMAL!
ROOOAR!!!
GASP
AAAH!
CRASH!

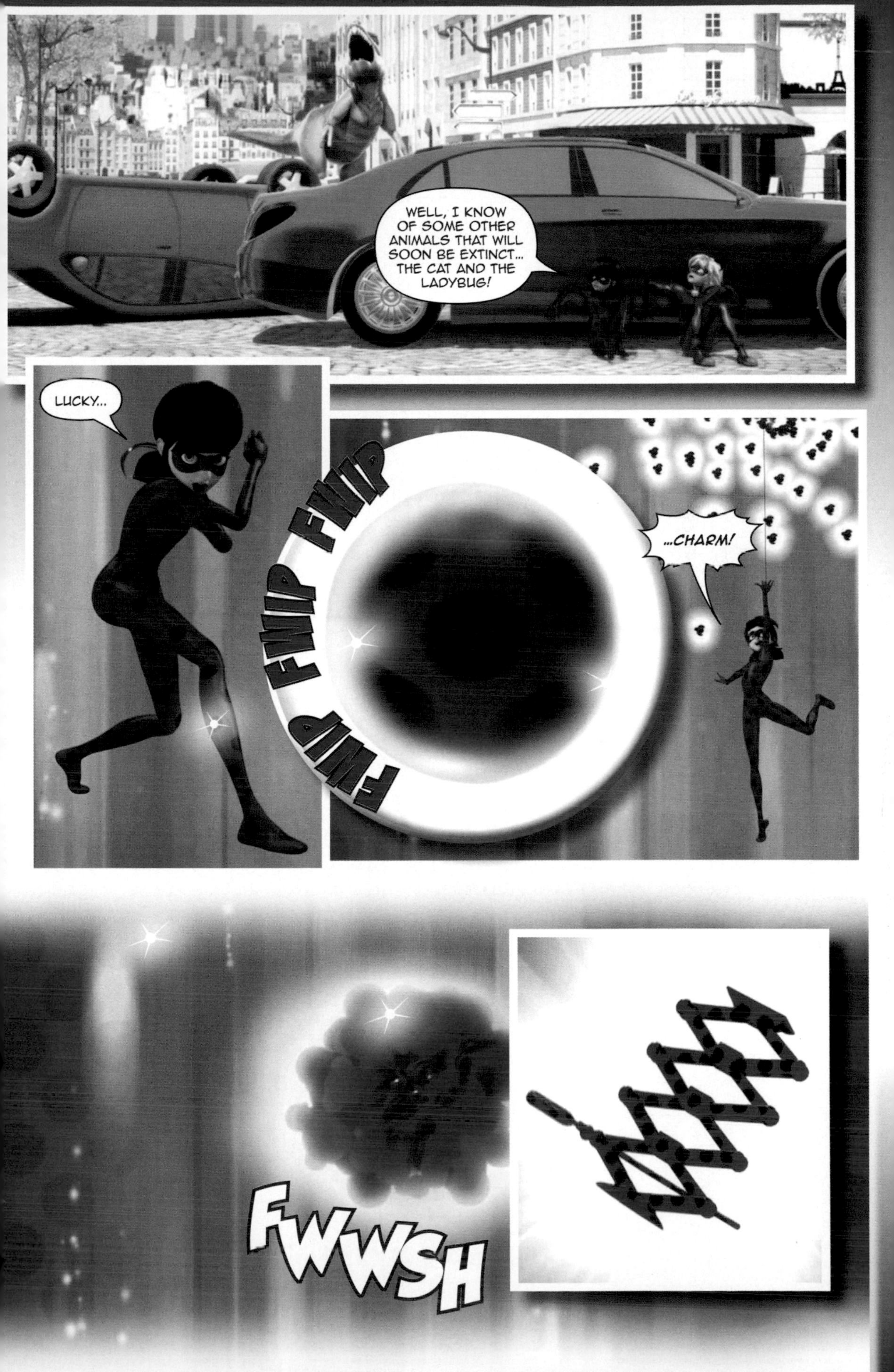
WELL, I KNOW OF SOME OTHER ANIMALS THAT WILL SOON BE EXTINCT... THE CAT AND THE LADYBUG!
LUCKY...
FWIP FWIP FWIP
...CHARM!
FWWSH

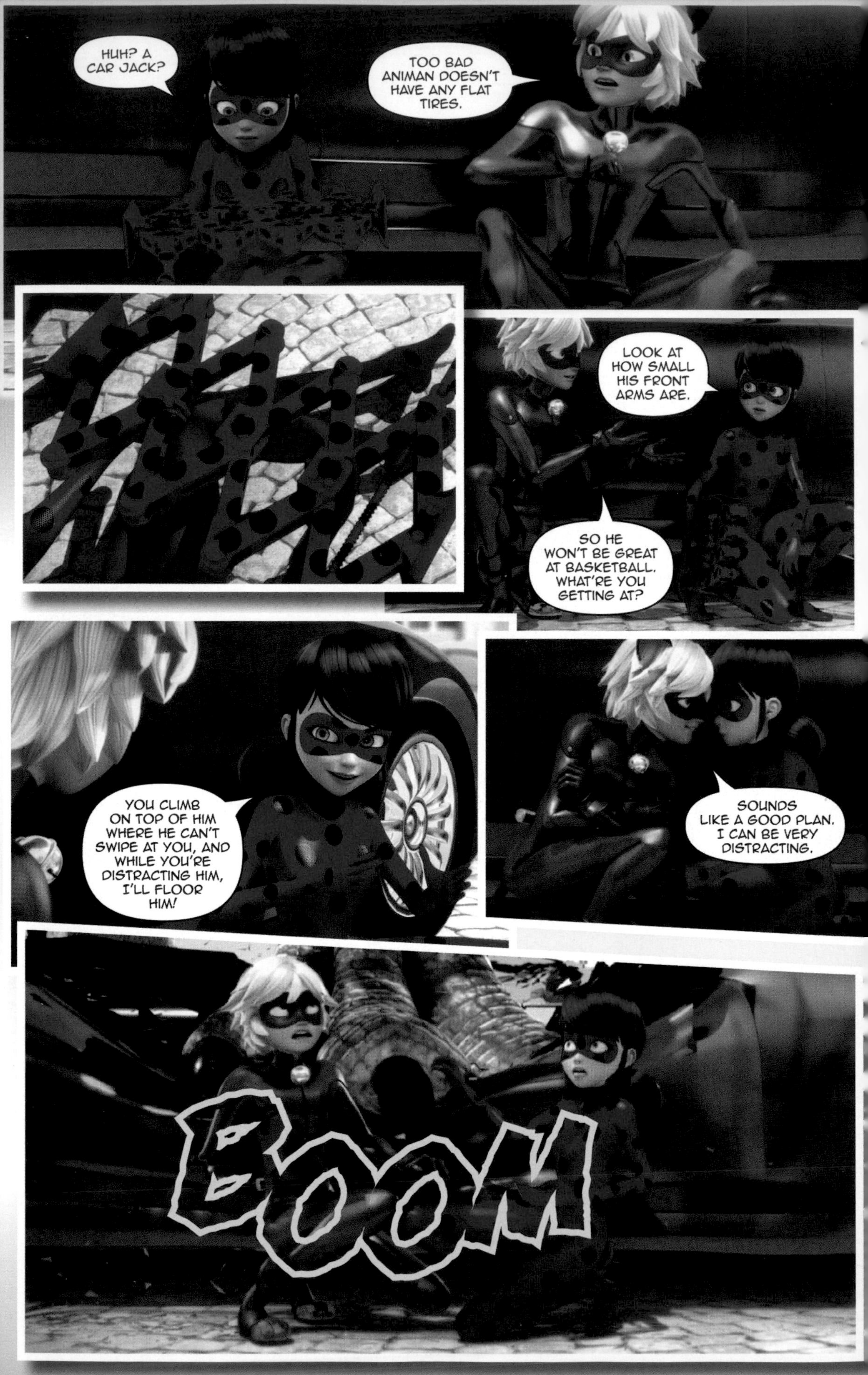
HUH? A CAR JACK?
TOO BAD ANIMAN DOESN'T HAVE ANY FLAT TIRES.
LOOK AT HOW SMALL HIS FRONT ARMS ARE.
SO HE WON'T BE GREAT AT BASKETBALL. WHAT'RE YOU GETTING AT?
YOU CLIMB ON TOP OF HIM WHERE HE CAN'T SWIPE AT YOU, AND WHILE YOU'RE DISTRACTING HIM, I'LL FLOOR HIM!
SOUNDS LIKE A GOOD PLAN. I CAN BE VERY DISTRACTING.
BOOM

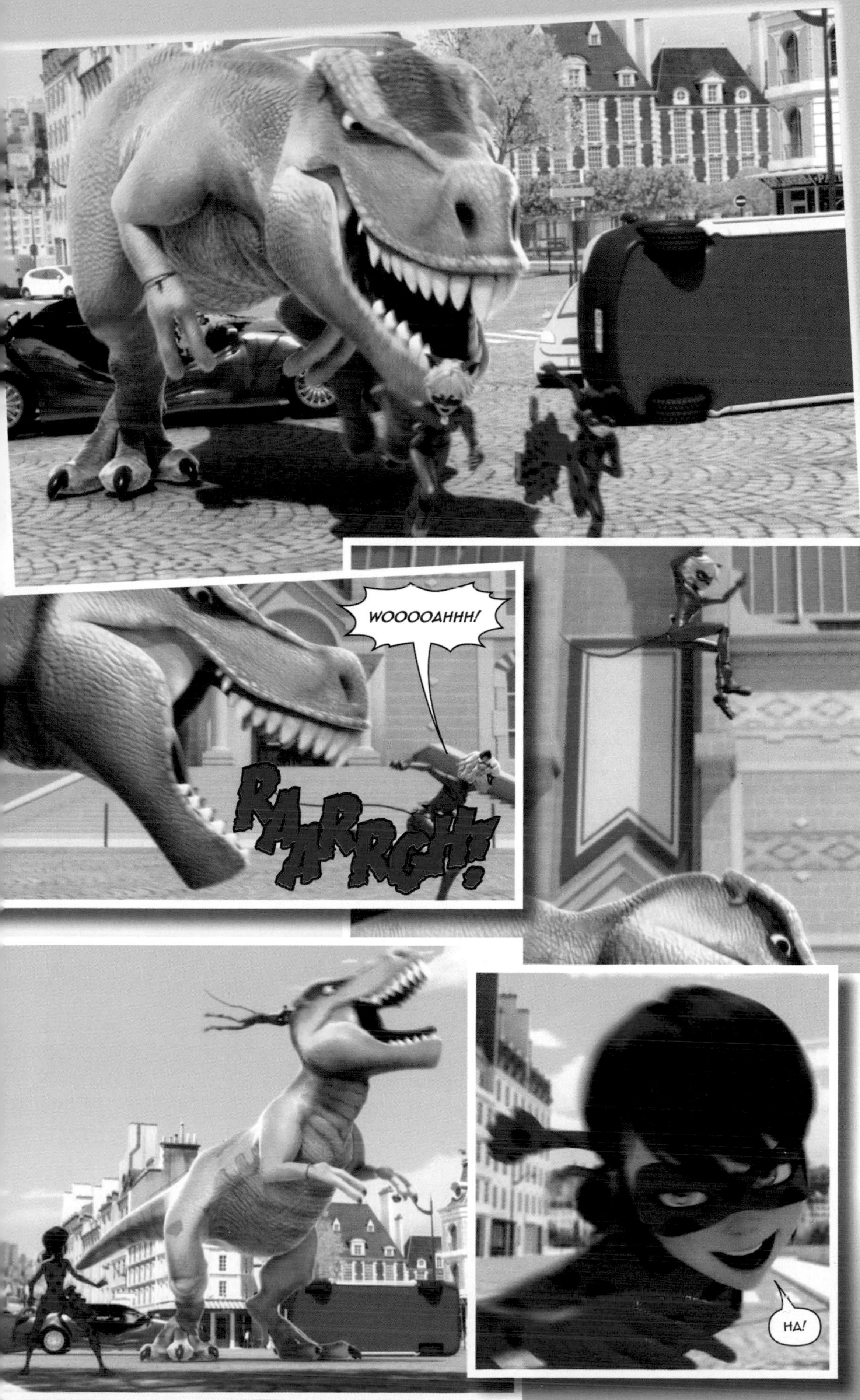
WOOOOAHHH!
RAARRGH!
HA!

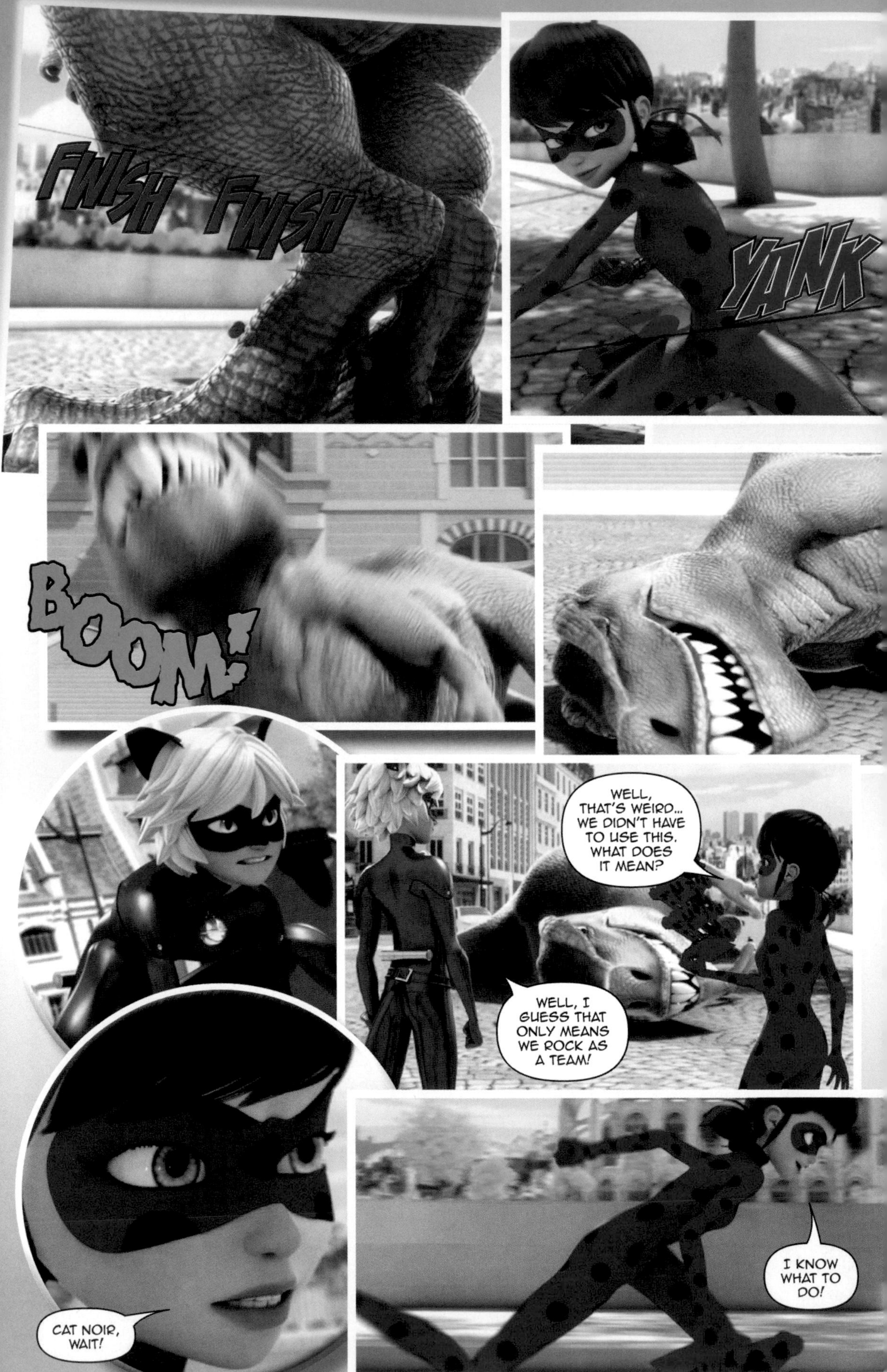
FWISH FWISH
YANK
BOOM!
WELL, THAT'S WEIRD... WE DIDN'T HAVE TO USE THIS. WHAT DOES IT MEAN?
WELL, I GUESS THAT ONLY MEANS WE ROCK AS A TEAM!
CAT NOIR, WAIT!
I KNOW WHAT TO DO!

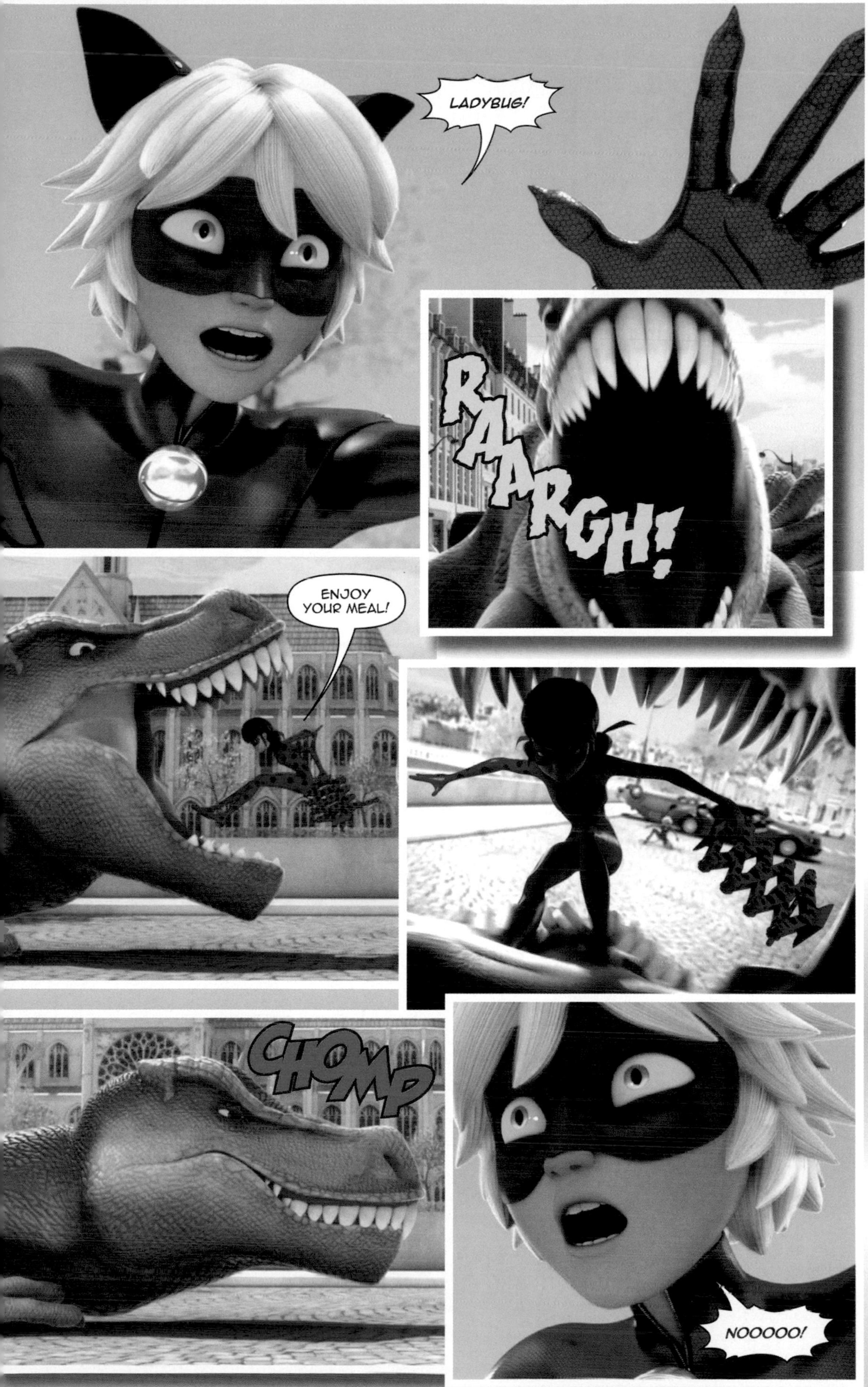
LADYBUG!
RAARGH!
ENJOY YOUR MEAL!
CHOMP
NOOOOO!

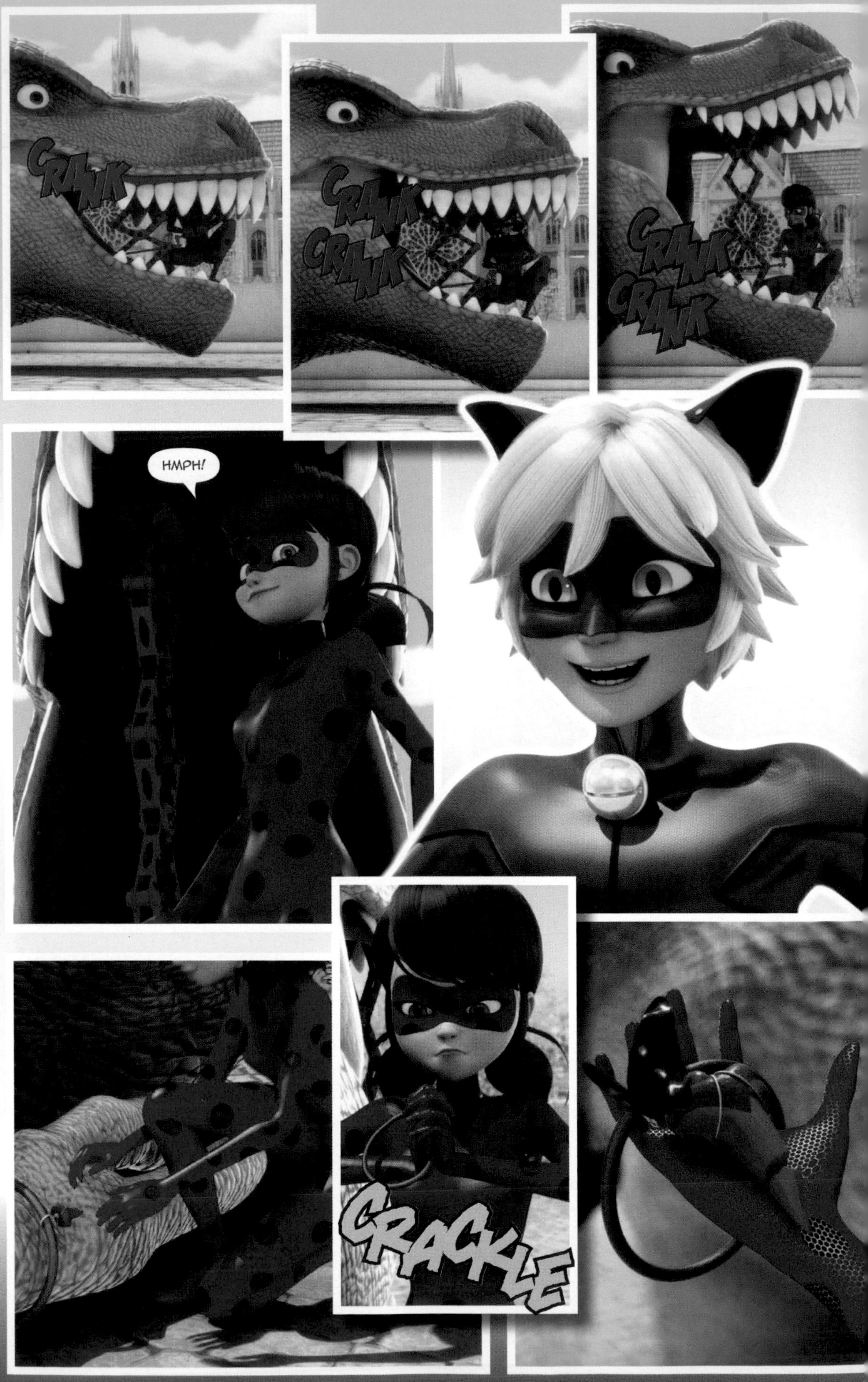
CRANK
CRANK
CRANK
CRANK
CRANK
HMPH!
CRACKLE

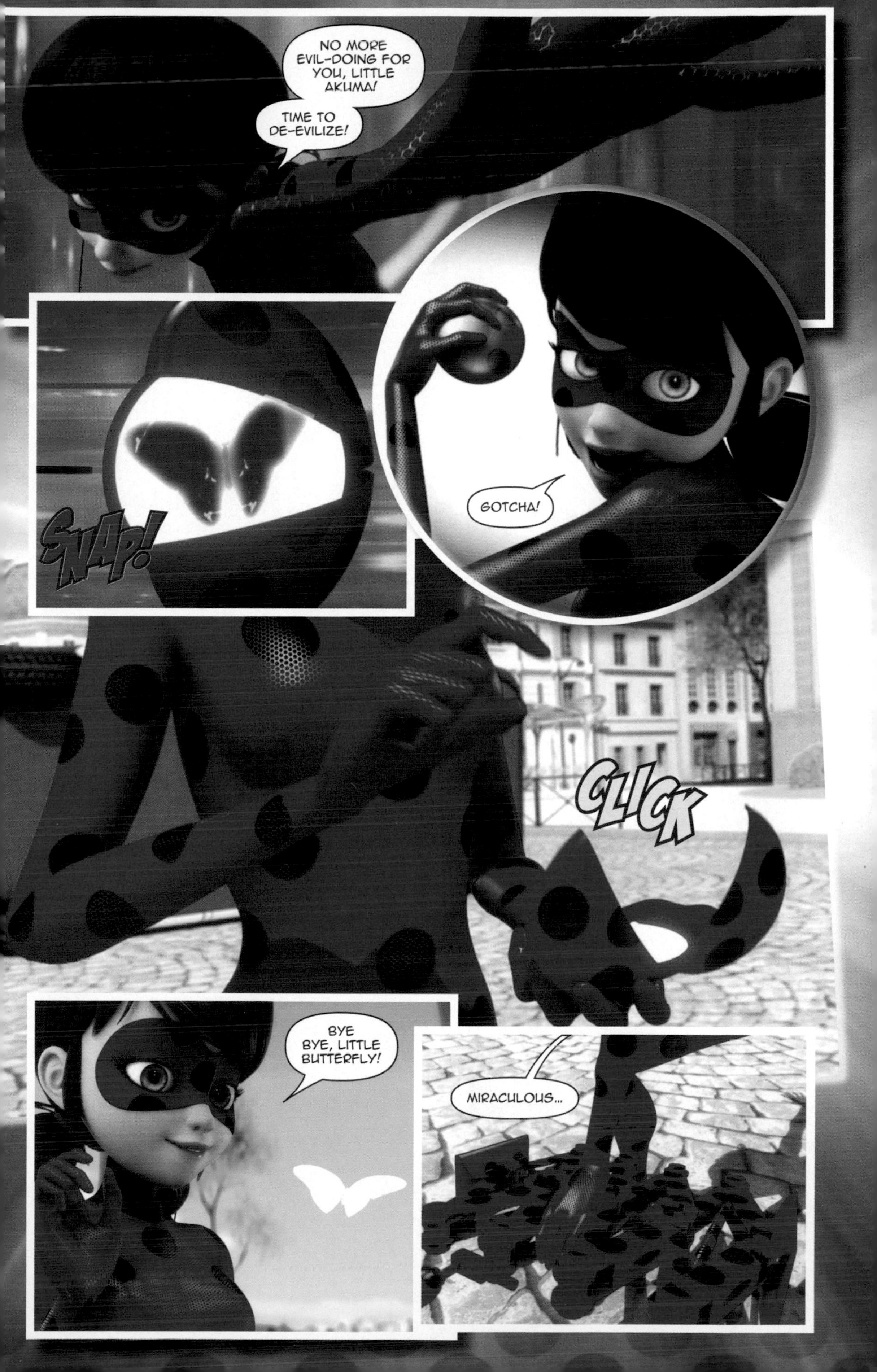

NO MORE EVIL-DOING FOR YOU, LITTLE AKUMA!
TIME TO DE-EVILIZE!
SNAP!
GOTCHA!
CLICK
BYE BYE, LITTLE BUTTERFLY!
MIRACULOUS...

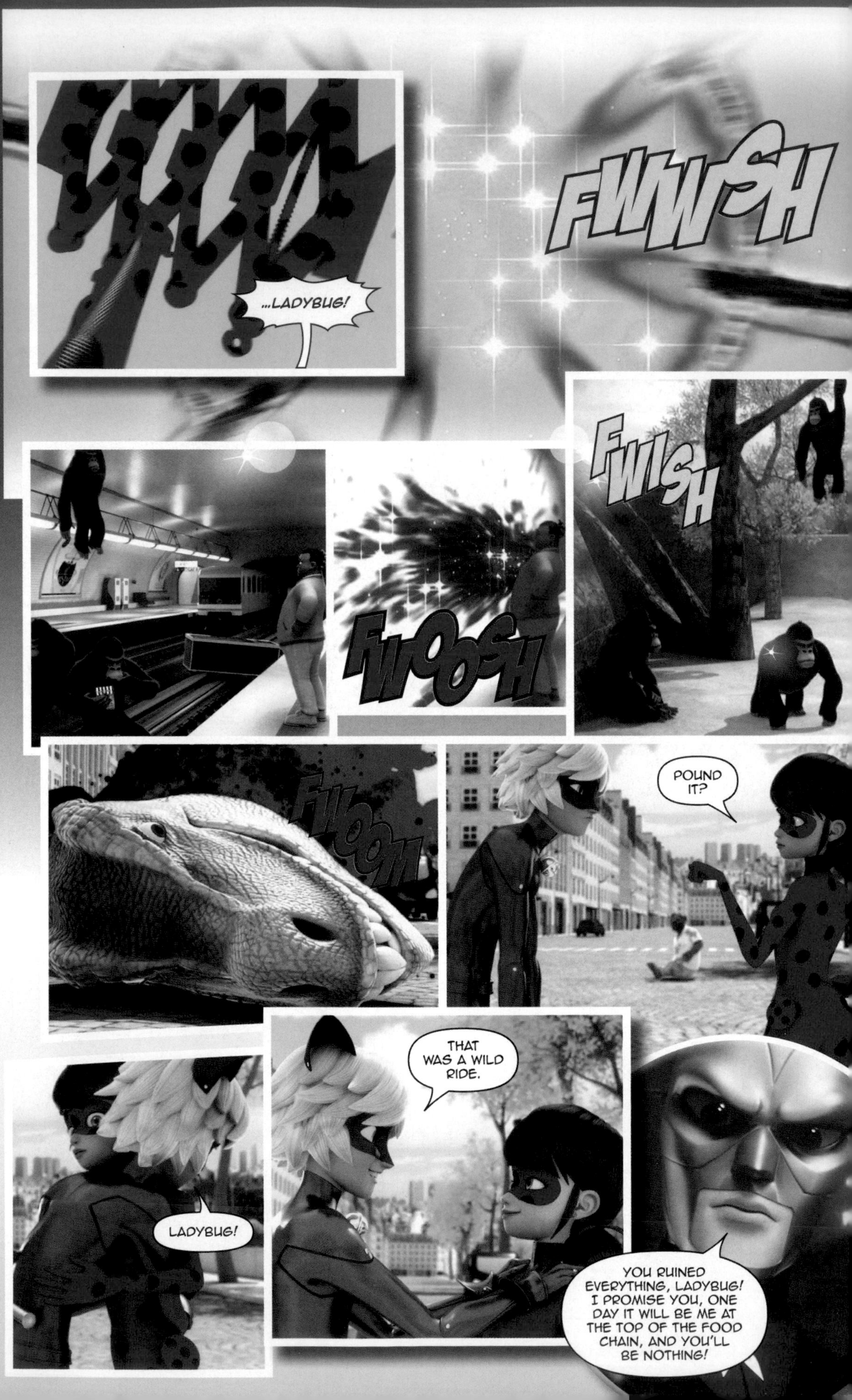
...LADYBUG!
FWWSH
FWISH
FWOOSH
FWOOM
POUND IT?
LADYBUG!
THAT WAS A WILD RIDE.
YOU RUINED EVERYTHING, LADYBUG! I PROMISE YOU, ONE DAY IT WILL BE ME AT THE TOP OF THE FOOD CHAIN, AND YOU'LL BE NOTHING!

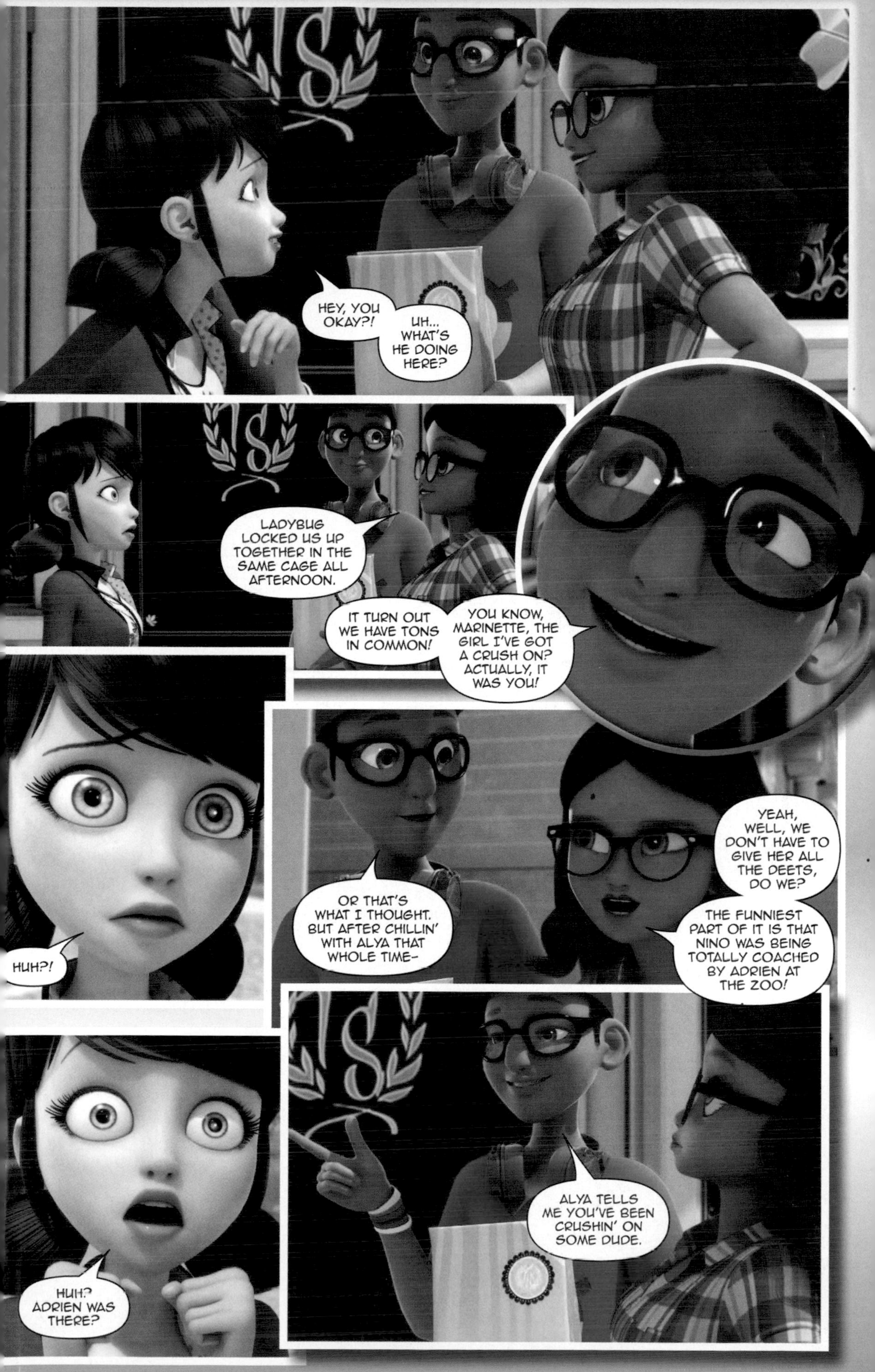
HEY, YOU OKAY?!
UH... WHAT'S HE DOING HERE?
LADYBUG LOCKED US UP TOGETHER IN THE SAME CAGE ALL AFTERNOON.
IT TURN OUT WE HAVE TONS IN COMMON!
YOU KNOW, MARINETTE, THE GIRL I'VE GOT A CRUSH ON? ACTUALLY, IT WAS YOU!
HUH?!
OR THAT'S WHAT I THOUGHT. BUT AFTER CHILLIN' WITH ALYA THAT WHOLE TIME-
YEAH, WELL, WE DON'T HAVE TO GIVE HER ALL THE DEETS, DO WE?
THE FUNNIEST PART OF IT IS THAT NINO WAS BEING TOTALLY COACHED BY ADRIEN AT THE ZOO!
HUH? ADRIEN WAS THERE?
ALYA TELLS ME YOU'VE BEEN CRUSHIN' ON SOME DUDE.

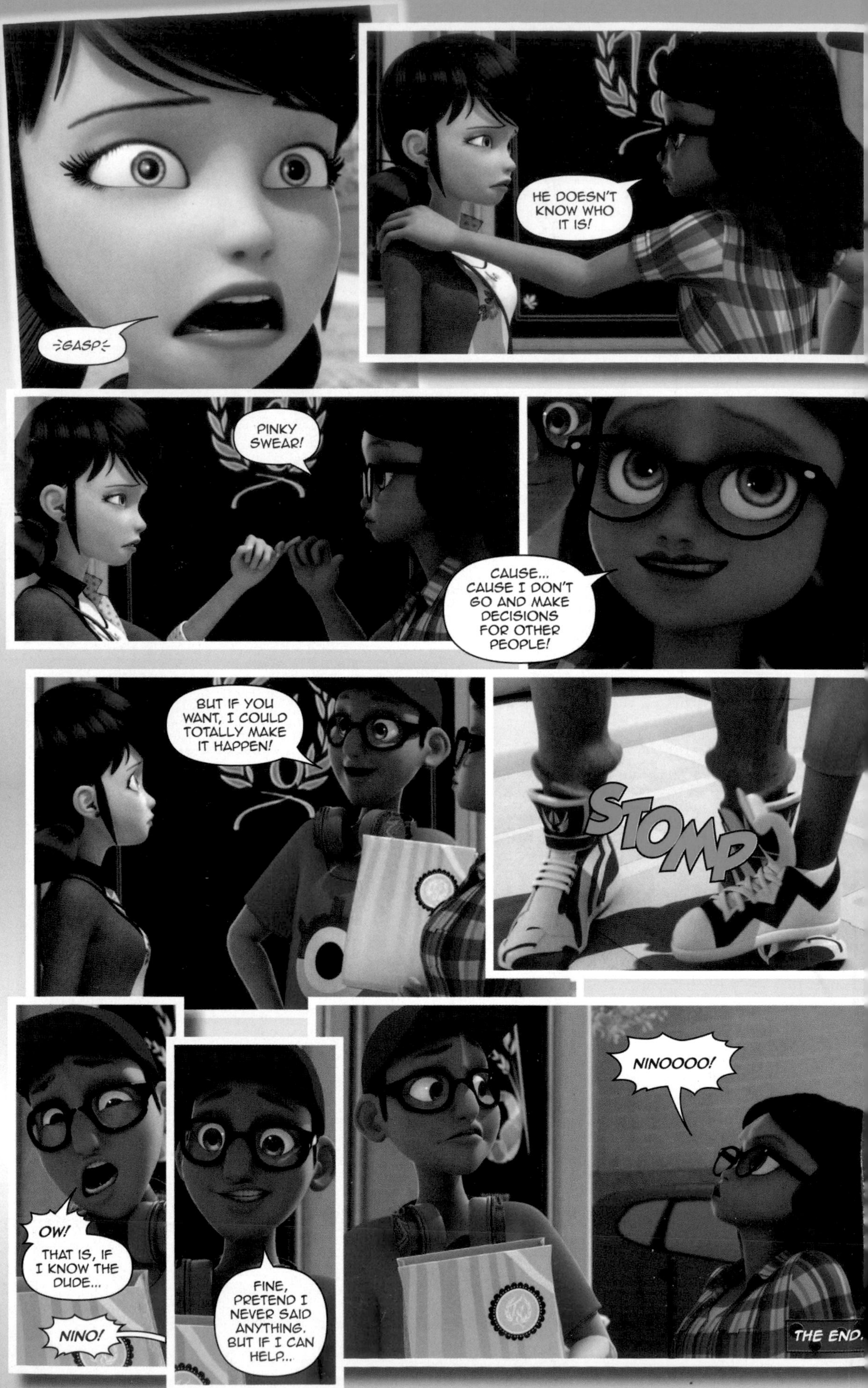

HE DOESN'T KNOW WHO IT IS!
GASP
PINKY SWEAR!
CAUSE... CAUSE I DON'T GO AND MAKE DECISIONS FOR OTHER PEOPLE!
BUT IF YOU WANT, I COULD TOTALLY MAKE IT HAPPEN!
STOMP
OW!
THAT IS, IF I KNOW THE DUDE...
NINO!
FINE, PRETEND I NEVER SAID ANYTHING. BUT IF I CAN HELP...
NINOOOO!
THE END.